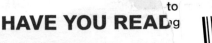
HAVE YOU READ...

Discover the entire Rober...

...le

THE CRUCIFIX KILLER

A body is found with a strange double cross carved into the neck: the signature of a psychopath known as the Crucifix Killer. But Detective Robert Hunter knows that's impossible. Because two years ago, the Crucifix Killer was caught. Wasn't he?

THE EXECUTIONER

Inside a Los Angeles church lies the blood-soaked body of a priest, the figure 3 scrawled in blood on his chest. At first, Robert Hunter believes that this is a ritualistic killing. But as more bodies surface, he is forced to reassess.

THE NIGHT STALKER

When an unidentified victim is discovered on a slab in an abandoned butcher's shop, the cause of death is unclear. Her body bears no marks; but her lips have been carefully stitched shut. It is only when the full autopsy gets underway that Robert Hunter discovers the true horror.

THE DEATH SCULPTOR

A student nurse has the shock of her life when she discovers her patient, prosecutor Derek Nicholson, brutally murdered in his bed. But what most shocks Detective Robert Hunter is the calling card the killer left behind.

ONE BY ONE

Detective Robert Hunter receives an anonymous call asking him to go to a specific web address – a private broadcast. Hunter logs on and a horrific show devised for his eyes only immediately begins.

AN EVIL MIND

A freak accident leads to the arrest of a man, but further investigations suggest a much more horrifying discovery – a serial killer who has been kidnapping, torturing and mutilating victims all over the United States for at least twenty-five years. And he will now only speak to Robert Hunter.

I AM DEATH

Seven days after being abducted, the body of a twenty-year-old woman is found. Detective Robert Hunter is assigned the case and almost immediately a second body turns up. Hunter knows he has to be quick, for he is chasing a monster.

THE CALLER

Be careful before answering your next call. It could be the beginning of a nightmare, as Robert Hunter discovers as he chases a killer who stalks victims on social media.

CHRIS CARTER
GALLERY
OF THE
DEAD

**SIMON &
SCHUSTER**

London · New York · Sydney · Toronto · New Delhi

A CBS COMPANY

First published in Great Britain by Simon & Schuster UK Ltd, 2018
A CBS COMPANY

1 3 5 7 9 10 8 6 4 2

Simon & Schuster UK Ltd
1st Floor
222 Gray's Inn Road
London WC1X 8HB

www.simonandschuster.co.uk

Simon & Schuster Australia, Sydney
Simon & Schuster India, New Delhi

A CIP catalogue record for this book
is available from the British Library

Hardback ISBN: 978-1-4711-5634-2
Trade Paperback ISBN: 978-1-4711-5635-9
eBook ISBN: 978-1-4711-5637-3

Typeset in the UK by M Rules
Printed and bound by CPI Group (UK) Ltd, Croydon, CR0 4YY

MIX
Paper from
responsible sources
FSC® C020471

Simon & Schuster UK Ltd are committed to sourcing paper
that is made from wood grown in sustainable forests and support the Forest
Stewardship Council, the leading international forest certification organisation.
Our books displaying the FSC logo are printed on FSC certified paper.

This novel is dedicated to all the readers out there for the most incredible support over so many years.

From the bottom of my heart, I thank you.

One

Linda Parker stepped into her two-bedroom house in Silver Lake, Los Angeles, closed the door behind her and let go of a heavy, tired breath. It'd been a long and busy day. Five photoshoots in just as many different studios scattered all across town. The work itself wasn't that tiring. Linda loved modeling and she was lucky enough to be able to do it professionally, but driving around in a city like LA, where traffic was slow-moving at the best of times, had a special way of exhausting and irritating the most patient of souls.

Linda had left home at around seven thirty that morning and by the time she parked her red VW Beetle back on her driveway, the clock on her dashboard was showing 10:14 p.m. She was tired and she was hungry, but first things first.

'Wine,' she said to herself as she switched on her living-room lights and kicked off her shoes. 'I so need a large glass of wine right now.'

Linda shared her single-story, white-fronted house with Mr. Boingo, a black and white stray cat she had rescued from the streets eleven years ago. Due to his advanced age, Mr. Boingo barely left the house anymore. Running around outside, chasing after birds he could never really get to, had lost its appeal several summers ago and Mr. Boingo now spent most of his days either sleeping or perched on the windowsill, catatonically staring out at an empty street.

As the lights came on, Mr. Boingo, who'd been asleep on his favorite chair for the past three hours, got up and stretched his front legs before letting out a long, carefree yawn.

Linda smiled. 'Hey there, Mr. Boingo. So how was your day? Busy?'

Happy to see her again, Mr. Boingo jumped to the floor and slowly approached Linda.

'Are you hungry, little one?' Linda asked, bending down to pick up her cat.

Mr. Boingo snuggled up to her.

'Have you finished all your food?' She kissed his forehead.

Linda had known it would be a long day, so she had made sure she left Mr. Boingo enough food, or at least she thought she had. Taking a step to her right, she checked the food and water bowls tucked away in the corner. Neither was empty.

'You're not hungry, are you?'

Mr. Boingo began purring; his sleepy eyes blinked twice at her.

'No, I'm not.' Putting on a silly, cartoon-like voice, Linda pretended to be Mr. Boingo. 'I just want cuddles 'cause I missed my mommy.'

She began gently scratching Mr. Boingo's neck and the underside of his chin. The cat's mouth immediately stretched into a happy smile.

'You love that, don't you?' She kissed his forehead again.

Cat in arms, Linda entered her kitchen, grabbed a clean glass from the dishwasher and poured herself a healthy measure from an already opened bottle of South African Pinotage. She let Mr. Boingo go before bringing the glass to her lips.

'Umm!' she said out loud, as her body finally began to relax. 'Heaven in liquid form.'

From her fridge, Linda retrieved her dinner – a small bowl of salad. She would much rather have a double cheeseburger with chili fries, or a large, extra-hot pepperoni pizza, but that would be breaking the rules of her strict low-calorie diet, something she only allowed herself to do once in a while as a treat, and tonight wasn't 'treat night'.

After another sip, Linda collected her wine and her salad, and left the kitchen.

Mr. Boingo followed.

Back in the living room, Linda placed everything on her dining table and powered up her laptop. While waiting for her computer to boot up, she reached inside her handbag for a tube of moisturizing cream. After carefully massaging a generous amount into her hands, she repeated the procedure with her feet.

From the floor, Mr. Boingo watched, unimpressed.

The next half-hour was spent replying to emails and adding several new bookings to her calendar. That done, Linda closed her email application and decided to log into her Facebook account – thirty-two new friend requests, thirty-nine new messages and ninety-six new notifications. She checked the clock on the wall to her left – 10:51 p.m. As she began debating if she was really in the mood for Facebook, Mr. Boingo jumped onto her lap.

'Hey there. You want more cuddles, don't you?' The cartoon-like voice was back. 'Of course I do. I've been left alone the whole day. Bad mommy.'

Linda had begun stroking her cat's chin again when she remembered something that she'd been meaning to do for a couple of days.

'I know what,' she said, staring straight into Mr. Boingo's tiny eyes. 'Let's take one of those Face Swap pictures, how about that, huh?'

A couple of days ago, Linda's best friend, Maria, had Instagrammed a Face Swap picture of her and her adorable little Bichon Frise. The dog had a congenital abnormality in its lower jaw, which caused its tongue to stick out all the time. To match it, Maria also stuck out her tongue as the picture was taken. The combination of fluffy white fur, bleached blonde hair, tongues sticking out, and Maria's always over-the-top makeup, amounted to a very entertaining image. Linda had promised herself that she would try something similar with Mr. Boingo.

'Yeah, let's do that,' she said, nodding at her cat, her voice full of excitement. 'It will be fun, I promise you.'

She picked up Mr. Boingo, grabbed her cellphone and tapped the icon for a Face Swap application she had already downloaded.

'OK, here we go.'

She readjusted her sitting position and considered the image on the tiny screen. A couple of framed paintings, together with a silver light fixture, could be seen on the wall directly behind her. To the left of the paintings was the doorway that led to a short corridor and the rest of the house.

Linda was very particular when it came to taking pictures, even the ones done just for fun.

'Umm, no, I don't like that,' she said, shaking her head at Mr. Boingo.

The lights in the hallway behind her were switched off, but the ones on the silver fixture were on, giving the image on her screen an odd background glare. She readjusted her position once again, this time moving a little to her left. The glare was gone.

'Yeah, much better, don't you think?' she asked Mr. Boingo.

His reply was a slow, sleepy blink of the eyes.

'OK. Let's do this before you crash out again, sleepyhead.'

Using the Face Swap application couldn't be any simpler. All she had to do was take a picture. That was it. The application would instantly identify the two faces on the screen, place a red circle around each of them and then automatically swap them around.

Linda picked up Mr. Boingo and sat back on her chair.

'There,' she said, pointing to the screen on her cellphone. 'Look there.'

Mr. Boingo, looking like he was about to doze off, let out another lazy yawn.

'No, silly cat, don't look at me. Look there. Look.' She pointed at her screen one more time, this time snapping her fingers. The noise seemed to do the trick. Mr. Boingo finally turned and looked directly at Linda's cellphone.

'There we go.'

Losing no time, Linda put on a bright smile and quickly tapped the 'photo' button.

On her screen, the first red circle appeared around her face, but as the second one quickly followed, Linda felt something constrict inside her chest like a tourniquet, because the application didn't place it around Mr. Boingo's tiny face. Instead, it placed it around something in the dark doorway directly behind her.

Two

'Good evening, everyone.'

Despite having the assistance of a microphone and a powerful PA system, UCLA psychology professor Ms. Tracy Adams understandably projected her voice a little louder than usual. She was standing before a full-to-capacity one-hundred-and-fifty-seater lecture hall, and the chit-chatter of so many animated voices made the place sound like a giant beehive. The audience comprised not only enthusiastic criminology and criminal psychology students, but also several other tutors, who were all very interested in hearing tonight's lecture.

Professor Adams' captivating green eyes, behind old-fashioned, black-framed cat-eye glasses, circled the auditorium.

'We're just about to start,' she continued. 'So if those of you who aren't already seated could please find a seat, that would be much appreciated.' She paused and waited patiently.

Professor Adams was no doubt a fascinating woman – intelligent, attractive, knowledgeable, charismatic, elegant and intriguingly mysterious. It was no wonder that so many of her students, male and female, had developed a somewhat adolescent-like crush on her, not to mention some of the faculty staff. But tonight, Professor Tracy Adams wasn't the reason why the large lecture hall, located on the northwest quarter of the UCLA campus in Westwood, was heaving with people.

A full minute went by before everyone had finally taken their seats.

'Well,' Professor Adams said. 'I would like to start by thanking everyone for being here. If only I could get this sort of turnout to all my classes . . .'

Subdued laughter broke out across the auditorium.

'OK,' she carried on. 'Before we begin, if I may, I'd like to give you all some background information on tonight's special guest.' Her eyes briefly moved to the tall and well-built man standing to the left of the stage.

The man, who had his hands tucked into his trouser pockets, replied with a timid smile.

Professor Adams' attention moved to the notes in front of her, resting on the speaker's podium, before returning to the audience.

'A psychology graduate from Stanford University,' she began. 'He received his first degree at the age of nineteen.' Her next three words were delivered with a deliberate pause between them. '*Summa cum laude.*'

A wave of surprised mumbling moved across the room.

'Also from Stanford University,' she continued, 'and still at the tender age of twenty-three, he received a Ph.D. in Criminal Behavior Analyses and Biopsychology. His thesis, which was titled "An Advanced Psychological Study in Criminal Conduct" became, and still is to this day, mandatory reading at the FBI's NCAVC.' A short pause. 'For those of you who don't know, or have forgotten what NCAVC stands for, that's the FBI's National Center for the Analysis of Violent Crime.'

She checked her notes then looked back to the crowd.

'Despite being offered a profiler's position with the NCAVC's Behavioral Analysis Unit several times, tonight's guest has never accepted the offer, choosing instead to join the Los Angeles Police Department.'

More surprised mumbling, this time a little louder.

Professor Adams waited for it to die down before continuing.

'As a member of this city's police force, he moved through its ranks at lightning speed, becoming the youngest ever officer to make detective for the LAPD. Since then, his crime-solving record has been second to none.'

She paused again, this time for effect.

'Our guest tonight is a highly decorated detective with the LAPD's HSS – the Homicide Special Section – which is an elite branch of the Robbery Homicide Division that was created to deal solely with serial and high-profile homicide cases requiring extensive investigative time and expertise.'

Professor Adams raised her right index finger to emphasize her next point. 'But that's not all. Due to his background in criminal behavior psychology and the fact that this beautiful city of ours seems to attract a very particular breed of psychopaths ...'

Laughter returned to the lecture hall.

'... Our guest was placed in an even more specialized entity within the HSS. All homicides involving overwhelming sadism and brutality are tagged by the LAPD as Ultra Violent Crimes. Our guest tonight does a job that most detectives in this country would give their right arm *not* to. He is the head of the LAPD's Ultra Violent Crimes Unit.' She turned and once again looked at the man standing by the side of the stage.

One hundred and fifty pairs of eyes followed hers.

'It took me a *looong* time to finally persuade him to come to UCLA as a guest speaker and to talk to all of you about one of the most intriguing subjects as far as criminology and criminal psychology are concerned – the modern-day serial killer.'

The room fell eerily silent.

'Tonight, it gives me great pleasure to be able to introduce to you Detective Robert Hunter of the LAPD.'

The place erupted in ovation.

Professor Adams motioned Hunter to join her.

Detective Hunter freed his hands from his pockets and slowly took the three short steps that led up to the stage. As he locked eyes with the professor, she gave him a confident smile, followed by a very sensual but almost imperceptible wink. He broke eye contact, faced the applauding auditorium and shyly bowed his head. Hunter really wasn't used to any of this.

'Break a leg,' Professor Adams whispered as she handed Hunter the microphone and left the stage the same way he had come up.

Hunter waited until the place had gone quiet again.

'I guess I would like to start by once again thanking all of you for being here. I must admit that this wasn't what I was expecting.'

It was Hunter's turn to give Professor Adams the eye.

'I thought that I'd be speaking to maybe twenty to twenty-five students, max.'

More laughter from the crowd.

Renewing her smile, the professor shrugged at Hunter from the edge of the stage.

'Before I begin, please allow me to explain that I'm no public speaker and I'm certainly no teacher, but I'll do my best to try to relate to you what I know, and to answer whatever questions you may have.'

Once again, the audience broke into applause.

Hunter was unsure what the audience's knowledge level was, so he started with some basic definitions – like the difference between a serial killer, a spree killer and a mass murderer. The explanation was substantiated by a few examples of incidents that had taken place recently in the USA.

He proceeded by giving his audience a seven-point list of the phases of a serial killer, from the Aura Phase – the very beginning, where the killer-to-be starts to lose his/her grip on reality – to the Depression Phase – the great emotional letdown that in most cases follows the murder act.

'Before I move on,' Hunter said as he finished explaining the final phase, his voice taking a much more serious tone. 'When it comes to serial homicides, the most important thing I'd like you to remember is that . . .'

He was interrupted by his cellphone vibrating inside his jacket pocket.

He paused and reached for it.

'I'm so sorry about this,' he said, raising his right hand at the intrigued audience. 'If you could all give me just a minute.' He switched off the microphone and placed it on the podium. 'Detective Hunter,' he said into the mouthpiece. 'UVC Unit.'

As he listened to the caller on the other end of the line, his eyes found Professor Adams'. No words were necessary. She could read the expression on his face. She'd been by his side before when a similar call had come in.

'You've got to be joking.' She mumbled the words in disbelief before taking to the stage again and approaching Hunter. 'Why am I not surprised this is happening tonight?'

Hunter disconnected from the call and faced her.

'I'm terribly sorry, Tracy,' he said, his voice low and constricted. He could see her disappointment. 'I need to go.'

She nodded her understanding. 'It's OK, Robert. Go. I'll explain it to everyone.'

As Hunter rushed off the stage, Professor Adams grabbed the microphone from the podium, let out a sad sigh and faced a very confused crowd.

Three

Hunter's watch read 9:31 p.m. by the time he got to the address he'd been given over the phone. Even at that time on a Wednesday evening, it had taken him around three quarters of an hour to cover the almost nineteen miles between Westwood and Silver Lake – an ethnically highly diverse neighborhood, just east of Hollywood. As he joined Berkeley Avenue, heading west, he immediately saw the cluster of police vehicles surrounding the entrance to North Benton Way.

Hunter knew that in a city like Los Angeles, nothing could gather a crowd of curious onlookers faster than the combination of flashing police lights and black-and-yellow crime-scene tape. With that in mind, he wasn't at all surprised to see the ever-growing mob of nearby residents that had already assembled by the perimeter – cellphones firmly in hand, hungry for a few seconds of video footage, or even just a decent picture so it could all be displayed on their social-media pages, like Pokémon trophies.

The press had also beaten Hunter to the punch. With tripods and cameras mounted onto their rooftops, two news vans had taken positions on the sidewalk, just across the road from the police cordoned-off area. A couple of reporters were trying their best to obtain whatever information they could out of anyone who would talk to them.

As he finally cleared the crowd, Hunter rolled down his window and presented his badge to one of the uniformed officers guarding the road's entrance. The officer nodded before clearing the way for Hunter to drive through.

North Benton Way was a quiet residential street just south of the famous Silver Lake Reservoir. Fully grown sycamore trees flanked both sides of the road, shading it from the sun during the day, but casting ominous shadows just about everywhere come dusk. The house Hunter was after was the sixth one along the right-hand side. A red VW Beetle and a blue Tesla S occupied both spaces on the driveway. Parked on the street, a little to the right of the house, Hunter could see three more black-and-white units, together with an LA County Coroner's forensics van.

Hunter pulled up in front of the van and stepped out of his car, his six-foot frame towering high above the sun-beaten roof of his old Buick LeSabre. He took a moment and allowed his gaze to run up and down the street. The neighboring houses were all lit up, with most of their residents either peering out their windows, or standing by the front door with a look of total shock and disbelief on their faces. As Hunter clipped his badge onto his belt, another car cleared the police barrier at the top of the road. Hunter immediately recognized the metallic blue Honda Civic. It belonged to his partner at the UVC Unit, Detective Carlos Garcia.

'Just got here?' Garcia asked as he parked next to one of the police cruisers and jumped out of his car.

'Less than a minute ago,' Hunter confirmed.

Garcia's longish brown hair, still damp from a late shower, was pulled back into a tight ponytail.

Both detectives turned and faced the white-fronted house. Three solemn-faced officers were standing on the sidewalk across the road. Just behind them, a CSI agent, dressed in a hooded Tyvek coverall and armed with a ProTac flashlight, was meticulously scrutinizing the well-cared-for front lawn. At the house's front porch, half sheltered by a blue forensics tent, a second agent was dusting the door handle and its frame for latent fingerprints.

Noticing them, the oldest of the three police officers on the sidewalk broke away from the group and crossed the road in the direction of the two detectives.

Hunter instantly noticed the single metal pin on the officer's shirt collar, which identified him as a first lieutenant with the LAPD.

'You guys must be UVC.' The officer's raspy voice sounded tired.

'Yes, sir,' Garcia replied. 'That would be us.'

The lieutenant, who looked to be in his early fifties, was about three inches shorter than Hunter and at least forty-five pounds heavier, all of it around his waist.

'I'm Lieutenant Frederick Jarvis with the Central Bureau,' he said, offering his hand. 'Northeast Area Division.'

Hunter and Garcia introduced themselves.

'Were you first at the scene?' Garcia asked.

'No,' Lieutenant Jarvis replied, turning around and indicating the two policemen he had left behind on the sidewalk. 'Officer Grabowski and Perez were. I'm the one who decided to escalate this whole mess up to you guys in Ultra Violent Crimes.'

'So you've been inside?' Hunter asked.

The lieutenant's demeanor changed as he breathed out. 'I have. Yes.' He scratched his right cheek. 'Thirty-one years in the force and in those years I have seen way more than my fair share of crazy, but if before I die I'm allowed to choose just one thing I could unsee . . .' His chin jerked in the direction of the house. 'That right in there would be it.'

Four

Hunter and Garcia signed the crime-scene manifest, collected a disposable forensics coverall each and began suiting up. Lieutenant Jarvis didn't reach for one, clearly indicating that he had no intention of reentering that particular crime scene.

'So what sort of information do we have on the victim so far?' Garcia asked.

'The very basic sort,' the lieutenant replied, reaching for his notepad. 'Her name was Linda Parker,' he began. 'Twenty-four years old from the Harbor, right here in LA. She made a living as a model. Her record was squeaky clean as far as we can tell – no arrests, no outstanding fines, no court orders ... nothing. Her VW Beetle had only a few more months to go on finance before it was all paid off. Her taxes were also all paid on time and in full.'

'Did she live here alone?' Garcia again.

'As far as we know – yes. No other names show on any of the utility bills or accounts.'

'Any known boyfriends? Relationships?'

The lieutenant shrugged. 'We've had no time to gather that sort of information. Sorry, guys, you're going to have to do the digging work on that.'

Once again, Hunter allowed his stare to run up and down the street.

'Anything at all from the neighbors?' he asked. He knew the lieutenant would've already ordered a door-to-door of the neighboring houses.

'Nothing. No one seems to have seen or heard anything, but my guys are still asking around, so maybe with a bit of luck—'

'Unfortunately lady luck doesn't seem to like us very much,' Garcia said. There was no humor in his voice. 'But who knows? Every day is a new day.'

'It looks like the perp gained access to the house through the victim's bedroom window at the back,' Lieutenant Jarvis said. 'It's been smashed from the outside.'

'How did he get access to the backyard?' Garcia asked.

The lieutenant nodded at the wooden door on the left of the house. A third forensic agent was dusting it for prints. 'No signs of forced entry, but it wouldn't take an athlete to climb over that.'

'Is that the person who found the body?' Hunter asked the lieutenant, his head tilting in the direction of the official vehicles parked on the road just to the right of the house.

As soon as he'd stepped out of his car, Hunter had noticed a female officer kneeling by the opened passenger door of the black-and-white unit furthest from them. The officer wasn't alone. A very distressed woman in her late forties, maybe early fifties, sat in the passenger seat in front of her.

'That's right,' Lieutenant Jarvis replied. 'At least you won't have to go through the ordeal of informing the parents. She's the victim's mother.'

Hunter and Garcia paused, their eyes going from the lieutenant to the woman sitting in the cruiser. Neither detective could think of a more soul-destroying experience for a mother to go through than to discover the brutally murdered body of her own daughter.

'Understandably, she's in shock,' the lieutenant explained. 'And not making a lot of sense right now, but from what we understand she used to speak to her daughter on a daily basis, either in person or on the phone.' He rechecked his notes. 'Last time they spoke was two days ago – on Monday after-noon. That was a phone conversation. They were supposed to have met for lunch yesterday, but her mother had to call and cancel. According to her, she called her daughter at around nine in the morning, but got no reply. The call went straight into voicemail. She left a message, but her daughter never called back. The mother tried calling again about forty-five minutes before they were supposed to meet, just to make sure her daughter had gotten the message and didn't waste the trip. Again, straight into voicemail. She tried again last night and then again this morning and in the afternoon.' Lieutenant Jarvis gave the detectives a confirming nod. 'Voicemail every time. That was when the mother got worried. She said that, though unlikely, maybe her daughter had gotten upset because she had to cancel their lunch meeting yesterday, but according to her, even if that had been the case, her daughter would've called back by now. The mother called again and left one last message saying that she would drop by tonight.'

'So what time did she get here today?' Hunter asked.

'Around seven o'clock.'

'How did she get in?' Garcia this time. 'Was the door unlocked?'

'No, the door was locked, but her mother kept a spare key with her.'

Hunter turned toward the CSI agent dusting the front door.

'Break-in?' he asked.

'If it happened at this door, it wasn't forcefully,' the agent replied, looking back at Hunter. 'The lock, the doorframe, nothing here has been tampered with, but this door has got a simple deadlock. It wouldn't really take an expert to breach it.'

Hunter and Garcia pulled their hoods over their heads and zipped up their coveralls.

'Through the living room,' Lieutenant Jarvis explained, gesturing as he did. 'Onto the hallway on the other side and into the bedroom at the end of it. If you get lost, just follow the smell of blood.' The lieutenant didn't phrase his last sentence as a joke. 'And if I were you, I wouldn't disregard the nose mask.'

Linda Parker's front door opened straight into a spacious living room, pleasantly decorated with a mixture of shabby-chic and traditional furniture, all of it complemented by pastel curtains, which matched the room's rugs and cushions. Nothing seemed out of place. Nothing suggested a struggle.

Another forensics agent, also searching for latent prints, was working her way through the many surfaces in the room. She acknowledged the detectives with a subtle nod.

The wooden-floor corridor that led to the rest of the house was short and wide, with a single door on the right-hand side, two on the left and one at the end of it. Only the second door on the left-hand side was shut. The walls were adorned by several framed photographs – fashion-magazine-cover style. They all showed the same striking model – slender and toned with a heart-shaped face, full lips, a delicate nose, upturned eyes that were almost aquamarine in color and cheekbones most women would pay a fortune for.

Hunter and Garcia made their way toward the room at the end of the hallway.

A quick peek into the open door on the right – bedroom.

The open door on the left – bathroom.

They would check the shut door later.

As they finally got to the crime-scene room, they paused at the door in flustered silence.

Of one thing Hunter and Garcia were both absolutely sure – Lieutenant Jarvis's wish would never come true. He would never be able to unsee what was inside that room.

Five

The man was jolted awake by the loud sound of a motorcycle in the streets outside. For a while he lay on his back, immobile, staring up at the ceiling. The room he was in was illuminated only by the weak moonlight that came in through the large window on the wall to his left, but he didn't mind the darkness. Actually, he preferred it. The way he saw it, it matched the color of his soul.

The man concentrated on his breathing, trying to calm it down. *In through your nose,* he mentally told himself as he breathed in. *And out through your mouth.* He exhaled. *In through your nose.* Breathed in. *And out through your mouth.* Exhaled.

Slowly his rapid breathing began to steady itself again.

The man was soaking wet, drenched in cold sweat, just as he always was when he woke up from 'the nightmare'. The visions were always the same – violent ... grotesque ... painful – but he didn't want to think about them. He never did. So while focusing on his breathing, he banished the images back to the darkest places in his mind, with one certainty – sooner or later they would come back again. They always did.

It took him ten minutes to finally move from lying down to

sitting up. Most of the cold sweat had dried against his skin, making him feel sticky and filthy. He needed a shower. He always needed a shower after 'the nightmare'.

In the bathroom he turned on the water and waited until steam began clouding the room before stepping under the strong and warm jet. The man closed his eyes and allowed the water to splash against his face ... his skin. He could practically feel his pores dilating, welcoming the cleansing.

He adored that sensation.

The man thoroughly washed his entire body twice over before retrieving a razorblade and a bottle of baby oil from the shower caddy. He poured some of the oil onto the palm of his right hand and slobbered it all over his left leg. The process was then repeated – left hand, right leg. It was always done in that sequence. He placed the razorblade under the water jet for a couple of seconds before bending down and bringing it to his right shin.

Years ago, a prostitute had told him that to avoid skin rashes when shaving off body hair, especially underarms and around his groin area, he should use baby or coconut oil.

'You should try it,' she had told him. 'Rashes and skin burns will be a thing of the past, trust me.'

She was right. It really did work. Not only did it free him from rashes and skin burns, but it also made his skin feel smoother than ever.

The man shaved his body daily, sometimes even twice a day, from his head all the way down to the little hairs on his toes. He did it not because he was irrational, or a fanatic, or because voices told him to. He did it simply because he enjoyed the way his skin felt in the absence of hair. How so much more sensitive it became. The only part of his body he wouldn't shave was his eyebrows. He'd tried it once before, but he didn't like the result. It made him look odd ... creepy even, and he was yet to find fake eyebrows that looked as good as real ones, unlike wigs and fake beards, which he had quite a collection of.

The man finished the long shaving process, turned off the water, stepped out of the shower and toweled himself dry. Back in the bedroom, he stood naked in front of a full-sized mirror, admiring his own body.

Full of pride, he turned to his left and switched on the large pedestal fan he kept there. As the gust of air came into contact with his smooth skin, his whole body shivered, sending a wave of ecstasy up and down his spine more powerful and pleasurable than any drug was ever able to achieve. It was as if the shaving ritual had enhanced his skin's sensory receptors tenfold.

The man bathed in that bliss for several minutes before finally switching off the fan.

'I guess it's time to go get ready,' he told himself, his body shivering one more time, this time from the pure thrill of anticipation.

The man just couldn't wait to do it all over again.

Six

When it came to crime scenes, it was no real surprise that Hunter and Garcia were known for having 'thick skin'. They had witnessed more bloody and brutal homicide aftermaths than most detectives in the entire history of the LAPD. Very few acts of violence still had the capacity to shake them. What they saw inside Linda Parker's bedroom that evening was one of them.

'What the hell?' Garcia uttered those words almost unconsciously. Despite all his experience, his brain was having trouble comprehending the images his eyes were capturing.

Everything about that crime scene was unsettling, starting with the temperature inside the room.

In Los Angeles, the average high temperature in April was around twenty-one degrees Celsius, but the room felt a lot more like two, five at a push.

Garcia folded his arms in front of his chest to keep some of his body heat, but the unusual cold temperature was only the beginning. The room before them was plastered in crimson red – the floor, the rug, the curtains, the furniture, the bed, the walls . . . everything, and still, all that blood amounted to nothing more than a silly joke when compared to the centerpiece in the room.

Linda Parker's body had been left on the bed, which had its headboard pushed up against the south wall. She was lying on her back, on blood-soaked sheets that had once been white. Her arms were resting by her torso, with her legs naturally extended, but the extremities to all four of her limbs were missing. Her feet had been hacked off at the ankles and her hands at the wrists, but that too played second fiddle to the killer's main disturbing act.

Linda Parker's body had been skinned, leaving behind a grotesque mess of brownish-red muscle tissue, naked organs and exposed bones. The smell of rotting flesh toxified the air inside the room.

'Welcome to your new nightmare, guys.'

The odd greeting came from Kevin White, the forty-eight-year-old lead forensics agent who was standing to one side of the bed. He was five-foot-ten with light brown eyes under thick, unruly eyebrows. His hair, currently covered by the hood of his Tyvek coverall, was fair and thinning at the top. His mask hid a long nose and a thin mustache that looked more like peach fuzz than facial hair. He was a very experienced agent, who had worked with Hunter and Garcia at a handful of crime scenes before. Kevin White was also an expert in forensic entomology.

Across the bed from White, a CSI photographer was clicking away at the body, trying to capture it from all possible angles. With every two or three clicks, before resuming his job, he would stop, shake his head, then look away for an instant, squinting, clearly fighting the urge to be sick.

Hunter and Garcia finally stepped into the room and, being careful to avoid the scattered pools of dried-up blood on the floorboards, approached the bed.

White gave them a few more seconds to fully take in the scene before he spoke again.

'We've been here for just a little over half an hour,' he explained. 'And as you can clearly see, this crime scene will take a while to process in full, but I'll give you the little we've come up with so far.' He nodded at the AC unit on the wall across the room from him. 'The aircon was on full blast when we got here. That's why the room feels like a fridge.'

'The killer wanted to preserve the body?' Hunter asked.

'Possibly,' White agreed. 'But if that was the killer's intention or not, the low temperature has done just that.'

Intrigue danced across both detectives' faces.

'You'll have to wait for the official autopsy result for a more precise estimate of the time of death,' White continued. 'But at this temperature, the normal decomposition process would be delayed by about thirty to forty hours. Given the fact that her body is just entering full rigor mortis, I'd say that she was murdered somewhere between forty to fifty-two hours ago.'

'That would take us back to Monday evening,' Garcia said, looking at Hunter. 'Lieutenant Jarvis told us outside that her mother last spoke to her on Monday afternoon.' He turned and addressed White again. 'It sounds like your estimate is pretty much on the money, Kevin.'

Pride lit up in White's eyes. 'The temperature, together with the shut windows all around the house, would also explain the lack of blowflies buzzing away in here.' He paused and looked back at the body on the bed. 'Her body should've been much smaller by now.'

In normal circumstances, even at nighttime, if a body were left at the mercy of the elements either outside or inside, blowflies could settle on it in a matter of minutes. They would've concentrated their efforts in the mouth, the nose, the eyes and any open wounds. In the case of a skinned body, the entire body became an open wound and therefore a breeding ground for blowflies. In just a few hours, there would have been as many as half a million eggs laid all over the corpse. Those eggs would have hatched within twenty-four hours and in a single day, the maggots that those eggs produced would have reduced a full-grown human body to half size. Hunter and Garcia knew that well enough.

'Unfortunately,' White carried on, 'for the cause of death you'll have to wait for the autopsy report. What I can tell you is that there are no visible stabbing or bullet wounds. No apparent blunt trauma to the head, either. No bones seem to be broken, with the obvious exception of the severed hands and feet. Her ribcage looks intact and her neck hasn't been snapped.'

'Bled out?' Garcia ventured.

'There's a high possibility that that was how she died,' White accepted. 'But as I've said, the autopsy report will clear it up.'

Both detectives went silent for a moment.

'We haven't found any of the missing body parts,' White added. 'No hands, feet, or skin, but we haven't had time to check the whole house yet.'

'Any way of telling if any of this savagery was done while she was still alive?' Garcia asked.

'Not with any certainty,' White replied. 'I hate to sound repetitive here, Carlos, but you'll have to wait for the autopsy report for a more accurate answer.'

Garcia's eyes circled the room one more time. Judging by the amount of blood everywhere, he wouldn't be surprised if the post-mortem revealed that the victim was indeed alive when she was skinned. But even if that had been the case, something still made no sense to him.

'I don't get this,' he said. 'What the hell is all this blood everywhere?' His stare moved to Hunter, but the question was thrown at anyone who cared to answer it. 'And all the way across the room, too. This isn't arterial spray. We can all see that.' He stepped closer to the east wall, studying a long blood mark against it. 'All these marks look like smudges. As if they were done on purpose.'

'They could very possibly have been,' White agreed.

Hunter stepped closer to the bed and began studying what once had been Linda Parker's face. In the absence of skin, what was left behind was horrifying and hypnotic in equal measures.

As a consequence of over forty hours of exposure, even at low temperatures, the thin muscle layer that sat between her facial bone structure and her skin had darkened into an odd shade of brown, as if it had been lightly scorched by fire. Her nose cartilage was still in place, but the eyelids and lips were gone, completely exposing her gums, teeth, jawbone, skullcap and ocular cavity. Her eyes hadn't been removed by her killer, but they weren't there anymore either. Most of the vitreous humor – the transparent jelly-like tissue filling the eyeball behind the lens – had dried up. As a result, Linda Parker's eyes had deflated and practically disappeared into their sockets.

'Have you moved her yet?' Hunter asked.

'No, not yet,' White replied. 'I was waiting for you guys to get here so you could see the body in situ, because here's the catch – if you look closely, it doesn't look like the killer skinned her completely.'

Hunter took a step back, tilting his head to one side.

'You're right,' he said. 'It seems like there's still a patch of skin left on her back.'

Garcia joined Hunter. 'That's odd. Why would the killer skin most of her body, but leave a patch on her back?'

'Let's have a look, shall we?' White said, walking around to the other side of the bed. 'You guys want to give me a hand?' White asked Hunter and Garcia.

'Sure.'

The photographer got out of the way, moving over to the other end of the room.

'Let's just bring her up into a sitting position as much as we can,' White said, nodding at Hunter and Garcia, who nodded back. 'On three . . . one, two, three.'

As they brought the body up from the bed, Hunter, Garcia and White all angled their heads to one side to have a look at the victim's back.

As the patch of skin finally came into view, they all froze.

'Jesus!' White said. 'What the hell is this?'

Seven

Still bare of clothes, the man took a seat at his dressing table and studied his reflection in the three-way vanity mirror for a moment, checking his profile from both angles.

He loved the strange sensation he got every time he was about to start his transformation. It was a complicated feeling that not even he could properly explain, but it bizarrely filled him with a sense of accomplishment merged with something he could only describe as mind-numbing ecstasy.

The man savored that sensation for an extra full minute, allowing it to run through his body like blood running through his veins.

Elated, the man smiled at himself.

He knew that he could make himself look however he pleased. He could change the shape of his nose, the color of his eyes, the fullness of his cheekbones, the angle of his chin, the thickness of his lips, the contour of his ears, the quality of his teeth . . . it didn't matter. The man's knowledge of how to mold foam prosthetics coupled with his makeup expertise was second to none. Better yet, if he combined all that with just a few electronic gadgets, he could even change the sound and the strength of his voice, like he'd done before.

The man sat back on his chair and regarded the photo he had pinned to the top right-hand corner of his mirror. He had absolutely no idea who the man on it was. The picture had come from a random stock-photos website, but the person on it had a very interesting look about him – round nose, low cheekbones, full lips, blue eyes, and angled eyebrows that gave his whole face a somewhat sad look. For some reason the man liked that. The person's skin color was also a shade darker than the man's own.

The man had already molded several pieces of foam prosthetics to match the person's nose, lips and cheekbones, and as he applied a thin layer of special adhesive to one of the pieces, he began to imagine what that person would be like in real life – how he would talk, walk, smile, laugh . . . Would his voice be soft and subdued, strong and authoritative, or a combination of both?

How about his personality? the man wondered. *Would he be outgoing, talkative, shy, introvert, funny, serious, intellectual?* The possibilities were endless, and that thoroughly excited him. He loved the creation process of every new person he became. He loved it because there was no one better at it than he was. But the physical transformation, together with the personality conception, was only part of the fun. The real excitement, the real creative process would come later, for the man was undoubtedly an artist.

Eight

Hunter, Garcia and White were all surprised to see that a perfectly shaped, straight-edged patch of skin still remained attached to Linda Parker's back. In fact, the patch covered the whole of her back, from left to right side and from a couple of centimeters below her shoulders all the way down to the top of her buttocks, but the surprises didn't end there. Despite all the dried blood that covered most of that skin patch, all three of them could clearly see that something had been hastily carved into it, rupturing the skin and cutting into her flesh.

'What the actual fuck?' Garcia whispered as he squinted at the marks.

'Tommy,' White called, gesturing for the forensics photographer to join them. 'You need to come get this.'

Tommy looked back at White as if saying, *There's more to this freakshow?*

'Now,' White urged him.

Adjusting his glasses, Tommy walked around to the left side of the bed.

'Oh, man!' he said, shaking his head one more time. 'This just ain't right.'

The carvings to the victim's back looked like an odd combination of symbols and letters, forming four distinct horizontal lines. Those symbols and letters had been crudely carved using only straight lines, no curves.

It took the photographer a couple of seconds to recompose himself before he began clicking away. Despite the blinding brightness of his camera flash exploding from behind them, Hunter's attention never faltered.

As his gaze moved from letter to symbol and from straight line to straight line, a new shiver began at the core of Hunter's soul, gaining momentum like a rocket.

'Is this some sort of Devil-worship language or some bull-shit like that?' Garcia again.

Hunter slowly shook his head at his partner.

'Well, it's definitely not English,' White replied.

'Maybe it's alien,' the photographer offered. 'It would be easier to believe that than that another human being was capable of doing all this.'

'No.' Hunter finally broke his silence, his voice plain. 'It's Latin.'

'Latin?'

Both Garcia and the photographer frowned at Hunter before their attention returned to the markings on the victim's back. They re-studied them for another long moment.

White also didn't look so sure.

'I don't see it, Robert,' he said, tilting his head from one side to the other. 'And my Latin isn't bad at all.'

'If this is Latin,' Garcia asked, 'what do these symbols mean?'

'They aren't symbols,' Hunter replied, but he could easily see how his partner, or anyone else, would've mistaken some of the carved letters for symbols. 'It's just the careless way in which the letters were drawn.'

Neither Garcia nor White seemed to follow.

'Do you guys have her?' Hunter asked. 'Can I free my hands?'

'Yeah, we've got her,' White replied.

Hunter let go of the body.

Garcia and White kept her in place.

'These cuts to her skin,' Hunter began, indicating as he clarified. 'These lines used to form the letters, were made by what look like quick slashes from some sort of blade.' He reenacted the movement with his hand, his index finger sticking out.

'Yeah, OK,' Garcia agreed.

White also nodded.

'And as you can see,' Hunter continued, still indicating as he spoke, 'whoever did this used only straight lines, no curves, which gives us two options. One – he drew some of the letters this way on purpose, or two – he wasn't paying that much attention to precision as he drew them. Nevertheless, what we are left with here are several lines that fail to connect where they were supposed to, either by falling short or missing the target altogether. That's why some of these look more like symbols than letters.'

Garcia, White and Tommy, who had stopped taking pictures to concentrate on Hunter's explanation, still looked very confused.

Hunter tried to clarify.

'Like here, for example. This is supposed to be a "P".' Hunter used his finger to redraw the letter over the existing carved one without touching the victim, but this time he used a curved line. 'And this is a "D".' He repeated the process.

'Some are also very skewed and out of line, which makes it a lot harder to see it, like here – this is supposed to be an "H", this is an "M", this is an "S", and this is a "C".'

As Hunter redrew the letters with his fingers, his argument began to make a lot more sense.

'I'll be damned,' White said, his eyes widening at the markings. The puzzle was beginning to come together for him, but it still wasn't quite there yet.

'The next problem we have –' Hunter wasn't done yet, '– is that as everyone can see, we have four distinct horizontal lines here, which would suggest that we also have four different words, but we don't.'

Garcia was still staring at the carvings, but the look in his eyes was a very lost one.

'How many words do we have?' White asked.

'Three,' Hunter replied. 'But they've been split at completely random places to form four lines. If you give me a piece of paper and a pen I'll show you.'

'I can get you one,' Tommy said, walking over to his camera case, which he had left by the bedroom door. A couple of seconds later he handed Hunter a notepad and a pencil.

'So this is the first line.'

Hunter said each letter out loud as he first indicated it on the victim's back, before writing it on the notepad.

Finally Hunter showed them what he had written.

PULCHR.

ITUDOCI.

RCUMD.

ATEIUS.

'What the fuck?' Garcia said, as he and White placed the body back onto a lying position.

He knew that Hunter saw things differently than most people did. His brain worked differently too, especially when it came to putting puzzles together, but sometimes Hunter did more than surprise him, he scared him.

'How the hell did you manage to see all that from these crazy cuts to her back, and so fast, too?'

'I was just about to ask you the same thing,' White said. 'Have you seen something like this before?'

Hunter shook his head before playing it down. 'No, never. Maybe it was the angle I was looking at them.'

White's attention returned to the piece of paper Hunter had shown them. 'Pulchritudocircumdateius.' He first read it at an overly slow pace and as a single word before finally splitting the three words correctly. 'Pulchritudo Circumdat Eius.' His pronunciation was spot on.

Garcia's eyebrows arched, as his stare ping-ponged between Hunter and White. 'Unfortunately the last time I spoke Latin was – never. What the hell does it mean? Does anyone know? Is it supposed to be some sort of Devil incantation or something?'

'No.' This time it was White who shook his head. 'I don't think so.'

'So what is it?'

'If I'm not mistaken,' White replied, 'it means – Beauty is all around her.'

'That's correct,' Hunter confirmed. 'Beauty is all around her ... beauty surrounds her. The words in English may vary, but the meaning is the same.'

For a moment Garcia paused and looked around the room again in astonished disbelief, his gaze moving from blood smudge to blood smudge. 'Beauty is all around her? What beauty?'

White's stare followed Garcia's. It was then that a thought came to him. 'You wanted to know what all this was?' He addressed the detective. 'All this blood everywhere for no apparent reason? Maybe you're right. Maybe all these smudges *were* done on purpose. Maybe this killer believes he's ...' White cringed at his own suggestion, '... an artist or something. Maybe to him ...' He nodded at the skinned and mutilated body. 'All this – the victim, the room, the blood, the position he left her, all of it – is nothing more than a ... morbid art piece.'

Hunter could feel goose bumps kiss the back of his neck. He took a step back and tried to take in the whole scene one more time.

'The carvings to the victim's back ...' White said in conclusion, 'they could be just how the killer chose to sign his work.'

Before anyone could reply, the female forensics agent who had been dusting the surfaces in the living room for latent prints appeared at the door to the bedroom.

'Jesus Christ!' she said, her expression one of sheer disgust. 'Whoever this killer is, he's one sick sonofabitch.'

Everyone frowned at her.

'You guys better come and have a look at this.'

Nine

Hunter, Garcia and White followed the agent out of the bedroom and through the short hallway that led back into the living room, but contrary to what they were expecting, the agent didn't direct them to any of the surfaces she'd been dusting for prints, nor did she lead them to the front door or the outside of the house. Instead, she took a right as they entered the living room and guided everyone into a sharp-lined, modern-looking kitchen.

The kitchen was surprisingly spacious, with black granite worktops running along three of the walls and contrasting perfectly with the shiny white floors and cupboard doors. The chrome extractor unit above the black stove matched the stainless-steel sink and the wall-mounted oven. A large double window, directly above the sink, would no doubt bring more than enough sunlight into the kitchen during daytime. The fridge, the freezer and the dishwasher were all hidden behind cupboard doors, making the kitchen look and feel clean and decluttered, and that was exactly the first thing Hunter noticed as he stepped into the room – how clean it all seemed to be. There was no real mess anywhere. No crumbs or leftovers on any of the surfaces, including the floor. Nothing to be put away, except three items left inside the sink – a fork, a small salad bowl and a wine glass. The wine glass and the salad bowl were both empty. The glass showed residues of red wine and a very noticeable red lipstick smudge around its rim.

'I finished with all the surfaces in the living room,' the agent explained. 'Second in line was the kitchen.' She nodded at her equipment case on the floor, to the right of the door.

Despite her steady voice, Hunter picked up a sincere hint of distress in her tone. While she spoke, his eyes carried on scanning the room.

'As I'm sure you have already noticed,' the agent continued, 'every appliance in this kitchen, except for the oven and the microwave, sit hidden behind one of the cupboard doors.'

She indicated the first door on the far left, under the work-top that hugged the east wall.

'We have a dishwasher right here,' she said, before diverting their attention to the two tall doors that flanked the wall-mounted oven on the west side of the kitchen. 'Over there you'll find the fridge on the left and the freezer on the right.' She paused and took a deep breath. 'Why don't you go ahead and have a look inside the freezer?'

Kevin White's stare stayed on his agent for a couple more seconds before moving to Hunter and Garcia, who were standing to his left. He already had a pretty good idea of what he would find inside that freezer. His weight shifted from one foot to another before he finally took a step forward and pulled open the door.

'Oh ... Jesus Christ!'

The shock in White's voice was real. There was no question that he was expecting to find the victim's missing body parts stashed away in that freezer. But he was wrong. He was very wrong.

Hunter and Garcia had followed White and what they saw as he pulled the freezer door open added a whole new layer of cruelty to an already over-sadistic crime scene.

Two of the freezer shelves had been removed to create more vertical space. In that space, frozen in place, was a black and gray cat.

Ten

It was coming up to a quarter past one in the morning by the time Hunter finally got to his small one-bedroom apartment in Huntington Park, southeastern Los Angeles. Kevin White and his forensics team had stayed behind at the house. Despite how fast they were working they were still at least three to four hours away from processing it all, and that was only if they failed to stumble upon any more surprises. Hunter and Garcia had waited until Linda Parker's body had been taken to the county coroner's office before leaving the crime scene, but as Hunter closed his front door behind him, he wondered why he hadn't stayed with the forensics team. It would've at least kept him busy, since he could already tell that tonight, falling asleep would be a real struggle.

Insomnia is a highly unpredictable condition that affects one in every five people in the United States. It can manifest itself in a variety of ways and intensities, none of them kind. The disorder is usually linked to stress and the pressures of being an adult in modern society, but not always.

Hunter was only seven years old when he first started experiencing sleepless nights. They began shortly after cancer robbed him of his mother. Back then, with no other family for him to rely on other than his father, coping with such loss proved to be a very painful and lonely affair for the young Robert Hunter. At night, he would sit alone in his bedroom and lose himself in the memories of when his mother could still smile. Of a time when her arms were still strong enough to hug him and her voice loud enough to reach his ears.

With her death, it didn't take long for the ghastly nightmares to follow and they were so devastating, so psychologically damaging that insomnia was the only logical answer his brain could come up with. Sleep became a Russian roulette for Hunter – a luxury and a torment all rolled up in one. For a seven-year-old boy, his coping mechanism was as brutal as a battlefield amputation, but Hunter faced it the best way he could. To keep himself occupied during those endless, lonely, sleepless hours, Hunter took to books, reading everything and anything he could get his hands on as if reading somehow empowered him. Books became his sanctuary. His fortress. His shield against the never-ending nightmares.

As the years went by, Hunter learned how to live with insomnia instead of fighting it. On a good night he would find three, maybe four hours of sleep. On a bad one, not even a second.

Hunter had just finished pouring himself a glass of water in the kitchen when he heard his cellphone vibrate on top of the small dining table that doubled as a computer desk in the living room. He checked his watch again – 01:17 a.m.

'Detective Hunter, UVC Unit,' he said, bringing the phone to his ear.

'Robert . . .'

For a moment the female voice threw him. At that time in the morning, especially after just coming back from a crime scene where the forensics team had stayed behind, Hunter didn't even check the display screen, already fully expecting to hear Kevin White's voice, bringing him even more bad news.

'Robert?' the voice said again, this time as a question.

Hunter had completely forgotten about his unfinished UCLA lecture. He had completely forgotten that he had promised Professor Tracy Adams that he would call her.

'Tracy,' he said, his voice low and apologetic. 'I'm so sorry I haven't called you. I ...' Hunter saw no point in lying, '... forgot.'

'No, don't worry about that,' Tracy replied, her tone sincere.

Hunter and Professor Adams had met for the first time a few months ago at the twenty-four-hour reading room of the historic Powell Library Building inside the UCLA campus. The attraction on both sides had been immediate and though they'd been out on a few dates where romance had certainly threatened to blossom, Hunter had chosen to keep it just a little over an arm's length away.

'Is everything OK?' Tracy asked, and instantly regretted the question. She knew Hunter's LAPD unit dealt solely with extreme violent crimes, which meant that every time he received a call where he had to drop everything and just go, everything was never OK.

'I'm sorry. I mean ...' Tracy tried to think where to back-pedal to.

'It's all right. I know what you mean,' Hunter said, hoping Tracy wouldn't pick up on the concern in his voice, but knowing that she was way too attentive not to.

Hunter never discussed his cases with anyone outside the realms of the investigation, no matter how close to him they were, but he had to admit that he had come close to confiding in her more than once before. Not only was Tracy one of the most grounded people he had ever met, she was also a very well-respected criminal psychology professor at UCLA. If there ever were a civilian who would understand the pressures of what he went through with the Ultra Violent Crimes Unit, Tracy Adams would certainly be that person.

'I'm so sorry about the lecture last night,' Hunter said, moving away from the subject. 'I was actually looking forward to it.'

'No you weren't,' Tracy replied, the quirkiness in her tone giving away the smile on her face. 'Did you forget that I was the one who spent weeks trying to convince you to do it?'

Hunter said nothing.

'But admit it, Robert. You were having fun, weren't you? I saw it. You felt that teaching bug bite.'

Hunter nodded to himself. 'It was a lot less painful than what I'd expected.'

'Well, I do love what I do,' Tracy said. 'But I'll tell you this, I'd give just about anything for the attendance numbers and the level of undivided attention you got in those few minutes. Everyone in that room was completely transfixed by everything you were saying. Including me.'

Hunter laughed. 'And the really interesting part was still to come.'

'Yes, I can imagine.'

Hunter walked over to the large window in his living room. Outside, clouds had started gathering up in the sky, slowly ridding the night of all its stars.

'Robert . . . are you still there?'

Hunter caught a glimpse of his reflection in the window. He looked tired.

'Yes. I'm here.'

'Are you at home?'

A short pause.

'Yes, I just got in about five minutes ago, but I can't help thinking that I should've stayed. CSI is still at the scene, and they'll be there for at least another two to three hours.'

'Wow, is it that bad?' Tracy's question ran away from her and for the second time in less than a minute, she found herself regretting her choice of words, but before she had a chance to apologize, Hunter surprised her.

'Worse, Tracy,' he confirmed in a heavy voice. 'A lot worse.'

Tracy's initial impulse had been to ask Hunter if he wanted to talk about it, but this time thought finally preceded action and she quickly rephrased the question in her head before actually asking it.

'Would you like some company? Do you want to come over?'

Hunter hesitated.

'I'm still wide awake,' she added. 'Will be for hours. I can tell.'

As coincidence had it, Tracy Adams also suffered from insomnia, albeit not as severely as Hunter.

'And I've got a late start tomorrow. My first class is only at eleven.'

The truth was, Hunter would have loved her company, but he thought about it for an instant, more than enough time for his logical side to take over.

'Is it OK if I take a rain check on that one? Tonight I won't be good company to anybody.'

Hunter meant every word, but that was only part of the reason. Something had been really bothering him since he had entered Linda Parker's bedroom a few hours back, and before the night was over he wanted to run a couple of searches against a few different databases.

'Of course,' Tracy replied after a silent moment. 'If you change your mind, you know where to find me, right?'

'I do. I'll call you, OK?'

As soon as they disconnected, images of the crime scene began tumbling over each other inside Hunter's head – avalanche style. He looked up at the sky again. The stars were now all gone. Darkness, it seemed, had come to Los Angeles in more ways than one.

Eleven

Dr. Carolyn Hove, the Los Angeles Chief Medical Examiner, was an early riser. She'd been so for as long as anyone could remember, including herself. Back when she was a schoolkid, even during summer breaks, and to her parents' dismay and annoyance, young Carolyn would be up and ready for action by the crack of dawn. One of her earliest memories of her late father was of him telling her that if she looked up the definition of 'morning person' in a dictionary, she would probably find a picture of herself.

That morning, like every morning throughout the year, Dr. Hove arrived at the County Department of Medical Examiner – Coroner in North Mission Road at least an hour before any other pathologist in her team. That first quiet hour by herself was her favorite part of the working day.

At the reception counter, inside the lobby of the architecturally stunning old hospital-turned-morgue, Frank, the night watcher, who was built like a tank, greeted her with a warm smile.

'Good morning, Doctor,' he said in his natural baritone voice.

Dr. Hove smiled back at him. Despite being in her late

forties, she still looked like a woman in her early thirties, tall and slim, with piercing green eyes, full lips, prominent cheekbones and a delicate nose. That morning, her long chestnut hair had been tied back into a tidy ponytail.

Frank pushed a large cup of coffee across the counter in her direction.

'Brewed less than a minute ago,' he said.

Every morning, as soon as Frank saw Dr. Hove driving into the parking lot through one of the many surveillance monitors, he would make a brand-new pot of strong Colombian coffee. Her favorite. By the time she'd parked and walked through the main entrance doors, he'd always have a fresh, steaming cup waiting for her.

'I have no idea what my mornings would be like without you, Frank,' the doctor said as she took the cup. Her voice had the sort of velvety and calm tone usually associated with experience and knowledge, and Dr. Hove possessed plenty of both. 'Did you watch the game last night?' she asked, already knowing the answer. Just like her, Frank was a huge Lakers fan and, if time and work allowed, would never miss a game.

'But of course,' he replied. 'Did you?'

The doctor made a face at him. 'Does Dolly Parton sleep on her back?'

Frank's smile brightened. 'What a game, wasn't it? And we're now one step closer to the playoffs.'

'Oh, we'll get there,' Dr. Hove said with conviction. 'The way we've been playing, there's no doubt about it. I'll see you tomorrow, Frank. Have a good morning and a good sleep.'

'Have no doubt of that, Doc.'

Dr. Hove approached the double metal doors just past the

reception counter and waited for Frank to buzz her in. Once she got to her office, she fired up her computer, sat back on her chair and sipped her coffee. It tasted absolutely perfect.

As her computer finally came to life, the event and autopsy rota was the first application to automatically load onto her screen.

She studied it for a short moment.

Several autopsies from the previous day had taken longer than the examining pathologist had anticipated, which was nothing new. Due to the incredible workload of the Los Angeles County morgue, such delays happened a lot more often than Dr. Hove wanted. The main problem was, those autopsies would have to be reentered into today's schedule, pushing back the ones that had originally been planned for the day. It was a vicious cycle and at the moment, the backlog added up to roughly a week and a half.

Dr. Hove had another sip of her coffee and went to work. As the Chief Medical Examiner, it was her job to reschedule the autopsies each and every morning, reassigning examination rooms and pathologists if necessary. She had to push back five post-mortems originally scheduled for the end of the day, but after twenty minutes she had it all sorted out. Unfortunately that was only half of the battle.

Dr. Hove's stare moved to the pile of folders that had been left inside the 'entry' tray on her desk. Those files belonged to the bodies that had arrived overnight. They would have to be entered into the system and added to the autopsy schedule.

'Never a dull night in the City of Angels,' she whispered to herself, reaching for the files.

Unknown to Dr. Hove, in the early hours of the

morning, there had been two retaliation drive-by shoot-outs in Westmont. Nine males had lost their lives, and four of them were under the age of eighteen. Add five other adult bodies to that tally – three male and two female – who had all died under mysterious circumstances, and Dr. Hove was looking at fourteen new arrivals; but again, that didn't really bother her. What did bring a worried frown to her forehead was the annotation that had been made to the cover sheet of one of the two female body files.

New entries marked as 'urgent' were a common trade in her line of work. Understandably, every LAPD or county sheriff homicide detective saw practically every single one of their cases as urgent, and since the results from a post-mortem examination could very easily change the entire course of an investigation, they would all like to have them back as fast as humanly possible. Dr. Hove and every pathologist in her team were more than used to handling cases tagged as urgent. But the file she had in her hand wasn't marked as urgent. It was marked as a Level Zero autopsy.

Twelve

In Los Angeles, every post-mortem examination where, even after death, the victim could still pose some sort of risk of contamination – radiation, poisoning, contagious diseases, etc., were tagged as 'dangerous' or 'hazardous'. Those examinations were conducted exclusively inside Autopsy Theater Zero, which was the only autopsy theater located in a sealed-off area down in the basement of the main building of the Medical Examiner complex. Those autopsies were known as Level Zero and they could only be performed by a specialist team, or the Chief Medical Examiner herself.

'Interesting,' Dr. Hove said, flipping open the file.

She was instantly surprised.

Usually, requests for a Level Zero autopsy only came to her if the investigation was either being handled by the FBI, or had the involvement of the CDC – Center for Disease Control and Prevention – but that wasn't the case. This investigation belonged to the LAPD. More precisely, to the Ultra Violent Crimes Unit. The name of the lead detective assigned to the case was Robert Hunter.

As the doctor read that piece of information, her interest

increased. She leaned forward and placed her coffee cup on her desk.

Dr. Hove and Detective Hunter's professional relationship went back several years and she was yet to meet a more enigmatic man than the head of the LAPD's Ultra Violent Crimes Unit, but that wasn't the only characteristic that differentiated Hunter from every other homicide detective inside the LAPD, and every other law-enforcement agency she had ever worked with. In twenty-one years as a pathologist, Dr. Hove had never come across anyone who could read a crime scene or get inside the mind of a killer quite the same way Detective Hunter could.

Even without seeing the body, Dr. Hove was sure that this would be an interesting post-mortem examination.

Due to the fact that the female body in question had only been discovered in the early hours of last night, the file Dr. Hove was looking at held a limited amount of information – victim's name and address, a basic description of the crime scene, the name of the unit and the detectives assigned to the case, and the name of the lead forensics agent who had attended the scene. There were no CSI photographs. Not yet. Those would be added later, together with several different forensics lab reports.

Dr. Hove's attention returned to her computer screen and she rechecked her roster. Level Zero autopsies always took priority over absolutely everything.

After rescheduling a private post-mortem examination and postponing a late-morning meeting, she was able to slot the new entry into her first autopsy of the day. Half an hour later, she had suited up and was ready to start.

Autopsy Theater Zero was more than just a post-mortem examination room. It was a completely self-contained pathology examination area, with its own cold-storage chamber and an individual lab facility. Its restricted access database also sat separate from the Department of Medical Examiner's main databank, which meant that the results of any post-mortem examinations conducted inside Theater Zero couldn't be accessed by general personnel and therefore could be kept a secret, at least for some time.

Linda Parker's body, still sealed inside a body bag, was brought down to Theater Zero by one of the autopsy technicians, who also helped Dr. Hove move it from the gurney to one of the three stainless-steel examination tables inside the large white-tiled room.

'Would you be needing anything else, Doctor?' the athletic-looking technician asked as his gaze moved around furtively. He'd never been inside this room before. 'Would you like me to help you wash and prepare the body?'

'No, I'll be fine on my own,' the doctor replied, pushing her dark-framed glasses up the bridge of her nose. 'If I need anything else I'll call.'

She waited until the technician had exited the theater before unzipping the body bag.

Despite all her experience, despite the hundreds and hundreds of murdered bodies she'd examined throughout her career, the brutality of certain cases that ended up on her autopsy table still had the capacity to disturb her. This certainly was one of those.

The full examination lasted just a little under two hours and as Dr. Hove finally identified the cause of death, she took a step back from the table and regarded the savagely mutilated and skinned body on it one more time.

'This doesn't make any sense.'

Thirteen

Hunter and Garcia's office was at the far end of the Robbery Homicide Division's floor, inside the famous Police Administration Building in downtown LA. The office was a claustrophobic twenty-two-square-meter concrete box, with barely more than two desks, three old-fashioned filing cabinets and a large white magnetic board pushed up against the south wall, but it was still a completely separate enclosure to the rest of the RHD, which, if nothing else, kept prying eyes and the loud buzzing of voices locked out.

Hunter had received an email from Kevin White less than an hour ago, enclosing a copy of the crime-scene forensics report together with a .zip file containing all the images captured by the official photographer. Hunter had spent the last half-hour printing them all out and pinning them to the magnetic board, when Captain Blake pushed open their office door and stepped inside.

Barbara Blake had taken over the LAPD Robbery Homicide Division's leadership several years ago, after the retirement of its long-standing captain, William Bolter. Elegant, attractive, with long black hair and mysterious dark eyes that could make most people shiver with a single stare, Captain Blake wasn't easily intimidated. After so many years and so many different roles within the force, very little ever unsettled her, but for the next full minute she didn't say a word to either of her two detectives. All she did was study the pictures on the white board with a disbelieving look.

'The victim was skinned?' she finally asked in a breath that nearly failed her.

'Almost entirely, Captain,' Garcia replied, letting himself slump back on his chair.

'Alive?'

'Couldn't be determined at the scene.' This time the reply came from Hunter. 'We're still waiting for the autopsy report to confirm it. If we're lucky, we might still get it this morning.'

'The killer also took her hands and feet,' Garcia added.

The captain's stare paused on him for an instant before returning to the board. She stepped closer and her eyes found the close-up photograph of what the killer had carved into the victim's back.

'What the actual hell?' Among the carvings, Captain Blake was able to identify a few letters. 'Is this supposed to say something?'

Garcia got to his feet. 'It's actually Latin, Captain.' He approached the board and showed her how several of the lines should have connected but didn't. When he was done, Captain Blake shook her head as if she had been temporarily stunned. Her eyes narrowed, trying to make out the words.

'It means – "beauty is all around her", Captain.'

Blank turned into skeptical.

'I don't get it,' she finally said.

Garcia didn't suffer from insomnia but, just like Hunter, he too had had very little sleep overnight. After returning from Linda Parker's crime scene, he had spent most of the early hours of the morning trying to understand at least a fraction of the madness he had seen inside that house . . . the blood, the carvings, the skinned body, the missing feet and hands . . . No matter which path he tried to follow inside his head, they all seemed to end up at the exact same well.

'It's early days, Captain,' Garcia said, walking back to his desk. 'But a half theory sort of emerged last night at the crime scene.'

'All right,' the captain said with interest. 'And what is this half theory?'

Garcia knew that he was about to enter Crazyland. He sat back on his chair, rested his elbows on the armrests and touched fingertip against fingertip.

'That maybe this killer thinks of himself as an artist.' He paused and indicated the photos on the board. 'And that craziness you see there would be nothing more than his "art piece", which he considers to be a work of beauty.'

The captain's gaze had returned to the photos on the board, but it slowly moved back to Garcia.

'Are you joking?' She almost choked on her next words. 'An artist? A work of beauty? What?'

Garcia nodded. 'To the killer – maybe – yes.'

'That's absurd.'

Garcia looked at Hunter for help.

He got none.

'Indeed it is,' Garcia agreed. 'And to be honest, no matter how inventive we might believe we are, we would never have come up with such a crazy theory if not for the message the killer carved into this poor girl's back.'

On the board, Captain Blake found the picture that showed the carvings.

'Beauty is all around her?' she asked. 'Is that what you said all that nonsense translates to?'

'That's it. And I know how crazy it all sounds, Captain, but it also makes some sort of crazy sense.'

Glaring at her detective, the captain threw her hands up. 'Well, I'm all ears, Carlos. Please, by all means, enlighten me.' She grabbed a fold-up chair that was leaning against one of the walls and took a seat.

Garcia got up and walked back over to the picture board.

'Have a look at these, Captain,' he began, indicating the photographs taken of the walls, the furniture and the floor inside Linda Parker's bedroom, all of it completely smeared in blood.

Captain Blake shrugged. 'Yeah, so? This is the Ultra Violent Crimes Unit, isn't it? Ninety-eight percent of all crime scenes you investigate look like that or worse.'

'That's true. But in all of them there's an obvious reason for all the blood.' He shook his head. 'Not here.'

'What? You're telling me that you can't find a reason to justify all those blood smears?' Her questioning stare ran from Garcia to Hunter then back to Garcia. 'How about a struggle?' she suggested. 'A desperate victim, covered in blood, trying to get away from her attacker and stumbling everywhere: the walls ... the furniture ... isn't that a possibility?'

'Our first thought too,' Garcia agreed. 'But have a closer look at these pictures.' He indicated a group of three photographs showing furniture pieces inside Linda Parker's bedroom – a chest of drawers, a dressing table and a bedside table – the pieces all had blood smeared against them. 'If all this blood was the result of our victim desperately running away from her killer, then what's missing from these photos?'

The captain studied the images for a long moment.

'A mess,' she said, finally understanding what Garcia was referring to. 'There's no mess.'

'Precisely,' Garcia confirmed. 'Nothing was out of place. Nothing had been knocked over anywhere. The vase, the alarm clock, the reading lamp, the picture frames, her makeup, her jewelry . . . every object in that room seemed to be exactly where it was supposed to be. There was nothing on the floor, either. Not even a hairclip. Trust me, we looked. If she'd been running for her life, leaving bloodstains all over the place while colliding with her furniture, her stuff should've been all over the room.'

The captain couldn't fault Garcia's logic, which right then began to scare her a little bit. 'So what you're saying is you think that all those blood smears and smudges everywhere were done on purpose? To transform the room into a . . . piece . . . a sculpture . . . a canvas . . . whatever.'

Once again, her stare played between her two detectives.

This time, Hunter finally replied.

'Right now, that's what it looks like, Captain.'

Fourteen

The man had always preferred to travel at night. The low temperatures were a lot kinder, not only to the car's engine, but also to its tires, not to mention how so much lighter traffic was everywhere, but that was only part of the reason.

Ever since he was a little kid, the man had always been a creature of the night. There was no denying that. He had always loved its sounds, its smell, its mystery. He loved the way nighttime scared and liberated him at the same time, but most of all, he loved the darkness and how perfectly it was able to hide him.

The man could easily remember when his mother used to order him to bed – 9:00 p.m. on the dot, every day. No exceptions. Ever.

The man would never argue, either. There was no point because there would never be an argument. If he ever tried talking back to her, or contradicting her in any way, the gates of hell would open before him. So instead of arguing, as soon as the clock struck nine o'clock, the man would quietly and calmly retire to his bedroom. His mother didn't even need to say anything. The trick was – he wouldn't really go to sleep. All the man would do was lie on his bed and pretend.

Pretend that he was somewhere else. Pretend that he was someone else.

And his imagination was powerful.

A lot more powerful than the gates of hell.

A lot more powerful than hell itself.

But that had been a long time ago. Those particular gates were now forever shut.

Unfortunately, newer, improved and a lot more powerful ones had opened.

The man was dragged away from his memory by a barking dog somewhere down an alleyway. The nighttime drive had made a seven-hour trip last just under five and a half and he had made it to his destination with plenty of time to spare.

The man checked his watch. The center would open in a few hours.

Still sitting in the driver's seat, he stretched his back and massaged his neck. The movement of people on the streets was starting to pick up, as regular office hours were just around the corner. Bus stops were filling up, strolls were becoming more hurried and traffic noise seemed to be doubling by the minute.

The man sat back and thought about what to do. Maybe he would go get some breakfast in a café somewhere and strike up a conversation with the person behind the counter or at the next table. It would give him a chance to test his new character: Mike – that was the name he had chosen for this particular one.

Yes, he thought. That was a good plan.

After that, he would get back to his car and start bandaging his arm.

Fifteen

Captain Blake took a moment, allowing her thoughts to try to catch up with what Hunter and Garcia were suggesting. It didn't take an expert to read the hesitation in her demeanor.

'As Carlos has pointed out, Captain,' Hunter said, grabbing her attention again. 'It's way too early in the investigation to assume anything with any degree of certainty. All this really means is that we'll all have to keep an open mind here. Someone who is capable of something like this, will, I'm sure, also have a very distorted vision of reality.'

'Why doesn't that surprise me?' the captain said. Very little ever made sense at the LAPD's Violent Crimes Unit.

'So who is she?' Captain Blake asked, crossing one leg over the other. 'Do we have any background info on her yet?'

'We do, but nothing in great detail,' Garcia replied, reaching for the notepad on his desk. 'Her name was Linda Parker, born on March ninth, 1994 in Harbor City. She was the only child of Emily and Vincent Parker. Emily was a housewife and Vincent an accountant running his own private firm in Rolling Hills. Linda went to Newport Harbor high school, where she graduated in 2011. Apparently she managed to escape most of the downfalls of puberty because she started modeling for catalogs when she was only thirteen years old. In school, she was voted Newport Harbor Prom Queen for three consecutive years. As a senior she was also voted "most likely to become a supermodel". By the time she graduated from high school, she was doing quite well as a catalog model, bringing in nearly as much money as her father. After high school, she decided to skip going to college to concentrate on her modeling career. I guess the main idea was to move on to international modeling and big-name designers. She managed to land a few catwalk spots on some well-known international fashion shows, all of them in Europe, but the big top-model career was still to materialize.'

'When you say catalogs,' Captain Blake asked, 'what do you mean?'

Garcia flipped a page on his notepad. 'Clothes, shoes, swimwear, sportswear, lingerie, jewelry – that sort of thing. Like I said, we don't have anything in much detail at the moment, but we have a team working on it.'

'Any X-rated material?' the captain asked.

'Not from what we found out so far.'

'Nevertheless, she was a model,' the captain said. 'That was her profession.'

'That's right.'

'So I'm assuming that she probably had fans.'

'Yes, and quite a lot of them,' Garcia confirmed, checking his notes once again. 'She had a very prominent online presence. All the usual suspects – Facebook, Twitter, Instagram and even a YouTube channel where she gave viewers tips about makeup, hair styling and fashion. In total, over a quarter of a million followers.'

Captain Blake used two fingers to massage her left temple. She could already feel a headache coming on.

'Over a quarter of a million followers?' she said, making a face. 'That blows the scope wide open, doesn't it? Because correct me if I'm wrong here, but doesn't a murder where the killer specifically disfigures the victim, especially the face, suggest an obsession with her? More specifically, with the way she looked, with how pretty she was.' Her eyes paused on Hunter for confirmation.

'Theoretically, yes,' he agreed.

'So with that many followers,' the captain continued, 'with all her social-media exposure, photos, videos, catalogs and who knows what else, any number of those followers could've developed such an obsession; isn't that so? And out of those, any number of them could've been psychopathic enough to carry out a murder of this magnitude. We all know how crazy fans can get.'

'Yes,' he agreed again. 'Because the victim was a celebrity in her own right with so many fans, the scope for who the killer might be is wide open. An obsessed but disillusioned fan with psychopathic tendencies could've very well been capable of something like this. And since the advent of the internet, with more and more social-media websites popping up everywhere, developing obsessions, not only toward celebrities but anyone, really, has become a lot easier.'

'Great!' Captain Blake said. 'Two hundred and fifty thousand possible suspects spread all around the world. You guys should have this wrapped up in no time, then. Was she married? Did she have a boyfriend? A lover?'

'She wasn't married,' Garcia replied. 'And according to her mother, she wasn't seeing anyone either, but we'll dig a little deeper into it.'

The captain stood up and took a couple of steps back to get a wider view of the board.

'Beauty is all around her,' she said to herself, now fully considering the half theory Garcia had suggested.

'That's what the killer wrote,' Garcia reaffirmed. 'Which means that he's clearly trying to tell us something.'

'I get that,' Captain Blake agreed. 'But why write the message in Latin?'

'We're not sure,' Hunter replied.

'Care to venture a guess?'

Hunter stayed quiet, but Garcia didn't.

'It could be a clue to where he's from,' he said.

The captain turned to face him, pondering that idea for a second. 'In which way, Carlos?'

'You've said so a moment ago – over two hundred and fifty thousand fans spread all over the world. A hurt, disillusioned and psychotic enough fan could've flown in from anywhere, killed her, and since her body wasn't discovered for a couple of days, be back to where he came from by now. In which instance, we'll probably never catch him.'

Captain Blake's thoughtful look deepened.

'A less pessimistic scenario,' Hunter added, 'is that this is LA, one of the most diverse cities on the planet when it comes to its residents' nationalities. Maybe her killer lives here, but isn't an American citizen.'

'But Latin isn't spoken anywhere anymore,' the captain came back. 'So to follow this line of thought, by carving his message in Latin he's telling us what? He's from Italy? Latin America?'

'It could be,' Hunter said.

Captain Blake brought her right thumb and index finger to her forehead. *Yes*, she thought. *A headache is definitely on its way.* She considered not asking her next question, but her curiosity proved too strong. 'So why the message? Just to give us a hint of where he's from?'

Both detectives stayed quiet.

'Anybody?' she pushed.

'Delusions of grandeur,' Garcia suggested.

'I'm sorry?' Captain Blake turned to face him.

'Delusions of grandeur, Captain. One of the main traits of psychopaths. You know this. They see themselves as superior to everyone else. They think they are more intelligent, better looking, stronger, more talented, more creative, smarter, and so on. Due to such delusions, a great number of them also believe that whatever it is that they're doing ... whatever it is that they're trying to achieve with their murders, just can't be understood by us, mere mortals, because our vision and intellect doesn't reach as high as theirs.' He paused, once again giving the captain a moment. 'The killer knew, and rightly so, that no one in their sane mind would see that crime scene as a work of art, unless he told us to.'

Garcia indicated a couple of photos on the board.

'These carvings on her back,' he continued. 'This is him telling us that those aren't just blood smears on the walls. They are brush strokes. The message on the victim's back could be more than just a taunt. It could be his signature on a canvas. He could be gloating. Praising his own work.'

Captain Blake let go of a heavy breath. The more she looked at the photos on the board, the less crazy the art-piece theory appeared. She knew that if this had been an absurd crime of passion, a murder for revenge, a robbery gone wrong, an explosion of bad temper, even a sick and sadistic rape act, with a little stretch of the imagination, maybe the bloody mess around the room could have been expected – but not the carvings on the victim's back.

In silence she walked the length of the board, her eyes moving from photograph to photograph.

'Cause of death?' she asked.

'Probably bled out,' Garcia replied. 'But that's not official.'

'So that's why you requested a Level Zero autopsy.' Captain Blake addressed Hunter. 'Because if this nut-job has really done all this just to create some demented art, then one thing is for sure: this guy didn't jump on a plane and go back to where he came from. If this freak thinks he's creating art, then we all know that this isn't going to be his solo "piece", don't we? If we don't stop him soon, this isn't going to end here. This is going to turn serial.'

Hunter's concerned stare met his captain's.

'That's what worries me. There's a possibility that it already has.'

Sixteen

Risk of contamination wasn't the only factor that could trigger a request for a Level Zero autopsy. There was another type of risk that most authorities around the world would do anything to avoid – the risk of citizen panic. The Los Angeles press, who tended to sensationalize most stories to high heaven, paid people for information, and they paid well. They had informants inside the police, the fire brigade, hospitals, government security agencies, and of course the Department of Medical Examiner.

The media would have a field day and no shame about instigating widespread frenzy inside the City of Angels if they were to report the news of a new serial killer on the loose. Hunter and the LAPD's best chance of keeping the story under wraps, at least for the time being, was to keep as many details as they could as secret as they could.

Los Angeles was no stranger to violent crimes. A mutilated and skinned body left inside a room that had been practically redecorated with the victim's blood would certainly raise eyebrows and trigger an avalanche of questions, but it wouldn't necessarily sound the 'serial killer' alarm, unless the press got word of the carvings on the victim's back. If there was one thing about serial killers that every crime reporter in LA knew, it was that they were the only ones who tended to taunt the police with messages, riddles, puzzles, drawings, phone calls, or whatever. Back at the crime scene, due to the position in which the victim had been left on the bed, only four people had seen the carvings on Linda Parker's back – Hunter, Garcia, Kevin White, and the forensics team photographer, Tommy. Dr. Hove and Captain Blake brought that number up to six and none of them would pass that knowledge onto the press.

Hunter's comment was met by a very concerned look from Captain Blake.

'I'm sorry, Robert, already has what? Turned serial?'

Hunter nodded before sending one last photo to the printer.

'OK, you guys just lost me. Is there another body that I don't know about?' Instinctively, her eyes searched the board one more time.

'If there is,' Hunter replied, 'none of us know about it.'

Captain Blake's eyebrows shot up in an arch.

'OK,' she said. 'So if we don't have any bodies other than this one, where's this idea coming from, Robert? What makes you think there's a possibility that this killer has killed before?'

'It's not one thing in particular, Captain. It's the entire crime scene, but again, it's too early in the investigation to be certain of anything, and to be honest, all I have is a hunch.'

Captain Blake waited, but Hunter didn't offer much else.

'All right,' she pushed. 'Let's hear this hunch of yours then.'

Hunter knew his captain well enough to know that he had no other way out of this. He drove her attention back to the picture board.

'OK,' he said. 'Let me start with the level of violence and how skilled the killer was. He severed his victim's hands and feet clean off her body.' He indicated the photographs as he spoke. 'And the optimal word here is "clean".' He gave Captain Blake an extra millisecond. 'The autopsy report should give us a better idea of the tool used, but according to the forensics team at the scene, it wasn't an ax or any sort of sharp blade where the killer could've achieved that with a single blow.'

The captain stepped closer and regarded the pictures Hunter had indicated.

'So what are we talking about here?' She speculated. 'Some sort of saw?'

'Almost certainly,' Hunter agreed. 'But the detail here is that he probably used a handheld saw. Not an electric one, and that would only add to his skillset.'

'How do you know it was a handheld saw instead of an electric one?'

'An electric saw would've caused the victim's blood to spray in all different directions and in a very distinctive pattern – tiny spit-like drops, if you like,' Hunter explained. 'Forensics scrutinized every blood smudge they found at the victim's house. No spray pattern of any sort was found anywhere.'

Captain Blake tucked a strand of loose hair behind her left ear before Hunter redirected her attention to the next group of photographs.

'Not wanting to state the obvious here, but he also skinned his victim, which – if nothing else – takes knowledge. But in this case, the skinning was done so proficiently it suggests experience. At least some.'

'Something like this,' Garcia commented, 'with this level of competence, isn't easy to achieve first time out.'

Captain Blake scratched her left cheek uneasily. 'I understand that, but couldn't this killer have gained that sort of experience in some way other than having killed before?'

'Yes, of course,' Hunter admitted. 'A trained butcher would easily qualify. Doctors, ex-doctors, medical students with hands-on training . . .' He shrugged.

'Not to mention the real sickos,' Garcia butted in. 'The ones with no experience, but who'd take the time to practice on animals first.'

Captain Blake's jaw dropped half open. 'You mean, skinning them?'

Garcia nodded. 'The skin property of certain animals, like pigs, rats, mice and rabbits, are similar enough to that of humans to allow for that kind of practice.'

That thought made Captain Blake grimace.

'As sick as all that sounds,' she said, 'the two of you just argued against your own case – this killer's proficiency at skinning and mutilating his victim doesn't necessarily equate to him having killed before. He could be a butcher, an ex-medical student and so on.'

'That's true.' Hunter accepted it. 'The killer could've gained that sort of experience in several different ways without having murdered anyone before, but so far we've only discussed the level of violence and skill used by the killer.' He indicated the photographs that showed the carvings to Linda Parker's back one more time. 'But we also have this.'

Captain Blake drew in a deep breath. 'Yes, I know, and that's the main reason why I asked you about this turning serial. We all know that not all serial killers like to taunt the police, but *only* serial criminals do so.'

She stabbed one of the photos on the board with her index finger.

'A message, a signature, alien code, whatever the hell this is – this is without question a taunt and therefore has "serial" written all over it, but the series has to start somewhere, doesn't it?' Captain Blake opened her arms wide, as if she was about to hug the board. 'So let me ask you again, Robert. Why do you think that this isn't his first victim?'

'Like I said, Captain, it's just a hunch, but once I started adding everything together – the level of violence, the killer's proficiency, the message he left behind, the crime scene as a whole, it just doesn't feel like this is his starting point.'

'Great,' Captain Blake said with a quick shake of the head. 'Every time you have one of your hunches, Robert, we need to brace ourselves for a shit storm, and this is already starting to look like a hurricane.'

'There's one more thing as well,' Garcia said.

She turned to face him. 'Will this nightmare ever end? What is it now?'

Garcia made a face at Hunter, who finally collected the last photo printout from the printer tray and pinned it to the board. It showed Linda Parker's cat frozen solid inside her fridge.

Captain Blake had to do a double take and even then she doubted her eyes. 'What . . . the hell . . . is that?'

'That's the victim's cat,' Garcia replied. 'We found it inside the freezer.'

A pit began forming somewhere inside the captain's stomach. She had always loved cats. She had had Pee-a-lot, her green-eyed, ginger Ragamuffin, for eight years. His original name had been Furmuffin, but within the first couple of months and after several very wet 'accidents' around the house, Captain Blake decided to change his name to a more becoming one.

'The killer . . .' Her voice caught in her throat. '. . . Killed her cat?'

'He froze it to death,' Garcia confirmed. 'There were scratches to the inside of the freezer door, together with fur and bits of the cat's nails.'

'Why?' the captain asked, her stare wandering between Hunter and Garcia. 'What's the point in torturing and killing a defenseless animal like that? It's not like it was a guard dog and the killer had to take it out before getting to the victim, is it?'

She waited, but neither detective offered a reply.

'It's not a rhetorical question, guys,' she pushed. Anger had cracked into her voice. 'Does anyone have any kind of theory as to why this bastard had to kill the goddamn cat?' Despite it being an open question, she pinned Hunter down with a laser stare.

He shrugged. 'He could've done it just to prove his resolve.'

'What?' The captain's eyes widened. 'So breaking into the victim's house, chopping off her hands and feet, skinning the body and transforming the entire room into a blood party wasn't enough evidence of his resolve? He had to freeze the poor cat to make it clear? Who the hell is this guy – Satan?'

Hunter stepped back from the board and leaned against the edge of his desk. When he spoke, his voice seemed to carry all the calm in the world.

'Just look at your reaction, Captain. Until a moment ago you sounded concerned, but there was no real anger in it. As soon as you found out about the cat . . .' Hunter didn't need to finish his sentence.

'And you're not alone in your reaction either,' Garcia added. 'It happened to all of us at the crime scene. As soon as we discovered the cat in the freezer, everyone's mood took a turn, even Robert's, and you know how calm and collected he always is.'

Captain Blake kept her eyes on the picture for just another second before turning away in disgust. 'It takes a different kind of "sick" to mutilate and skin a body in the way that it was done here, but to do something like this to a tiny animal, who would've posed absolutely no threat whatsoever—'

'It's shocking, but not surprising,' Hunter interrupted.

She glared at him.

'Many psychopaths start to show signs of psychopathy at a very young age,' Hunter reminded her. 'Cruelty to animals and predisposition for arson are the two top items on that "early signs of psychopathy" list. Many modern serial killers have graduated from hurting and killing animals to hurting and killing people. It's a fact. So yes, this is shocking, but not surprising.'

'So what you're telling me here is that we are probably dealing with a completely emotionless freak. Someone whose level of emotional detachment toward life in general is off the scale – human . . . animal . . . it doesn't matter because he couldn't care less.'

'I have no doubt of that, Captain,' Garcia replied.

'There's another possibility,' Hunter said, but before he was able to explain, the phone on his desk rang.

Seventeen

Before sharing the results of Linda Parker's post-mortem examination with Hunter and Garcia, Dr. Hove decided to once again go over a couple of her findings, just to be absolutely sure. Thirty-five minutes later, still sitting inside Autopsy Theater Zero, she finally called the detectives at the Police Administration Building.

'Robert, it's Carolyn Hove,' she said as Hunter picked up the phone at the other end. 'I'm done with the Level Zero autopsy you've requested.'

'Oh, that's great, Doc,' Hunter said. 'So what have you got for us?'

Dr. Hove's stare wandered back to the body on the examination table. The familiar Y incision that ran from the top of each shoulder to the lower part of the sternum had already been sewn shut. Thick black stitches now ran the entire length of the cut, adding a whole new layer of grotesqueness to an already alien-looking body.

'Something quite intriguing, I must say,' she replied.

Hunter paused for a second. 'Give me a moment, Doc. Let me put you on speakerphone . . .'

Dr. Hove heard a muffled click come through on her earpiece before Hunter spoke again.

'OK, Doc. Go ahead.'

'Well,' she began. 'Given the mutilated state the body is in and the gravity of its wounds, I was expecting to find that the victim had been severely tortured prior to her death, but that isn't the case at all.'

'How do you mean?' The question was asked by a somewhat distant female voice, which made Dr. Hove frown.

'Sorry, who is this?' she asked with concern.

'Sorry, Carolyn, it's Barbara Blake.' Her voice strengthened as the captain stepped closer to Hunter's desk. 'I should've said hello when Robert placed the call on speakerphone.'

'Oh no, not at all. Sorry I didn't recognize your voice, Barbara. It sounded a little distant. How are you doing, anyway?'

'Not too bad, but something tells me that that's about to change.'

'Just to avoid any more surprises,' Dr. Hove said, 'whom else am I speaking to?'

'Just me, Doc,' Garcia called out. 'It's just the three of us in here.'

'Carolyn, what did you mean when you said that that wasn't the case?' Captain Blake asked again.

'Well, as we all know, appearances can be quite deceiving, and that indeed is the case here, because despite how violent this murder looks to have been, the victim didn't suffer.'

Dr. Hove's announcement was met by an awkward silence from the other end of the line. In her mind, she could picture the stare that Hunter, Garcia and Captain Blake would be exchanging between them.

'She didn't suffer?' Captain Blake asked at last, her voice coated with doubt.

'Nope. Not according to what I found out. All the barbarism

that was done to her – the skinning of the body, the amputation of the hands and feet – it was all done post-mortem.'

There was another long, uneasy silence before Garcia asked the next question.

'So the victim didn't bleed to death from her wounds?'

'No. She died of asphyxiation. And here comes another surprise – the asphyxiation was done by suffocation, not strangulation.'

'Hold on, Doc,' Garcia said. 'Can you please run that by me again?'

'The muscles on her neck show no bruising,' Dr. Hove explained. 'Her larynx and trachea aren't crushed and the hyoid bone isn't fractured. Actually, I found no damage whatsoever to her neck, throat, or her respiratory system.'

'So how did she suffocate?' This time the question came from Captain Blake. 'The killer put a pillow over her face while she slept?'

'Something like that,' the doctor replied. 'But it wasn't a pillow, Barbara. When the body senses it's asphyxiating, its automatic physiological response is to try to draw in the deepest breath it possibly can. As it realizes that that breath is lacking in oxygen, it panics and instantly tries again. This time, a lot more desperately, I should add. A pillow, a gag, a shirt . . . anything made out of any sort of textile fabrics would release fibers, which, with the victim's frantic deep breaths, would've been sucked into her mouth and nostrils and lodged themselves all over the place.' Dr. Hove paused for breath. 'I found nothing. No fibers. No residues. Nothing. Not inside her nose or in her mouth and throat.'

'A thick plastic bag, maybe?' Garcia suggested.

'Very possible,' Dr. Hove agreed. 'But without being able

to examine the victim's facial skin, there's no way I can tell you with any plausible certainty what the killer used as a suffocation tool. What I can tell you is that it didn't take long for her to die. A minute . . . a minute and a half, tops. I've been as meticulous as I could've been with this particular post-mortem examination, and I found nothing to suggest that she had to endure any sort of physical pain prior to her death. Other than, of course, the sheer panic that comes with asphyxiation.'

'So all that sadism occurred post-death?' Garcia asked.

'That's correct.'

'Well this makes absolutely no goddamn sense,' Captain Blake said.

'My thoughts exactly, Barbara.'

Eighteen

The National Center for Analysis of Violent Crimes (NCAVC) was a specialist FBI department conceived in 1981 and finally officially established in June 1984. Its main mission was to provide assistance in the investigation of unusual or repetitive violent crimes to law-enforcement agencies, not only inside US territory, but also across the globe. Though its headquarters was located at the famous FBI training academy near the town of Quantico in Virginia, the head of the NCAVC department, Adrian Kennedy, coordinated most of its investigations from his large and comfortable office in Washington DC. Kennedy was in the middle of a call to the US Attorney General when, without knocking, Special Agent Larry Williams, one of the NCAVC's most decorated agents, pushed open Kennedy's office door and stepped inside. Following him, with a frustrated look on her face, was Clare Pascal, Kennedy's PA/secretary.

From behind black-framed glasses, the NCAVC director's concerned eyes moved to both people at his door.

'The Surgeon has resurfaced,' Williams said in a tone of voice as urgent as the look he carried with him.

Kennedy held Williams' stare just long enough for his brain

to process the severity of his words. He felt a muscle flex in his jaw.

'Sorry, Loretta,' Kennedy said into the phone. 'Let me call you back in an hour or so. Something just came up.' He disconnected from the call and his attention returned to Special Agent Larry Williams.

'I'm terribly sorry, Director,' his secretary said, finally positioning herself in front of Agent Williams' athletic frame. 'I told him you were on an important call, but he didn't care to listen and I failed to stop him in time.'

'It's OK, Clare,' Kennedy said with a hand wave. 'I'll take it from here. Thank you.'

Clare, still disappointed with her performance, exited Kennedy's office in silence, closing the door behind her.

Kennedy took off his glasses and placed them on his antique mahogany pedestal desk. Despite how spacious and luxurious his office was, Adrian Kennedy was no career bureaucrat.

Freshly out of law school, Kennedy had begun his journey with the FBI at quite a young age and immediately demonstrated that he had tremendous aptitude for leadership, coupled with an exceptionally analytical mind and a natural ability to motivate people. It didn't take long for those qualities to get noticed and Kennedy was soon assigned to the prestigious US President Protection Detail team. It was then that he was hailed as a hero. During his fourth year with the protection team, Kennedy managed to foil an assassination attempt by throwing himself in front of a bullet that no doubt had the President's name on it. After receiving a high commendation award for bravery and a personal 'thank you' letter from the President himself, Adrian Kennedy was asked by the director of the FBI at the time to head a new department that was still taking its baby steps back in Quantico – the National Center for the Analysis of Violent Crimes. Kennedy deliberated on his decision for less than a day before accepting the position.

It was also he who, just a few years later, suggested that a new department within the NCAVC be created – the Behavioral Analysis Unit, or BAU for short. Its mission was simple and complex in equal measures – to help with the investigation of certain violent repeat crimes through the use of psychology, psychoanalysis and behavioral sciences. Adrian Kennedy was not only the director of the NCAVC Department; he was also the head of the Behavioral Analysis Unit.

'The Surgeon?' Kennedy asked in a naturally hoarse voice that had been made worse by years of smoking. 'Are you sure?'

Agent Williams stepped forward and his conviction wavered a fraction. He scratched the underside of his chin.

'Not one hundred percent, sir, but we should be getting confirmation very soon.'

Kennedy sat back on his Chesterfield winged chair, rested his elbows on its arms, and interlaced his fingers in front of his chin. His eyes were a remarkable shade of blue – dark, yet luminous and absolutely overflowing with knowledge and experience.

'So let me get this straight, Special Agent Williams. You stormed past my secretary, almost kicked my office door down – without knocking, I must add – interrupted a very important call to the US Attorney General, just to give me a "maybe"?'

Williams shifted his weight from one foot to the other. His dark eyes avoided the director's stare for just a second.

'Are you out of your goddamn mind?'

'I'm sorry, sir, but it's him, I know it. We just need official confirmation.'

'And how exactly do you "know it"?'

Agent Williams pulled a piece of paper from his pocket.

'At around two o'clock this morning,' he began, 'there was an official search into the VICAP database for homicides where the perp had left any sort of written messages at the scene. More specifically, messages written in Latin.'

Kennedy still looked unimpressed. 'And in your mind, that fact alone gave you the right to burst into my office unannounced.'

'There's more.'

'Well, I sincerely hope so.' Kennedy nodded sarcastically.

'The search returned zero hits,' Agent Williams continued. 'So a new search followed – messages that had been carved somewhere on the victim's body.'

Kennedy's chin moved up a fraction. 'Go on.'

'Once again, and we know why, the VICAP database returned no hits, so a third, more refined search followed – bodies found with an odd combination of letters and symbols carved into their backs.'

The muscle on Kennedy's jaw flexed harder this time.

'It has to be him, sir,' Agent Williams insisted. 'There's no other reason why anyone would search the VICAP database for that sort of information – a message, in Latin, which looks like an odd combination of letters and symbols, left carved into the victim's back.' He allowed that thought to hang in the air for an instant. 'I know you don't believe in that sort of coincidence, sir. It's got to be him. It can't be anyone else.'

Kennedy accepted it with a single head movement. 'OK. Where is Special Agent Fisher?'

Williams consulted his watch. 'On her way there as we speak. I'm joining her as soon as I leave here, but I had a feeling that you'd maybe want to come.'

Kennedy breathed out and got to his feet. 'So where are we going this time?'

'Los Angeles, sir.'

Kennedy was about to reach for the phone on his desk to tell his secretary to clear his calendar for the next two days, when it dawned on him.

'Wait a second,' he said, his left hand up in the air in a stop sign. 'Los Angeles, California?'

Williams's eyes squinted at the NCAVC director.

'I'm . . . not aware of a different Los Angeles, sir.'

Slowly but steadily, Kennedy's lips stretched into an enigmatic grin.

Unsure, Special Agent Williams turned and checked behind him before facing Kennedy again.

'Have I missed something, sir?'

'If you're right . . . if this is indeed The Surgeon, then he might've just made his first and worst mistake.'

'I don't follow, sir.'

Kennedy picked up his cellphone. 'I'll explain it to you when we get to LA.'

Nineteen

Hunter sat back on his chair, his brain trying hard to process what Dr. Hove had just told them.

How could such a violent-looking crime scene be lacking in exactly that – violence? It really did make no sense, unless ...

'Was the victim sexually assaulted at all, Doc?' Hunter asked.

'I found no indications of it, Robert. There's no bruising to any of the groin muscles, the vagina or the anus. No semen or lubricant residues either, which would be left behind if her attacker had used a rubber.'

'And you're absolutely sure that the victim was asphyxiated *before* she was skinned?' Garcia jumped in again.

'Yes. One hundred percent.' Dr. Hove sounded a little irritated by the question. 'She died first. No doubt about that. Why?'

'Carolyn.' Captain Blake, who had moved the fold-up chair closer to Hunter's desk, took the floor one more time. 'Have you seen the crime-scene photos?'

'No. Not yet. I got here very early this morning and I was greeted straight away by Robert's Level Zero request, which, as you know, takes precedence over everything. The forensics file that accompanied the body was pretty basic – no photographs – and I haven't had a chance to check my email yet. Why?'

'Well, the crime scene is covered in blood,' the captain explained. 'The floor, the walls, the furniture, everything. There're a couple of theories being thrown around here in the office and one of them is the possibility that the blood smudges at the scene were the result of a desperate victim, drenched in blood, trying to get away from her attacker, but if you're really sure she died before all this brutality that was done to her body, then that blows that theory straight out of the water.'

'Not exactly, Barbara,' Dr. Hove came back.

'What do you mean?'

'The victim's hands,' Hunter said.

'That's correct,' Dr. Hove agreed. 'As I've said, I haven't seen the crime-scene photos yet, so it's hard for me to voice an opinion without analyzing these blood smudges that you're referring to, but when we take into account that we don't have the victim's hands or feet, which could've been bleeding from defensive wounds before they were severed from her body, then yes, the scenario you just described is quite possible.'

'Yes, but that still wouldn't explain why nothing was tipped over or out of place,' Garcia said.

'Sorry, what was tipped over or out of place?' Dr. Hove asked.

'Oh, nothing, Doc,' Garcia replied. 'It's to do with these theories the captain mentioned. By the way, do you have an estimated time of death?'

'Yes, of course. By my calculations, the victim lost her life somewhere between fifty-eight and sixty-five hours ago, which takes us to Monday night, somewhere between nine in the evening and midnight.'

'Could you give us a better idea of what her attacker used for the amputations?' Hunter asked.

'It was a small, serrated blade,' the doctor replied, her voice full of certainty. 'Judging by the type of serration I found on her fibula and tibia – her ankle bones – the blade used was thin, with tiny teeth, very close together. From that alone I'd say it was a saw, not a kitchen knife. I can also tell you that the cuts are too uneven for them to have been made by an electric instrument. He used a handheld saw. Something like a coping saw, or similar. Unfortunately, too common to be able to trace it.'

'Well, nothing new there,' Captain Blake commented. 'One more thing, Carolyn, any indications of drug abuse?'

'We'll have to wait for toxicology to be absolutely sure, but if she did use drugs, it was probably only recreational. This girl was no junkie. I found no track marks on any of her veins. She wasn't a smoker, either. If she were a regular user of inhalable substances like crack cocaine, crystal meth, or even heroin, I would've found indications of it. Her gums and teeth were in perfect condition. Best I've ever seen.' Another short pause. 'Why the question? Were any drugs found at the crime scene?'

'No. Nothing at all, Doc,' Hunter answered. 'We're just going through all the initial motions of the investigation.'

'Did any of this blood at the crime scene look like arterial spray?' Dr. Hove asked.

'No. None of it.' Garcia, who was sitting at the edge of Hunter's desk, replied. 'There were a few blood splatters, but no arterial spray.'

'Palm prints?'

'That would be "no" again. All the bloodstains we found

on the walls and on the furniture looked a lot more like smears than anything else.'

That knowledge further intrigued Dr. Hove.

'Smears?'

'That's right,' Garcia confirmed. 'We're still waiting for the forensics results.'

It was Dr. Hove's turn to go silent. To her, this case was getting more and more bizarre by the second. She now couldn't wait to have a look at the crime-scene photographs.

'The carvings to the victim's back,' she finally said. 'Does anyone have a clue what any of that means? All those letters and symbols together?'

'That's the catch,' Garcia replied, making a face at Hunter and Captain Blake. 'They aren't symbols.'

'I beg your pardon?'

It took Garcia a few minutes to run Dr. Hove through the whole explanation.

'I ... completely missed that,' she said, her voice a little less steady than moments ago. 'I could tell that some of it was or looked to be Latin, but I never really put it together. *Pulchritudo. Circumdat. Eius.*' She whispered the words to herself. 'Beauty ... surrounds ... her.'

'Well,' Garcia said. 'The translation that we've all agreed on here is "Beauty is all around her".'

'Yes,' the doctor agreed. 'Surrounds her, it's all around her; the meaning is the same, isn't it?'

'I guess.' Garcia accepted it.

'Let me ask you something else, Doc.' Hunter took over again. 'Taking into consideration the amputations and the skinning of the body, how skilled would you say her attacker was?'

'Very good question, Robert, and I'd say that he is way

above average. The amputations could've been done a little better, but they were certainly good enough. The cuts were done at the correct position – in other words, if the victim really had needed her hands and feet amputated, that's pretty much where a doctor would have made the incisions, though with an electric saw instead of a handheld one. And despite them being post-mortem, like I've said, the interesting thing is that the incisions were still made with all due care.'

Hunter, Garcia and Captain Blake all considered the implications of what Dr. Hove had just told them.

'How about the skinning?' the captain asked.

'Again, Barbara, done proficiently enough.'

'Proficiently as in "not bad for a first-timer", or "he's probably done this before"?'

The doctor went quiet. It was clear that she hadn't thought about it in those terms.

'Carolyn?' Captain Blake pushed.

'Yes, sorry, Barbara, I'm here. Do you think this killer has killed before? I mean, in this way?'

'I don't know. You tell me. Do you think he has?'

'It's hard to tell with any degree of certainty if he's killed before or not. He could very well have. Like I said, the amputations were skillful enough and so was the skinning of the body. Though both of those actions could've been practiced on animals, this guy knew very well what he was doing.'

'And what makes you say that?'

'Skinning a human body isn't as difficult as it might sound,' Dr. Hove told everyone. 'Human skin is very strong and quite tough. I'll skip all the bio-medical details, so as not to bore everyone, but in short all one would need to do would be to make an incision, grab the skin and simply pull it off. If any of you have ever bitten into a mango and then pulled its skin from the fruit, the experience would be pretty similar.'

'Thanks for the visual image, Doc,' Garcia said, making a disgruntled face at the phone. 'When I lived in Brazil we had a mango tree in our backyard. Probably one of the fruit I ate the most as a kid. That new piece of information will go very well with my childhood memories.'

'Sorry, Carlos, but with that said, let me add that being able to remove all of someone's skin in one go, ending up with a kind of skin bodysuit, is something you would only really see in movies. That is practically impossible to do. The easiest way to skin a human being is to do it in patches. You would cut delimiting lines into the skin – and that is exactly what this killer did.'

'Delimiting lines?' Captain Blake asked.

'Yes, and here's why I said that this killer knew very well what he was doing. In this case he has divided her body into top and bottom, by making a thin but long incision that surrounded her entire waist. The skinning of her legs and arms would also be made a lot easier by removing their extremities – hands and feet.' The doctor paused for a moment. 'Now imagine deshelling a hard-boiled egg. For you to pull away tiny bits of shell is easy – everyone can do it – but for you to pull the entire shell away in one go, or even in two large pieces, is a lot harder. One might even say that it takes experience.'

'So you're telling us that this killer ended up with two large patches of the victim's skin,' Garcia asked. 'One from her waist down – something that would look like a pair of human-skin trousers – and the other from her waist all the way up to her head, like a human-skin hooded and masked sweatshirt.'

'If he took the time and had the patience that such a procedure requires,' Dr. Hove replied. 'Yes, he probably would've ended up with something very similar, with the exception that the "hooded and masked sweatshirt", as you put it, would have a very large patch missing from its back.'

Hunter's next question made Captain Blake cringe.

'Would those be wearable, Doc?'

'Wearable?'

'Yes. If the killer ended up with something similar to a pair of human-skin trousers and a human-skin hooded and masked sweatshirt, despite the missing patch from the back, could he possibly wear them?'

Dr. Hove hadn't considered that possibility until then.

'If he preserved them with the right solutions then yes, Robert, he could.'

Twenty

After their meeting with Captain Blake and the conference call with Dr. Hove, Hunter and Garcia decided to return to Linda Parker's house. Both of them wanted to have a second look at the crime scene, but this time they would do it undisturbed and by themselves.

'So,' Garcia said as he pulled into the driveway. 'What was this other possibility you were talking about?'

'Excuse me?' Hunter looked back at his partner, a little unsure.

'Back in the office,' Garcia said, his head tilting slightly to his left. 'When it was suggested that we are probably dealing with a psychopath who is off the scale when it comes to emotional detachment, you said that there was another possibility, but you never got to tell us what.'

They got out of the car and began making their way toward the house.

'The most disturbing of them all,' Hunter said. 'That this killer isn't really as heartless and emotionless as he appears to be, but he's mentally strong enough to be able to *consciously* break through that threshold whenever he wants to.'

Garcia paused by the house's front lawn. 'For what reason?'

Hunter shrugged. 'Maybe just to prove to us or, even worse, to himself, that he is capable of doing it if he wants to.'

'Prove it to himself?'

Hunter nodded. 'Some human minds are funny like that, Carlos. Some people will push themselves to the limits of just about anything, including savagery, for no better reason than to prove to themselves that they can do it. That they have it in them. Like a self-dare.'

Garcia pointed to Linda Parker's house. 'Someone could self-dare himself to do that?'

'Even worse,' Hunter said. 'You've heard of the Chessboard Killer, right?'

'Yes, of course. Russian guy. Alexander . . . something?'

'Pichushkin,' Hunter confirmed. 'Yes, that's him. Do you remember his story?'

Garcia took a moment. 'From what I remember he was an absolute freak. He gained that nickname because he wanted to kill as many people as there were squares on a chessboard, right? Sixty-four?'

Hunter nodded. 'He didn't actually gain the nickname. He gave it to himself. And you're right – he *wanted* to kill as many people as there are squares on a chessboard. The problem with him was that, unlike most serial killers in history, Pichushkin wasn't driven by some crazy monster inside of him that he couldn't control. He wasn't fighting an uncontrollable urge that slowly overwhelmed him over time. He simply one day decided that he would be a serial killer, just like you and I decided a long time ago that we wanted to be cops. To him it was a conscious choice, not the consequence of an internal battle.'

'Like a career choice?'

'One can put it that way, yes, but it gets stranger still. There was a reason why he wanted to become a serial killer.'

'Which was?'

'A very simple one. He wanted to follow in his hero's footsteps.'

They reached the house's front door.

'Hero?'

Hunter nodded. 'His biggest idol was a murderer. One of Russia's most infamous and prolific serial killers, actually – Andrei Chikatilo.'

'The Butcher of Rostov?' Garcia said.

'One and the same,' Hunter agreed. 'After he got caught, Chikatilo confessed to murdering fifty-six people between 1978 and 1990.'

'Yes, I remember his story. Very sadistic, pedophile, necrophiliac predator, right? He only raped his victims after mutilating their bodies, including several children.'

'Yes, that's him,' Hunter confirmed. 'Now here's the thing about the Chessboard Killer: when the Russian police finally arrested Pichushkin, they asked him why he had done it, why he had killed all those people.' Hunter paused just to emphasize the lack of logic in what he was about to say. 'He told them that it had been because he wanted to beat Chikatilo's record of fifty-six murders. Alexander Pichushkin's big desire in life was to be remembered as the most prolific serial killer in Russian history. That was the reason he started killing. His victims were whoever was around at the time – men, women, old, young, black, white – it didn't matter. He was never driven by a compulsion to kill based on the kind of victim or the level of violence. What he was doing was number crunching. That was his motivation.'

All Garcia could do was shake his head at how unbelievable that story was. 'That's just a whole lot of crazy inside one small head.'

Hunter used a penknife to break the police seal at Linda Parker's front door. 'Indeed. And because all he wanted was to beat the record, Pichushkin simply picked a number. Any number would do, as long as it was higher than fifty-six. A very good chess player, Pichushkin decided on the number sixty-four, because it would also allow him to pick a great nickname for himself. A nickname that would surely get the attention of the press, not only in Russia, but worldwide.'

'The Chessboard Killer,' Garcia agreed. 'It was quite an intriguing name, I must admit.'

'It certainly worked for him.'

'So . . . did he?' Garcia asked.

'Kill sixty-four people?'

'Yes, or beat Chikatilo's record?'

'Well, that's where the story gets even more ironic. Pichushkin told the police that he had killed sixty people. Not a whole chessboard, but it would've beaten Chikatilo's record, making him the most prolific serial killer in Russia's history until then. The problem was, despite what he told the police, the police could only confirm forty-nine murders, which fell a little short of Chikatilo's mark. The icing on the cake was that that was only revealed in court, not before. So, inside the courtroom, when Pichushkin heard that information for the first time and realized that officially he did not beat the record and he would not be known as "most prolific serial killer in Russian history", he went absolutely ballistic.'

'What, really?'

'I kid you not,' Hunter confirmed. 'The trial wasn't that

long ago – 2007. If you search the internet, you'll find several videos of him, in court, inside a sealed glass defendant cage, going absolutely mental, screaming at everyone, punching the glass, the works. But he wasn't protesting the guilty verdict. He was protesting the number of murders. He kept on yelling at the judge that he had committed more than fifty-six murders. That the record was his and not Chikatilo's.'

'That's just insane. I will have to check that out.'

'Alexander Pichushkin is a prime example of the kind of evil a man can do when guided by nothing but sheer determination. His psychopathy wasn't inherent, it was induced. He didn't start life as an emotionally detached person, he forced himself to become one just so he could achieve a goal. And if this is the kind of killer we're dealing with here . . .' Hunter allowed his thought to go unfinished.

Garcia shook his head once again. 'Do you know what, Robert? I just don't think I understand this crazy world anymore.'

Hunter finally unlocked the door and pushed it open. 'I never did.'

Twenty-One

'You're all done, Mr. Davis,' the petite nurse said as she pulled the needle from Timothy Davis's right arm. Despite being thirty years old, that was the first time Timothy had given blood. The whole process had been surprisingly painless and stress-free, though he did blink awkwardly a couple of times as he first set eyes on the needle.

'Oh, please don't let the size of the needle scare you, Mr. Davis,' the nurse had said, offering him one of the most comforting smiles he had ever seen. Her nametag read *Rose Atkins*.

Timothy Davis had used a home kit to find out his blood type and, before registering online less than three weeks ago, he'd read all about blood donation. The explanation he'd found said that the reason sixteen- to seventeen-gauge needles were used was that they minimized the damage that could sometimes occur to red blood cells as they traveled through the needle. The explanation didn't make them look any less scary, though.

'No, ma'am,' Timothy had replied in a whispering voice. 'The needle doesn't scare me none.'

'Ma'am?' The nurse's light-blue eyes had shined with doubt as her smile turned questioning. 'Please tell me that I don't really look that old.'

'Oh, no, ma'am,' Timothy replied, his tone sincerely apologetic. 'Please take no offense. I didn't mean anything by it. It's
just the way I talk.'

Timothy Davis really just couldn't help the way he
addressed others, for that was how his parents had brought
him up.

Despite now living in Arizona, Timothy had been born in
the city of Madison, Alabama, to an African American father
and an Asian-Indian-American mother. His parents were dirt
poor and both of them had had to work two jobs each just to
feed and clothe Timothy and his two younger sisters, Iris and
Betsy. In school, Timothy had been a way-above-average student, maintaining a 3.8 GPA throughout his high-school years,
but for a poor African American kid living in Madison, being
above average still wasn't good enough.

No matter what the press might want people to believe,
or what the world might think, race inequality was still alive
and well in the USA, especially in Alabama, which ranked at
number four in the list of most racist states in America, something that Timothy, his sisters and his parents knew only too
well. Timothy had inherited almost all of his father's physical
traits, with the exception of his hazel eyes. His eyes had definitely come from his mother's side of the family.

'Always be polite, son,' his father had told him when
Timothy was still a young kid. 'Always be polite. Don't matter
who you grow up to be, rich or poor, big or small, always
treat others with respect, you hear? Black folks, white folks,
yellow folks, it don't matter none, but especially white folks.
Don't give them a reason to hate you even more, son, you
hear? Women is always "ma'am", men is always "sir". Don't
be weak, son, but don't be arrogant either. In this life, folks

will try to put you down, oh, yes, sir, they will. They'll try and they'll try hard too, so you do your best, you hear? Always do your best. And when they tell you that your best ain't enough, because they *will* tell you that, you do better, you understand, Tim? You do better, son.'

His father's words didn't fall on deaf ears, because Timothy Davis always tried his best at everything he did, and when he became the first ever person in his family to graduate from high school, his father begged him to leave Alabama.

'Don't you stay around this godforsaken land, son. You deserve better, you hear? You deserve much better than Alabama and the Deep South. You're a man now. You've paid your dues here and ain't nobody gonna tell you you owe nobody nothing ... cause you don't. Oh, no, sir, you don't. Your ma ain't here no more, but she's watching from up there and she's as proud of you as I am, son. She wants you to know that it's time for you to go on to better things, you hear? Go far away from this land. You have a chance that none of us ever had, so you listen to your pa and you listen good. You go and you find a college far away from here. Some place where white folks and black folks don't hate each other none, or at least not like they do here, son. Some place where the color of your skin won't stop you from being whoever you want to be.'

Timothy did listen to his father's words; he only applied to colleges inside what was considered to be the least racist state in the whole of the USA – California. After being accepted by all five universities he had applied to, Timothy chose to join the College of Mechanical Engineering at the University of California in Berkeley. It was there, during his second semester, that he met Ronda, the girl who was to become his wife five years later.

'That wasn't so bad, was it?' the nurse asked, cleaning away the small blob of blood that had surfaced on Timothy's arm once she had extracted the needle.

'No, ma'am. Not bad at all. I thought that it would hurt some, but I was wrong.'

The nurse smiled one more time. She actually found it cute the way he called her ma'am, specially dressed in his strong Alabama accent, but there was a certain sadness about him, a dark gloom inside his eyes that was hard not to notice.

'Is everything all right, Mr. Davis?' she asked, as she applied a plaster onto Timothy's arm before pressure-bandaging it.

'Oh, yes, ma'am, everything is just fine.'

Timothy Davis had always been a terrible liar and it didn't take an expert to see through him, but despite her concern, Nurse Atkins didn't see it as her place to push it any further.

'You should keep the bandage on for about half an hour,' she advised. 'And the plaster for about six, OK?'

'Yes, ma'am. I'll do just that.'

'For the rest of today,' she continued, as she helped Timothy to his feet. 'You might feel a little tired, maybe even a little weak, so no heavy lifting or strenuous work of any kind, you hear?'

Timothy nodded. 'Absolutely, ma'am.'

Nurse Atkins guided him into a short corridor and to the next room along – the 'snacks deck', as everyone who worked at the blood bank liked to call it.

'Please help yourself to as many cookies and as much juice as you like. It will help bring your blood-sugar level back up. Are you vegetarian, by any chance?'

'Oh, no, ma'am.'

'OK, so once you get home try to stick to food that's full of iron like red meat, fish, chicken, or even cereal with dried fruit, preferably raisins. Get some rest, drink plenty of hydrating fluids and by tomorrow you'll be as good as new.'

'Thank you so much for all your help, ma'am. I really appreciate it.'

As Nurse Atkins walked away, Timothy Davis felt a comforting kind of warmth spread through his body. A single act of kindness, that was all it took. His blood could now help save a life. Maybe even more than one.

Twenty-Two

Hunter waited until Garcia had stepped into Linda Parker's living room before closing the door behind them. For a moment neither of them moved, neither of them said a word; they simply stood there, as if for some reason they needed to acclimatize themselves to the inside of the house.

Most people would be surprised at how different an indoor crime scene could look once the circus show created by the police and the forensics team had moved on.

The first very noticeable difference was always the lighting. Gone were all the overly powerful forensics lights, used mostly to help CSI agents identify fibers, residues and sometimes even dust that didn't seem to belong there. In its place they had the scene's original lighting, be it natural, as it came in through the windows, or artificial, from all the light fixtures in the house. The significance of that difference was that the crime had occurred under a combination of those two types of lighting, not the blinding brightness of the forensics ones.

The second major factor that would alter the perspective of an indoor crime scene was how much the space seemed to change once everyone was gone. Without the human dynamics of agents and officers moving around the place, every room inevitably appeared a lot more spacious, not to mention how much quieter the entire house became. For a profiler trying to put together a mental picture of what might've happened on the night of the crime, those factors alone could sometimes make all the difference.

'I know I probably say this every time.' Garcia broke the silence. 'But this room really does seem a lot bigger than what I remember.'

'Yes,' Hunter replied, walking over to the window on the east wall and drawing the curtains shut. 'You do say that every time.'

'What are you doing?' Garcia asked.

'Dr. Hove told us that the victim lost her life sometime between nine in the evening and midnight on Monday, right? There would've been no natural light in here. I just want to try to get a better feel for the—'

'Yeah, sorry, I forgot about the whole sensory thing you do,' Garcia said, nodding in acceptance before closing the curtains on the other living-room window. He had never met anyone who could visualize a scene in the same way Hunter could.

Both detectives took their time re-examining the living room and the kitchen before moving on to the corridor and finally reaching the main crime scene at the end of the hallway.

Just like the impression they got as they entered the living room a little earlier, without all the agents moving around and their CSI equipment crowding up the place, Linda Parker's bedroom appeared to be twice as big as they remembered it – and darker, a lot darker. But the lighting and the space weren't the only difference. The air inside the house felt heavy and stale, almost unbreathable, laden with an odd, indescribable odor that went beyond the metallic smell of blood and the stomach-churning stench of decomposing flesh. Hunter and Garcia made an effort to breathe mostly through their mouths and from the bedroom door they once again allowed their eyes to circle the room.

'Now that the autopsy report has told us that the victim wasn't tortured prior to her death,' Garcia said, 'that there was no suffering involved, the chaos in this room is starting to look a little less chaotic, don't you think?'

Still being careful to avoid the pools of dried blood on the floor, Hunter moved deeper into the room. 'You're talking about the art-piece theory, right?'

Garcia nodded. 'As crazy as it sounds, it makes sense, doesn't it? Everyone's first impression as they stepped inside this blood-drenched room was that this crime scene was nothing but overly sadistic. Some sick freak who took pleasure in torturing and mutilating his victim for hours before she was finally allowed to die, and from experience alone, you and I would've gone with that theory any day of the week and twice on Sundays. But according to what Dr. Hove told us, our killer didn't get his kicks that way. No torture, Robert. None. No suffering, either. On the contrary, she was dead in less than two minutes. Now look at this crime scene and think about it. If the killer wasn't a sadistic freak who got a hard-on from torturing his victim and watching her suffer, then why do all this? Why turn the room into a blood fest? Why mutilate her body way beyond recognition? It makes no sense. Even if this guy is a complete nut-job, crazy enough to try to *wear* her skin like some ill-fitting suit, it still wouldn't explain these blood smears everywhere.'

Hunter began studying the blood-covered walls one more time.

'Now,' Garcia continued. 'If we consider the possibility that the killer saw this whole scene as an art piece, that this entire room was nothing but a canvas to him, then the apparent brutality in here starts to make sense, because it loses its sadistic connotation. In the killer's eyes, what happened in here wasn't evil or vicious; it was art. There probably was no anger toward the victim. This killer didn't thrive in the power or the dominance of the murder act. He didn't feed off her fear or suffering. That's why he killed her quickly. And what did he do immediately after suffocating her? He took off her hands and feet. Why? Because he wanted to keep them? I don't think so. To make skinning her body a little easier, like Dr. Hove suggested? Maybe. But I think there was another reason, too. I think he took them because they were the extremities to her body's major arteries and veins.'

Hunter paused and thoughtfully looked back at his partner.

'To create his brush strokes,' Garcia explained, indicating the walls around the room, 'he needed her blood, Robert. It was his paint, so to speak.'

Hunter was still staring at the walls. He took two steps back, one to his right, tilted his head sideways and began studying them from a different angle.

Garcia carried on with his analysis.

'The skinned body on the bed was simply the centerpiece in his live canvas. To the killer, her suffering, if there was any, her death, all of it, was secondary – collateral damage so he could create his masterpiece.'

Hunter looked back at the bed pushed up against the south wall. Though Linda Parker's body wasn't there anymore, he could easily see the whole scene in his head as if it were.

'Just like the Chessboard Killer example you gave me a

moment ago,' Garcia concluded. 'This killer's pleasure didn't come from the murder or the violence in it, it came from accomplishing something he had set out to accomplish. In the Chessboard Killer's case – beating a record. In this case – creating a sick and grotesque art piece.'

'How about the victim?' Hunter asked.

'What do you mean?'

'How was she chosen? You said that to the killer, her suffering, her death, all of it was secondary, right? How about the victim herself? Do you think that *she* was also secondary? I mean – any person would do as long as the killer could create his art? Or did he pick Linda Parker for a specific reason?'

Garcia paused by the bed. The blood-soaked sheets were still on it. 'I'm not sure. He could've picked her because it was convenient for him.'

'I don't think so,' Hunter disagreed. 'If he really thinks of himself as an artist, and this is the kind of art he creates, his centerpiece wouldn't have been chosen for convenience, Carlos. Artists are usually very specific in their vision of what they want to create. Something must've brought him here. Something must've made him choose her.'

'OK, so what do you think it could be? It couldn't have been anything to do with her looks because it doesn't feature in the final composition. She was skinned, remember? If she had been black, Asian, blonde, brunette, drop-dead-gorgeous, diarrhea-ugly, whatever, it wouldn't have mattered. The final effect would still have been the same because all we could see was muscle tissue.'

'That's true,' Hunter agreed. 'But I wouldn't discard her looks just yet. Maybe it doesn't matter to us – spectators – because we only really got to see the finished work. Or maybe that was exactly the killer's intention – for us to think that the victim didn't really matter; but it mattered to him.' Hunter paused, as with Garcia's suggestion a new thought entered his mind. 'She was a model, right? Clothes catalogs, catwalks, that sort of thing.'

'Yes, that's right.'

'How about art modeling? Posing for paintings, sculptures, art photos . . . whatever. Anything to do with art, not fashion.'

Garcia's eyes lit up as he reached for his cellphone. 'I don't know, but I'll get someone on it right now.'

While Garcia spoke to Operations, Hunter changed position again. This time he walked back toward the bedroom door and placed his left cheek against the wall.

'Robert, what the hell are you doing?' Garcia asked as he disconnected from the call.

'Clutching at straws, I guess.'

'By doing what?'

'I'm not really sure. Maybe I'm just trying to see something where there isn't anything to be seen.'

'See something? It looked like you were trying to listen to the wall.'

'I was looking at the blood smears, actually.'

Garcia walked over to where Hunter was. 'You picked a really weird angle to look at them.'

'Exactly. I was thinking about the letters carved into the victim's back and how some of the lines didn't connect properly. If this whole scene really is a canvas, then maybe just like the carvings, all these smears aren't what they initially appear to be. Maybe they all add up to something else – an image, another letter, another message – something other than just blood marks on the walls.'

Garcia hadn't thought of that, but it made a lot of sense.

'Maybe the reason why we can't see it,' Hunter continued, 'is because we're not looking at it the right way, using the correct perspective, the correct angle . . . I'm not sure. Some works of art are like that – the image changes as you change your point of view, but hey, like I've said, I'm clutching at straws here because nothing really makes sense.'

'Maybe you *are* clutching at straws,' Garcia agreed. 'But I say that that's definitely worth a try.'

He walked over to the north wall and placed his right cheek on it.

Twenty-Three

The snacks room at the blood center in downtown Tucson wasn't very big, but it was spacious enough to accommodate three small tables and the two other people already in it reasonably well.

Despite having no appetite, Timothy Davis walked over to the table in the corner that displayed a very small selection of cookies and biscuits. His eyes scanned the few packets on the table and his mouth twisted awkwardly.

'Not really a varied choice, is it?'

The question came from the tall man who had just joined Timothy by the table. He too seemed to be struggling with a decision.

'No, sir,' Timothy replied with a slight headshake. 'The problem is, I'm not very big on cookies or biscuits.'

'Yeah, I hear you, buddy, me neither, but unfortunately this is all the Red Cross can afford. Actually, I think that even these packets have come from donations.'

'Yes, sir, they probably have.'

The man studied Timothy for a brief second. 'I'm Mike,' he said, extending a strong and firm hand. His arm had also been bandaged, but his dressing seemed quite different from the one

Nurse Atkins had applied around Timothy's arm. Timothy failed to notice that.

'Timothy Davis. Pleasure to meet you, sir.'

'OK, what's with the "sir" thing?' Mike asked, his brow creasing under his baseball cap.

'Oh, please take no offense, sir. Where I come from I just . . . got used to calling everybody either "sir" or "ma'am", that's all. I don't mean anything by it.'

'Where you come from?' Mike said, running his thumb and forefinger over his thick walrus mustache. 'Let me take a wild guess here – somewhere in the Deep South.'

Timothy smiled. 'That's right, sir. Alabama, born, bred and raised.'

'Alabama? That's a looong way away. So what brings you to Tucson?'

'Mostly work,' Timothy replied, extending and flexing his arm a couple of times. 'This gets quite itchy, doesn't it?'

Mike chuckled. 'It sure does. Is this your first time?'

Timothy nodded. 'I should've done it before, but . . .' his voice was padded by melancholy. 'Anyway, I've promised myself that I'll be a regular from now on. Yes, sir. Got to try and help others when we can, you know? At least some. People just don't seem to care about each other anymore.' Timothy raised a hand. 'I'll admit that I've been guilty of that myself for a long time. But I'll do better from now on, sir. Yes I will.'

The melancholy was still there, but before Mike could ask anything else, Timothy moved the subject along.

'How about you, sir? Is this your first time?'

'Oh no. This is my . . . eighth.'

At that exact moment, Timothy's stomach growled so loudly Mike took a step back.

'Wow,' he said, making a face, his blue eyes paused on Timothy's stomach. 'It sounds like you have something alive and very angry in there.'

'I apologize, sir. I'm not sure where that came from.'

'From being hungry,' Mike said. 'That's where. Didn't you have some food before coming here?'

Timothy hesitated. When he spoke again, his voice was barely louder than a whisper. 'I know I was supposed to, but ...'

Despite the hunger noises coming from his stomach, Timothy didn't feel like eating anything. In fact, he hadn't had much of an appetite for the past three and a half weeks and he had dropped a considerable amount of weight in that time.

'Well,' Mike said, 'I'm afraid that cookies and biscuits just won't be enough to silence that dragon living in your stomach. Have you had breakfast this morning?'

'Umm ... I did, I just didn't eat very much.'

'Are you nuts?' Mike asked. 'That's a crazy thing to do on the morning you're giving blood. I'm surprised they allowed you to donate.'

Timothy's eyes averted.

'You never told them, did you? Of course not. If you had they would've sent you home and asked you to come back tomorrow or the day after.'

'I know, sir, but I haven't had much of an appetite lately and I doubt that that will change in the next few days.' The sadness in Timothy's eyes was heartbreaking.

'Why?' Mike asked. 'Are you ill? Have you been to a doctor?'

'No, sir, I'm not ill. I'm just ... reevaluating my choices in life, I guess.'

'Well, your stomach is begging you for some food, my friend, and now that you have just given blood, you *need* to listen to it, unless you enjoy passing out without much warning.'

Timothy shook his head. 'Not particularly, sir, no.' He looked back at the cookie table.

Mike consulted his watch. 'I have an idea. Do you like Mexican food?'

Timothy curbed a smile. It was his favorite kind of food.

'Yes, sir, very much.'

'OK, the "sir" thing will have to stop. Please. It's making me feel ancient. Just call me Mike, OK?'

Timothy nodded in agreement. 'Sure, Mike. Please call me Tim.'

Mike smiled. 'That's much better. I already feel young again. So now back to the subject at hand, Tim: just around the corner from here there's a fantastic little Mexican café. They do the most incredible burritos. That will certainly fill you up, I promise you. How about you and I go grab ourselves some proper food, Mexican style. I'm buying. What do you say?'

Timothy looked unsure.

'C'mon,' Mike insisted. 'Neither of us can really go into work today, especially you, no matter what it is that you do, and we both need food. Doctor's orders.' He grinned. 'So we might as well eat something we enjoy, don't you think?'

As if on cue Timothy's stomach growled again.

'OK, we have one "yes",' Mike joked. 'Any more takers?'

Timothy smiled as he also checked his watch. He didn't really have anywhere to go back to. He had quit his job, and home . . . well, home just didn't feel like home anymore.

'Yes,' he finally replied. 'Mexican sounds mighty fine right now. Lead the way and I'll follow.'

'Great,' Mike said. 'But first let's grab some orange juice. We both need the fluids and the sugar.'

'I guess that's a good idea.'

As the man walked across the room and grabbed two cups of orange juice from a small table, Timothy never noticed him emptying the contents of the tiny bottle he had palmed into his right hand into one of the cups.

Twenty-Four

Once Hunter and Garcia left Linda Parker's house, they decided to split the afternoon's interview workload. Hunter was seeing Linda's parents in Cheviot Hills while Garcia was dropping by her model agency in West Hollywood. By pure chance, they both made it back to the Police Administration Building just seconds apart. Hunter had just locked the door to his old Buick when Garcia pulled up next to him.

'Did you just get here?' he asked as he jumped out of his car. 'Or are you going out again?'

'No, I just got back.'

'So how was your interview?'

'Tough,' Hunter replied. 'Her parents are in shock. Getting any sort of information out of them was a very slow and tactical affair.'

'That's why you went to them while I checked out her model agency,' Garcia said. 'You're much more tactful than I am. Anyway, did they give you anything?'

'Nothing ground-breaking,' Hunter explained. 'As we were told, it does sound like Linda Parker's mother was also her best friend. They hung out together. Went places together. Took holidays together. Did most things best friends do together.

She was adamant that Linda always told her everything that was going on with her personal life. Including about guys she was seeing.'

Garcia tilted his head sideways in a 'not so sure' way. 'Did you buy that?'

'No. Nobody ever gets told *everything*. No matter how good a friend they think they are. We all have secrets.'

'Especially when it comes to mother-and-daughter relationships,' Garcia agreed. 'I just can't see a daughter telling her mother *everything*, regardless of how open-minded they both are.'

'But we've got to go with what we have,' Hunter said. 'Which is, according to her mother, Linda Parker wasn't seeing anyone. Actually, her mother told me that she'd never really had a steady boyfriend.'

'Never? Really?'

They entered the PAB, crossed the reception lobby and cleared security.

'She told me that Linda just didn't have time for relationships,' Hunter clarified. 'And that since high school she had always concentrated all her efforts on her career and getting into the international fashion world. She said boyfriends were a distraction that Linda knew very well how to live without.'

They reached the elevator.

'Actually,' Garcia said, 'the people at her model agency told me pretty much the same thing – that Linda Parker wasn't the dating type and that she was very focused on her career.'

'But I did get something else that might help us,' Hunter added.

'Oh, and what's that?'

'Emily Parker wasn't only Linda's mother and best friend.

She also helped Linda with her online presence – Facebook, Twitter, Instagram, YouTube and email.'

'OK.'

'That means that she had the username and password to all of Linda's accounts,' Hunter said.

'Wow. We won't have to hack into anything?'

'Not this time.'

'Damn, that's got to be a first.'

'Her mother also told me that on the day she was murdered, Monday, Miss Parker had a very busy day – five photo-shoots in five different studios scattered all over LA.'

'Yep. I got the same info from her agency. We're going to have to check them all.'

As they crossed the Robbery Homicide Division's floor in the direction of their office, they both frowned as they noticed that their door was ajar.

'Did you forget to lock the office?' Hunter asked.

Garcia looked back at him sideways. 'You were behind me when we left, remember? If anybody forgot to lock anything, it was you.'

'I never forget to lock the door.'

'Maybe the captain is in there,' Garcia came back.

'Yeah, but why?'

As they at last got to their office, Hunter and Garcia stopped by the open door. Captain Blake wasn't in there. Instead, standing directly in front of their picture board with her back toward them and seemingly studying all the photographs that had been pinned onto it was a five-foot-eight woman. Her black hair had been elegantly styled into a shoulder-length beach wave. She wore a perfectly cut dark-gray suit jacket and a matching knee-length skirt.

Hunter didn't need to ask to know who she was.

Garcia, on the other hand, had no clue who the woman was. He was much more impulsive.

'Excuse me,' he said, his tone firm and demanding. 'Who the hell are you and how did you get in here?'

'He skinned her?' the woman asked without turning around and completely disregarding Garcia's question. 'And he severed her hands and feet?' The surprise in her voice was undeniable.

Garcia's head jerked back momentarily as his eyes widened with wonder. 'Sorry, lady, are you hard of hearing? This office is out of bounds to *everyone*. You can't be in here.'

'And what the hell is this?' she asked, still facing the board. 'Is this a frozen cat? What the hell is going on here?'

Garcia looked at Hunter. 'Is she for real? Who the hell is this woman? And how do we turn on her hearing aid?' He addressed the woman again. 'Hey, crazy lady, over here. I've got chocolate.'

'She's FBI,' Hunter replied.

The woman finally turned to face the detectives.

'Well spotted,' she said with a head nod. 'I'm Special Agent Erica Fisher with the NCAVC's Behavioral Analysis Unit.' She took two steps toward them before offering her hand. She had a small beauty spot above the left corner of her upper lip that added an extra pinch of charm to an already very striking heart-shaped face. Her eyes, which were as dark as her hair and as enigmatic as a coded message in wartime, locked with Hunter's.

Neither detective shook her hand, but Hunter held her stare.

'Well,' Garcia said, walking past her and placing himself between her and the picture board. 'Regardless of who you are, Special Agent Erica Fisher, you still can't be in here.'

'I guess that's where you're wrong,' she replied before finally breaking eye contact with Hunter and turning to face Garcia. 'Let me guess. You must be Detective Carlos Garcia, right? Born in São Paulo, Brazil. Your mother was American and a history teacher. Your father was Brazilian and a federal agent for the Brazilian government. After your parents divorced, you and your mother relocated to Los Angeles. You were ten years old at the time. Your father stayed in Brazil, where he still lives. You joined the police force straight out of high school and your progress was pretty much outstanding.'

Garcia frowned first at her, then at Hunter, but Special Agent Erica Fisher still wasn't finished.

'After busting your ass for two years as a detective in North LA, you were given a choice of divisions. That doesn't happen to many young detectives. You chose to join the Homicide Division. You married your high-school sweetheart, Anna Preston, and you have no kids.'

'Are you thinking about writing my biography?' Garcia asked.

Agent Fisher smiled as her eyes returned to Hunter. 'And the quiet guy over here can only be Detective Robert Hunter. You look a little different from the pictures in our archives.'

Hunter stayed silent.

'I've heard an awful lot about you, Detective Hunter. In fact, I've read your book. Every NCAVC agent has. It's part of our training. Very impressive stuff.'

Still not a word from Hunter.

'You guess that's where we're wrong?' Garcia said, dragging her attention back to him. 'That's what you said, right? And what exactly do you mean by that?'

Once again, Agent Fisher didn't seem to take notice of

Garcia's words and for a moment she looked like she was debating what to do.

'Hello?' A new quirkiness found its way into Garcia's voice. 'Is she really deaf?' he asked Hunter.

Agent Fisher let go of an irritated breath. 'No, I'm not deaf, Detective Garcia, and what I meant by "that's where you're wrong" is that this whole investigation is being taken over by the FBI. You guys can . . . move on to your next case, go get some donuts, or whatever it is that you do.'

One second of stunned silence.

'Come again?' Garcia said, frowning at Agent Fisher.

'Which part?'

'The one about the FBI taking over *our* investigation.'

'You heard it right, Detective Garcia,' she confirmed. 'My orders were to wait before breaking the news to you, but you seemed a little too eager to find out so . . . there you have it. This case doesn't belong to the LAPD anymore.'

'Who ordered you to wait?' Hunter finally broke his silence.

'Excuse me?' Agent Fisher repositioned herself so she could see both detectives without having to rotate her body every time.

'You just said that you were ordered to wait,' Hunter said. 'Who gave you those orders?'

'I did.'

The reply caught everyone by surprise, because it came from the person who was now standing at the door to Hunter and Garcia's office.

Twenty-Five

Hunter, Garcia and Special Agent Fisher all turned at the same time to face the hoarse, gravelly voice that had come from behind Hunter. Standing just outside the door to their office was not one person, but three.

'The orders came from me, old buddy,' Adrian Kennedy confirmed, his eyes fixed on Hunter. He was flanked by Captain Blake on one side and Special Agent Larry Williams on the other.

Garcia's surprised face was a picture. 'Oh, I didn't know that we were having a party. I could've gotten us all some party horns.' His questioning stare moved to Kennedy. 'And you are . . . ?'

Kennedy didn't laugh at the joke. 'My name's Adrian Kennedy,' he replied as he stepped into the office. Captain Blake and Special Agent Williams followed him inside. 'And you must be Detective Carlos Garcia.' Kennedy walked over to him and offered Garcia his hand. As he walked past Agent Fisher, Kennedy gave her a stern sideways look. 'It's a pleasure to finally meet you, Detective.'

Garcia stood still, though he did frown at the word 'finally'. 'Sorry, but is your name supposed to mean something to me?'

'Adrian Kennedy is the FBI's NCAVC's Director, Carlos,' Captain Blake explained as she positioned herself by Hunter's desk. 'He also heads the NCAVC's Behavioral Analysis Unit.'

'Great,' Garcia replied, unimpressed, before addressing Kennedy again. 'Congratulations. It sounds like you've done well for yourself.' He threw an even more inquisitive look Captain Blake's way.

Her reply came in the form of a single shrug.

Kennedy finally retracted his hand, which had been hanging idle in midair until then. He turned and faced Hunter.

'How are you, old friend? It's nice to see you again.'

Hunter did shake Kennedy's hand.

'This is Special Agent Larry Williams,' Kennedy said, taking care of the formal introductions. 'And obviously you've already met Special Agent Erica Fisher.' His gaze found hers. 'Who should've followed orders and waited.'

'I apologize, sir. I was just trying to—'

Kennedy's slight shake of the head was enough to bring an early end to Agent Fisher's excuse.

'What's going on, Adrian?' Hunter asked. 'Why's the NCAVC taking over this investigation?'

'Well,' Kennedy said, scratching the underside of his chin. 'It's complicated.'

'Simplify.' Hunter's tone was firm.

Special Agents Fisher and Williams looked at each other doubtfully. They had never heard anyone talk back to Director Kennedy that way, let alone a PD detective.

Before Kennedy could answer the question, his attention traveled to the picture board to his left and he paused. The expression on his face went from surprised to confused in record time.

That was when Agent Williams also took notice of the board.

'What the hell?' he said as he stepped closer, his eyes jumping from picture to picture before settling on Kennedy. 'He skinned the victim?'

'Adrian,' Hunter called in a firm voice. 'Why's the NCAVC taking over this investigation?'

Kennedy breathed out as he looked back at Hunter.

'Well,' he finally said. 'What you're looking at here, my friend, isn't this killer's first victim.'

Twenty-Six

As Timothy Davis finally regained consciousness, confusion set in almost immediately. He had no idea of what had happened to him or why. He had no idea of where he was or how he'd gotten there. Right then, the only thing he knew, the only thing he could tell was that the darkness that surrounded him seemed absolute, so much so that for a second he wondered if his eyes were really open. But even so, a strange feeling of familiarity slowly began engulfing him, as if he knew he'd been to that place before.

Despite how numb his mind seemed to be, Timothy begged his memory to help him, but the images he got were broken and incoherent. The last thing he was able to remember was ... leaving the Red Cross blood-donation center downtown?

Yes, that *was* the last thing he could remember.

He'd given blood for the first time, but when did that happen?

Today?

Yesterday?

Last week?

As he searched for an answer a new memory took shape inside his head and he remembered something else – he hadn't been alone as he left the center. There was someone else with him. A tall man he'd met in there, but the man's name evaded him. Timothy tried but the mother of all headaches had built a solid wall between him and most of his memories.

'Where the hell am I?'

As soon as he uttered those words, his throat exploded in the most agonizing of pains, as if he had swallowed a ball of angry fire ants. Reflexively his hands shot up to his neck and to the source of the pain, except they never got there. They never even left the side of his body.

'What the hell?'

The fire ants got angrier inside his throat and he clenched his teeth so tight it felt like they were about to crack. For a moment he concentrated on his breathing, trying to steady it as much as he could.

In.

Out.

In.

Out.

The pain finally subsided and Timothy realized something that he had somehow failed to until then – he'd been lying on his back on some hard, uncomfortable surface. His legs were fully extended, with his feet side by side, touching each other. His arms were flat against the side of his body, his palms facing up. He tried his arms again and that was when he understood why he couldn't move them – something was tugging at his wrists, firmly restricting his arms. He tried his legs – something tugged at his ankles.

'Goddamn it, what the hell is going on?'

Pain exploded in his throat for the third time, but Timothy didn't care anymore. He needed answers. He needed to understand what was happening to him. He tried lifting his body into a sitting position, but something tugged at his waist. He'd been immobilized with incredible accuracy and precision. He could still move his head and neck, but what good would that do? In absolute darkness, looking right, left, or center made no difference at all. He began feeling sick, as if something putrid was sitting inside his stomach, slowly rotting everything around it.

Think, Tim, think, he told himself. There was no reason for him to keep on messing with the fire ants in his throat. 'You're a mechanical engineer. Problem solving is what you do. Think, goddamn it, think.'

That was when he noticed a new pain, something that for some reason, his mind had chosen to block out until then, but not anymore. The pain exploded from his left leg, crawled past his torso and chest, taking hold of his neck before crashing like a ferocious wave of thorns inside his head. The mother of all headaches was suddenly introduced to its evil twin sister.

What the hell is this? he thought. *Why am I tied down like an animal? Where the hell am I?*

Timothy felt everything around him begin to spin out of control. Nothing made sense. He closed his eyes and all of a sudden his mind was flooded with memories of his wife.

Timothy and Ronda had met at the end of his second semester at Berkeley, northern California. He was a Mechanical Engineering freshman and Ronda a Computer Sciences sophomore. It was at a sorority party – Sigma Nu. Timothy was standing out back by the swimming pool, sipping on a bottle of beer, when Ronda spotted him from the balcony. He was about an inch shy of six foot and very attractive, but she couldn't help thinking that he looked almost out of place, too shy to be at a party where all kinds of crazy seemed to be going on.

'Not really enjoying the party?' she had asked him as she joined him by the pool. The smile on her lips had been too enigmatic for Timothy to figure out.

'No, ma'am,' he had replied, putting down his beer. 'The party is just fine. I just needed to get me some fresh air.'

'Did you just call me ma'am?'

'Umm . . . sorry, ma'am. Please make nothing of it. I'm from out of town and it's just the way I talk.'

And talk they did, for hours on end. They ended up leaving the party together, but they didn't go back to their rooms. They walked all the way to Albany Beach, where they sat and watched the first rays of sunlight crack the night. It was against that backdrop – sun coming up where the ocean met the sky – that they kissed for the first time. Timothy had never forgotten that first kiss, or how it made him feel.

From that day onwards, they became almost inseparable, only being away from each other during class time. They even got a job together in a restaurant on Jefferson Avenue. Ronda worked the tables while Timothy displayed his culinary abilities in the kitchen. Near the end of Timothy's sophomore year, Ronda took him to Idaho to meet her parents and he surprised her by asking her father for her hand in marriage. With her parents' blessing, Timothy married Ronda three months after his graduation.

The move from California to Arizona came during that same year, when a highly regarded technology company, specializing in civil government defense, offered Timothy a fantastic position with their weapons engineering team.

It was shortly after they moved to Tucson that Ronda began experiencing terrible pains around her pelvic region, especially during her menstrual cycles, but Ronda, being the stubborn African American Idahoan that she was, only agreed to see a doctor after the fifth consecutive month of debilitating pain and heavy bleeding. That was when their world was shattered for the first time. At the age of twenty-five, Ronda Davis was diagnosed with endometriosis of the ovaries, which had also rendered her infertile.

The news of Ronda's inability to bear children devastated the couple, but it didn't lessen their love for each other; in fact, it seemed to somehow strengthen their bond.

'There are other ways of starting a family,' Timothy had told her, and he promised Ronda that once they were settled and their careers were a little more established, they would start theirs. He told her that nothing in this world would stop them from having their family and being happy, but Timothy was wrong. Just before her twenty-ninth birthday, Ronda began feeling ill again and after a battery of tests and exams, their world was shattered for the second time. Ronda was diagnosed with stage-three pancreatic cancer and given a total of eighteen months to live.

Maybe it was her stubbornness, or maybe it was the love that Timothy and Ronda had for each other. No one really knows, but Ronda fought her cancer with everything she had and she turned those eighteen months into thirty-four. She finally passed away, in their home, three and a half weeks ago.

Another surge of pain, coming from his left leg, tore Timothy away from his memory, but the guttural scream he let out didn't derive from his physical agony. It came from how much he missed Ronda. It came from how angry he was with life and with a God that he had believed in and prayed to for most of his life. But not anymore.

Clunk. Clunk.

The distant, muffled sound came from somewhere on Timothy's right and his eyes shot in that direction like a couple of missiles, but all he saw was darkness.

'Hello?' he said, totally disregarding the fire ants in his throat. 'Is someone there?'

No reply.

Still as a statue, Timothy waited, concentrating extra hard on his hearing.

Nothing.

He was beginning to believe that his ears had played a trick on him when he heard it again.

Clunk. Clunk. Closer this time, but still not close enough.

'Hello?' he said again. 'Who's there?'

No reply.

'Please. I'm in here. Can anyone hear me? Please, help me. Please.'

The next noise Timothy heard sounded like a door handle being turned.

'Yes, in here. Please, help me. I'm in here.'

Timothy held his breath. A couple of seconds later he heard the creaking of a door being opened. Still, darkness clothed him like a tailored suit.

'Hello?' he said in an unsteady voice.

Suddenly, directly above him, a light bulb flicked into life, bathing the room in brightness.

The sharp light burned at his eyes like fire, forcing Timothy to squeeze them shut.

A quick blink.

Still too bright.

He waited a couple more seconds before blinking again.

That was a little better, but still the light hurt him.

A few more seconds.

Blink.

Better.

Blink.

His pupils finally adapted to the light.

Timothy turned his head in the direction of the opened door. As he did, a figure took shape – tall and slim, standing there, looking back at him.

Timothy squinted, doing his best to make out the man's face.

'You weren't supposed to be awake,' the man said. Despite his voice sounding calm, there was a tingle of preoccupation in his tone. 'How come you're awake? I'm sure I've dosed everything correctly.'

Timothy tried searching his memory for that voice, but the mother of all headaches and its evil sister seemed to be having a party in his head, and they were wrecking the place.

The man was still standing by the doorway.

'What?' Timothy said, his voice fragile.

The man finally moved from the doorway, taking a single step into the room.

'Please, sir . . . I don't understand what's happening.'

Timothy strained to keep his eyes on the figure now approaching him, but a new stream of pain shot up from his left leg like fireworks, making every muscle in his body tense as if they were cramping. Instinctively, his eyes left the man and moved to his leg. Darkness was gone and Timothy could finally see why it hurt so much.

'Oh my God.'

Twenty-Seven

If Adrian Kennedy and his two FBI agents were expecting to surprise Hunter, Garcia and Captain Blake with his revelation that Linda Parker hadn't been this killer's first victim, they were severely disappointed.

'You called it, buddy,' Garcia said, nodding at his partner.

'What?' Kennedy asked.

'Robert had a hunch that this killer had offended before,' Captain Blake replied.

'How many victims so far, Adrian?' Hunter asked.

Kennedy looked back at him and his reply was a simple head tilt accompanied by an eyebrow movement.

'How many victims, Adrian?' Hunter pushed, his voice calm albeit demanding.

'I'm sorry, Detective.' This time the reply came from Special Agent Fisher. 'But that information is on a need-to-know basis and since this isn't an LAPD investigation anymore, you don't—'

'Special Agent Fisher,' Kennedy cut her short. 'Why don't you go get a coffee or something? I noticed they have a machine right at the end of the corridor. I'll call you back in here when I need you.'

Agent Fisher paused, her mouth semi-open in dismay.

'But sir, I was just replying to—'

'*Outside*, Agent Fisher.' Kennedy's hoarse voice seemed to gain a new depth. 'I'll call you back in here when I need you.'

'Ooooohh,' Garcia said playfully. 'Someone just got handed the keys to the dog-house.'

Agent Fisher faced him while pretending to scratch the tip of her nose with her right middle finger.

Garcia winked back at her. 'That's cute. Did you learn that at the FBI Academy?'

As she exited the office, Agent Fisher had to call on all her willpower not to slam the door behind her.

'How many murders so far, Adrian?' Hunter asked one more time.

'I was harsh on her, Robert,' Kennedy replied. 'But Special Agent Fisher was right, and you know it. That sort of information is on a need-to-know basis and, officially, this investigation doesn't belong to the LAPD anymore.'

'Hey, wait a second there,' Captain Blake cut in. 'How about a little professional courtesy, huh? You guys want us to hand over everything we've got on this investigation so far, right? How about you guys give us a little before taking everything?'

Kennedy peeked first at Special Agent Williams and then at the picture board. For a moment he looked deep in thought.

'OK, I guess that's fair,' he finally replied. 'But I have a better proposal.' The pause that followed was clearly deliberate and Hunter could already guess what was coming next. That was why he refrained from asking the obvious question, unlike Captain Blake.

'And that is?'

'Why don't the FBI and the LAPD join forces on this one?'

'Excuse me, sir?' The surprise in Special Agent Williams' voice was almost tangible.

'Remember when I told you that The Surgeon might've just made his first and worst mistake?'

'Yes?'

Kennedy's chin jerked in Hunter's direction. 'That's his mistake right there.'

'The Surgeon?' Garcia asked, frowning at Hunter. 'Mistake . . . ? What . . . ?'

'Sorry, sir,' Agent Williams said. 'But I don't follow either.'

'The Surgeon's last victim was murdered inside Los Angeles,' Kennedy explained. 'Which obviously falls under LAPD jurisdiction. And because he used excessive violence,' he indicated the board, 'the investigation was automatically assigned to the LAPD's Ultra Violent Crimes Unit, which is headed by Detective Hunter.'

'Yes . . . so?' Agent Williams still looked puzzled.

'Well, Robert Hunter is the best criminal profiler I've ever worked with,' Kennedy said. 'He's the best criminal pro-filer the FBI has *never* had. I've tried to recruit him into the NCAVC so many times I've lost count.'

'And flattery won't get you there this time either, Adrian,' Hunter said.

'But that's the thing, Robert,' Kennedy replied. 'I'm not trying to recruit you, not this time. What I'm offering here is a joint effort between the FBI's NCAVC and the LAPD's UVC Unit. This is not a job offer. You will not become an FBI agent. You'll still be an LAPD detective, but you'll gain nationwide jurisdiction for the entire length of the investigation. What I'm offering you here is a chance to stay in this investigation and to catch this sick freak.'

'I'm sorry, sir,' Agent Williams said. 'I don't mean to interrupt, but bringing outside help into this investigation isn't
necessary. I respect Detective Hunter's work. I really do. I read
his book and all, but if I may speak frankly, he doesn't have the
training or the ability for something of this magnitude. He's
just a PD detective and all he'll do is slow us down.' He looked
at Hunter. 'No offense.'

'None taken,' Hunter replied.

'Well, I got offended,' Garcia cut in, raising a hand. 'Just a
PD detective . . . ?'

Kennedy lifted his right index finger to silence them for a
minute. 'What do you say, Robert?'

Hunter stayed quiet.

'I know you, old buddy,' Kennedy pushed. 'I know that
when you sink your teeth into a case, especially when it's
something as intriguing as this, you just can't let go that easily.'
He paused again, studying Hunter. 'I want you on this case,
Robert. That's the reason why I'm here. I didn't fly all this way
just to tell you that the FBI was taking over your investigation.
I came here because I wanted to talk to you person to person
and because I am the only one who can make this happen. I
can make it official in less than fifteen minutes. All you've got
to do is say the word.'

Hunter kept his eyes on Kennedy but his mind took him
back to just a few hours ago, when he had been sitting face to
face with Emily Parker, Linda Parker's mother. As Hunter was
getting up to leave, Mrs. Parker had reached out and placed a
trembling hand on his shoulder.

'Detective,' she said in a voice strangled by tears. 'Please
promise me that you will catch him. Please promise me that
you will make this sonofabitch pay for what he's done to my

daughter. She was my only child.' With those words, Emily Parker broke down in sobs again.

'We'll do all we can to bring the person responsible for your daughter's death to justice, Mrs. Parker,' Hunter replied.

'No,' Emily Parker came back, her voice angry. 'That's not good enough, Detective. I don't want to hear the kind of crap you feed the six o'clock news reporters. You can save that bullshit for the press. I want your personal promise that you will catch this sonofabitch. That you won't rest until this sick freak is behind bars. Promise me, Detective. Promise me.'

Hunter wasn't one to promise anything he wasn't absolutely sure he could deliver, but right then he knew that Emily Parker was hurting in a way she'd never hurt before, and all she was really after was some reassurance that the people tasked with catching her daughter's killer would not give up on her. Hunter phrased his answer the best way he could without having to lie.

'Mrs. Parker, I give you my word that I won't rest until the person who took your daughter from you is behind bars. That I can promise you.'

The conviction in Hunter's voice brought a new barrage of tears to Mrs. Parker's eyes.

'How many victims, Adrian?' Hunter asked again.

Kennedy could sense that Hunter was on the brink of giving in. It was only fair that he conceded some ground as well.

'This is his third victim,' Kennedy finally replied.

Hunter and Garcia exchanged a concerned look.

'Where were the others located?' Garcia this time. 'We know they weren't in LA, probably not even in California, so where has this guy struck before?'

Kennedy faced him.

'Sir, please,' Agent Williams intervened. 'We really don't need any help here.'

'Yes, I know,' Garcia addressed the agent. 'We're just mere PD detectives, right? All we're going to do is slow you guys down.'

'What do you mean "we"?' Agent Williams replied, trying to suppress a sarcastic chuckle. 'Did you think that Director Kennedy was talking to you too?'

Hunter questioned Kennedy with a simple stare.

Kennedy nodded. 'I'm sorry, Robert, but Special Agent Williams is right. The offer for a joint operation is extended only to you.'

'You have got to be kidding me,' Garcia said in disbelief.

Hunter signaled his partner to give him a moment. 'That's not what you said, Adrian.'

'What do you mean? I never said anything about your partner.'

'Yes, you did.'

'What?' Agent Williams intervened again. 'When?'

Hunter was still addressing Kennedy. 'You proposed a joint operation between the NCAVC and the LAPD's UVC Unit, right? Those were your words. Well, Detective Garcia and I are the LAPD's UVC Unit, not me by myself. The only reason why this unit has the reputation it has, is because we work together.' Hunter's turn to pause for effect. 'So if you want this joint operation to go ahead, Adrian, you better make room for the two of us.'

Kennedy hesitated for a moment and Agent Williams took over one more time.

'Well that's just not going to happen, is it? If you think—'

'Special Agent Williams,' Kennedy stopped him. This time the gravel in his voice was coated with annoyance. 'If you interrupt me one more time, you'll be removed from this investigation and on a plane back to Quantico in the next hour, am I clear?'

'But sir!'

'Am I clear, Special Agent Williams?'

Agent Williams looked down at his shoes like a schoolboy who'd just been severely reprimanded.

'Yes, sir.'

'Maybe you should borrow the dog-house keys from your partner,' Garcia said.

'Detective Garcia,' Kennedy said, his whole demeanor booming with authority. 'If you are to be part of this operation, you will have to tone that sarcasm of yours way, way down.'

Garcia was about to come out with a new dig, but he caught a glimpse of the way Hunter and Captain Blake were looking at him.

'OK,' he finally conceded. 'I think I can do that. No problem.'

Kennedy readdressed Hunter. 'So you're in?'

Hunter peeked at his partner.

Garcia nodded once. 'Oh, I'm definitely in. I want to catch this sicko.'

'This will be a joint operation,' Hunter told Kennedy. 'The NCAVC and the UVC Unit will have equal levels of authority, command and clearance throughout the investigation. No one keeps anything from anyone.' His stare moved to Agent Williams. 'This is not a competition. We're all after the same end result. Can you work with that?'

Agent Williams took a deep breath to steady himself. 'Yes, I can work with that.'

'Carlos?'

'Yes, of course. I have absolutely no problem with that.'

Hunter looked at Linda Parker's skinned body photographs pinned to the picture board.

'OK, Adrian, we're in. You've got your joint operation.'

Twenty-Eight

'What?' Special Agent Fisher said once she was allowed back into Hunter and Garcia's office. The look on her face was as if the world had turned upside down during her absence. 'A joint operation?' Her stare sought Agent Williams for help, but all he could do was shrug.

'That's right, Special Agent Fisher,' Kennedy confirmed.

'But sir, that's absolutely unnecessary. We have this whole investigation under contr—'

'Special Agent Fisher,' Kennedy stopped her yet again. This time he sounded angry. 'We're not going to keep on doing this and if you are to stand a prayer of being a part of this operation, you better snap out of this superior attitude of yours, and you better do it pronto, do you understand me?'

Agent Fisher looked like she was about to breathe out fire.

'If I hear that even a single second of this investigation has been jeopardized due to your attitude, you'll be stuck with office work for the rest of your FBI career. Have I made myself clear?'

Agent Fisher's stare went from Kennedy to Agent Williams, to Hunter and finally back to Kennedy.

'Have I made myself clear, Special Agent Fisher?' Kennedy's voice was resolute.

'Yes, sir,' she replied with a nod. 'Crystal. You'll get no problems from me.'

Garcia was about to let fly a new sarcastic comment when Hunter gave him an almost imperceptible headshake.

'OK,' Kennedy said, addressing his agents and positioning himself behind Hunter's desk. 'Now that we're all in agreement, how about we get everybody up to speed on what we've got so far?'

'That'd be a good start,' Garcia said.

Kennedy nodded at Special Agent Williams, who retrieved a blue file from the briefcase he had brought with him.

Kennedy stepped back from the desk, as if to give everyone more space.

'OK,' Agent Williams began. 'The Surgeon first came to our attention a little over two months ago, on February fifteenth to be exact.'

'The Surgeon?' Garcia asked.

'That's the moniker the FBI is using on this creep,' Agent Williams explained. 'The reason, I think, is pretty obvious.' He indicated the board. 'But I'll get there in time, anyway.'

From the blue file, Agent Fisher obtained an eleven- by eight-inch colored portrait of a woman and placed it on Hunter's desk.

'The Surgeon's first victim was Kristine Rivers, a twenty-year-old college student from Wayne State University in Detroit.'

Hunter, Garcia and Captain Blake stepped closer to examine the photograph. As they did, Hunter felt an uncomfortable knot begin to tie itself up at the back of his throat. Though the girl in the photo looked to be no older than seventeen, she reminded Hunter of Professor Tracy Adams. Her gentle heart-shaped face was stylishly framed by long red hair. Her almond-shaped eyes were blue and they seemed to carry a naive sparkle in them. Her lips were full and adorned by a deep red lipstick. Her nose was pointy but delicate, and her cheekbones were prominent and smooth-curved.

'Miss Rivers was born and raised in Hamilton, Ohio,' Agent Williams continued. 'Where her family still lives. She was accepted into law school at Wayne State two years ago.' He flipped a page on the file he was reading. 'Miss Rivers shared a small apartment, located on the outskirts of the university campus, with two other sophomore law students: Susan Temple, also twenty years old and from Michigan, and Rosanna Rodriguez, twenty-one years old from Iowa. On the night of February thirteenth or morning of the fourteenth, Miss Rivers failed to come back home from her waitressing job in an All-American Diner in Springwells Village.'

'Springwells Village is about three miles from where she lived,' Agent Fisher added.

'How did she usually get home from work?' Garcia asked. 'Did she walk?'

'No, she took the bus,' Agent Fisher replied. 'We checked all the buses' CCTV footage, talked to all the drivers who had worked that route that night – nothing. It doesn't seem like Miss Rivers ever boarded the bus home.'

'What time did she finish work?' Garcia again.

'The Diner closed at half past midnight,' Agent Williams answered. 'According to everyone who was working that night, Miss Rivers left, by herself, ten to fifteen minutes after closing time. No one noticed her talking to anyone in particular, either. No customers or anyone else who could've invited her out once her shift was over. In fact, some of them were grabbing a beer after work, but Miss Rivers said that she needed to get home because she had class early the next morning.'

'How far away was the bus stop from the diner?'

'About a block away, and before you ask, there were no CCTV cameras anywhere on that stretch.'

Agent Williams paused and waited for any more questions. None were forthcoming, so he finally carried on with his accounts.

'The next morning, Miss Rivers' body was discovered by Detroit PD inside an abandoned wooden shed on the banks of the Detroit River, not that far from the university campus.' He retrieved four new photographs from his blue file, placing them all on Hunter's desk. 'And this was how she was found.'

'What the hell?' Garcia said. His surprise was mirrored on Hunter's and Captain Blake's faces.

'Yeah, exactly,' Agent Williams replied.

Twenty-Nine

'Shhhhh,' the man whispered as he stared straight into Timothy Davis's eyes. His tone of voice was comforting and reassuring. 'It will be OK, Tim. It will all be OK now. Trust me.'

Timothy blinked once ... twice ... three times. The movement was slow and lethargic and though his eyes were still open they were fading fast. The images they registered came in blurry and distorted, as if he were looking at the world through a thick sheet of plastic.

His ears weren't doing much better, either. Though he could still hear the man's voice, the words he spoke failed to make much sense, not because they were incoherent or spoken too softly, but because Timothy's brain, now starved of blood, lacked the capacity to understand them.

The man took a step back and grabbed a lungful of soiled air. It had been a very slow-moving and difficult couple of hours, especially because this had been the first ever time that the man had tried anything like this. The procedure had been a lot harder and taken a lot longer than he had anticipated, but it was all paying off with dividends.

The man had to admit that he'd had his doubts. When he'd

first come up with the concept for Timothy Davis, he wasn't sure it would actually work, and because there was absolutely no way he could test the procedure beforehand, doubts had begun creeping up on him, so much so that the man had considered using a completely different method to achieve what he had set out to achieve. A method that would've been almost impossible to properly keep under control. But now he was glad that he had stuck with his original plan. In the man's eyes, what he had just done was a masterpiece – a work of pure art – and he still wasn't done yet. For his concept to be absolutely perfect, there were still a couple of finishing touches he had to add, but there was no rush. The man knew that he had all the time in the world, so for a moment he allowed himself to indulge in his own self-glorifying ecstasy.

'Ple . . . please.'

Not even Timothy knew where the strength to utter that word had come from, and though his plea had been barely louder than a whisper, it had been enough to shatter the man's invisible vanity mirror and drag him back to the moment.

His stare rested on Timothy's now pale face. Life was draining from it fast.

'It really is OK, Tim,' the man replied. 'You don't have to fight it anymore. Just relax and let it happen.'

Timothy tried to look back at the man, but his unfocused eyes were losing direction. Around him, the room, the air, all of it seemed to be getting colder and colder.

'Do go gentle into that good night, my friend,' the man insisted, but by then Timothy's ears were incapable of discerning sounds.

Timothy felt his heart drumming against the inside of his chest as if he had just run a marathon at top speed. Breathing was getting harder and harder. He couldn't feel his toes anymore. In fact, he couldn't feel his legs either ... or his fingers ... or his hands ... or even his arms. Timothy's whole body seemed to have deserted him, while his heart was literally beating the life out of him.

'Rejoice, Tim,' the man said. 'For this is actually our moment of glory. Yours and mine, and do you know why?' The man smiled proudly. 'Because when I'm done, you'll be immortalized.'

A second later, Timothy Davis took his last breath on this earth.

Thirty

For several silent seconds, Hunter, Garcia and Captain Blake kept their stunned eyes on the two photographs that Special Agent Williams had placed on Hunter's desk. They now understood why Adrian Kennedy and both FBI agents had acted so surprised when they first laid eyes on Linda Parker's crime-scene pictures.

The first two photographs on Hunter's desk were full-body shots of Kristine Rivers, The Surgeon's first victim. She had been stripped naked and left lying on her back on what looked to be a dirty floor. Her arms were resting naturally by her torso, with her legs extended, her heels practically touching each other, the same position in which Hunter and Garcia had found Linda Parker the night before. But that was where the similarities ended. Unlike Linda Parker's body, Kristine Rivers' hadn't been skinned, neither had her hands and feet been severed from her limbs. In fact, her body looked completely unharmed, which led everyone to focus their attention on the next two photographs – both close-ups of Kristine Rivers' face – and that was where it all got even more confusing, because this time the killer had taken the victim's eyes, leaving behind nothing but two terrifying dark holes caked in dry blood and a grotesquely disfigured face.

But that wasn't all.

Most of her skull, from halfway up her forehead all the way to the back of her neck, had also been completely exposed. Kristine Rivers had been scalped – Old West style.

Hunter repositioned himself to better study the images.

There was no blood whatsoever on the floor surrounding her body, not even by her head, which told everyone that the extraction of her eyes, together with the scalping, hadn't occurred inside that disused wooden shed.

'Wait a second,' Captain Blake interrupted, only then realizing something she had missed. 'Are you sure we're talking about the same perpetrator here? The MO in this case looks to be *totally* different.'

'My exact thoughts once I laid eyes on your picture board,' Kennedy replied.

'Same here,' Agent Fisher added.

'Which was no longer than fifteen minutes ago,' Captain Blake came back, half-surprised, half-annoyed. 'So you're telling me that the NCAVC's "A" team flew all the way down here from DC, put on this huge song-and-dance show about taking over our investigation, without being one hundred percent sure if we were talking about the same perp or not?'

'Well, not exactly,' Kennedy replied.

Captain Blake's annoyance heightened. 'And what does that mean?'

Kennedy nodded at Agent Williams.

'You are one hundred percent correct, Captain.' The agent took over once again, reaching inside his blue file for yet another photograph. 'The MO here seems completely different and none of us knew that until fifteen minutes ago or there-abouts. We tried patching into the LAPD's database to have a better look at your investigation files before flying over here, but we couldn't find anything – no pictures, no crime-scene description ... nothing. Hence our total surprise once we finally saw your crime-scene photographs.'

'The reason why you got nothing,' Garcia clarified, 'is that the UVC Unit keeps most of its investigations offline, for that exact reason.'

'It's a good strategy,' Agent Williams admitted, before bringing the subject back to the victims. 'So, at first look, the only similarities between these two victims is maybe the position in which they were left and the fact that they were both females in their early twenties, which, anybody in this room will agree, isn't nearly enough to even suggest that they were both victims of the same perpetrator.'

He finally placed the fifth photo on the desk.

'But then we've got this.'

Thirty-One

The new photo Agent Williams placed on Hunter's desk hadn't come from Kristine Rivers' crime scene. It came from her post-mortem examination. Her body had been washed clean and moved onto a large stainless-steel autopsy table. It was lying on its front.

'Looks familiar?' Though Kennedy's question was to every-one, his gaze landed on Captain Blake.

'I'll be damned,' she replied.

Carved into Kristine Rivers' back was what looked to be a carbon copy of the carvings the killer had made on Linda Parker's back – a seemingly odd combination of letters and symbols, forming four distinct lines, though everyone in that room already knew that those symbols would turn out to be badly drawn letters.

There were six characters in the first line, five in the second, seven in the third, and five again in the fourth and last one. The killer had once again used only straight-line slashes to create his letters, no curves. The markings began approximately two inches below Kristine Rivers' shoulders and ended about an inch above her buttocks. Just like the ones carved into Linda Parker's back, each letter was about two to three inches high and about one and a half inches long.

'The LA victim,' Agent Williams asked. 'When was her body discovered?'

'She was murdered on Monday evening,' Garcia replied. 'But her body was only discovered late last night.'

Agent Williams paused. 'Late last night? What time did you guys get to the crime scene?'

Despite failing to see the relevance of the question, Garcia looked at Hunter for confirmation. 'About nine thirty, maybe a quarter to ten. Why?'

'A quarter to ten? The surprise in Agent Williams' voice was reciprocated on the look Agent Fisher gave the LAPD detectives.

Kennedy, on the other hand, knowing why both agents looked surprised, held back on a smile.

'OK,' Agent Williams began. 'I know you have already figured out that despite these carvings looking like a strange combination of letters and symbols, they are actually just badly drawn letters that when put together correctly will form a sentence . . . in Latin. And the reason I know that is because someone from this office, at around two o'clock this morning, tried searching the VICAP database for a similar perpetrator signature – a killer who leaves messages, in Latin, carved somewhere on his victim's body.'

Garcia and Captain Blake both looked at Hunter.

The guilty look on his face was accompanied by a subtle nod.

'So the mystery is finally solved,' Captain Blake said.

'What mystery is that?' Agent Williams enquired.

'Well, since our victim's body was only discovered late last night and we did *not* request any help from the Bureau, I was wondering how the FBI found out about it so fast. So this was how. You were monitoring the VICAP database.'

'Correct,' Agent Williams admitted. 'Any searches containing certain words or combinations of them, get flagged up and we are notified immediately.'

'Not only monitoring it,' Hunter intervened. 'They were also filtering its responses, because no matter how I phrased my search, I got zero matches.'

'Correct again,' Agent Williams agreed. 'We suppressed the results coming out of VICAP. We didn't want anyone else knowing that this guy had killed before.'

'That's one of the many perks of being with the Bureau, Robert,' Kennedy cut in. 'The power to do things that regular police departments cannot.'

Hunter gave him a sideways look.

'Anyway,' Agent Williams said, bringing everyone's attention back to him. 'So you're telling me that you guys figured out that these carvings created a sentence in Latin in the space of just three, maybe four hours?'

'Three or four hours?' Garcia asked, making sure that the surprise in his voice was noted. 'It took us about a minute.' He looked at Hunter. 'Maybe less. I think you called it at the scene in just a few seconds, didn't you?'

Hunter didn't reply.

'What?' Agent Fisher asked, turning around and looking at the picture board one more time. 'At the crime scene? With all this dried-up blood on her back muddling everything up even more? Get real. There's no way.'

Kennedy bit his bottom lip. The suppressed smile was still there.

'Why?' Garcia asked. 'How long did it take you guys to figure that one out?'

Agent Fisher cleared her throat, but said nothing. Instead, she looked at Agent Williams.

'About eight hours.' The reply came from Kennedy.

'Seven actually, sir,' Agent Williams corrected the director as if he had made the gravest of errors.

Still, both FBI agents looked a little uncomfortable.

'Well,' Garcia said, staring straight at Kennedy. 'That's one of the many perks of being with a police department. We think faster.'

'All right,' Kennedy said, pinning Garcia down with a stare that could crack a mirror. 'This kind of childish behavior has got to stop.'

'Just saying.'

'Now, Detective Garcia.'

'Put a fucking lid on it, Carlos,' Captain Blake said. 'No more, do you hear me? Another sarcastic comment out of you and I will be transferring you into another unit, which means you're out of this investigation. Is that clear enough for you?'

He lifted up both hands in surrender.

'The dog-house keys are hanging just outside the door,' Agent Fisher said.

'How about we get back to what really matters here?' Hunter suggested.

'You took the words right out of my mouth, Robert,' Kennedy said, before addressing Captain Blake. 'So I guess this settles the argument that we are indeed talking about the same perpetrator here.'

The captain agreed with a nod.

From the way Hunter was looking at the photographs,

Garcia and Kennedy could tell that in his mind he was already working everything out. As his eyes moved from knife slash to knife slash, Hunter first put the straight-line cuts together to form the missing letters before grouping them into each of the four lines.

PULCHR
ITUDO
INCONIU
NCTIO

'*Pulchritudo in coniunctio*,' he read out loud.

There was no disguising Agent Williams and Agent Fisher's surprise.

As Hunter read the Latin phrase out loud, Garcia and Captain Blake squinted at the photo on his desk, trying to see what he'd seen.

Hunter moved his right index finger over the picture to show them how the lines connected, before linking the words.

'You frighten me sometimes, Robert, do you know that?' Captain Blake commented.

'All right,' Garcia said with a nod. 'I see it but I don't understand it. What does it mean?'

'Beauty is in the . . . combination . . . relationship . . . connection . . .' Hunter replied. 'It could be any of those. The Latin language has a very limited vocabulary. A single word, when translated into English, could have five, six, seven different meanings. Sometimes more. It all depends on the context.'

'That's correct,' Agent Fisher jumped in. 'But we believe that in this case the killer meant "relationship" – "Beauty is in the relationship".'

Garcia scratched his forehead. 'Well, that sure as hell isn't the same phrase we got.' He indicated the board.

Everyone in the room turned to face it.

'The truth is,' Kennedy said, 'we weren't really expecting it to be. It seems like the killer changes the Latin phrase with each murder.'

Agent Fisher was staring at the pictures of Linda Parker's back a lot harder than anyone else, clearly trying to make out the phrase the killer had carved into her body, but straight away she encountered one big problem. Hunter hadn't had time to put up the official autopsy photographs yet. The ones on the board were taken at the crime scene, showing the carvings partially covered by dried blood, which made identifying the cuts, the letters and the words considerably harder. Still, she gave it her best try.

'The first word is the same – *Pulchritudo*.' She indicated with her finger. 'Which means "beauty". Then we have a "c" then an "r . . ." No. "C" then an "i" then a "p . . ." No.'

'*Pulchritudo Circumdat Eius*,' Hunter said.

Agent Fisher looked at him with fire in her eyes. 'I was getting there. I just needed a little more time.'

'My Latin is rusty,' Kennedy said with a shrug.

'It means "beauty is all around her", sir.' Agent Fisher translated it.

Immediately Kennedy seemed to enter pensive mode. His eyes focused on nothing at all as the gears inside his head began working overtime. Hunter recognized the blank look on his face.

'Not now, Adrian,' he said, dragging Kennedy away from his thoughts. 'You guys were supposed to be bringing us up to speed, remember? Once we have everything, then we can all sit down and try to understand the connection between the Latin phrases the killer has used for each victim, if there really is a connection. But for now, we still have quite a lot of ground to cover.' He addressed Agent Williams. 'You said that Linda Parker was his third victim, right?'

'That's correct.'

'So let's keep on going here. We'll revisit everything once all the facts are out.'

'Agreed,' Kennedy said.

Everyone else in the room nodded.

'All right.' Agent Williams took over again. 'So, moving on . . . as you can see from the photographs, her killer not only scalped her, but he also removed both of her eyes. According to Dr. Ramos, the pathologist who performed the autopsy back in Detroit – and this was later confirmed by one of our own pathologists in Quantico – this was no amateur job. The scalping isn't a very difficult or technical procedure, but the extraction of the eyes is, and this killer has performed an exenteration to professional standards.'

'Exenteration?' Captain Blake asked.

'The removal of the ocular globe together with all of the contents of the eye socket,' Hunter explained. 'Eyelids, muscles, lacrimal glands, optic nerves, everything. That's why all that was left behind were two empty holes.'

Both FBI agents looked at Hunter curiously.

'I read a lot,' he clarified.

'I'm sure you do,' Agent Fisher commented.

Kennedy shuffled his weight from one foot to another in a fidgety way for two reasons. One – he wasn't a man who was used to being on his feet for such a long time, and two – he could pretty much kill for a cigarette right then.

'But that wasn't the cause of death, right?' Garcia asked. 'She wasn't alive when the killer took her eyes.'

'No, she wasn't,' Kennedy confirmed.

'Let me guess,' Garcia continued. 'Asphyxiation, but not by strangulation. She was suffocated.'

'Was it the same here?' Agent Williams asked, his head tilting in the direction of the board.

Garcia nodded. 'In our case, her hands, feet and skin were taken from her after she passed, not while she was still alive. According to Dr. Hove, the Los Angeles Chief Medical Examiner, despite how brutal that crime scene looks, the victim wasn't tortured. She didn't suffer.'

'That was exactly what the post-mortem revealed in Kristine Rivers' case as well,' Agent Williams agreed. 'No torture. No suffering. She was suffocated. The exenteration and the scalping came later.' From his blue folder he retrieved Kristine Rivers' autopsy report and placed it on the desk.

'How about victim number two?' Hunter asked. 'I know we haven't got there yet and I don't want to jump the gun here, but was the victim also suffocated?'

'Yes. Just like Kristine Rivers. No torture. No suffering.'

'So we've made a wrong assumption,' Hunter said.

'Which assumption was that?' Kennedy asked.

'About the killer's MO being different from one murder to the other. It's not. It's the same across the board. He suffocates his victims. What differs is his signatures, both in what he does to them after they pass and in the messages he leaves behind.'

Everyone paused for a heartbeat.

'Did forensics find anything at the crime scene?' Captain Blake asked.

'Nothing that could give us any leads,' Kennedy replied. 'Kristine's body was found inside an old and disused shed by the river. The shed had been out of operation for many years, during which it was used by hobos as a shelter, by addicts as a shooting-up spot, and God knows who else and for what else. There was a lot of debris, dirt and rubbish everywhere, which gave forensics a bucketful of fingerprints. They also recovered DNA from urine stains, discarded needles, used rubbers and other sources. Through those we were able to identify and track down several individuals. Through them we tracked down several more.' He shook his head. 'All of them were either homeless or junkies. No one with the kind of knowledge or skill required to pull off something of this magnitude.'

'Was she sexually assaulted?' Hunter asked.

Agent Fisher peeked at Kennedy before replying. 'No. Miss Rivers wasn't touched that way.'

'Why?' Kennedy asked, his voice full of concern. 'Was the LA victim raped?'

Hunter locked eyes with the NCAVC director. 'No, she wasn't sexually assaulted either.'

The room went silent again for a couple more seconds.

'Any more questions?' Agent Williams asked. 'Or am I OK to carry on?'

'Let's carry on,' Hunter suggested.

'All right,' the agent continued, pushing all the photographs on Hunter's desk to one side. 'Our killer's second victim.' He returned to his blue folder.

'Wait a second,' Garcia interrupted him. 'How about the rest of the photographs?'

'What rest of the photographs?' Agent Fisher asked.

'The crime-scene ones from the disused shed? The blood on the walls?'

'What?'

'There was no blood on the walls, right?' Hunter asked,

reading their puzzled looks. Once again, he called everyone's attention back to the picture board. 'Unlike Kristine Rivers,' he explained, 'Linda Parker's body wasn't found inside a shed or any random abandoned place. She was murdered inside her own house. Her body mutilated inside her own bedroom. And as you can see . . .' he indicated a specific group of photographs, 'the killer made a point of smearing most of the walls and the furniture with her blood.'

Kennedy and his agents stepped closer to have a better look at the photos.

'So the killer didn't do the same at your crime scene?' Garcia asked.

'No,' Agent Williams replied. 'Kristine Rivers wasn't murdered inside that shed. Her eyes and scalp weren't taken there either. There was no blood anywhere. The only blood we found had dried on her skin.'

'The pattern here is all wrong for these to be blood splatters from arterial spray or something similar,' Agent Fisher said. She was the only one still staring at the board. 'What they look like is "get away" smears. A victim trying to escape her attacker.'

'Yes, we know what they look like. Thank you.' Garcia didn't try to keep the sarcasm out of his tone. 'But we don't think that's what they are.'

'You think the killer put them there on purpose? Why?'

'We'll get to that later,' Hunter said, stopping Garcia before he was able to explain. 'Let's carry on with the original sequence of events. We all know that serial murders follow a certain progression inside the killer's mind. So for now we should stick with that as well, even if we don't understand it. Covering things out of order, without having all the facts first, will just generate unnecessary questions and confusion. Let's move on to the killer's second victim before we get to the third, how about that?'

Everyone agreed and Agent Williams returned to his folder for a new eleven- by eight-inch photograph, a full-body shot.

'OK,' he said, placing the photo on Hunter's desk. 'The Surgeon struck again almost a month after Kristine Rivers, on March eleventh.'

If the photographs of Kristine Rivers had surprised Hunter, Garcia and Captain Blake, the second victim shocked them.

Thirty-Two

Before he began, Special Agent Williams allowed Hunter, Garcia and Captain Blake a few seconds to study the new photograph he had just placed on the desk.

'I can see by the expression on your faces,' he said, 'that The Surgeon's second victim has surprised you as much as it surprised us.'

The man in the photo was looking up from an open newspaper he'd been reading. The smile on his lips was gracious, but it was a sad smile, probably put on just for the sake of the photograph. His old-looking and ill-fitting clothes were clean but scruffy, as if they'd been slept in at least a couple of nights. The little hair he had left, two small islands just above his ears, were as white as milk, matching the color of his bushy eyebrows and his thick mustache. His deep, dark-brown eyes, just like his smile, seemed full of sorrow and the white in them, over their many years on this earth, had acquired a light-yellow tint, losing much of the sparkle that had once lived in them. His rosy face, together with his bony hands, seemed to be held together by a messy web of capillaries and thinning veins, running behind wrinkled and tired skin. He had the look of a man who was used to hard work and suffering. The look of a man who had accepted his destiny.

'This was Albert Greene,' Agent Williams reported. 'An eighty-four-year-old, ex-school janitor from Wichita, Kansas.'

'He was eighty-four years old?' Captain Blake asked in a tone coated by a mixture of disbelief and disgust.

'That's correct,' the agent confirmed, his voice solemn. 'Mr. Greene was born and raised in Northeast Millair, one of the most impoverished and underprivileged neighborhoods in Wichita. His father passed away from pneumonia when he was only thirteen years old. Due to how poor his family was and the fact that he was the oldest of four children, Mr. Greene was left with the task of being family breadwinner; he had no choice but to drop out of school halfway through seventh grade and find a job to help his mother bring up his two brothers and one sister. He was never able to return to school.'

Agent Williams paused and made a somewhat sorry face. 'Well, not as a student, anyhow. Between the ages of thirteen and twenty-three Mr. Greene helped his family in any way he could, jumping from odd job to odd job until, call it "life irony" if you will, he was employed as the school janitor at the same school he had dropped out of ten years earlier. He spent fifteen years at that school until it was closed down in 1972. By then, Mr. Greene had married and had had a daughter of his own – Jody Elena Greene. By the beginning of the next school term, Mr. Greene had secured a new job, again as a school janitor, but this time in Maple Hills, one of the most affluent neighborhoods in the city, working for one of the best high schools in the whole of Kansas. When he hit the age of sixty, he stopped being a janitor and became the main CCTV control-room operator. He stayed at that same job until he retired, at the age of sixty-nine, and probably only because arthritis had gotten the best of him by then.'

'Jesus Christ!' Captain Blake said, taking a step back from Hunter's desk. 'Are you telling me that this killer went after an eighty-four-year-old man ridden with arthritis?'

'Yes, Captain. As sick as it sounds, that's exactly what I'm telling you.' Agent Williams turned to address Hunter. 'Detective, you said that the LA victim, Linda Parker, was found inside her own house?'

'That's right.'

'Well, so was Mr. Greene.'

Agent Williams reopened his blue folder and retrieved another four photographs, placing them on Hunter's desk. Once again they were divided into two full-body shots and two facial close-ups.

'You've got to be kidding me,' Garcia said, uneven lines creasing the edges of his eyes as he cringed.

Captain Blake looked like she was about to say something, but words failed her.

Hunter stayed silent, his analytical stare moving slowly from one photo to the other.

'I guess that now you really understand the reason for our surprise once we discovered what this killer had done to victim number three,' Agent Fisher said.

The first two photographs on Hunter's desk revealed that Albert Greene had also been stripped naked and left lying on his back, but not on some sort of dirty floor. This time, the killer had left his victim lying on a bed, in the exact same position he had left Kristine Rivers and Linda Parker – arms resting naturally by his torso, with his legs extended, ankles practically touching each other. But just like Kristine Rivers,

Albert Greene's body hadn't been skinned, neither had his hands and feet been severed.

'As you can see,' Agent Williams proceeded, pointing to photos three and four, the facial close-ups taken at the crime scene, 'the killer also took away Mr. Greene's eyes, using the same method he'd used with Kristine Rivers, but this time, no scalping.'

The skin on Albert Greene's face looked even more wrinkled and fragile than it did on the first photo they were shown. His mouth was contorted out of shape and his eyes ... his eyes just weren't there. The killer had once again extracted both ocular globes, leaving behind two dark holes caked in dried blood.

'Another orbital exenteration?' Hunter asked.

'Of the same professional standard he'd shown with Kristine,' Kennedy replied.

'And that's why victim number three,' Agent Fisher took over, pointing to the picture board, 'caught us completely off guard. Two victims. Two asphyxiations. Two expertly performed eye surgeries. One scalping. Then, about a month later, we've got this – complete mutilation. Hands and feet hacked off, the body skinned like an animal's, but the eyes ...' She indicated one of the facial close-up photographs of Linda Parker. 'The eyes weren't touched. No exenteration.' She shook her head. 'We weren't expecting this.'

'How about the carvings?' Hunter asked.

Agent Williams reached for another photograph from his folder and placed it on the desk. Once again, the killer had carved his message into his victim's back and, just like before, the message was divided into four distinct lines, containing what at first would appear to be an odd combination of letters and symbols. This time the killer had divided the lines as follows: First line – six characters. Second line – eight characters. Third line – eight characters. Fourth line – eight characters.

'Mr. Greene's skin was old and thinning,' Agent Williams explained. 'Very tenuous, and we believe that that's the reason why this message looks a little messier than the previous one.'

This time Agent Fisher didn't give Hunter any time to decipher it.

'This time we have four words instead of only three – *Pulchritudo in oculis aspicientis*,' she revealed, before addressing Garcia. 'It means "beauty is in the eye of the beholder".'

After a silent moment, Kennedy took the floor again.

'So now you can probably understand our frustration, Robert. We've been working on this for over two months. Due to the similarities of the first two murders, we've been drawing up a few theories and pursuing some specific investigative avenues, but this third victim is like a dagger through the heart of most of what we've been working on so far.'

Hunter, Garcia and Captain Blake could clearly see why.

'You said Mr. Greene was found inside his own house?' Hunter asked.

'He was,' Agent Williams confirmed, displaying six new photos. These ones showed details of the room in which Albert Greene had been found – his own room. There was no blood on any of the walls. No blood on the floor. No blood on the furniture.

'Any signs of a break-in?' Garcia this time.

'None,' Agent Fisher replied. 'And no signs of a struggle either, but then again, what sort of struggle could an eighty-four-year-old man with aching joints put up anyway?'

'What about Mr. Greene's wife?' Hunter asked. 'You said he was married, right?'

'He was for many years,' Kennedy replied. 'But his wife, Elena, passed away six years ago. Mr. Greene lived alone in a small one-bedroom house in Murdock, another poor and rough neighborhood in Wichita. His daughter lives in Colorado with her husband and two kids. She would visit him twice a year, sometimes more, if time and money allowed. Mr. Greene never had a caregiver. Despite his age, he was still able to do everything himself, from going to the shops to cooking and cleaning the house. According to everyone we talked to, he was a very simple but proud man. He was alone in the house when the attack happened.'

'So who found the body?' Garcia asked. 'And how long after the murder?'

'One of his neighbors,' Agent Williams replied. 'Two houses down – Mr. Morales, who is sixty-nine. He's also a widower and he and Mr. Greene were best friends. They tended to spend most of their days together. Each had a key to the other's house. On the morning of the twelfth of March, Mr. Morales didn't see his old friend sitting outside on his front porch like he did every day, so he got worried and went knocking. No answer, he used his key and . . .'

Garcia nodded, his attention back on the photographs on the desk.

'We can talk details later,' Agent Williams added. 'Or you guys can read the files to your heart's content, but this is the bulk of what we have.' He stepped back from Hunter's desk, placed his blue folder on top of a metal cabinet and faced the picture board. 'I guess now it's your turn. Tell us about Linda Parker.'

'Before we do that,' Hunter suggested, 'how about we all take a twenty-minute break? We've been locked in this office for over an hour. I, for one, could use a trip to the bathroom and a cup of coffee.'

'And a cigarette,' Kennedy added. 'I certainly could do with a cigarette right now.'

Everyone in the room agreed.

Outside the Police Administration Building, Hunter caught up with Kennedy as he lit his first cigarette.

'We need to talk, Adrian.'

Hunter's tone concerned Kennedy, but he kept a straight face. 'Sure. What's up?'

Hunter handed the NCAVC director the first portrait photograph they had been shown of Kristine Rivers.

Kennedy took a long drag of his cigarette.

'OK,' Hunter asked. 'So who is she?'

'What? What do you mean? We've told you that upstairs. Her name is Kristine Rivers.'

'That I know. What I want to know is *who she is*.'

'I don't follow.'

'Yes you do. You know exactly what I'm talking about, Adrian. No more bullshit. Who is this woman . . . *really*?'

Thirty-Three

'I'm starting to get a little hungry,' Officer Jack Palmer from the Tucson Police Department in Arizona said as he turned right on East Sunrise Drive. 'How about we grab a couple of tacos or something?'

'Not a bad idea,' his partner, Police Officer Diana Bishop, replied as she adjusted her police belt. 'I could certainly do with a burrito right now.'

'Blanco Tacos?' Officer Palmer asked.

'Sure, either there or El Pueblito. They're both great.'

'Blanco Tacos is closer,' Palmer replied, performing a quick U-turn.

Five minutes later they had ordered an Al Pastor burrito and a double portion of fully loaded tacos.

'What do you want to drink?' Palmer asked.

'Just a bottle of water, thanks.'

'No coffee?'

'Nah, I'm drinking too much of that stuff. I need to cut down a little. I practically have coffee running in my veins.'

Palmer chuckled. 'Yep, that happens when you keep on getting stuck with night shifts.' He turned and addressed the stocky Mexican man behind the counter. 'Can I also get a bottle of water and a large coffee to go, please?'

'Sure, Officer.' The man didn't ring it through. 'The water and the coffee are on the house.'

'Oh, thank you very much. That's very kind of you.'

Right then the police radios on both of their belts cracked into life.

'*Any units in the vicinity of East Miraval Place – Catalina Foothills. We have reports of a possible armed 10-62.*'

Both officers exchanged an anxious look. '10-62' was the police code for 'breaking and entering'. Instinctively they both turned and looked out the shop window. East Miraval Place wasn't far.

Palmer nodded at his partner. 'We'll take it.' He faced the Mexican attendant one more time. 'Sorry, but can you hold on to that food? We'll come back for it. Trust me.'

As the two of them rushed out of the restaurant, Officer Bishop reached for her radio.

'This is unit three-two-two, Tucson PD. We're just around the corner from East Miraval Place and en route. Requesting full address.'

With the sirens blaring, it took them less than three and a half minutes to get to the address dispatch had given them.

East Miraval Place was a dead-end street on the north side of Catalina Foothills, an affluent neighborhood on the north quadrant of Tucson. The street, like most of the neighborhood, had a minimalist style, where paving and concrete blended nicely with the desert landscape of cactuses, desert flowers and even the occasional tumbleweed, giving it a truly Old West feel. Sticking with the minimalist approach, most of the roads and streets in Catalina Foothills had no illumination, and over fifty percent of them had no nameplates or signs of any kind, making it very easy for even residents to miss their

street or get a little lost in the process of getting home once the
sun had set.

Despite knowing the area well, Officers Palmer and
Bishop took no chances, following their sat nav all the way to
their destination.

There were only five houses in the wide but short street,
and the address they were given took them to the last house
on the right – a large, single-story brick building with a three-
car garage and overgrown desert vegetation as a live fence.
Parked at the end of the driveway, just outside the garage,
was a metallic silver Buick Encore. The lights on the outside
of the house were on, but inside everything seemed to be in
complete darkness.

'According to dispatch the house belongs to Timothy
and Ronda Davis,' Bishop said, reading the information
displayed on the in-car computer screen. 'He's a mechanical
engineer and she's a computer programmer. They both work
for Raytheon.'

'The weapons company?'

Bishop shrugged. 'Must be. Do you know any other
Raytheons around here?'

That made Palmer pause for thought. 'All right,' he said, a
few seconds later. 'Let's go check this thing out.' He jumped
out of the car.

Bishop followed suit.

As they passed the Buick on the driveway, Palmer tried
the door – locked. He then placed his hand on its hood – no
warmth whatsoever. He shook his head at his partner.

Both officers unholstered their weapons.

To get to the house's front door, they needed to circle
around the left side of the garage building, following the

driveway. They did so in single file and as stealthily as they could. Palmer took the lead. As they rounded the corner, even from a few yards away, Palmer and Bishop could tell that the front door had been left ajar.

'Crap,' Bishop said. 'Not a great sign. So are we going in or waiting for back-up? Dispatch said that this is a possible *armed* 10-62.'

Palmer's eyebrows arched at his partner. 'I'm not waiting.'

'Going in it is, then,' Bishop said, and quickly crossed herself.

They positioned themselves one on each side of the door. Palmer used his fingers to run down a silent count of three and slowly pushed the door until it was fully open.

With their weapons and flashlights drawn, they both took a deep breath and entered the house. Palmer swung right while Bishop went left.

The front door opened into a large anteroom with a teardrop crystal chandelier hanging from the ceiling, a circular mirror on the wall to their right and two large vases flanking a double door a few paces in front of them. Not many places to hide.

'Clear,' Palmer announced.

'Clear,' Bishop replied.

The next room was an impressive entry foyer, with check-ered black-and-white granite flooring and white wainscoting running along all the walls. Directly in front of them was a sumptuous turned staircase, leading up to the second floor. The opened double door to their right clearly led into a massive living-room area. To their left they saw another double door, this one shut. Just past the staircase, also on the left wall, there was a single wooden door that had been left a couple of inches ajar.

'Shit,' Bishop whispered. 'What do we do now?'

Palmer allowed his stare to crawl around the foyer while he figured out their next move.

'Maybe it would be best if we split up.'

'What, really?'

'What do you suggest?'

'Sticking together, that's what. This is too much like one of those horror films.'

'What? What horror film?'

'Those where the *girl* cop dies first.'

'Are you for real?'

Click. Click. A muffled noise echoed throughout the room.

'Shhhh,' Palmer said, his eyes like an owl's. 'Did you hear that?'

'Damn straight I did. Where did it come from?'

'Not sure.' He signaled for them to wait and listen.

Two seconds.

Four seconds.

Five seconds.

Click. Click. The sound came again and this time they both turned to face the single door along the left wall, just past the staircase.

'I think it came from over there,' Bishop said, nodding at the door.

'Yeah, that was my impression as well.'

Being extra cautious, Officers Palmer and Bishop approached the door.

Click. Click. They heard it again, but it still sounded somewhat distant, which meant that it wasn't coming from directly behind the door.

Palmer first brought a finger to his lips, then reached out

and very slowly pushed the door open, hoping to God that the hinges wouldn't creak.

They didn't, but it didn't matter. There was no one there. Instead the door got them to a concrete staircase that led down to the house's basement. At the bottom of the stairs there was a second door, also a couple of inches ajar, but this time there was light coming from behind it.

Palmer signaled Bishop that they should go down together. He would go first.

Bishop agreed with a head nod.

They took the steps down one by one and very carefully. As they finally reached the second door, Bishop could swear her heart was about to explode out of her chest.

They heard a new noise come from behind the door. This time it sounded like movement.

Palmer signaled his partner one more time. The message was for Bishop to get ready. He would push the door open, but he wouldn't do it slowly like before. The move would be fast and sudden with the intention to catch by surprise whoever was behind the door.

Once again, Bishop indicated her understanding with a head gesture.

Up came the three-finger silent countdown one more time.

Three . . .

Two . . .

One.

Thirty-Four

With a drag that seemed to last an eternity, Adrian Kennedy lit his second cigarette from the first.

Hunter waited.

'I knew it would be hard to get it past you, old buddy,' Kennedy said, as he exhaled a thick cloud of smoke. 'But even I wasn't expecting you to figure it out so quickly. So what gave it away?'

'You, Adrian,' Hunter replied. 'You gave it away.'

'Really? When?'

'The first time,' Hunter explained. 'When I flipped through Kristine Rivers' investigation file upstairs.'

Kennedy questioned with a stare.

'It said that you attended the crime scene.'

The stare was still there.

'C'mon, Adrian, I know you, and I know how the NCAVC works. You won't travel anywhere unless it's absolutely mandatory. Most of the NCAVC's operations are coordinated either from your office in Quantico or the one in DC; there's rarely a need for you to become field active.'

Kennedy watched the smoke curl up in the air as it left the tip of his cigarette. He looked like he was enjoying Hunter's assessment.

'Sure,' Hunter continued, 'this killer's first murder was intriguing, but not enough to get the NCAVC's director so worked up about it that he had to attend the scene himself. There was nothing there you hadn't seen before, Adrian – a killer who takes body parts from his victims? A killer who carves messages into his victims' flesh? A killer who likes to position his victims in a specific way? The Bureau's archives back in Quantico are littered with similar cases.' Hunter shook his head. 'No, there had to have been some other reason why you went to Detroit and so fast. Don't tell me Detroit PD requested the FBI's help, because I know they didn't. Not within just a few hours of the body being discovered.'

'I see your logic, Robert,' Kennedy said. 'And it makes total sense, but the reason we turned up in Detroit doesn't necessarily have to be linked to the victim. It could be linked to the killer.'

'That was actually my first thought,' Hunter admitted. 'A dormant killer. Someone who the NCAVC were already looking for. A killer who perhaps had gone into a long cool-off period and had finally decided to resurface. But that still wouldn't completely justify your presence at the crime scene. Then your body language gave it away again.'

Kennedy looked a little surprised. 'Did it? When?'

'When Kristine Rivers' crime-scene photographs were displayed,' Hunter explained. 'Your composure wavered fractionally and your eyes averted from the images. The more we talked about her, the more fidgety you got.'

Kennedy looked like he was trying to recall the moment.

'Then, just a while later,' Hunter added, 'I asked if she'd been sexually assaulted. Agent Fisher exchanged a flash look with you before responding, and immediately after that you reciprocated the question, this time concerning the LA victim. There was more than just apprehension in your voice, Adrian. There was pain. After I told you that the killer didn't touch Linda Parker in that way either, the pain in your voice turned into relief.' Hunter paused, studying the NCAVC director.

Kennedy held steady.

'Pain for Miss Rivers' death and relief for the fact that she hadn't been sexually assaulted.'

Another pause.

Again Kennedy kept his poker face.

'I know you well enough to know that you never allow yourself to get involved, Adrian. Add to that the fact that you referred to the victim by her first name at least a couple of times and something here isn't quite right. Rule number one of the NCAVC when working brutal serial-murder cases: never let it get personal, never get emotionally attached to anything or anyone, especially the victims.'

Kennedy flicked the filter of his cigarette with his thumb, tipping the ash before looking back at Hunter.

'What if I told you that Kristine Rivers was with the FBI's Witness Protection Program and that is why we got involved so fast?'

'Then I would tell you to get your agents, get the hell out of my office and stop wasting my time.'

'Why?'

'Because she wasn't with the Witness Protection Program, Adrian.'

'How can you be so sure? The names on the FBI's WPP are highly classified.'

'Are you kidding me?' Hunter sounded half-offended. 'If Kristine Rivers was part of the WPP she wouldn't have been relocated to a major city like Detroit, or allowed to enroll into a top university like Wayne State – too much exposure. The risk of her being recognized by a fellow student, a teacher, or even on the streets of Detroit by a stranger would be too great. WPP subjects always get relocated to obscure little towns somewhere in the back of beyond, not to huge metropolises. Plus, neither you nor your agents have a clue who this killer could be. If Kristine Rivers had been murdered because she was with the WPP, you would know where to start looking.'

Kennedy gave Hunter a lifeless smile while nodding.

'So can we please drop the bullshit now?' Hunter said. 'Who was she, Adrian?'

Kennedy gazed at the photograph Hunter was holding. 'You probably read in the file that her mother's name is Suzanne Rivers, right?'

Hunter nodded once.

'What the file doesn't show is that Kristine's mother's maiden name is Suzanne Kennedy. She's my sister. Kristine was my niece, Robert.'

Thirty-Five

In finally hearing Kennedy's revelation about Kristine Rivers' true identity, Hunter's face fell. He knew that this time Kennedy had come clean.

'I'm ... so sorry, Adrian. I didn't mean to ...'

Kennedy looked away for an instant.

'I know you didn't, Robert. I know you well enough, old buddy.' One more puff of his cigarette.

'So why didn't you tell me from the start? Did you really think you could keep that sort of information hidden from us throughout the investigation?'

'Of course I didn't think I'd be able to keep it hidden,' Kennedy replied. 'Even if I wanted to, I know you would find out. I just didn't expect it to be within the hour. I thought I had done a great job up there when those pictures came out.' He shrugged. 'Obviously not. But I would've told you everything once this initial meeting was over, anyway. Before I fly back to Washington tonight.'

'Why after the meeting?' Hunter asked. 'Why not come clean from the start?'

Three uniformed police officers on their cigarette break exited the PAB and stopped a few feet from Hunter. As they lit up, Kennedy motioned Hunter to walk with him.

'Because I didn't want you to get onboard just as a favor to me,' Kennedy said, once they were out of earshot. 'I didn't want you to think that I was using my niece's murder as a reason to bring you into this investigation.'

He finished his cigarette and stubbed it out against the wall.

'I wanted you on this case, Robert. I wanted you on this case from day one because you can read these scenarios better than anyone I know, and to be very truthful, there's no one else inside the FBI or any other law-enforcement agency whose professional ability I trust and respect more than yours.'

Kennedy took a second and his next words came out dusted with emotion. 'This bastard took my niece. He mutilated her face. He took her eyes. He *scalped* her. Who the fuck does that? And then he left her body inside a dirty and disgusting shed, amidst junkies' discarded syringes and used rubbers, but you know what the funny thing is? Despite all my anger and hatred, I'm almost grateful to this bastard for not raping her.'

Out came cigarette number three.

'I know you didn't know her, Robert, but she was the sweetest girl you could ever meet. Always smiling. Always positive about everything. Happiness was just part of her.' A new sadness danced across Kennedy's face. 'She was only twenty years old. She had her whole life still in front of her. She had so much to live for and some sick fuck took it away from her. He took her away from us.'

Hunter had never seen Kennedy that emotional.

'Her family ... my sister, they're all in pieces. Me? I'm in pieces too, but I'm also pissed the fuck off, and I will not stop until this sack of shit is caught. Believe me, I came this close to calling you more than once.' He indicated with his thumb and index finger. 'Then, early this morning I got the news that The Surgeon's possible third victim had been found right here in Los Angeles. I didn't even have to check. I knew that the LAPD's UVC Unit would have the case. I knew that *you* would have the case.'

Hunter leaned back against the wall.

'With three victims,' Kennedy proceeded, 'the carvings he makes into his victims' backs, the words in Latin and the puzzle that this creep leaves us, I had no doubt that the case itself would intrigue you enough for you to want in, especially when one of the victims was taken inside your own turf. But I wanted to talk to you face to face. I didn't want to do this over the phone. That's why I'm here. If you hadn't agreed to the joint investigation, I would've asked to talk to you in private and I would've come clean.'

Hunter looked back at Kennedy.

'Yes, I probably would've bagged you for your help. Not that you haven't already figured this out, but we've got nothing, Robert. For the past two months or so, I've had practically every agent at my disposal working endless hours in some aspect of this investigation and we haven't moved an inch. And you already know why, don't you?'

Hunter said nothing in reply, but Kennedy knew he knew.

'Yes,' Kennedy admitted. 'We threw ourselves head first into a single theory – that Kristine had been no random victim. Her murder just couldn't have been a coincidence. In my eyes and consequently the eyes of the FBI, there could've been only one reason why she was chosen, and that reason was me. I had no doubt of that. After all, I'm the Director of the FBI's National Center for the Analyses of Violent Crimes *and* the Behavioral Analysis Unit. By default, I'm responsible for the imprisonment and even the death of hundreds upon hundreds of criminals. The list of people out there who'd love to hurt me as a payback for something they deem me responsible for is probably longer than the Mississippi River. And then there were the carvings on Kristine's back. Once we finally deciphered them, my certainty that she had been murdered just because she was my niece grew exponentially – "Beauty is in the *relationship*".'

Kennedy allowed those words to propagate through the air for a moment.

'In my mind,' he continued, 'there was no ambiguity to the meaning of that phrase. The killer could only be referring to one kind of relationship – family.'

Kennedy paused again, giving Hunter a second to think about it.

'The beauty of family, Robert, shattered by the hands of a sick sonofabitch. The way I saw it, the carvings were just the killer's way of making sure I didn't miss the real reason my niece lost her life.'

'But why not just come out and say it?' Hunter asked. 'A letter sent to you . . . an anonymous phone call . . . even a text message. There were loads of different ways the killer could've let you know. Why write the phrase in Latin? Why make it into a puzzle with most of the letters looking like symbols and the words broken out of place?'

'Why do you think, Robert?'

Hunter realized how silly his query had been. 'Because that's what you and the NCAVC do.' He answered his own question, nodding at himself.

'That's correct,' Kennedy agreed. 'It's our job to figure out clues, riddles, puzzles, taunts . . . anything perpetrators leave behind, purposely or not. He wanted to make sure I knew, but he wasn't about to do my job for me. Everything fitted perfectly for Kristine's murder to have been a "payback" job.'

'Were you two close?' Hunter asked. 'You and Kristine?'

'With my job?' Kennedy shook his head. 'It's hard to be a family man of any sort. Why do you think I have two ex-wives? I barely have time to take a piss. But I did make an effort. Kristine was my only niece. I saw her once, maybe twice a year. She was a law student and criminal law was definitely her thing, so sometimes she would come visit me in Quantico. She loved the whole academy thing – the archives, the stories, the photos, the forensics lab . . . everything.'

Hunter stayed quiet and Kennedy had another puff of his cigarette before continuing.

'Trust me, Robert, I had a platoon of agents and cadets going through old cases, name lists . . . everything we could think of. Then out of the blue we got a call from the Wichita Police Department. I'm sure you can already imagine the sort of havoc a second victim brought into our investigation. Not once, while investigating Kristine's murder, did the word "serial" get mentioned. We were all positive that her murder had been a direct attack on me.' For a second Kennedy looked almost angry with himself. 'When Albert Greene got added to the equation, we were forced to reassess our theory, but even then I was so blinded by anger, so sure that Kristine's murder had been a retaliation act that we just carried on making mistakes and losing time. We expanded our payback theory and we never stopped knocking at the wrong doors.'

'Expanded the payback theory?' Hunter asked. 'How?'

Kennedy shrugged. 'Before I leave today I'll make sure that you and Detective Garcia have full copies of our entire investigation so far into both murders, including every single photograph we have, crime scene and otherwise. You guys can have a look for yourselves.'

'All right.'

'But my stubbornness stops now,' Kennedy reassured Hunter. 'With Linda Parker being taken here in LA ...' He shook his head. 'This isn't about me. It can't be because Albert Greene and Linda Parker simply don't belong. Despite how angry I am, I have to accept that unfortunately Kristine was simply in the wrong place, at the wrong time.'

Thirty-Six

Given what Adrian Kennedy and Special Agents Williams and Fisher had already seen on the picture board, it didn't take Hunter and Garcia too long to run them through the little they had on Linda Parker's investigation so far.

'That's pretty much it,' Garcia announced, leaning against the left side of the picture board. 'Robert and I were regrouping here in the office to discuss our next move when we walked into Special Agent Erica Fisher here snooping around. Officially, our investigation into the murder of one Linda Parker only started a few hours ago.'

Captain Blake checked her detective with a suspicious look. 'You're not going to mention the "art" theory?'

'Art theory?' Kennedy asked. The surprise in his tone was directed at Hunter. 'You guys have formed a theory already?'

'I wouldn't go as far as calling it a theory,' Hunter replied. 'But after we discovered the carvings to the victim's back, something was suggested by the lead forensics agent at the scene last night that did seem to link a few loose dots.'

'Can we hear it?' Kennedy asked. He was already craving another cigarette.

Hunter let Garcia guide the FBI crew through that specific

bumpy ride. When Garcia was done, the entire room went quiet one more time. Captain Blake was the first to break the silence.

'Nuts? Yes, but whatever that is –' she referred to the picture board, '– that's not the work of a sane person.'

'Agreed,' Agent Fisher said, as she and Agent Williams re-studied the photographs taken of the walls and the furniture inside Linda Parker's bedroom. 'And I'll admit that in a stand-alone situation it makes a kind of crazy sense. If these really aren't the result of a bleeding victim trying to get away from her attacker – and given the message the killer has carved into the victim's back – I can clearly see how that theory would've surfaced. But ...' she turned and faced Hunter and Garcia, '... when put into context – The Surgeon's first two victims, the state of their crime scenes and the carvings to their backs – this "art" theory kind of loses all of its momentum, don't you think? No blood on the walls in either of his first two crime scenes. No "bloody brush strokes", to quote Detective Garcia. One victim was left in a dirty shed, the other inside his own bedroom, which I might add was squeaky-clean. Nothing artistic about that.'

'And then we have the phrases the killer has carved into the backs of his first two victims,' Agent Williams added. '"Beauty is in the relationship" and "beauty is in the eye of the beholder". They also don't fit this art theory.'

'Sure,' Garcia accepted, folding his arms in front of his chest. 'If you're asking me for an on-the-spot flash assessment, right here, right now, I'd have to agree with you. This art theory was suggested when we had only one victim, one scen-ario, not three, and we all know that theories can easily change during the course of any investigation, but we're not prepared to discard any possibilities just yet.

'The FBI has been running with this for over two months, but we've just been invited to the party. We haven't had a chance to do anything yet – read over the investigation files, listen to any of the interview tapes, talk to any POIs … We haven't even had a chance to properly scrutinize any of the photographs you've shown us, but from the little I've seen and heard so far, if this killer really turns out to be mad enough to believe that he's an artist, if he turns out to be mad enough to see murder as an art form and to treat his crime scenes as a canvas, that wouldn't really surprise me. Would it surprise you?'

Kennedy paused and looked back at his agents. Neither of them said anything back, but the vacant look in their eyes gave away how deep in thought they were.

'One thing we all know when it comes to serial offenders leaving behind messages,' Garcia continued, 'cryptic or not, is that there's always a deeper meaning to them than to simply taunt the police.' He picked up one of the photographs that showed the carvings to Linda Parker's back. 'Sure, we have deciphered these, but we haven't yet figured out the real meaning behind any of these phrases, because I think that this is the killer reaching out. Whatever it is that he thinks he's accomplishing with these murders, he wants us to understand him, however crazy his reasons might be. He wants us to understand why he's doing what he's doing.'

In silence, Kennedy and both of his agents breathed in Garcia's argument.

'Look,' said Hunter, joining the conversation, breaking the tension that was clearly building up inside their office. 'All we're saying here is that we can't be sure of *anything* at this point and for that reason we can't discard any possibilities just yet. With someone like The Surgeon, The Artist, The Doctor, or whatever name anyone wants to call him, we need to keep an open mind, we need to think out of the box, because one thing is for certain – whoever this guy is, he's resourceful, knowledgeable, skilled, and he plays by no rules.'

'And I know I can't speak for you folks at the FBI's NCAVC.' Garcia finished Hunter's thought. 'After all, we're just PD detectives here, but just by looking at all this, I can tell you one thing – this guy's like no other killer we've ever encountered before.'

Thirty-Seven

In one fast movement, Officer Palmer pushed the second basement door open and immediately rotated his body into the room, both hands firmly gripping the handle of his gun, his heart double-timing every beat, his eyes wide open – twenty percent scared, eighty percent searching the room like a hawk.

Bishop took a deep breath, swallowed dry and followed directly behind her partner.

It took both trained police officers just a fraction of a second to find their target – a man standing across the room from them.

The man, who was tall and slim, was no doubt caught by surprise. The fright made him jump back awkwardly.

A whole new slow second went by before Officers Palmer and Bishop realized that the man had something in his hands, but his arms were low, denying both officers a clear view of what it was.

Police training kicked in as it should.

'Drop it,' Palmer called out in a loud, nervous voice, his weapon now aimed at the man's chest.

The man hesitated.

'I said drop it,' Palmer shouted one more time, hoping his voice sounded a little steadier than it had just a second ago.

The man's gaze quickly bounced from one police officer to the other.

'Drop it,' Palmer ordered one last time. 'Or I swear we'll drop you.'

Outgunned and outnumbered, the man finally complied, letting whatever he had in his hands fall to the ground. Both officers heard something heavy hit the floor with a loud clunk, but their view was obstructed by a metal-framed hospital-style bed.

'Hands where I can see them,' Palmer instructed the man, who hesitated again before taking a step back.

'Easy there, partner,' the man said in return, clearly trying to buy himself some time.

Palmer's finger tightened on his trigger. 'Hands where I can see them . . . now.'

The man planted his left foot next to his right one, being sure to keep them shoulder-width apart.

'Let me see your hands.' Palmer's voice was still a little shaky. 'Now.'

Despite all his training, curiosity got the better of Palmer and for a fraction of a second, the officer's eyes wandered down toward the bed.

The man noticed Palmer's eye movement.

It took Palmer another second to understand what he was looking at and as he did, adrenaline exploded into his veins, making his whole body tense up.

Officer Bishop, who was a step behind Palmer and a little to his right, also finally registered the entire scene.

Her heart took a break from beating.

'Jesus Christ!'

Thirty-Eight

At the end of their meeting, it was decided that instead of cramming everyone into a cell-sized sweatbox at the Police Administration Building (Hunter and Garcia's office), it would be better for everyone to coordinate their joint investigation from the Los Angeles FBI Headquarters in Westwood. The original suggestion had been to move the whole operation to Quantico and into the offices of the NCAVC, but Captain Blake put a swift end to that conversation. Unless absolutely necessary, she needed her detectives to stay in Los Angeles.

'Jesus!' Garcia said, sitting back on his chair and rubbing his tired eyes with his thumb and forefinger. 'The sheer number of documents in these files is mind-boggling. How can they accumulate so much in only two months?'

'Well,' Hunter said, without diverting his attention from his computer screen. He had already told Garcia about the private conversation he'd had with Kennedy during his cigarette break. 'Adrian has had an army of agents working the case from the get-go.'

'Yeah, well that certainly shows,' Garcia came back. 'I've been reading solidly for the past three hours. My eyes are about to melt in their sockets here and I've barely made a dent in either of their two murder investigations.'

Hunter was beginning to feel just as frustrated. In accordance with their payback theory, the NCAVC had compiled a list of all the investigations Adrian Kennedy had personally been a part of in the past twenty-five years – four hundred and forty-four cases. From that list they'd conducted a staggering number of 'whereabouts' checks, interviews and surveillance operations. If Hunter and Garcia were to read every record . . . every transcript word for word, it would take the two of them a month just to get through the interviews, never mind the remaining documents.

'This payback theory of theirs,' Garcia said, opening two documents on his screen at the same time. 'They just didn't want to give up on it, did they?'

'Apparently not,' Hunter said.

'Completely understandable at first,' Garcia agreed. 'After all, someone had murdered the niece of an FBI director, so payback would be the first theory on any investigator's mind, but check this out.' He repositioned himself on his chair. 'Just a little over a month later, as we both well know, they were presented with their second victim – Albert Greene. Same MO. Same signature, but a new message, which we all know isn't that unusual for a serial murderer. After the FBI turned up in Wichita and scrutinized the whole scene for a full day, there was superficial talk about this being the work of a serial killer. *Superficial.*' He looked at Hunter sideways. 'What they concentrated most of their efforts on was expanding the payback theory so Albert Greene would fit into it.'

Hunter nodded. 'From payback murder to payback rampage.'

'Exactly,' Garcia confirmed. 'A killer trying to punish not only Director Kennedy, but everyone who worked on a specific investigation. Everyone who the killer considered responsible for either sending someone to prison, or to his/her death.'

'Which to be fair, Carlos,' Hunter came back, 'was still a very plausible theory. The NCAVC helps countless law-enforcement agencies all over the country every year. Not to mention the cases that they take on by themselves. In any one of their investigations, a number of special agents, detectives, officers and people from the District Attorney's office will get involved.' Hunter got up and walked over to the coffee machine. 'Revenge, as we both know, is a very powerful motivator. If in his mind the killer really held Adrian responsible for the outcome of an investigation, it stands to reason that he would also hold everyone else linked to that investigation responsible – or at least the main players.' He poured himself a fresh cup. 'Coffee?' he offered.

'No, I'm OK, thank you,' Garcia replied. 'I'm definitely not arguing that point, Robert. Yes, payback rampage was still a very plausible theory, but they plowed through Albert Greene's family tree to see if he was directly related to anyone in law enforcement, or even to someone in a District Attorney's office, and they got nothing. No matter which way they looked at this, they just couldn't slot Albert Greene into their theory. So one would've thought that they would finally push that theory to the sidelines and start considering other possibilities.'

Hunter had a sip of his coffee before going back to his desk. 'But that's what they did.'

Garcia chuckled. 'Yeah, they came up with a spinoff of the payback theory. The possibility that Mr. Greene's murder could've been a "throw-off" – something to get the NCAVC off the path they were pursuing. In short, they began investigating the chances of this killer going after a complete stranger, in this case, Albert Greene, using the same MO and signature used to kill Kristine Rivers, just so it would *look like* her murder had been the work of a serial killer.' With wide-open eyes, Garcia held Hunter's stare.

'I can see how most people would think that that was a crazy thing to do,' Hunter said. 'But if you take a second, it isn't nearly as crazy as it sounds.'

'And how's that?'

'You know how united the LAPD, or any PD in the country gets as soon as a cop-killer surfaces, right? The entire department would stop at nothing to chase him down.' Hunter shrugged. 'You kill the niece of an FBI director and there's no doubt that you'll get the wrath of one of the most powerful law-enforcement agencies in the world chasing you with everything they've got – every resource, every ally. And Adrian Kennedy won't give up . . . *ever*. But if you make it look like she was the unfortunate victim of a fanatical serial killer, in time the whole thing might just become another investigation in the FBI archives. See the logic?'

Garcia chewed on that thought for several long seconds. 'OK, I admit, it makes a weird sort of sense, but not enough for the FBI to make it their top theory. They spent two months and countless man-hours talking to the wrong people and looking in the wrong places. There's a reason why Director Kennedy told you that they haven't moved an inch since they've begun investigating this.'

'I know,' Hunter replied. 'And yes, they've made mistakes, but we've all been there before, Carlos. Adrian admitted that he was blinded by anger and, unfortunately, that anger stirred the investigation the wrong way. But talking about what should've been done won't help us. The only thing we can do now is forget about those mistakes and move on.'

PING.

The text-message beep came from Garcia's cellphone. He interrupted their conversation and quickly checked his display screen.

'Oh shit!' he said. The look in his eyes was pure fear.

'Everything OK?' Hunter asked.

The message Garcia had just received had come from his wife, Anna, and it contained three words, followed by an angry emoji.

Are you coming? ☹

'I'm dead,' he said. 'I'm so dead they're going to have to bury me twice.' He quickly typed a message back.

On my way. ☺

'What happened?'

'I've got to go.' Even Garcia's tone of voice had changed. 'I'm supposed to be having dinner with the in-laws tonight and I completely lost track of time.'

Hunter checked his watch – 7:12 p.m. He too hadn't noticed the time go by so fast.

'This is going to be like the tenth time I'm late for dinner with Anna's parents.'

'Oh, that can't be good.'

Garcia reached for his jacket. 'Are you staying?' he asked as he got to the door. 'It's past seven, Robert, and it's been a hell of a long day for everyone, not to mention that you got no sleep last night.'

'Yeah, I know. I'm going to stay just a little longer. There are still a few more things I want to go over.'

'You're not superman, you know? You need to disconnect and give your brain some breathing time before that big vein across your forehead pops. Plus, your eyes are tired. I can tell. You look like you've just smoked a big doobie.'

'Really?' Hunter tried to catch his reflection against the window glass.

'There's no point in exhausting yourself on the first day of an investigation. I know we're starting from the beginning again, but the forty-eight-hour rule doesn't really apply to this guy. He's been killing for months.'

'I know, but I'm really not going to stay long.' He tapped his watch with his index finger. 'You, on the other hand, better get going.'

'Yep. I'm out of here.'

'Say hello to Anna for me, will you?'

'I will, if she's still talking to me, that is. By the way, if I disappear without a trace, please check my backyard for a shallow grave. If not, I'll see you tomorrow at the Feds.'

Thirty-Nine

Anyone driving down Wilshire Boulevard would be forgiven for mistaking the Los Angeles FBI Headquarters for some sort of special federal prison, where the window bars couldn't be seen from the outside. Despite its prime real-estate location, one thing was absolutely clear to everyone: the seventeen-story-high concrete box structure hadn't been built with aesthetics in mind, a feature that repeated itself across every FBI building in the country.

Inside a corner office, on the eighth floor of that nondescript and enigmatic building, Special Agents Fisher and Williams had taken no time settling in. The room they were given was about four times the size of Hunter and Garcia's office back at the PAB and equipped to the walls with high-tech monitors, lightning-fast computers and gigantic curved 4K screens.

Both FBI agents had spent the last three hours looking over all the photos belonging to Linda Parker's crime scene, as well as revising a series of files concerning their investigation into the murders of Kristine Rivers and Albert Greene – two victims whose life stories couldn't have been any more different from each other.

'Shit!' Agent Fisher said, as she pushed her chair away from her desk. She stared at her computer screen for another second before hurling the pen she had in her hand at it.

'Are you all right, Erica?' Agent Williams asked, angling his body to look past his own screen at his partner. He was used to Agent Fisher's sudden outbursts.

'I don't have a clue what I'm doing anymore, Larry.' The tips of her fingers came up to her temples. 'I keep on rereading all these files, but I have no idea what I'm looking for.'

But that wasn't true at all – Special Agent Erica Fisher knew very well what she was looking for as she reread file after file and studied photograph after photograph. She was trying to identify anything that could shed some sort of light, no matter how faint, on why the killer had picked those three people as his victims.

At first they had thought that the reason The Surgeon had taken Kristine Rivers' life had been because she was Director Kennedy's niece, but that theory had now been blown completely out of the water. Nevertheless, Kristine Rivers had been chosen, together with Albert Greene and now Linda Parker, and there had to have been a reason for that.

Chance? Being in the wrong place at the wrong time?

Just like Hunter and Garcia had said earlier, they just couldn't afford to discard any possibilities, but Agent Fisher had never worked a serial-murder case, or even heard of one, where the killer had picked his/her victims absolutely at random. Even in a case like this one, where all the victims seemed to be complete strangers to each other, living in different parts of the country, there was always something that would somehow drive the killer to them – a physical or personal characteristic, something in their past, a location, a preference, a desire, an object, a possession . . . It didn't matter if it made sense to anyone or not. It could be something easily identifiable, or something completely obscure, but there was always something.

Even if Detectives Hunter and Garcia had stumbled upon something with the art theory and this killer was indeed mad enough to think that what he was doing was transforming his crime scenes, his victims, into sick works of art, something made him go knock on Kristine Rivers', Albert Greene's, and Linda Parker's door. Agent Fisher was sure of that, but what was it?

The more Agent Fisher thought about it, the more something Detective Garcia had said earlier kept on coming back to her – that they hadn't yet figured out the real meaning behind any of the carved phrases, and that the killer was reaching out, wanting them to understand why he was doing it.

'Here,' Agent Williams said, coming up to Agent Fisher's desk and placing a new steaming cup of coffee on it. 'This should help a little.'

'Thanks, Larry.' Agent Fisher leaned back on her chair as she looked up at her partner. 'Though I'd much rather have a bottle of wine right now.' A soft tilt of the head. 'Vodka would do just as fine, too.'

'That could be easily arranged.' Agent Williams checked his watch.

'Yeah, I wish. You've seen me drunk, right?'

'Uh huh.' Agent Williams smiled at her and their eyes locked.

There was no denying that Special Agent Larry Williams was an extremely attractive man, but that was only the tip of the iceberg. Looks aside, he was intelligent, dedicated, accomplished, a total gentleman, and the best agent she had ever worked with.

He was also completely in love with Agent Fisher.

Despite all his efforts to keep it secret, Agent Fisher saw it in his eyes every time he looked at her. She heard it in his voice. She felt it in his touch.

Truth be told, in different circumstances, Special Agent Erica Fisher would've probably fallen for him as well, but her heart belonged to someone else. Someone very, very different.

After a quick bathroom break, Agent Fisher returned to her files. As her brain played with different thoughts, she began separating all the photographs they had into three distinct groups – victims, carvings, and crime scene. That done, she got up from her seat, took a couple of steps back from her desk and let her eyes slowly walk those columns once . . . twice . . . ten times.

We have deciphered these, but we haven't yet figured out the real meaning behind any of these phrases.

'This is so pointless.'

Her brain felt numb, her eyes felt tired, her body felt drained.

This killer is reaching out.

'There's nothing here. Detective Garcia was wrong.'

He wants us to understand him. He wants us to understand why he's doing what he's doing.

'Maybe I'll try again tomor—'

As Agent Fisher began turning away from her computer screen, something in one of the photos caught her eye and she paused.

One second . . .

Her body revitalized.

Two seconds . . .

The brain numbness was gone.

Three seconds . . .

There it was.

Forty

Despite how tired he felt, Hunter decided that before driving home he would stop by The Thirsty Crow Lounge in Silver Lake. The place, which had once been a novelty truck-stop dive called Stinkers, had undergone a massive transformation and was now an easy-going, throwback bar, worlds away from the seedy watering hole it used to be. Its vast selection of Scotch, bourbon and spirits, together with its diverse cocktail menu, owed nothing to any of the more famous whisky and cocktail lounges in downtown LA. It was also a lot more reasonably priced, which considerably added to its appeal, and considering that Hunter's biggest passion was single malt Scotch whisky, The Thirsty Crow Lounge had become one of his favorite places in recent years.

Back in his apartment, Hunter had a small but impressive collection of Scotch that would probably satisfy the palate of most connoisseurs. He would never consider himself an expert, but unlike so many of his friends, who also claimed to enjoy single malt Scotch whisky, he knew how to appreciate the flavors and robustness of the malts, instead of simply getting drunk on them. Though sometimes getting drunk worked just fine.

Hunter sat at the far end of the shiny white-topped bar, which together with the polished dark-wood paneled walls and the music of Parov Stelar playing out of the old-fashioned juke-box gave the place a cozy speakeasy look and feel. He had just ordered his first shot of Scotch when Professor Tracy Adams walked through the lounge doors. Her bright red hair fell loose past her shoulders, with her fringe styled into a charming 1940s victory roll. She wore a halterneck black-and-white rockabilly swing dress, which exposed both of her tattoo-covered arms. The silk bow around her waist matched her black, low-heel Mary Jane shoes perfectly. As she made her way toward Hunter, several patrons turned on their seats to look at her.

'Have I missed much?' she asked, nodding at the tumbler sitting on the bar in front of Hunter. The question came accompanied by a smile that could make even the most confident of men stutter.

'Not really,' Hunter replied, getting to his feet.

She gave him a peck on the lips. 'I'm surprised, but very pleased you called.'

By choice, Hunter had been a loner for most of his life, and for that reason he had always been very comfortable in his own company. He didn't mind drinking by himself, having dinner by himself, or even going places by himself. It gave him a chance to relax with his own thoughts. But sometimes, being alone with his thoughts wasn't such a good idea. Plus, Garcia was right. Hunter knew he needed to disconnect from the case, even if only for a few hours. He needed to give his brain some breathing time, and he could see no better way of doing that than to be in the company of someone like Tracy. Not only was she intelligent, funny, and terribly attractive, but she certainly could keep up with the drinking as well.

He waited until Tracy had taken her seat before returning to his.

'So what did you go for tonight?' Tracy asked, referring to Hunter's choice of Scotch.

He simply slid his glass her way.

She took it and even before bringing it to her nose she could smell the strong peat smoke.

'Laphroaig?' she asked, but immediately corrected herself. 'No, Ardbeg.'

Hunter smiled. He knew she would get it right.

Just like Hunter, Tracy Adams loved Scotch whisky and her nose and palate were as refined as any expert's, something she had learned from her father, a true Scotsman from the Highlands.

'Is this Uigeadail?' she asked as she brought the glass to her lips. 'No.' She corrected herself again, after the smallest of sips. 'Corryvreckan, right?' Her Scots Gaelic pronunciation was impeccable.

Hunter nodded.

'Wow.' She sat back as she slid the glass back to Hunter. 'And with no water, either. That bad a day?'

Hunter didn't have a favorite malt. He usually chose his dram according to how he was feeling, and though he was a mystery to everyone, Tracy had managed to pick up a few of his telltale signs. One of them was that if he'd had a bad day, Hunter would always choose a smoky malt, and one couldn't get much smokier than Ardbeg Corryvreckan.

'Not one of the best,' he confirmed.

The bartender, who was at least six-foot-three, with a gleaming smile and blond hair tied back into a hipster ponytail, placed a black paper napkin on the bar in front of Tracy.

'So what can I get you tonight?' he asked in a baritone voice that could've belonged to a documentary narrator.

'I guess I'll follow suit,' she replied, nodding at Hunter. 'I'll have the same, please.'

One of the bartender's eyebrows lifted slightly. 'Really? That's quite a heavy, smoky malt. A lot heavier on the alcohol too. Are you sure you wouldn't prefer something a little smoother?'

'It's OK, Alex,' Hunter said. 'She can handle her Scotch better than anyone in here, including you and me.'

The bartender smiled as he looked back at Tracy. 'Is that a fact?'

She shrugged.

'In that case, welcome to The Thirsty Crow. I'm Alex.'

'Tracy. Pleased to meet you.'

They shook hands.

'An Ardbeg Corryvreckan coming up. Any ice with that?'

'No, but if you give me just about a fifth of water in it I'd appreciate it.'

'Oh, I like her,' the bartender said, nodding at Hunter before pouring Tracy her drink.

Tracy and Hunter touched glasses.

'I know you don't talk about your work,' she said, once the bartender had returned to his duties. 'So I won't even ask, but if you feel like talking about anything, you know I'm a great listener, right?'

They both had a sip of their drinks.

'We're joining forces with the FBI for this one,' Hunter said, after a short pause.

His revelation almost made Tracy choke – thirty percent because of the unexpected news and seventy percent because

Hunter had chosen to share something about one of his investigations with her. He had never done that before.

She quickly had another sip of her Scotch. 'Are you talking about the same case you had to rush out of UCLA for?'

Hunter nodded.

'But you barely—' She paused, as she finally realized what she was missing. 'You didn't go asking for help, did you? They invited themselves in.'

Another nod.

Tracy taught psychology and forensic psychology at UCLA. She knew exactly how the FBI worked. She knew that, bar a few exceptions, the FBI would only provide assistance with a homicide investigation if the primary law-enforcement agency involved officially requested their help.

'So that means that whatever this is,' Tracy continued, 'it's not the first in the series and it has crossed city boundaries, probably even state ones.'

Hunter's reply was an eyebrow movement, followed by a sip of his Scotch.

'Well, if you guys haven't asked for help, they surely found out about it fast enough.'

'That was my fault,' Hunter said.

Despite being curious, Tracy decided not to dig any deeper. If Hunter wanted to tell her anything else, he would. 'Have you ever joined forces with the FBI before?'

'Not in this capacity. I've helped them out on a case not that long ago, but I was on leave from the LAPD. It wasn't a joint effort.'

'Will you have to relocate to Quantico?'

'No chance,' Hunter replied. 'We'll be working out of the LA FBI Headquarters in Westwood.'

Tracy didn't try to disguise how pleased she was with that answer. 'Oh, OK. So we're still on for dinner tomorrow night?'

Hunter had forgotten all about their dinner plans, but neither his eyes nor his facial expression gave his memory lapse away. 'Yes, of course.'

Tracy renewed her smile. 'Are the bathrooms at the back?'

Hunter nodded.

'I won't be a minute.' She had one more sip of her Scotch before grabbing her handbag.

The bathrooms were at the end of a short corridor, past a very stylish decorated sitting area. Tracy chuckled as she saw the signs on the doors.

The one on the right said 'Whisky'. The one on the left said 'Vanilla vodka and cranberry'.

No wonder the bartender was so surprised, she said to herself.

At that exact moment, a six-foot-two man who looked to be in his mid-thirties exited the men's bathroom. He wore a dark T-shirt, blue jeans and black boots. As his eyes settled on Tracy, he stopped and smiled.

'Wow,' he said, his stare moving slowly from her face down to her breasts, then all the way to her shoes. 'You're a pretty one, aren't you? And I loooove your ink.'

His words slurred a little, giving away how inebriated he was.

'Thank you,' Tracy replied politely.

The skin on the man's face was tanned and weather-beaten. His hair was short, crew-cut number one, and his broad chest and shoulders indicated a build packed with muscle.

As Tracy tried to move into the ladies' room, the man took a step to his right, blocking her path.

She looked up and into his dark-brown eyes. There was mischief in them.

'Could you please excuse me?'

'Look,' the man said. His voice sounded like it was coming from a water-filled tube. 'I saw you sitting with some douchebag at the bar, but that's probably because you don't know any better. But let me tell you, a pretty girl like you deserves someone who can really show you a good time. Someone like me.' The man's right hand moved in the direction of Tracy's hair, forcing her to quickly take a step back.

'Look,' she replied, not shying away from the man's stare. 'Since it's quite obvious that you've had a little too much to drink tonight, I will disregard your insulting comment about my date at the bar. That's clearly the alcohol talking. My advice to you is – go get a drink of water and ask the bartender to order you a taxi. More drinking will probably only make your night worse, not to mention how you'll feel in the morning.'

She tried to get past the man, but he blocked her path once again.

'I have a much better idea,' he said. 'Why don't I follow you in there.' He threw his thumb over his shoulder. 'And you and I can get properly acquainted. You know what I'm talking about, right?' His hand moved to his crotch and he gave it a long and slow rub.

Tracy chuckled. 'I don't know if I should laugh or puke. You are nauseatingly abominable.'

'Huh?'

'Oh, sorry, honey,' she said, with pity eyes. 'Too many big words for you? I can rephrase if you like.'

'What I'd like is for you to come in there with me. Then

I'll show you what "big" really is. Why would you want to drink with a VW Beetle ...' he pointed toward the bar area, '... when you can party with a limousine?' He used both hands to point at himself.

Tracy made a pain-stricken face. 'Did you learn the art of conversation out of a fortune cookie?'

'I'll tell you what I've learned.' The man reached for Tracy's arm.

Big mistake.

With her left hand, Tracy pushed the man's arm to one side, while her right one moved to his stomach.

The man's T-shirt was stretched thin against his muscly torso, which would have made it even easier for Tracy to find the correct spot, had she not already known exactly where to apply the pressure. As her fingers came into contact with the man's abdomen, his eyes widened and he gasped at the intense pain that shot through his body. Reflexively, he tensed his stomach muscles to try to repulse the attack, but it was all too late. Tracy's fingers were already applying pressure against the linea alba, the thin band of connective tissue that ran vertically down the center of the man's abdominal muscle.

His face contorted out of shape.

Tracy pushed a tiny bit harder.

The pain was so powerful, so debilitating, even the man's voice failed him.

Tracy smiled.

The man's legs trembled under his huge body and Tracy could tell that he was about to go down. Immediately she released some of the pressure to prevent him from collapsing.

His eyelids flickered oddly.

She pushed him back against the wall, using it to help her hold him upright.

'You'll be a little woozy after I let go here, OK?' Tracy said, her voice gentle and caring. 'But you'll be fine in a minute or two.'

The man looked at her with pleading eyes.

'So,' she continued. 'Once again, my advice is that you get a drink of water, then call a taxi and go home. You've done all the drinking you were supposed to do for tonight, all right?'

All the man could do was nod.

'And please,' Tracy added. 'Don't try that approach with anyone else . . . *ever.*'

She finally let go of him and entered the ladies' bathroom. A few seconds later she heard him collapse to the ground.

Back at the bar, Hunter finished his Scotch and swerved around on his bar stool.

Tracy had been gone for a few minutes now. Also, the tall, muscle-mount he had noticed going into the corridor that led to the bathrooms just a little before Tracy still wasn't back either.

Hunter began wondering if he should go check on her when he saw the six-foot-two man stumble out of the back. The man had his right hand pressed against his stomach, as if he'd just been punched. The look on his face was sheer agony. As the man got to Hunter, he paused.

'You should keep her on a leash, buddy,' he said in a weak, half-drunk voice.

'Excuse me?' There was no one else next to Hunter, so the man must've been talking to him.

'She's fucking lethal, that's what she is.'

Shrouded in confusion, Hunter watched as the man

stumbled away, grabbed his jacket from the back of a chair, and exited the lounge.

'What was that all about?' Alex asked Hunter.

'I have no idea, but I'd better go check on Tracy.'

Hunter didn't have to. As he turned on his stool, Tracy finally reappeared and returned to her seat.

'What happened?' Hunter asked.

'What do you mean?'

'Well, this WWF reject just came out of the bathroom, walked past me and said something about keeping you on a leash and how lethal you were.'

Tracy laughed. 'Is that what he said?'

'Who is he? And what did you do?'

'No one, really,' Tracy replied. 'Just someone I met back there. He asked me for my advice, so I gave it to him.'

'Advice?'

'Yes. I told him that he should go home. He'd had enough to drink for tonight. Where is he?' She turned and looked around the lounge but failed to spot the man.

'He left,' Hunter told her.

'Oh, so he did take my advice.'

Hunter found all this too bizarre, but decided not to ask any more questions.

Tracy finished her drink. 'Another one?'

Hunter considered it for a short moment. 'How about if we go get something to eat? Have you eaten already?'

Tracy smiled as she glanced at her watch. 'Given that it's past eleven in the evening . . . yes, I've had dinner already, but I can keep you company.' She paused and looked back at Hunter invitingly. 'Or how about we go back to my place and I'll cook you something?'

Tracy was a fantastic cook. Hunter knew that very well.

'Are you sure?' he asked. 'It's quite late and I wouldn't want to impose.'

'Yes. Positive. And you're not imposing.'

As they smiled at each other, Hunter's cellphone rang in his jacket pocket.

Tracy looked back at him, incredulous that this was about to happen again.

'Detective Hunter, UVC Unit.' Hunter took the call.

It was Special Agent Williams.

As Hunter listened in silence, his expression changed to something considerably more somber.

'Where?' he said into the mouthpiece, checking his watch. 'I'm not home right now, but I can be there in fifteen minutes.' He listened for another few seconds. 'OK, I'll be ready.' He disconnected from the call and his stare moved to Tracy.

She didn't need to ask. She knew that a call coming into Hunter's phone at that time of night could only mean one thing.

'I'm so terribly sorry,' he said, reaching for her hand.

She smiled through her disappointment.

'It's OK,' she said. 'It's your job.' She sipped her drink. 'Same perp again?'

Hunter nodded.

'Wow, he's not losing any time, is he?'

Hunter placed a couple of bills on the bar counter and reached for his jacket. 'Once again,' he said to Tracy. 'I'm so very sorry.'

'As long as you make it up to me, I don't mind,' she replied in a half-joking, half-serious tone.

'You can count on that.' He kissed her on the lips before rushing out of the bar.

Forty-One

A black SUV picked Hunter up from his home address exactly forty-five minutes after he'd left The Thirsty Crow Lounge, enough time for him to have a shower and grab a change of clothes. Sixty-five minutes after that, he met Garcia and both FBI agents at Van Nuys airport, in San Fernando Valley. The look on everyone's faces was a testimony to how little sleep they'd all had.

'Coffee?' Garcia asked as Hunter walked through the doors, offering him one of the cups he had in his hands.

Hunter gladly accepted it. 'You read my mind.'

'Perfect timing,' Agent Williams said, joining the two of them. 'The plane will be ready in under five minutes.'

'Do we have any more information other than what you told me over the phone?' Hunter asked.

All he was told was that The Surgeon had claimed a new victim and that he had about an hour to get ready before a car picked him up to take him to the airport.

'I also know very little,' Agent Williams replied.

'But surely more than we do,' Garcia said. 'Do we at least know where we're flying to?'

'Tucson, Arizona,' came the reply from Agent Fisher, who

had just come off her cellphone. 'Yesterday morning, after we learned about The Surgeon's third victim here in Los Angeles, it became crystal clear that he isn't sticking to a specific city, or even a specific state.'

Took you guys long enough, Garcia thought, but the thought didn't make it to his lips.

'So,' Agent Fisher continued, 'before flying over here, we made sure that every police department and every coroner and sheriff's office in the country received a top-priority bulletin, informing everyone that if a body is found with missing parts, and/or bearing certain marks to its flesh, the FBI is to be notified immediately and no investigation is to be initiated by local detectives. About two hours ago, our headquarters in Quantico received a call from the Tucson Police Department in Arizona. A male body was found early yesterday evening, bearing some strange carvings to its back.' She paused just to heighten the suspense. 'The information we were given was that the markings to the victim's back look like an odd combination of letters and symbols. Sounds familiar?'

'Is that all we have on the victim?' Garcia asked.

Agent Fisher shrugged. 'At this point, yes . . . Oh, one more thing,' she added before making her way toward the boarding gate. 'Tucson Police also have a man in custody.'

'A man in custody?' Hunter asked, surprised.

Agent Fisher nodded. 'I was just told. He was arrested at the crime scene. Police officers found him standing over the body.'

Forty-Two

Homicide Detective James Miller of the Tucson Police Department pushed his silver-framed glasses up the bridge of his nose before tucking his hands deep into his trouser pockets. For the next five minutes he attentively observed the handcuffed man sitting alone at the metal table on the other side of the two-way mirror.

'James, what are you doing?' Detective Edward Hill asked, as he joined his partner inside observation room one. After six years in the force, Hill had finally made detective for the Tucson PD just under a year ago. He was nine years Miller's junior.

'What does it look like I'm doing, Rookie?' Miller replied, without looking back at Hill. Since their captain had paired them together eleven months ago, Miller had never called Detective Hill by any name other than 'Rookie'.

'What you always do before interrogating a suspect,' Hill said, pausing by Miller's side. He too rested his eyes on the enigmatic tall man with a shaved head, sitting at the metal table.

'That's why I like you, Rookie. You're sharp. No wonder you made detective.'

Hill didn't laugh at the joke. 'Didn't you hear what the captain said? The suspect is not to be interrogated by us. This isn't our case, James. All we've got to do is keep him here until the FBI arrives.'

'Yes, I heard the captain,' Miller replied. 'And if you want to play puppet to those jerks in black suits and stupid-looking aviator glasses, be my guest, Rookie, but I didn't work my ass off to make homicide detective just so I could chaperone a murder suspect for the goddamn FBI. This guy was arrested in Catalina Foothills. If you've forgotten, that's our jurisdiction. As far as I know, until we see any official paperwork, this is our case, not the Fed's.' Miller finally turned and faced Hill. 'Have you seen any paperwork yet?'

Hill made a face at Miller. 'No, but we both know it's coming, so why do you want to waste time interrogating him, when we know that there will be nothing else we'll be able to do after this? The case will be taken from us before the sun comes up. From what I've heard, the Feds are already on their way here.'

'So we'd better get in there fast,' Miller said, consulting his watch.

'Are you dying for a kick in the balls?' Hill asked, scratching his designer goatee. 'Captain Suarez will have our asses for this. You know that, right?'

'No he won't. Actually, if we manage to piss off the FBI enough, he will probably take us out for a drink.'

Hill looked back at Miller dubiously.

'The captain hates the Feds, Rookie. It's something that goes back a long way. Someday you can ask him to tell you the story.'

Hill could believe that. He knew too many cops who didn't see eye to eye with the FBI. For the next full minute, he observed the man on the other side of the two-way mirror.

'Is he asleep?' Hill asked with a frown.

'That's only one of this guy's intriguing factors,' Miller replied. 'I've been standing here for almost ten minutes now and, apart from blinking, that guy hasn't moved a muscle.'

'What, really?'

'Not a fucking inch, Rookie. No hand movement . . . No twitchy leg . . . No bouncing of the knee . . . No nervous scratch of the chin . . . No rotation of the neck . . . No tongue across the lips . . . Nothing. Not even the eyes moving from side to side. All he's done since I got here is sit in that exact same position and stare at his hands. It's like he's in a trance or something. I have never seen anyone with that much focus, that much control, let alone a dude facing murder in the first.'

Hill bit his bottom lip and crossed his arms in front of his body.

'Do we have a name yet?' Miller asked.

Hill shook his head. 'No. Nothing. He had no identification on him. No driver's license. No credit cards. No wallet. Nothing.'

'Fingerprints? Face recognition?'

'Gave us zilch. He's not in the system.'

'And he isn't talking.'

'No,' Hill confirmed. 'Hasn't said a word yet. We can't even book him because we don't have a name to book him under.'

'That's why this is a one-chance-in-a-lifetime kind o' thing, Rookie,' Miller said. 'This is the kind of serial killer you only find in Hollywood movies; do you understand what I'm saying?'

'Serial killer?' Hill's mesmerized eyes shot toward Miller. 'That escalated fast. Why do you think he's a serial killer?'

'Rookie, don't be so naive. Why do you think the Feds are on their way over here at this time of night, just hours after Mr. Solid Statue here has been arrested?' Miller paused for a second. 'Let me give you a tip – it's not because he's a wanted shoplifter.'

Hill's attention returned to the man sitting in the interrogation room.

'Let's not lie to ourselves here, Rookie,' Miller added, as he took off his blazer jacket and began rolling up his sleeves. 'People like him are one of the main reasons why we joined the police force ... why we fought so hard to become homicide detectives. I don't know about you, but when I was a kid, I couldn't get enough of movies about serial killers. I watched everything there was to watch because it fascinated me. It still does.'

Hill got a little closer to the glass.

'This is Tucson, Rookie,' Miller continued. 'Sure, we've got crime here. We even have homicides, but we just don't get this kind of stuff.' He pointed at the man. 'This is the kind of stuff books are written about and movies are made from.' He unholstered his weapon and placed it on the table inside the observation room. 'And here he is, sitting inside *our* interrogation room. Call me curious, but I for one would love to get inside his mind, even if for just a few minutes. Plus, I'm a great interrogator, you know that.' He reached for the door.

'Are you really going to go in there?' Hill asked.

'You bet.'

'And you don't think that the first thing he's going to do is lawyer up? Actually, I'm surprised he hasn't done that yet, but then again, he hasn't said a word to anyone since he was arrested, James.'

'I guess we'll see, won't we? By the way, there's no need to hit the record button.'

Forty-Three

The twenty-four-feet-long passenger cabin inside the Dassault Falcon 2000EX jet was divided into three very luxurious areas – Forward, with four seats, Middle, with three seats, and Aft, also with three seats. All ten 360-degree swivel seats were finished in soft beige leather, each with its own media center, individual climate controls, and power outlets. There was a fully stocked bar up front, near the cockpit, together with a locked weapons cabinet. At the back, past the Aft cabin was a spacious bathroom, with impressive shower facilities. Low-heat, fully controllable LED overhead lights allowed the passengers to set the mood either individually, per cabin, or for the entire airplane.

'Wow,' Garcia commented as he and Hunter finally boarded the aircraft. 'The Feds do have it much better than we do.'

'Oh, you can certainly bet on that,' Agent Fisher said, as she squeezed past them to take one of the seats at the front of the plane.

Agent Williams took the one facing her.

'You can stop drooling now, Detective.' Agent Fisher couldn't help the dig. 'It's only a plane.'

Staying in the forward cabin, Hunter and Garcia took the two seats across the aisle from the agents.

'Did you make it in time for dinner with the in-laws?' Hunter asked, after fastening his seatbelt.

'Nah,' Garcia replied. 'I missed dinner completely, but I made it in time for dessert and drinks, which, thanks to my charming personality, made everything OK again.'

Hunter smiled. 'I'm sure.'

Within minutes of everybody boarding the private jet, the Dassault Falcon taxied its way up the runway. Two minutes later the control tower gave the go-ahead for takeoff, which it did very smoothly before climbing up to a cruising altitude of 28,000 feet. Through the speakers, the pilot quickly announced that flying conditions were good, the sky was cloudless and that their flight time would be around one hour and twenty-five minutes.

'How about you?' Garcia asked. 'What time did you leave the office?'

Hunter's head tilted to one side. 'A lot later than I wanted to.'

'Yeah, somehow I sort of knew that that would happen.'

Agent Fisher waited until the pilot had finally turned off the "fasten seatbelt" sign before swerving her seat around to face everyone.

'There's something that I would like to show everybody,' she said, retrieving several photographs from her briefcase and placing them on the large retractable table that sat between her and Agent Williams.

Hunter's and Garcia's attention gravitated toward the images.

Just like she had done back in their temporary office, Agent Fisher separated the photos into three groups – victims, carvings, and crime scene.

'Yesterday in your office,' she began, 'you guys mentioned the possibility of this killer being crazy enough to see murder as an art form, remember?' She nodded at Garcia. 'The possibility that maybe he treats his crime scenes as some sort of canvas, some sort of window for his work.'

Garcia looked almost shocked. He found it hard to believe that Agent Fisher had actually taken notice of something he had said, never mind considered it.

'Well,' she continued, 'once we got settled into our office, we began revising a few files, including all the photographs belonging to The Surgeon's first two crime scenes.' Her gaze moved to the photos on the table, dragging everyone else's with it. 'And I think that we might have something.'

'Something?' Garcia leaned forward, resting his elbows on his knees. 'Like something that might link the first two crime scenes to this art theory?'

'Possibly.'

Even the air inside the private jet seemed to stand still in anticipation.

'There's something you said yesterday,' Agent Fisher said, once again addressing Garcia, 'that kept on repeating itself inside my head over and over.'

'And what was that?' Garcia asked.

'That though we had deciphered the Latin phrases, we hadn't yet figured out the real *meaning* behind them. So, as I reassessed the photos of the first two crime scenes, I realized you were right. Blinded by our initial theory, we perhaps made a grave mistake.' Her voice took on an almost apologetic tone. 'That mistake was that we looked exclusively at the victims and disregarded everything else.'

'Everything else?' Garcia asked. 'As in the scene itself?'

'Exactly. Our sole concern was always the victim.' Agent Fisher lifted her right hand in a 'wait' gesture. 'Let me ask you all a question here – are any of you big into art? I mean, do you read about it, go to galleries, museums, expositions, that sort of thing?'

'No, not really,' Garcia replied.

'Rarely,' Hunter admitted it.

'Why?' Garcia again.

From her briefcase, Agent Fisher grabbed three printouts she had obtained from the internet. None of them were related to any of the crime scenes or the victims.

'Well, I have never really been an art buff,' she said. 'But yesterday, in your office, you mentioned that art is subjective. It depends on your point of view.'

She placed the first photo on the table. It displayed a perfectly made bed, with crisp white sheets, at the center of a very dirty and messy room.

'What may look like art through someone's eyes . . .'

She displayed the second printout. It was almost the reverse of the first – a messy and dirty bed at the center of a totally white, sterile room.

'. . . can look like nothing but junk through someone else's.'

The last of the three printouts showed exactly that – a pile of junk that had been dumped at the center of an art gallery.

As Agent Fisher placed the printouts on the table, the thoughtful look on Hunter's and Garcia's faces deepened.

'These are only three quick examples, but art galleries just about everywhere seem to be littered with similar pieces. Art used to be something people would cherish, but in our modern world, just about anything can be considered art. This pile of junk,' she once again indicated the last of the three printouts she had shown them, 'sold for half a million dollars.'

'No way.' Garcia looked surprised and upset at the same time. 'I'm definitely in the wrong line of work, because that I can do.'

Agent Fisher left the printouts on the table while she selected a photo from the 'victim' pile.

'So, with that in mind, like I said, perhaps we made a grave mistake by looking at the victims in isolation. Take our first victim, for example.' She presented the photo she had selected. It was a full-body shot of Kristine Rivers lying on the shed's dirty floor. The rest of the shed could not be seen. 'If you isolate the victim, this is pretty much what you see.'

Agent Fisher returned the photo to the table and selected a new one, this time from the 'crime scene' pile. It was a wide-angle shot where Kristine Rivers' body could be seen against a backdrop of vibrant graffitied walls and a floor packed full of colorful debris. The agent took several steps back, placing herself in the Middle cabin before showing everyone the photo.

'But if you take in the entire crime scene as a whole, or better yet, a single image . . .'

The distance added a whole new perspective to the photograph.

'. . . then you just might be able to see the big picture.'

Forty-Four

Detective James Miller stepped into interrogation room one inside the Alvernon Way Police Station in downtown Tucson and closed the door behind him. Instead of approaching the small metal table at the center of the claustrophobic, underground chamber, he stood by the door in complete silence, hands tucked into his trouser pockets, eyes firmly locked on the man sitting at the table.

Despite the door closing with a loud enough bang, the man didn't look up. He kept his stare on his cuffed hands, which were chained to the tabletop.

The whole 'standing by the door in silence' act was all part of Miller's interrogation technique, a technique he had developed over twelve years as a homicide detective in Arizona, but in spite of all his experience, Miller did feel a tad nervous.

Yes, in those twelve years he had interrogated hundreds of suspects, many of them violent murderers, but as far as he knew he had never been face to face with a serial killer, let alone one wanted by the FBI. He'd read many books and watched a ton of documentaries on them and, truth be told, Miller had always hoped that he would one day be the lead detective in a serial-murder investigation – the kind of investigation that would generate nationwide interest and press coverage. In his head, he had pictured time and time again being the person in charge of the interrogation – the one whose task was to extract the truth from the killer. But as soon as that door closed behind him, Miller felt an uneasiness he hadn't felt in many years. There was definitely something very different about the man sitting at that table, something that Miller couldn't yet tell, but whatever it was it seemed to chill the air inside the room.

Miller's eyes moved to the two-way mirror on the east wall. He knew his partner would be on the other side of it, watching.

Miller kept his composure.

The man kept his head down.

Miller waited.

Inside that same room, Miller had played several variations of that game before – the silent, 'I will not move, I will not lock eyes with you' game. From experience, the detective knew that that was nothing more than a mental tug-of-war. A strength-of-mind game. Would the man acknowledge the detective first, either verbally, by movement, or by eye contact, or would Miller give in to the man's resolve and speak first?

To an outsider, something that trivial could easily sound childish, but Miller knew better than to disregard the import-ance of such psychological games inside an interrogation room, and that was why he had spent time studying the man from the other side of the two-way mirror. Just like a profes-sional poker player tries to read his opponents and adapts his game tactics accordingly, Miller had tried to do the same, but the man gave nothing away, except the fact that his resolve seemed to be flawless.

Who, Miller thought, *after being arrested at the scene of a*

*homicide, spends all that time sitting alone inside an interro-
gation room without moving a muscle or saying a word?* Miller
had never encountered anybody with that much self-control
before. The man's discipline, he had to agree, was watertight.

Miller kept his eyes on the man.

The man kept his eyes on his hands.

To his surprise, the first part of Miller's tactic – the door
closing behind him with a loud enough bang – had failed
gloriously. The bang was supposed to break the man's concentration, forcing him to look up and acknowledge the detective's
presence. It was a shock tactic that, until then, had never
failed Miller.

Maybe I should've slammed the door harder, Miller thought.

He pulled his hands from his pockets and took four steps
forward, placing himself directly in front of the metal table.

The man didn't look up.

Miller took a seat.

The man didn't look up.

Miller sat back, crossed one leg over the other and casually
rested his hands on his lap. That movement was also planned.
It placed Miller in a relaxed, carefree position, while the man
sat at the edge of his chair with his shoulders slightly hunched.
Clearly a much tenser position.

Miller waited.

Ten seconds.

The man didn't look up.

Fifteen seconds.

The man didn't look up.

Twenty seconds.

The man's eyes, and only his eyes, crawled across the table
and finally paused on the detective sitting before him.

Gotcha.

Miller felt like jumping up and punching the air, but he kept his cool. All he did was lock eyes with the man. Only then did he notice that the man's eyes were deep set and as dark as coal.

'Good evening,' Miller finally said in a calm and collected tone. The greeting was complemented by a delicate head bow.

The man said nothing.

'My name is Detective James Miller of the Tucson Police Department, Homicide Division.'

The man said nothing.

'We could start with you giving us your name. It would make things a lot easier, you know.'

The man said nothing.

'Well, I know that you can speak because according to the arrest report, when the two officers found you standing over the body of Timothy Davis and told you that they needed to see your hands, you replied, and I quote: "Wait a second, I can explain." So we know you're not a mute.'

That had been another trick from Miller. He knew very well that according to the arresting officers' report, the man had replied, 'Easy there, partner' – but Miller had deliberately told him something different to try to trigger a reaction, maybe even a response. 'That's not what I said' would do fine. It would be the beginning of a conversation, something Miller could work with. But once again, the man said nothing in return.

Miller maintained his relaxed position.

'You can play the silent game all you want, buddy, but we both know that in the end you will sing like a bird. You're not the first to play that game and you won't be the last, and the common denominator between all of you is that in the end you all talk. You might not talk to me, but you will talk. I promise you that. I'm just the first in line here and I can guarantee you that I am the easiest one to talk to, but you've got some heavy hitters coming for you. You know what I'm talking about, don't you?'

The man finally moved his head, lifting his chin just enough so he could properly look Miller in the eye. They held each other's stare for several long seconds and Miller saw no indication that the man was about to forfeit his silence. He tried one more time.

'How many have you killed so far?'

No reply.

'Three? Four? Five?'

No reply.

'How many?'

Silence.

This clearly wasn't working, not for Miller. He was about to change tactics once again when the interrogation-room door behind him swung open.

'What the hell are you doing?'

While Detective Miller turned on his chair, the cuffed man barely moved. All he did was tilt his head slightly to one side so he could see past the detective.

'Have you lost your goddamn mind?'

The booming, authoritative voice belonged to Captain Suarez, a short and full-figured man whose temper seemed to always be at the end of a very short fuse. As he spoke, his thick Mexican-style mustache bounced up and down over his lips in a somewhat comic fashion.

'Who authorized you to transfer the prisoner from his cell to the interrogation room? Did I fucking stutter when I told you that the suspect was not to be interrogated? This is not our case, Detective Miller. It belongs to the fucking Feds. I thought I had made myself very clear.'

Miller uncrossed his legs and looked at the man. 'Did you hear that?' His voice was a gentle murmur. 'The FBI is coming for you.'

'Detective Miller.' Captain Suarez' voice got even louder.

'I was just being friendly, Captain. You know, having a little chat with our guest here.'

'I'll tell you what I know,' the captain replied. 'I know that you'd better get your ass off that goddamn chair and out of this room right now, unless you have a dying urge to shovel horse shit with your bare hands for the next month. Gloves not allowed. And I *will* make that happen, Detective.'

'Yeah, yeah,' Miller said, calmly getting to his feet and looking back at the man. 'It was a boring conversation anyway.' But as the detective got to the door, the man sitting at the metal table surprised him, because he spoke for the first time.

He uttered four simple words.

Forty-Five

For five silent and unblinking seconds, Hunter and Garcia stared at the photo Agent Fisher had in her hand. From a distance, despite her facial mutilations, the colorful picture where Kristine Rivers' body could be seen against a backdrop of graffitied walls and a floor full of debris looked more like an art-gallery painting than a crime-scene photograph. In fact, the missing eyes and the scalped head added a macabre layer to the image.

'Holy shit!' Garcia felt the hairs on the back of his neck stand on end.

Hunter stayed quiet, but he did feel a rush of adrenaline run through him.

'Now you might be thinking that there's no way we'll get a similar effect with the second crime scene – Albert Greene's bedroom,' Agent Williams said, taking over from Agent Fisher. 'If you remember, there was nothing on the walls, nothing on the floor. No blood absolutely anywhere.'

Agent Fisher returned to the three groups of photographs she had arranged over the retractable table and selected two new images from the 'crime-scene' pile – both wide-angle shots taken from two separate perspectives, showing Albert

Greene's body on the bed inside his bedroom. Once again she put some distance between the photos and the group, but the effect was nothing like the one they got with the previous image she'd showed them. Even from a distance, neither picture looked anything like a painting. They looked exactly like what they actually were – crime-scene photographs.

'Definitely not the same effect, right?' Agent Williams pushed.

'Definitely not,' Garcia agreed.

'But what if the killer wasn't looking for the same effect?' Hunter suggested.

'Our thoughts exactly,' Agent Fisher said, her voice lifting with excitement.

'I don't follow,' Garcia said. 'Wouldn't that contradict the idea that the killer wants his crime scenes to look like paintings, like works of art?'

'Not necessarily,' Agent Fisher replied, the smirk on her lips revealing how much she was about to enjoy schooling the detective. 'If you think about it, it's impossible to create the same piece twice, but what you really have to remember here is that art is subjective.' She winked at Garcia, knowing full well that he had been the one who had brought that knowledge to the table in the first place. 'Now keep that in mind and tell me what you think of this.'

Agent Fisher once again took a few steps back, stopping halfway through the Middle cabin. This time she showed everyone two pictures side by side. On the left, the same photo she had showed them a minute earlier – Kristine Rivers' crime scene – and on the right, one of the two wide-angle shots from Albert Greene's bedroom.

Garcia's stare moved from one picture to the other a couple of times.

'You've got to be joking,' he said as he finally saw it. 'They're practically opposites of each other.'

'Indeed they are,' Agent Fisher confirmed. 'There's hope for you yet, Detective.'

It was Garcia's turn to scratch his nose using only his right middle finger.

Agent Fisher ignored the gesture. 'So what if for his first piece, the killer selected a place where he didn't need to paint the walls, or the floor, or anything else because the location, a disused shed by the river, already provided all the crazy "modern art" he needed – food wrappers, dirty rags, discarded drug paraphernalia, graffitied walls and so on. All he needed to do to make it his own was place the main piece – the victim's body with a disfigured face – at the center of it.'

She once again indicated the printout with the perfectly made bed at the center of a messy room.

'Then,' she continued, 'for his second "piece", the killer moved from a dirty shed to a squeaky-clean room and from a young female victim to an old male one; can you see?' She did not give Garcia any time to reply. 'If you disregard the fact that these are crime scenes, the two "pieces", just like you've said, are practically opposites of each other. Maybe *that* was the effect that the killer was going for.'

Garcia had to chew on all that for a second.

This time it was Agent Williams who selected a picture from the crime-scene pile. Another wide-angle shot, but this one from the Los Angeles crime scene, where Linda Parker's skinned body could be seen on blood-soaked sheets, against a background of blood-smeared walls.

'His third "piece" needs no introduction,' the agent said.

'Here he ups the shock factor, skinning the body and smearing the walls with blood.'

He handed the photo to Agent Fisher, who once again took a few steps back. Just like with the photo of the first crime scene she had shown everyone, from a distance, the picture she had in her hand looked almost like a gallery painting, where crimson red clashed headfirst with brilliant white walls and bright bed sheets.

'But the best part,' Agent Fisher said, reclaiming Hunter and Garcia's attention, 'is still to come.'

Forty-Six

Pima County's Chief Medical Examiner, Dr. Keith Morgan, had received the surprise call from FBI Special Agent Mike Brandon just as he had finished eating dinner. Once he disconnected, he placed a couple of calls of his own to find out exactly when the body of Timothy Davis would be arriving to the coroner's office downtown. With that taken care of, he prepared himself a strong cup of coffee, took another shower and got dressed.

Dr. Morgan didn't mind starting early or finishing late. As a matter of fact, he did both almost every day. Since his wife of twenty-five years had passed away four years ago, his job was all he had to keep him from constant loneliness. Dr. Morgan would gladly grab any opportunity he was offered to keep his mind busy, to keep him from losing another night to solitude.

At that time in the evening and with very little traffic to speak of, it took the doctor just ten minutes to cover the almost five miles between his home in the neighborhood of Southern Heights and the Pima County's Office of Chief Medical Examiner on East District Street.

'Have you forgotten something, Doc?' the tall, Hawaiian-looking attendant sitting behind the reception counter asked, looking up from the comic book he was reading. He didn't look very surprised to see Dr. Morgan back so soon.

'Not quite, Nathan,' the doctor replied, approaching the counter. 'How's the comic?'

'It's not a comic, Doc,' Nathan replied, his tone of voice almost defensive. 'It's a graphic novel, but this is a really good one. You would probably enjoy it.'

'Yeah, maybe I should give it a go sometime.'

'All you have to do is ask, Doc. I've got a room full of these.'

Dr. Morgan smiled passively. 'We should have just received a body in the last hour or so – African American male, thirty years of age, identified as Timothy Davis?'

Nathan put down his graphic novel and turned his attention to the computer on the counter in front of him.

'We have indeed,' he replied after performing a quick search. 'Apparent homicide. The body came in about fifty minutes ago.'

Dr. Morgan nodded. 'Yes, that'll be the one. Can you please get somebody to take it to theater one for me?'

The attendant checked the clock on the wall behind him. 'You're going to autopsy him now?'

Usually, when Dr. Morgan stayed late or came in early, he dealt mainly with paperwork.

'That's the idea.'

'But ... the body hasn't been prepped yet,' the attendant announced, looking slightly surprised.

Before any post-mortem examination, every body needed to be properly prepared. That meant undressed, if the case called for it, then sprayed with fungicide and thoroughly washed with disinfectant soap before being moved into an autopsy theater. That job usually fell to morgue orderlies, but since

Timothy Davis's body had arrived after closing time, it had simply been moved into a cold chamber.

'Do we have anyone around who would be able to prep the body while I get ready?' the doctor asked.

'Sure. Minika and Ralph are on night duty tonight. I'll get one of them to prep it for you, Doc. Theater one, you said?'

'That's right.'

'Consider it done.' Nathan gave Dr. Morgan a firm head nod. 'Would you like me to find you an assistant for the autopsy? I could give Patrick a call.'

Patrick Wilson was the intern who usually assisted Dr. Morgan with his autopsies.

'No. No need to bother anyone, really. I'll be fine on my own.'

Forty-Seven

As the private jet finally crossed the invisible line that separated South California from West Arizona, the stars that so brightly encrusted the night sky seemed to acquire a different kind of shine, hazier perhaps, less full of life, as if their brightness lost a fraction of its strength the further east they flew.

Hunter and Garcia both waited for Agent Fisher to continue, but she offered little else.

'The best part is still to come?' Garcia pushed. 'What do you mean?'

'The carvings the killer makes to his victims' backs,' Agent Fisher finally clarified. To emphasize her point, she called their attention back to the photo she had just showed them moments earlier, the one where Linda Parker's skinned body could be seen against a background of blood-smeared walls.

'Regardless of how much experience anyone has,' she began, 'this is without a doubt one of the most vicious-looking crime scenes any investigator could've walked into. Everything about it screams "brutality and sadism".'

Garcia chuckled. 'You don't have to tell us, we were there.'

'But despite what this looks like,' she advanced, 'pathological evidence tells a very different story – no pain ... no suffering . . . no torture. Death came fast and through suffocation, which doesn't make a lot of sense, not here . . . and not with any of this killer's previous victims either.'

'Until you look at it from a different perspective,' Hunter added.

'Absolutely.' Agent Fisher smiled at Hunter as if they shared some sort of telepathic bond. 'It explains why, despite how brutal this killer's crime scenes may look, he's actually merciful toward his victims. He has no reason to hurt them or make them suffer because he's not after them as people. He's after them as objects.'

Garcia made a face at Hunter. Despite him not uttering a single word, Hunter could read his expression like a book – *Is she late to the party or what? We've been through all this yesterday. It's like she's repeating everything I said.*

'One thing is for sure,' Agent Fisher carried on. 'This killer isn't dumb. Far from it. Delusional, maybe, but certainly not dumb. He knew that no matter who you were, no matter how much experience you had or even which law-enforcement agency you worked for . . . no one in their sane mind would've looked at any of these crime scenes in any way other than a sadistic shitshow.'

'Unless he told us to,' Garcia said, repeating what he had told Captain Blake the day before.

'Exactly.' Agent Fisher was clearly getting excited now. 'There really is hope for you yet, Detective.'

She indicated one of the 'carvings' photographs. It showed Linda Parker's back – *Pulchritudo Circumdat Eius* – 'Beauty is all around her'.

'With this,' she said, 'the killer covers the walls around her with blood.' Agent Fisher rotated her wrists so the palms of her hands faced the ceiling. 'If we believe that the killer used the Latin phrase he carved into his third victim to guide us to *his* view of the crime scene, it's only logical that he would've at least tried to do something similar with his first two as well, isn't it?'

She indicated a second photo in the 'carvings' group. It showed Kristine Rivers' back – *Pulchritudo in coniunctio.*

Garcia blinked first.

'Hold on a second,' he said. 'What does that mean again?'

'"Beauty is in the relationship",' Agent Williams replied.

'Or better yet,' Hunter broke in, '"Beauty is in the combination."'

Garcia looked at him.

'Remember that most Latin words will translate to more than a single word in English? "*Coniunctio*" can mean relationship, connection, combination, conjunction . . . it depends on the context.'

'And that was the bit we missed,' Agent Williams admitted, his index finger pointing at Hunter. 'The context. That was our big mistake. We believed that the killer meant to say "beauty is in the relationship" because it fitted with our original theory – Kristine Rivers' and Director Kennedy's family relationship. We believed that the carvings were just the killer's cryptic way of letting us know that her murder was payback for something that the killer considered Director Kennedy responsible for.'

'But you were wrong,' Garcia said.

'Yes, we were,' Agent Fisher said. 'We now know that her murder had nothing to do with revenge. The killer probably doesn't have a clue who Director Kennedy is. If we reanalyze the context of the crime, and by context I mean the crime scene as a whole, it becomes clear that what the killer meant was "beauty is in the combination".'

'As in the combination of the body and the rest of the shed,' Hunter said, immediately seeing the finishing line Agent Fisher was paving the way for.

She smiled and picked up the crime-scene photo that showed only Kristine Rivers' mutilated body on the floor. 'No other combination would work. Look at this – the body by itself . . . nothing but a grotesque, sadistic image, right?' She picked up the same wide-angle photo that she had showed them moments before. 'But in combination with the graffitied walls, the dirty floor and everything else . . . you tell me.'

For an instant, Garcia held his breath.

'The killer's message was cryptic, all right,' Agent Fisher continued. 'But once deciphered and viewed in the correct context, the message was nothing more than instructions on how he wanted us to look at his crime scene . . . his "art".' Agent Fisher once again pointed at Hunter. 'As we all know, certain serial murderers firmly believe that what they're really doing is "making the world a better place" or "giving the world a gift" or any old crazy nonsense. And those types of murderers, despite believing that they are more intelligent than everyone else, despite doubting that others could see things the way they see them, despite all their delusions, deep inside they don't want to be misunderstood. They want us . . .' The agent reconsidered her last statement. 'No, they want *the world* to know how great they are.'

Not wanting to lose her momentum, Agent Fisher selected one of the two wide-angle shots from the second crime scene – Albert Greene's bedroom.

'Mr. Greene's body was left on his own bed,' she said. 'Inside his own, *spotless* bedroom. There was no mess, no blood.'

The next photo Agent Fisher presented everyone showed Albert Greene's back – *Pulchritudo in oculis aspicientis.* Next to it, she placed the printout she had showed them earlier – a messy, unmade bed at the center of a sterile, empty room.

'"Beauty is in the eye of the beholder",' she said. 'His second message was as much a set of instructions as it was a challenge.'

'Challenge to do what?' Garcia asked.

'To see the beauty in his work.' The reply came from Hunter. His tone of voice was steady and pensive.

'Precisely,' Agent Williams agreed. 'We think that this time he *was* challenging us to see the beauty in his work. Why? Because he's accepting the fact that we might never see beauty in what he does, in what he considers to be art. He's accepting that what looks like art through someone's eyes – his eyes – might look like nothing but heartless murder through someone else's. "Beauty is in the eye of the beholder." We are the beholders.'

Agent Fisher addressed Garcia. 'You told us you believed that what the killer was doing through his carvings, his messages, was reaching out, remember?'

Garcia nodded.

'And I think you're right. The killer is reaching out. He's trying to show us his vision. Now please bear in mind that all we have are crime-scene photos, which were snapped by a forensics photographer, whose sole concern was to document the scene, nothing else. An art photographer, on the other hand, would look for the perfect angle to bring the composition – the "piece" – to life. Now I have no doubt that that's exactly what The Surgeon does. He photographs his scenes for his own pleasure. He maybe even films them. What this guy is doing is creating his own gallery of the dead.'

Forty-Eight

The Dassault Falcon jet touched down on runway three at Tucson International airport exactly one hour and twenty-one minutes after leaving Los Angeles.

'I've already instructed one of our teams back in Quantico to prepare an art-history search,' Agent Fisher told Hunter and Garcia, as the private jet taxied up the runway. 'If this killer really sees murder as an art form, if he really is using the crime scenes as his canvases, then there's also a chance that his inspiration comes from someone else's work. I instructed the team to search for artists who portrayed violence ... decapitation themes, skinning of the body, gouging of the eyes, scalping, torture methods ... anything on those lines.'

'I hope your team won't mind the heavy workload,' Hunter commented. 'Violence and torture have featured in most art periods in history. From ancient and medieval art to Renaissance, to neoclassical ... all the way until now.'

'Not to mention religious art,' Garcia added. 'Which depicts plenty of violence and torture.'

'Our team is the best at what they do,' Agent Fisher reassured everyone. 'If this killer has based his crimes on any existing work of art, they will find it.'

As the plane engines came to a full stop, a black GMC Yukon pulled up by the aircraft. The driver, a tall African American man who looked more like an NFL superstar than an FBI agent, greeted everyone by the air-stairs.

'Special Agent Williams?' he asked, as the four passengers alighted.

'Yes, that's me.' Williams stepped forward.

'I'm Mike Brandon, Special Agent in Charge of the Phoenix FBI field office. We spoke on the phone.' They shook hands. 'Welcome to Arizona and to Tucson.'

The official FBI Headquarters was located at number 935 Pennsylvania Avenue in Washington DC, just a few blocks away from the White House and directly across the road from the US Attorney General. The FBI Academy and research center, considered by many its true headquarters, was near the town of Quantico in Stafford County, Virginia. Aside from those, the FBI had fifty-six field offices scattered around the fifty American states. Many of those offices also controlled a number of satellite cells in a few selected cities known as 'resident agencies'. There was no FBI resident agency in Tucson and the closest field office was in Phoenix, 107 miles away.

'I'm hoping you have some more information for us,' Agent Williams said, as they all made their way toward the car.

'I have some,' Agent Brandon replied. 'Information is still trickling in. The body was only found a few hours ago and it's a big house. Forensics is still at the scene and they will probably be there until tomorrow, maybe longer. Too soon to tell right now. They have recovered a desktop computer and a laptop. Both password protected. Both already on their way to our IT experts in Quantico.'

'Cellphone?' Garcia asked.

'No, nothing yet.'

As everyone took their seats inside the vehicle, Brandon handed each of them an FBI file.

'The victim's name was Timothy Davis,' Agent Brandon began. 'A thirty-year-old mechanical engineer for Raytheon.'

Hunter's eyes narrowed at the name. 'Raytheon? The weapons company?'

'Technically they are a defense and national security company, sir,' Agent Brandon replied. 'But yes, they do produce weapons, among other things.'

'The victim was a mechanical engineer working for a defense and national security company?' Garcia asked.

'That's correct.'

'Well, good luck trying to breach his computer and laptop password then.'

The files Agent Brandon had handed everyone opened with a portrait photograph of the victim.

The image made them all pause at a brand-new fact.

Until then, none of them had any idea that The Surgeon's new victim had been an African American citizen.

Having interracial victims was a rare trend among serial killers. The ones who would go from one type of victim to the other tended to have their motives firmly grounded in sexual gratification. Their victims, regardless of race, more often than not, were either female sex workers – whom the killers could collect anonymously from the streets – or part of the LGBTQ community, whom they would usually pick up from clubs or bars. But even serial killers who selected interracial victims would usually stick to the same gender, targeting either only female subjects, or only male ones. The double crossover – from female to male and from one race to another – was extremely rare. Another fact that made The Surgeon unique.

'Around 5:40 yesterday afternoon,' Agent Brandon continued, 'Lady luck came knocking.'

'Lady luck?' Agent Fisher questioned.

'Tucson PD received a phone call from one of Mr. Davis's neighbors,' the agent clarified. 'A Mr. Christopher Pendleton, who from his window had seen a stranger breaking into Mr. Davis's property. Mr. Pendleton was supposed to be on vacation until the day after tomorrow, but had to return home this morning due to a work emergency.'

Quizzical stares were exchanged by everyone inside the SUV.

'You said 5:40?' Agent Williams asked.

Agent Brandon consulted his notes.

'Yes, 5:42 to be exact.'

'OK.'

'With the call,' Agent Brandon continued, 'Dispatch sent a black-and-white unit to Mr. Davis's address. After entering the property through its front door, which had been left unlocked, the two Tucson police officers at the scene heard a noise coming from the basement. They went down to investigate it and walked in on a man standing over Mr. Davis's lifeless body. The man was arrested on the spot.'

'Does this man have a name?' Agent Fisher asked.

'I'm sure he does,' Agent Brandon replied. 'But he hasn't said a word since he's been arrested, and since Tucson PD had specific orders not to question him, we don't have anything. They're waiting for you.'

'He hasn't said anything?'

'Not a word, apparently. He hasn't even lawyered up, yet.'

'And he didn't have any ID on him?' Agent Fisher insisted. 'Driver's license, a credit card, social security . . . anything?'

'Nope. No wallet, either. Just some cash on a money clip.'

'Fingerprints?'

A headshake. 'He's not in the system. We really have nothing on this guy.'

'And where's he now?'

'Tucson PD is keeping him at the Alvernon Way Police Station.'

'So let's go talk to this mysterious individual,' Agent Fisher said.

Agent Brandon turned on the engine and geared the SUV into drive. 'By the way, crime-scene photos are in the separate brown envelope at the back of the folder.'

As Hunter, Garcia, and both FBI agents retrieved the contents of the envelope, surprise covered their faces.

The first of the crime-scene photos showed Timothy Davis's body lying flat on a hospital-style bed. Just like all three previous victims, he had been stripped naked and left lying on his back, with his arms naturally by his torso. His legs were fully extended, with his ankles side by side almost touching each other. The hospital bed seemed a little odd, but what had really surprised everyone was that the body seemed untouched. Timothy Davis hadn't been skinned or scalped. His eyes hadn't been ripped from his skull. His hands and feet hadn't been severed either. At first look, there were no visible wounds, cuts, or even scratches to the body, until they flipped to the second of the crime-scene photographs – a close-up image of the inside of Timothy Davis's left leg. There, a small puncture and bruise could be seen around the groin region. The third photo was a facial close-up. Timothy Davis's eyes were shut, his mouth closed, but the look on his face was a peaceful one, as if death was something he'd been expecting for a while and was glad that it had finally arrived.

'The killer didn't take anything?' Agent Fisher asked. 'No body parts?'

Agent Brandon looked back at her inquisitively.

'Never mind,' she said with a shake of the head.

'If you're wondering about the hospital stretcher on the photo,' Agent Brandon said, as he drove toward the runway exit, 'it belonged to the victim.'

All eyes moved to the agent.

'His wife passed away three and a half weeks ago,' Agent Brandon explained. 'She'd been battling pancreatic cancer for some time. As I understand it, once it was confirmed that there was nothing anyone could do anymore, she chose to end her days at home with her husband, not in a hospital. Mr. Davis had a fully functioning setup in the house, hence the hospital bed. He quit his job so he could stay by her side.'

'Did they have any children?' Hunter asked.

'No, they didn't.'

Everyone's attention returned to the photographs in their files. The fourth and last photo was another full-body shot of Timothy Davis on the bed.

'What's happening with the post-mortem examination?' Agent Williams asked.

'Dr. Morgan,' Agent Brandon replied, 'the Chief Medical Examiner for Pima County, is probably working on it as we speak. I talked to him on the phone myself. He'll give me a call as soon as he's done.'

Forty-Nine

The seven-mile drive between Tucson International airport and the Police Department on South Alvernon Way was made in almost absolute silence. Everyone, except Agent Brandon, kept their attention solely on the files they were given.

'Here we are,' Agent Brandon said as he swung a right into the small visitors' parking lot to the right of the police station.

The building, which was set back from the road, was an unattractive two-story rectangular structure, with a well-kept front lawn. A short concrete walkway led them to a set of dark-glass automatic sliding doors and into a spacious entry hall. The young and slender officer sitting behind the security windows at the reception counter immediately stood up as the five visitors entered the building.

'May I help you?' he asked after sliding open part of the window.

'Yes,' Agent Brandon said, already producing his FBI credentials. 'Captain Suarez is expecting us.'

The officer blinked at the agent's ID card before furtively consulting his watch.

'At this hour?' He frowned. 'Are you sure you've got the time right?'

At that exact moment, the heavy door by the reception counter buzzed loudly before swinging open. At the other side of it, a short, overweight man stood at the entrance to a long corridor. He wore a dark suit that fit him like a sack of potatoes, over a light-blue shirt. No tie.

'It's OK,' he said, peeking around the corner at the young officer. 'I'll take it from here.'

'Yes, sir. Sorry, sir, I didn't know you were in.'

Captain Suarez faced the group. 'Special Agent Brandon?'

Agent Brandon stepped forward and they shook hands.

'If you'd all like to follow me, please,' the captain said after all the proper introductions. 'As I've told you over the phone,' he began, first leading everyone toward the end of the corridor before guiding them down a concrete set of steps, 'the subject isn't talking. He hasn't even given us his name.'

'He hasn't spoken a word since his arrest?' Hunter asked.

'Well, not exactly.'

The steps led them to another long hallway, this one a little darker than the one they'd just come from.

'One of my detectives tried to speak to him,' the captain explained. 'But all he managed to get were four stupid words – "This shall be fun".'

'One of your detectives tried to speak to him?' Agent Fisher stepped forward, her tone firm and annoyed. 'I thought your instructions were clear, Captain – the suspect was *not* to be interrogated by anyone. I hope you will agree that those weren't really a complicated set of instructions, were they? Nevertheless, you don't seem to have understood them. We'll need to hear the recording of this conversation between *your* detective and *our* suspect and we'll need to do that right away.'

Captain Suarez paused halfway down the corridor and looked back at the agent resolutely. He really didn't like her tone of voice.

'Look, Special Agent Bitchness, we're cooperating here. We have arrested a man at the scene of a homicide. A homicide that – though it *partially* matched a description received yesterday through an APB from the FBI – was committed *inside* our jurisdiction. Upon the arrest, we complied with the instructions in that FBI bulletin and, without asking "why", immediately contacted the Federal Bureau of Investigation. We have placed this man in a separate cell, isolated from everyone, as requested. Also as requested, no investigation was initialized from our side, though we had the right to do so. Since then, I have been sitting on my ass here until this godforsaken hour, waiting for you all to show up like heroes out of the dark dust because whatever this is, it just couldn't wait until the morning, right? Who knows? We're so incompetent at what we do here at Tucson PD that the suspect might've escaped before sunrise.'

The captain's eyes widened at Agent Fisher.

'There's no recording of the interview because there was no interview,' he continued. 'My detective walked in there and asked him a couple of questions, to which he never got a reply. As I've told you, the only words the suspect has spoken since his arrest were "This shall be fun." I could've omitted all that information from our little conversation here, but I didn't. Like I said, we are *cooperating*. If you don't like the way in which we are doing so –' he pointed down the corridor, '– you can walk back the same way you came in.'

Garcia almost danced a jig.

Agent Fisher took a deep breath, but before she was able to

reply, Agent Williams stepped forward, placing a hand on his partner's shoulder.

'I apologize, Captain. We definitely didn't come here to pick a fight or to rub anybody the wrong way. We're certainly grateful for your cooperation. It's been a very long and surprising day for all of us and we're a bit out of shape here. You're right. Maybe we should've waited until the morning when everyone would've been at least rested and less on edge, but since we're already here, do you mind if we carry on and talk to the subject?'

Captain Suarez held Agent Williams' stare for a couple of seconds.

'Right this way.'

As they carried on down the corridor, Garcia leaned over toward Hunter. 'Am I the only one who thinks that "This shall be fun" being the only thing the suspect has said since he was arrested is a little strange?'

'No,' Hunter said back. 'I'm with you on that one.'

Captain Suarez turned left at the end of the hallway and guided everyone past a door guarded by a young police officer before showing them all into a small observation room just around the corner. The air inside the concrete-walled room was uncomfortably warm.

'There he is,' Captain Suarez said.

Through the large two-way mirror on the wall directly in front of them, they could see a tall and broad-shouldered man sitting at a metal table. His hands were cuffed to the tabletop through a one-foot-long chain. He was sitting back on his chair in as much of a comfortable position as he could muster, given his predicament. His eyes were low, focusing on his lap. He wore a dark-blue T-shirt, blue jeans and black

All-Stars. His shoelaces had been taken from him as a precautionary measure.

For a long, silent moment everyone attentively regarded the man on the other side of the mirror, and if anyone in that observation room had ever imagined what The Surgeon might look like, that man would be pretty close to it.

'From what I understand,' Agent Fisher said, 'he had no identification on him when he was arrested.'

'That's correct,' Captain Suarez confirmed. 'All he had on him was a camera.'

'A camera?' The question came from Agent Williams, but the concerned look was uniform across everyone's faces. They had not known that fact until then, as none of them had seen the arresting report yet.

'That's right. When the two officers surprised him at the scene, they saw him drop a heavy object to the floor. They thought it was a weapon. It turned out to be a camera.'

One of Agent Fisher's eyebrows lifted as she turned to face the group.

'I said that he would probably be photographing his scenes, didn't I?'

'The camera has been bagged as evidence and it's sitting upstairs,' Captain Suarez announced.

'Has anyone looked through the photos yet?' Hunter asked.

'No,' Captain Suarez replied, purposely giving Agent Fisher a plastic smile. 'For two reasons. One – since this isn't our investigation, the evidence doesn't belong to us either, and two – it's not a digital camera.'

That fact surprised everyone.

'We're talking about an old-fashioned, thirty-six-millimeter film camera here. You'll have to get the film developed if you want to see the photos.'

'Not a problem,' Agent Brandon said, nodding at Captain Suarez. 'Let's go get the camera.' He addressed Agents Williams and Fisher. 'I'll have the pictures in an hour. Two, max.'

The captain looked at the rest of the group.

'It's OK, Captain,' Agent Williams assured him. 'We'll be all right by ourselves. We're just going to ask him a few questions.'

'Suit yourselves,' Captain Suarez replied before he and Agent Brandon left the room.

Everyone went back to regarding the man on the other side of the two-way mirror, but Agent Fisher seemed to be looking at him a little differently. There was a new shine in her eyes, as if she knew something the others didn't.

'We should let Robert talk to him,' Garcia suggested. 'He's an expert interrogator.'

'Oh, I really don't think so,' Agent Fisher said, taking a step back from the two-way mirror. 'Despite whatever title appears on the official report, Detective Garcia, this *is* an FBI investigation and as such, an FBI agent will be the first one to interrogate the suspect. And please rest assured that Detective Hunter isn't the only expert interrogator in this room.'

'So Agent Williams will interrogate him?' Garcia asked, his face as straight as a die.

'You probably think you're funny, don't you?' Agent Fisher asked back.

'I have my moments.'

'Well, this is definitely not one of them.'

Agent Fisher grabbed the notepad and the pen that were sitting on top of the small rectangular table inside the observation room. 'Please remember something, Detective: make no mistake, you're here as guests, nothing more, so you'd better get used to the view from the back seat. My advice to you is: get comfortable and try to pay attention, OK?' She reached for the door. 'Who knows? You might even learn something.'

Fifty

The door to interrogation room one closed behind Agent Fisher with an unrestricted bang, but once again the noise didn't seem to bother the man sitting at the metal table. He kept his eyes low, as if calmly reading some invisible book resting on his lap.

Agent Fisher studied the man from where she stood for a long moment before slowly approaching the table. The clicking of her low heels against the concrete floor echoed ominously throughout the room.

The man's eyes stayed where they were, but his lips stretched into a short, cynical smile, as if he knew exactly what was coming.

Click, clack, click, clack.

The man seemed to enjoy the odd suspense.

Agent Fisher finally paused before the table and waited.

No movement from the man. His eyes stayed low. His hands stayed on the table.

Agent Fisher half-placed, half-slapped the notepad she had with her on the tabletop. The noise it made didn't startle the man, but it seemed to get his attention, as he finally lifted his stare and locked eyes with the FBI agent.

'Hello there,' she said, her expression stern, her voice serene but firm, full of authority.

The look in the man's eyes was icy and calculating. No apprehension. No fear. He was studying her, Agent Fisher could tell. She'd seen that cold look many times before and it didn't scare her.

'I'm Special Agent Erica Fisher with the Federal Bureau of Investigation.'

If Agent Fisher was expecting even an ounce of hesitation to flash across the man's face as she mentioned which law-enforcement agency she worked for, she was bitterly disappointed. The man's demeanor didn't change, not even a little bit. He simply carried on analyzing the woman standing in front of him. In the mood she was in, Agent Fisher saw no point in wasting any time with frivolous conversation.

Trick number one – make the subject believe that you are the highest-ranking official in the investigation. The highest-ranking official he will ever talk to. Why? Many psychopathic serial killers, when they finally realize that the game is probably over, will do all they can to bargain their position, and they know that only the person at the very top has the power to conduct any sort of bargaining. Talking to anyone else is nothing more than a waste of breath. Agent Fisher could distinctly see that the man wasn't about to waste his.

'I'm the senior agent in charge of this entire investigation,' she lied.

On hearing those words, something finally changed inside the man's eyes.

Agent Fisher peeked at her image reflected in the two-way mirror to her left before taking a seat across the table from the man.

'This is the only opportunity you'll have to speak directly to me. After this, I'll be gone and I will not grant you another opportunity. Do you understand what I'm telling you?'

The man's stare seemed to intensify. He was still clearly trying to read her.

'So,' the agent continued. 'With that said, let's get through the introductions here, shall we? As I've said, I'm Special Agent Fisher . . . and you are?'

Nothing.

'Any name I can call you by, just for the sake of this conversation?' she insisted.

The man's poker face was almost as solid as his adversary's, but not quite. Still, there was no reply.

Agent Fisher sat back on the chair and crossed her legs. There was no agitation on her part.

The man clasped his hands on the tabletop.

Agent Fisher noticed that his nails were very clean and neatly clipped.

'Would you rather I come up with a name I can use until you decide to tell me your real one?' she asked.

For several seconds the man didn't move, then he gave her a barely noticeable shrug, which, despite being silent, was still a response. She was making progress.

Time to test some reactions.

'OK . . . let's see . . . I could call you . . .' she pretended to be thinking about it. 'Surgeon. How about that? Does that appeal to your skills?'

No reaction whatsoever from the man, which surprised Agent Fisher, but she kept a steady face, still not giving anything away.

'Don't you like that? Really? OK, I'm sure I can come

up with something else. How about ...' Another pause. 'Artist?'

A muscle flexed just under the man's left eye. It was a minute twitch, which Agent Fisher wasn't sure if the others on the other side of the two-way mirror had picked up on, but she certainly had.

'Is that better? Is that how you perceive yourself? As an artist?'

The man breathed in.

Agent Fisher gave him a somewhat sarcastic nod followed by a careless chuckle. 'You think that being silent will somehow help you?'

She waited.

Nothing.

'Well, I can guarantee you it won't. Why don't you try this: take a moment and look around you.' Agent Fisher waited a couple of seconds, but the man once again didn't move. 'Those are solid walls, and you're sitting down in the basement of a police precinct. I hate to break it to you, but ... you're fucked. You're going nowhere from here but to death row. You know that, don't you? Your only chance at anything is to talk to me.'

The threat didn't seem to bother the man.

Time to step things up a little.

Trick number two: push, challenge, or try to discredit the subject, but aim your punches at their overinflated egos. Due to their delusional belief that they are superior to everyone else, psychopaths will be much quicker to defend their egos than their actions.

'You know, for someone who thinks he's so smart, so creative, you sure screwed up fast, didn't you?'

The man blinked at her.

The punch got through.

Push again.

'Well, I've got some news for you. You're not smart. You're not an artist. You're just another crazy psycho who likes killing people and leaving stupid clues behind. Our archives are full of people like you.'

Silence.

Push further.

'Actually, no.' Agent Fisher made a face. 'Let me correct myself here. Our archives are full of people a lot smarter than you because they didn't get caught so quickly. They didn't forget that people have neighbors, and neighbors like to look out their windows.'

The man's eyes narrowed a touch.

Agent Fisher read it and chuckled again. 'Oh, you didn't know that that was how you got caught, did you?'

The man's jaw tightened.

'That's right, one of Mr. Davis's neighbors saw you breaking into Mr. Davis's house – a neighbor who was supposed to be on holiday, but had to cut it a few days short. Now how unlucky for you was that, huh?' She paused for effect. 'For someone who thinks he's so intelligent . . . so prepared, that's a stupid mistake to make, wouldn't you say? A last-minute check would've really come in handy for you.'

The cynical smile was back on the man's lips.

'You know what?' Agent Fisher calmly said, getting to her feet.

Trick number three.

'I'm actually done with this. I'm tired. I traveled a hell of a long way to get here and you definitely weren't worth it. Good luck on death row.' She turned her back on the man.

Click, clack, click, clack.

'So . . . Special Agent Fisher,' the man called out, halting the agent as she got to the door.

She didn't turn to face him.

'How many bodies have you found so far?' The man's voice was as powerful as his frame and as calm as Agent Fisher's.

She took a deep breath to suppress the smile that shadowed her lips before turning and allowing her gaze to settle on the man's face once again.

'How many?' he insisted.

She walked back to the table and retook her seat. It was her turn to stay quiet.

'Three . . . ?'

Agent Fisher studied him, trying to read his dark eyes.

'Four . . . ?' He tilted his head to one side ever so slightly.

Agent Fisher breathed out, sat back on her chair and re-crossed her legs.

The man gave her another simple and subtle nod.

Agent Fisher had finally got what she wanted.

'Why?' she asked. 'Are there more?'

The man's right eyebrow arched. 'There might be, but how about we go slowly, huh?'

The man practically admitting to more than four victims sent a chill down Agent Fisher's spine. *We have him,* she thought.

'Let's try to establish some key points here, shall we?' the man continued. 'Tell me, Special Agent Fisher, who was the first victim you found?'

She regarded the man with a hawk's stare. 'How about you tell me? Who was your first victim?'

The man ran his tongue over his top lip. 'I like you, Special Agent Fisher. You're not as dumb as you look.'

Agent Fisher blinked. 'As opposed to you, who so far has proven to be even dumber than you look.'

The man threw his head back and let go of a nervous laugh. 'Flattery will get you everywhere; isn't that how the saying goes?'

No reply from Agent Fisher.

'OK, let's forget about names for the time being; what do you say? Let's talk timeframes, how about that? Would that be better?' The man scooted forward on his chair and placed his elbows on the table. 'Tell me, Special Agent Fisher, when did the Bureau start this investigation? How long ago since you found the first body? Three weeks . . . ? Four, maybe . . . ?'

Agent Fisher kept as still as a statue.

The man shrugged. 'Maybe you don't know this, but things have been happening for a lot longer than that.'

'Really?' she challenged, still in a serene tone. 'Like what, for example? About two months, give or take?' As Agent Fisher mentioned the timeframe she noticed a thoughtful spar-kle in the man's demeanor.

'Give or take,' he said, as if admitting to something, but the way in which he phrased his reply gave Agent Fisher the impression that the FBI wasn't quite on the right track yet. She had to push for an answer.

'Longer?'

The man stayed silent.

Agent Fisher felt fear shake her core, because if The Surgeon had been killing for longer than two months, it meant that there was at least another victim. Someone prior to Kristine Rivers. Someone they hadn't found yet.

'How many victims?' she asked again.

The man said nothing.

'How many have you killed so far?'

All of a sudden the door to the interrogation room swung open and Agent Williams stepped inside. 'Agent Fisher, could I have a word, please?'

Agent Fisher turned to face her partner, finding the intrusion strange and completely unwelcome.

Agent Williams and Agent Fisher had worked together in countless investigations. As a team they had interrogated numerous suspects. Their act – good cop/bad cop – was one of the best in the Bureau, but she hadn't used any of her trigger words to signal Agent Williams in the observation room that it was time for "bad cop" to join the party.

She looked back at him grimly.

'Now, Agent Fisher.'

Agent Fisher frowned.

Something was definitely wrong.

Fifty-One

Fifteen minutes earlier

As soon as Agent Fisher left the observation room, Agent Williams moved a step closer to Hunter and Garcia.

'I'd like to apologize for Agent Fisher's behavior.' He sounded sincere. 'As I told Captain Suarez, it's been a very long and surprising day for all of us and it all seems to have gotten the best of her, at least for today. She never usually acts this way. She's a great agent. Very dedicated. Very in control. Very knowledgeable, but neither of us has ever worked on such a frustrating case.'

Hunter replied with a subtle nod. 'It's not a problem. I understand her frustration.'

'Frustration is just a small part of it,' Garcia said, sounding a lot less forgiving than Hunter.

Agent Williams looked back at him.

'C'mon, we can stop pretending here,' Garcia elaborated. 'It's more than obvious that what's really eating her is the fact that she feels threatened by us.'

Through the two-way mirror they all saw Agent Fisher step into the interrogation room and close the door behind her.

No reaction from the man at the table.

'The two of you were assigned as the lead agents in Director Kennedy's niece's homicide investigation,' Garcia continued. 'That's a huge responsibility, bestowed upon you by the director himself, which means that he not only trusts you, but he probably also considers the pair of you to be his best agents. Of course you guys want to do well for him, but after over two months of no results and a few downfalls, things have gone a little pear-shaped, haven't they? Tempers were probably already running high before Director Kennedy decided to invite us to join the investigation.' He shrugged as he corrected himself. 'And by *us* I mean Robert; I'm just a consequence. Anyway, Agent Fisher didn't like that at all, because in her head all it meant was that all of a sudden, in Director Kennedy's eyes, the FBI golden pair didn't seem to be shining so bright anymore.'

Agent Williams found it hard to retort.

'I'm not sure what she thinks is going to happen,' Garcia proceeded. 'But we're not here to discredit anyone or to tread on anyone's toes. We're not here to compete against you and we sure as hell aren't here trying to impress Director Kennedy or anyone else. We just want to catch this psycho as much as you do.'

The multidirectional microphone on the ceiling above the metal table inside the interrogation room picked up Agent Fisher's voice loud and clear, sending everyone inside the observation room into a deep silence. Through the speakers they all heard her introduce herself, then tell the man that she was the senior agent in charge of the entire investigation and that this would be his only opportunity to talk to her.

Hunter kept his arms folded in front of his chest and his full attention on the man sitting at the table. He would rather be inside the interrogation room, but even from the other side of the two-way mirror, he had a clear enough view of the man to be able to search his facial expressions and body movements for any telltale signs. He saw the man's stare intensify, as if he were weighing up what Agent Fisher had just told him. When she asked him for a name and upon his silence suggested that she come up with one for him, Hunter saw the subtle shrug the man had given her in reply.

When Fisher mentioned the word 'artist', there was a slight twitch to his left eye, which intrigued Hunter.

'Did you see that?' Agent Williams asked.

Both Hunter and Garcia nodded.

Inside the interrogation room, Agent Fisher countered the man's silence with a threat, but that also failed to produce any effect. She then began attacking his ego, but again the man's only reaction was an uneasy blink of the eyes. When she mentioned Mr. Davis's neighbor, the man's eyebrows moved down slightly. Not exactly a frown, but definitely a sign of curiosity. That intrigued Hunter, setting off the first alarm bell inside his head.

'Do we know if anyone has talked to Mr. Davis's neighbor?' he asked.

Garcia and Agent Williams turned to face him.

'The one who made the 911 call. Do we know if anyone has talked to him?'

'No idea,' Agent Williams replied. 'But we can find out. Why?'

'No reason, but I would just like to check,' Hunter answered. 'With the suspect being arrested on the spot and Tucson PD having orders not to initiate an investigation, that sort of detail could've easily been overlooked.'

Inside the interrogation room, Agent Fisher carried on with

her attack on the man's ego, but his curiosity seemed to fade way too fast, substituted by a faint, cynical smile.

A second alarm bell started ringing inside Hunter's head.

The man seemed to be pushing Agent Fisher just as much as she was pushing him. The only difference was that he was doing it in silence.

Agent Fisher got to her feet and began making her way to the door. There was no doubt that she was going through the interrogation-trick book one step at a time. As she got to the door, the man finally spoke.

'So ... Special Agent Fisher, how many bodies have you found so far?'

In the observation room, everybody's attention heightened exponentially as they watched Agent Fisher slowly walk back and retake her seat at the table, but it was the way in which the man threw the numbers at her that concerned Hunter.

Suddenly, the man surprised everyone when he practically admitted that there could be more than four victims.

'Sonofabitch,' Agent Williams said, making no effort to disguise the excitement in his voice. 'It's him. It's the fucking Surgeon. We've got him.' He reached for his phone, ready to call Director Kennedy, but Hunter stopped him by lightly placing a hand on his shoulder.

'Wait,' he said. 'Let this interview play out first.'

'Why? It's him. He's admitting to it.'

'Not exactly,' Hunter replied.

'What do you mean – "not exactly"?'

Back in the interrogation room Agent Fisher and the suspect began talking about the timeframe. The man shrugged before dropping the bomb: 'Things have been happening for a lot longer than that.'

More alarm bells, but they only seemed to be ringing inside Hunter's head.

'It's him,' Agent Williams said again. 'We've got him.'

'No, I don't think so,' Hunter said, shaking his head. 'This is wrong. This is all wrong.'

'Wrong?' Agent Williams queried. 'What do you mean, "wrong"? What's wrong?'

'What he's saying,' Hunter replied. 'He's not telling her anything; she is telling him.'

'What?' Agent Williams' entire forehead creased like an old piece of paper. 'I'm not following you, Detective Hunter.'

'He's cold-reading her.'

Fifty-Two

Agent Fisher closed the interrogation-room door behind her and pinned Agent Williams down with a stare that could've cut through steel.

'What the hell is going on, Larry?' she asked, half-confused, half-angry. 'I know that this isn't "bad cop" time because I didn't use any of our trigger words.'

'Could you give us a minute, please.' Agent Williams addressed the Tucson police officer who was guarding the interrogation-room door.

The officer nodded and walked over to the other end of the corridor.

'That's not him, Erica,' Agent Williams said, once the officer was out of earshot, pointing to the interrogation room. 'That's not The Surgeon in there.'

Agent Fisher's eyes widened at her partner. 'What? Have you been listening to the same interrogation?' She began numbering the events, using the fingers on her right hand to emphasize her points. 'His demeanor completely changed when I mentioned the word "artist". He practically told us that there are more than four victims and that he's been killing for longer than two months. All you need to do is read between the lines, Larry. Have you been asleep?'

'No I haven't, Erica, and you're not reading him. He's reading you.'

'What?' She chuckled nervously. 'What the hell are you talking about?'

'It's called "cold-reading", Erica,' Agent Williams tried to explain. 'It's a technique used by many—'

'I know what cold-reading is, Larry.' Agent Fisher's voice acquired an even angrier tone.

'Good, because that's what he's been doing in there,' Agent Williams replied. 'Very professionally, I might add.' He lifted both hands in a "please wait" gesture. 'Just try to think back to the moment you set foot in that room and the exact words you have used.' He gave her a second before recapping with her. 'You first introduced yourself, then asked him for a name. He stayed silent. You offered to come up with one just for the sake of conversation. His "go ahead" sign was a shrug. Not because he didn't care, but because he wanted to hear what you would come up with. Why? Because he knows that during an ongoing investigation, especially one involving a probable serial killer, law-enforcement agencies, including us, the FBI, tend to use some sort of moniker to refer to the perp. A moniker that is usually self-describing – The Tourniquet Killer, The Yorkshire Ripper, The Trailside Strangler, The Vampire of Sacramento, The Surgeon, The Artist. He wanted to know what we were calling the perp, Erica, because he was betting on the chance that the name alone would give him an idea of what this killer has been doing, how he's been taking out his victims. And his gamble paid off because you gave him two. You even asked him if The Surgeon appealed to his "skills".'

Agent Fisher's angry attitude lost a considerable amount of strength as her memory took her back to just moments earlier.

'If you had given him any other moniker,' Agent Williams carried on, 'The Blood Dancer, The Liver Cannibal, it doesn't matter – his reaction would've still been the same because he would've believed that that was what we were calling the killer. Why else would you have used a moniker?'

'And if I had just called him John, or Frank, or whatever?' Agent Fisher contested. 'For the sake of conversation.'

'Then his gamble wouldn't have paid off and he would've probably replied with another shrug as if saying "Suit yourself. Call me whatever you like." He had nothing to lose.'

Agent Fisher chewed on that thought for an instant.

'He finally let go of the silent game when you threatened to leave the room,' Agent Williams continued. 'But he didn't really give you anything. What he did was throw you a question about the number of victims. You gave him back some of his own medicine and stayed quiet. So what did he do to counter your silence? He used a simple cold-reading technique, Erica. He fed you possible answers to his own question – "three, four" – while at the same time paying close attention to your reactions. You might've not realized this, but you were absolutely still until he got to four. That was when you finally breathed out and sat back on your chair. He read your movement, stopped counting and smiled. You immediately countered with a double question, which simply confirmed the number on which he had stopped – "Why? Are there more?"

'After that, he didn't effectively tell you that there were more than four victims, like you thought he had. All he did was give you a very generic reply – "there might be" – a reply that, one: doesn't really implicate him in anything, and two: would trick you into believing that he was giving you the answer you wanted. How did he know that you would fall for it? Because that's one of the foundations cold-reading is built upon. It's pure psychology. When people are keen, when people *want* to believe, all you need to do is give them an ambiguous response and their brains will do the rest. It will make that ambiguous response sound exactly how they want it to sound because that's what they want to hear. So while he replied "there might be", your brain interpreted that as "yes, there are". How do I know that? Because my brain did the exact same thing back in the interrogation room.'

From the look in Agent Fisher's eyes, Agent Williams could tell that her memory was paging through the interrogation as quickly as it possibly could.

'He used the exact same trick when he asked you about the timeframe,' Agent Williams added. 'He fed you possibilities while studying your reaction – "Three weeks …? Four maybe …?" The problem he had was that he couldn't just carry on. He had no idea how far he would have to go before you picked up on his bullshit. Too risky, so he fed you another generic answer – "Things have been happening for a lot longer than that."' Agent Williams shrugged. '*Things?* What things? Murder? Corruption? Hate? Bigotry? Global warming? Pollution? The ozone layer? My back problem? All of those things have been happening for a lot longer than four weeks. But your brain interpreted his answer the way *you* wanted it to sound and you gave *him* the timeframe. He never gave it to you.'

Agent Williams reminded his partner of the words she had used.

'"Like what, for example? About two months, give or take?"'

Agent Fisher began to look a little lost.

'All he did,' Agent Williams said, 'was repeat the three last words you used – "give or take" – and once again, your brain took that as – "yes, longer than two months".'

There was a long, awkward pause. Agent Fisher avoided her partner's eyes by looking past him, down the corridor. The Tucson police officer was leaning against the wall. It looked like he was struggling to stay awake.

'Pure psychology?' she finally said. 'Did Detective Hunter fill your head with all this crap?'

Agent Williams ran a hand through his short dark hair.

'He was the one who called my attention to it, yes.'

Agent Fisher looked angry again.

'For Christ's sake, Larry. What the—'

'Erica, stop it.' The authority in Agent Williams' voice matched the anger in Agent Fisher's. She looked back at him, surprised. Agent Williams never lost his cool.

'This is not a competition,' he carried on. 'This isn't us against them. It isn't the FBI against the LAPD. This is all of us against The Surgeon. And we are losing.'

'If he's not The Surgeon,' she asked, 'then who the hell is he? And why would he allow himself to be wrongly arrested for multiple homicides without saying a single word in his defense?'

Agent Williams cleared his throat. 'The speculation, given that the only thing he had with him was a camera, is that he's a reporter, who somehow managed to find out about this investigation. He probably figured that by using a combination of silence and cold-reading, he would be able to extract enough information from the police . . . the FBI . . . whoever . . . to put together a news piece.'

Agent Fisher took a deep breath while her brain tried to come up with a reply, but before it was able to comply, Agent Williams challenged her.

'It's not him, Erica. If you think we're wrong, go back in there, give him something bogus about The Surgeon and see how he reacts.'

Agent Fisher allowed that thought to play in her head for several seconds. Had she been that stupid? Had she really not seen through the man's bullshit?

Anger threatened to choke her.

'All right,' she finally said, about to breathe out fire. 'Let's go test this sonofabitch.'

Fifty-Three

Agent Fisher reentered interrogation room one, but this time she closed the door behind her smoothly, as if she was walking into a library room.

The man at the metal table had gone back to focusing his attention on his lap.

Agent Fisher readjusted her ponytail and slowly made her way back to the table.

Click, clack, click, clack.

Maybe it was because the novelty of the silent and the no-eye-contact treatment had worn off, or maybe it was because every step Agent Fisher took was overflowing with determination, but this time the man's eyes moved straight back to her.

She paused before the vacant chair, but decided against taking a seat.

The man waited, his gaze carefully studying her every move.

'The coroner is done with the autopsy,' she lied, her face as steady as a surgeon's hand. 'Not that we weren't already expecting it, but since we're talking, I was wondering if you could help me understand something here. Why the different MOs? Why kill them all differently?'

The man's demeanor didn't change. He simply continued analyzing her with the same dead, cold stare as before.

'I mean,' she proceeded, 'you drowned your first victim, you strangled your second one, you slit the throat of your third, and now, death by poisoning. Why? Why jump from method to method? Why don't you stick with the same MO? I'm just curious here.'

Agent Fisher's performance could've gotten her a place at Juilliard. From the slight trepidation in her voice, to the confusion swimming in her eyes, her acting was absolutely flawless.

The man readjusted himself on his chair and looked back at Agent Fisher as if he knew something she didn't.

Their stares battled against each other for several seconds before Agent Fisher broke eye contact.

'You know what?' she said, without too much concern. 'I don't give a damn if you answer me or not. We've got you. It's over and you're going to rot in jail, starting from right now.' She turned on the balls of her feet and marched toward the door. 'Enjoy the rest of your pathetic life.'

'Well,' the man replied at last, once again stopping Agent Fisher just as she got to the door. 'One might like to experiment with different methods. Or each victim might request a different approach.'

Agent Fisher's stomach tightened inside her as if she'd been dropped from an airplane with no parachute.

'*One? Experiment?*' she asked as she turned around and walked back to the table, her eyes about to ignite. The man had once again used a generic reply. One that would not implicate him in anything.

The man shrugged. 'And why not? C'mon, Special Agent

Erica Fisher, do you want me to do your job for you? It's your job to figure these things out, isn't it?'

That was the straw that broke the camel's back.

'You sonofabitch.' She slammed her hands on the tabletop so hard it made the notepad on it bounce.

The man wasn't expecting that sort of reaction and despite his coolness, her aggressiveness startled him, making him jump back on his chair.

'Who the fuck are you?' she yelled as she leaned forward, her voice croaking with anger. 'There has been no change in the killer's MO, you lying piece of shit. I just made that up.'

There was no pretending anymore. The man knew that his game was up, but he still didn't lose his cool. His reply was a casual tilt of the head, which only served to bring Agent Fisher's blood to boiling point. She reached for the man's collar, grabbing it with both hands.

'I swear to God, if you're a reporter and you've done all this for a fucking story, I'll make your life a living hell, you dickless moron. You fucked with the wrong agent here.'

The door to the interrogation room swung open and Hunter, closely followed by Agent Williams and Garcia, stormed in.

'Erica,' Agent Williams called, getting to her and placing his hands on her arms.

Agent Fisher hesitated.

The man waited. His eyes showed no concern.

'Let him go, Erica.'

Agent Fisher breathed out, her stare glued to the man's face.

Agent Williams applied a little more pressure to her arms, trying to move them.

Finally, the agent let go of the man's shirt. She felt her whole body tremble with anger.

'You're so screwed,' she whispered to the man, before standing up straight again and taking a step back from the table. 'Somebody take this piece of shit out of my face before I teach him a lesson he'll never forget.'

'Not so fast, Special Agent Fisher,' the man said, his eyes slowly moving from her to the three new arrivals. 'I guess that this would be a good time for me to call my lawyer, don't you think?'

'Ha,' Agent Fisher chuckled. 'You won't get shit. You've committed a federal offense, you moron.'

'Have I?' the man asked, pretending to be oblivious. 'And which offense was that?'

Agent Fisher's eyes widened. 'You really are an idiot, aren't you? You should've thought this through, because wasting the FBI's time is a federal offense, you imbecile, and I will make sure you pay for this.'

'Really?' the man questioned, still in a carefree way. 'And how exactly did I waste the FBI's time, Special Agent Fisher? All I did was exercise my *constitutional* right to stay silent. When I spoke, I did not lie and I did not incriminate myself with any of my replies. If anyone has interpreted them wrongly, that isn't my fault. I also never once admitted to being . . .' His stare went back to Agent Fisher. 'I believe the FBI is calling this killer The Surgeon or The Artist – apparently according to his skills. So no, Special Agent Fisher, I did not waste your or the FBI's time. You did that all by yourself. All I did was sit here and listen.' The man sat back on his chair, with a new victorious air about him. 'Can I call my lawyer now? I'd really like to go home. I'm hungry, tired, and these handcuffs are quite annoying.'

Agent Fisher's hands clutched into fists.

'You are a freelance reporter, right?' Hunter asked, taking a step forward. 'Not really attached to any newspapers or news channels, correct? You just sell whatever story you have to the highest bidder.'

The man looked back at him curiously. 'Sorry, but you are?'

'My name is Robert Hunter.'

The man's head tilted back slightly. He spent a moment studying Hunter.

'You're not an FBI agent, are you?' His gaze moved around the room and paused on Garcia. 'And neither is he. That's easy to tell just by what you're wearing. Something, shall I say, much more relaxed than what Special Agent Fisher and Special Agent "grumpy face" here are wearing.' He nodded at Agent Williams.

'You're right,' Hunter agreed. 'We're not FBI agents.' He decided to leave it at that. 'You're very perceptive and your "silent" approach, together with your cold-reading technique, was quite an impressive trick. It did get you some information, but let's be honest here – not enough for any reputable news piece, especially when you consider the fact that the federal government has seized your camera and the film in it. You'll never get those pictures. You are aware of that, aren't you?'

'You have no right to seize my camera,' the man replied. This time there was concern in his voice.

'Unfortunately for you,' Hunter said, 'yes, we do. You can ask your lawyer when you call him.'

Once again the man's stare bounced from person to person in the room.

'But,' Hunter said, lifting his index finger, 'I have a proposal for you.'

Hunter's words caught everyone by surprise, making his

colleagues look back at him questioningly, but before Agent Fisher or Agent Williams could say anything, he signaled them both to give him a minute.

'A proposal?' the man asked.

'That's correct,' Hunter confirmed. 'Kind of – you help us, we help you.'

The man regarded Hunter with the same resolve he had regarded Agent Fisher throughout their interview. Hunter was much harder to read than she had been.

'OK,' the man said with a nod. 'I'm listening.'

Fifty-Four

Dr. Morgan took his time getting ready. By the time he finished scrubbing up and made his way to Autopsy Theater One, on the ground floor of the Pima County's Office of Medical Examiner, the body of Timothy Davis had already been washed, disinfected and transferred to the stainless-steel examination table at the center of the spotlessly clean, white linoleum floor.

The body was lying on its back, with its arms loosely by its side. As Dr. Morgan approached it, he paused for a moment.

Just minutes after death, due to the ceasing of heart function and consequently the lack of blood flow, human skin will begin to tighten and discolor, acquiring a grayish pale tone. Within thirty minutes of death, post-mortem lividity, which is the pooling of blood in the parts of the body that are closest to the ground, will start to settle, turning the skin purple and giving it a waxy feel, but Timothy Davis's body looked a lot paler than anyone would've expected for an African American subject. But that wasn't all – in his case, post-mortem lividity was practically unnoticeable.

'Interesting,' the doctor whispered to himself, adjusting his glasses on his nose to have a better look at the discoloration of the skin. He wondered if Mr. Davis had suffered from any dermatological conditions while alive.

Dr. Morgan checked the module directly behind him just to make sure he had all the instruments he needed. With everything in place, he finally turned on his digital Dictaphone, ready to start the official post-mortem examination.

He began by stating the date and time, followed by the morgue's internal case number. After that he described the general state of the body, detailing any wounds, marks, scratches, abrasions . . . anything that could be seen externally. Once Dr. Morgan flipped the body over to examine its back, something somersaulted inside his stomach.

'What the hell?'

Immediately he reached for his digital camera.

The marks to Timothy Davis's back practically sucked the air out of Dr. Morgan's lungs.

Arizona was not the most racist state, but unfortunately racial hatred was still going strong in pretty much every corner of America, regardless of which state you found yourself in. It was with that knowledge in mind that Dr. Morgan first considered the possibility of this being a racially motivated attack. The marks to the victim's back looked at first like some sort of castigation, applied to Mr. Davis by a whip, or similar instrument. But a closer examination made Dr. Morgan realize that was impossible. Not all, but several of the marks actually looked like letters. He could clearly identify a 'T', an 'R', an 'F', an 'M', and possibly an 'E'. That certainly was no coincidence and no matter how proficient one could be with a whip, Dr. Morgan just couldn't imagine anyone being so good as to be able to write letters with lashes. The rest of the marks looked random – just a mishmash of straight cuts.

'What in the world is all this?' Dr. Morgan asked himself, as adrenaline pumped his veins with excitement.

Then it finally dawned on him.

'I'll be damned. So this is why they needed this autopsy ASAP. This is a message.'

Dr. Morgan had been a pathologist for thirty-one years, twenty-one of them as the Chief Medical Examiner for Pima County. He had autopsied more than his fair share of bodies brought in from homicide crime scenes, some of them in an awful state, but he had never been the examining patholo-gist in a serial-murder case. In fact, as far as he knew, there had only been one serial killer active in Tucson, back in the sixties – Charles Schmid, also known as The Pied Piper of Tucson, who had murdered three people and buried them in the desert.

Dr. Morgan was now sure that this wasn't just any serial-killer case. This was a serial killer who had apparently left a cryptogram carved into his victim's flesh. That was something that happened plenty in Hollywood movies and crime-fiction books, but rarely in real life.

After photographing Timothy Davis's back and the mark-ings on it from a variety of angles, Dr. Morgan turned the body back around, ready for the Y incision and the internal organs examination. From the module behind him, he retrieved a long-handed scalpel and brought it to the body's right upper chest, starting the cut about an inch below its shoulder. As the laser-sharp scalpel ruptured through skin and muscle with tremendous ease, Dr. Morgan frowned.

Something didn't seem right.

'What is going on here?'

He proceeded with the incision and opened up the body's breastplate.

The doctor's jaw dropped open.

'This is . . . impossible.'

Fifty-Five

Once again, the man at the metal table scooted forward and placed his elbows on the tabletop.

'Before we start with this proposal you're talking about,' he said, addressing Hunter, 'how about a gesture of good faith? These handcuffs really are annoying. I would feel much more relaxed without them.'

'That can be easily arranged,' Hunter replied. 'But first, we would need to confirm your identity. Can we have your real name?'

The man exhaled while he weighed the odds. 'OK,' he finally said. 'My name is Owen. Owen Henderson.'

Hunter waited, but the man offered nothing else. 'You're going to have to give us a little more than that if you want those removed with any urgency. If you're not bothered and you don't mind keeping them on for another few hours, we can go with just Owen Henderson and hope for a quick match.'

The man now had four different faces to study instead of just one, which made the task infinitely harder. He concentrated his efforts on Hunter's.

'Before we go there,' he began. 'What sort of deal are we talking about? What are you offering and what do you expect back?'

Agent Fisher, who had turned her back on the man and was now facing Hunter, managed to ask him four different questions with a single look: 'Yeah, what sort of deal are you talking about here? What are you offering? What do you expect back and under whose authority are you able to offer anyone a goddamn deal?'

Hunter disregarded Agent Fisher's frosty look and approached the table. 'Somehow you ended up at a crime scene even before the police got there.'

The man could already guess where this was going.

'There are only two ways in which that would be possible,' Hunter continued. 'One: you really are the person we're after, in which case you're screwed and this case is over, or two: you were tipped off, in which case we need to know every detail about that tip.'

The man broke eye contact with Hunter while he scratched the back of his left hand. 'OK, I see what you need from me, but what do I get in return?'

'You'll get more than enough information for a very credible news piece,' Hunter said. 'Victims' names, locations, dates . . . you know how it goes.'

The man continued regarding Hunter with the utmost attention. So much so that he missed the angry look Agent Fisher gave the LAPD detective.

'And I get my photos back,' the man said. 'All of them.'

'You'll get your photos back,' Hunter accepted.

Agent Fisher looked like she was about to put a stop to the entire conversation, but Agent Williams signaled her to hold on for a while longer.

'But there's one condition,' Hunter added.

'Oh really?' The man didn't look very impressed. 'And what condition would that be?'

'You'll have to give us a few days before the piece is published,' Hunter revealed. 'Or else you *will* jeopardize the entire investigation and there's no way we will allow that to happen.'

The man drummed his fingers against one another. 'How many days are we talking about here?'

'We need a week,' Hunter replied.

The man shook his head. 'No. I can give you three days.'

'This is not a negotiation,' Hunter came back, his voice so commanding it made the man blink. 'I will not put this investigation in harm's way for you or anyone else. That's the deal. It's that or nothing. No information. No pictures. No anything. Good luck trying to find anyone who will publish your flimsy article.' As Hunter made his way toward the door, everyone else turned their backs on the man and followed suit.

'OK, fine,' the man called out. There was a little defeat in his voice. 'I'll give y'all seven days from today. It will give me more time to write the article, anyway.'

Everyone stopped and turned to face him.

'So how about we speed this up?' Hunter said.

The man nodded once. 'Owen Henderson, 531 West 17th Street in Clark Park, Phoenix, Arizona. I'm a freelance investigative reporter and photographer. I've had articles and photographs published by the *New York Times*, the *LA Times*, the *Chicago Tribune*, the *Washington Post*, and the *Miami Herald*, to name a few.'

From the corner of his eye, Hunter saw Agent Williams reach for his cellphone before exiting the room.

'OK,' Hunter said. 'Give us five minutes.'

'Hey,' the man called out. 'How about my handcuffs?'

Hunter paused by the door. He was the last one of the group. 'If everything checks out, Owen, I'll take those handcuffs off myself. I'll be back in five minutes.'

'Seriously? C'mon, man. Why the hell would I lie now?'

Hunter wasn't listening anymore.

Fifty-Six

Hunter, Garcia and both FBI agents had just returned to the observation room when Agent Williams received the callback from the FBI field office in Phoenix.

'Great,' he said into his cellphone after listening for all of ten seconds. 'Just email me the lot.' Once he disconnected he turned and addressed the rest of the group. 'It's a match.' With a head gesture he indicated the man on the other side of the two-way mirror. 'We are indeed looking at one Owen Henderson – thirty-six years old from Phoenix. He also didn't lie about his address or profession. Right now, I have two agents on the way to his house. In the meantime, I should be getting an email with all his basic info any second now.'

'Fine,' Agent Fisher said, leaning against one of the corners of the table at the center of the room and looking at Hunter. 'But you're not giving this sack of shit any deals. You do not have the authority to do so. Not without Director Kennedy's explicit authorization.'

'I know,' Hunter replied with an accepting nod.

Before Agent Fisher could say anything else Garcia jumped in.

'There will be no deals, Special Agent Fisher.' Garcia's

words came out slower than usual just to emphasize that he was stating the obvious. 'He played us,' he explained, but immediately took a second to rethink his words and decided to add a little dig. 'Actually, he played you, but that's beside the point. Now we play him.'

'Screw you,' she replied. 'He didn't play me.'

'Nevertheless,' Garcia said. 'Even if we don't give him anything, the rabbit is out of the hole now. There's no way we'll be able to keep a lid on this story anymore. So, before he or any other reporter comes up with a bullshit article about a brand-new serial killer who has claimed victims in four different states, I would suggest calling a press conference in the next day or two and feeding the press the story *we* want them to publicize. That's the only way we'll have any control over this now.'

Agent Fisher exchanged a new look with her FBI partner. They both knew Garcia was right.

'I'll give Director Kennedy a call in the morning,' Agent Williams said.

'Do you mind if I go back in there to talk to him?' Hunter asked.

'Since you were the one who offered him the bogus deal,' Agent Williams replied, 'it's only logical that you do the talking.'

They all looked at Agent Fisher.

'Fine,' she said bitterly. 'Someone else would have to do it anyway, because if I go back in there, I will slap that silly smirk off his idiot face.'

'OK,' Hunter said. 'I'll be right back.'

Before Hunter got to the door, it was pushed open by Special Agent Mike Brandon. He brought with him a tray with five steaming cups of coffee.

'I thought these would come in handy,' he said, placing the tray on the table.

'Damn straight,' Garcia said, reaching for a cup. Special Agents Williams and Fisher followed.

'We'll have the photographs from his camera in about half an hour,' Agent Brandon announced, as he dropped four cubes of white sugar into his cup. 'I also just got a call from Dr. Morgan,' he continued, stirring the sugar into the coffee. 'He's done with the autopsy, but he needs to know if we'll be dropping by the morgue tonight still, or in the morning.'

Hunter checked his watch. 'This won't take long. Ten minutes, max.'

'Call him back,' Agent Williams told Agent Brandon. 'Tell him to please wait. We'll be there in a tick or two.'

Fifty-Seven

Owen Henderson was sitting forward on his chair, staring at his cuffed hands, when Hunter reentered the interrogation room.

'Coffee?' Hunter offered, nodding at the cup he held in his right hand.

Owen's eyes burned a little brighter. 'I'd love some.'

Hunter closed the door behind him, placed the cup on the metal table and used the keys he had picked up from the officer outside to finally free Owen from his restraints.

'Thanks for that,' Owen said, rubbing his wrists vigorously. 'These were really very uncomfortable.'

'They weren't designed with comfort in mind,' Hunter replied calmly.

Owen gave Hunter a humorless smile before reaching for the coffee.

'It's black,' Hunter said. 'No sugar, no cream.'

'That's just fine.'

As Owen had his first sip, his eyes closed and his face softened as if inside that cup was the best-tasting liquid in the world.

'Sorry to interrupt your moment with the coffee,' Hunter

said. He had also decided to stand instead of taking the seat across the table from Owen. 'But we have zero time to waste here. You've already done a great job in that department.'

Owen sipped his coffee again and sat back on his chair.

'So how about we start from the very beginning,' Hunter continued. 'How did you hear about Timothy Davis? How did you get his address?'

'Through a phone call.'

Hunter waited, but Owen went quiet again.

'I said no more time-wasting, Owen.'

The odd gravel in Hunter's voice made Owen pause halfway through his next sip. His stare gravitated toward Hunter.

'No more games.'

'All right. I was having some food at Kaleidoscope Juice – it's a . . . coffee shop, juice and salad bar, and restaurant.'

'And where's that?'

'Downtown Phoenix. Not that far from where I live.'

'So you were having some food when you got the call?'

'That's right.'

'Were you by yourself?'

Owen chuckled. 'Story of my life.'

Hunter's expression remained blank.

'Yes,' Owen rephrased. 'I was by myself.'

'And at what time was that?'

'The call came in at around . . .' He looked down at his coffee cup as his memory went back. 'Two fifteen . . . Two twenty in the afternoon.' Owen's voice showed no excitement. No trepidation.

'Is the cellphone on which you received the call registered in your name?'

Owen frowned at the question. 'Of course.'

Hunter didn't look at the two-way mirror, but he knew that since Agent Williams and the FBI were already compiling a file on Owen Henderson, they would no doubt also already have any cellphone numbers registered to his name. With that, they could contact the cellphone provider and possibly retrieve a copy of the conversation.

'So what was said?' Hunter asked, but at the same time signaled Owen to wait just a moment. 'With as much detail as you can remember.'

Owen breathed out and placed his cup on the table. 'It wasn't a very long conversation,' he began. 'The phone rang, I answered it and the first thing he asked was if I would be interested in the biggest story of my life.'

'Hold on,' Hunter said, lifting a hand. 'Was that really the first thing the caller asked? Didn't he first ask who was speaking?'

'Well,' Owen replied with a half shrug. 'Not in so many words.' He decided to explain before Hunter had a chance to push him. 'I always answer my phone by announcing who I am.' He demonstrated by bringing his right hand closer to his face. His thumb became the earpiece and his pinky the mouthpiece. "Owen Henderson speaking".'

Hunter nodded. He always answered his phone in a very similar manner.

'But you're right,' Owen admitted. 'Once I told him my name, his first words were – "the investigative reporter, Owen Henderson?".'

'Did you ask him how he got hold of your cellphone number?'

'No, because that wouldn't be too hard. I'm listed, plus I have a website, a Facebook account and a LinkedIn account. Several newspapers have me on file as well. Getting hold of my cellphone number wouldn't be a problem to anyone.'

'All right, how about his voice? Did you notice if there was anything odd about it – too much bass ... ? Husky ... ? Deep ... ? Soft ... ? Could you tell if it was being put through a pitch shifter? A voice modifier?'

Once again, Owen took his time as he thought back.

'No, not at all. To be honest, it sounded as normal as normal voices go, and by normal I mean there was nothing about his voice, or even his tone, that I would call memorable. Nothing that would stick out. And I really don't think that he was using any sort of voice effect.' He shrugged. 'It just sounded normal.'

Hunter kept his disappointment completely hidden.

'OK, so tell me about the rest of the conversation, and as I've said, in as much detail as you can remember.'

Owen finished his coffee before picking up from where he'd left off. 'So he asked me if I was indeed the investigative reporter. I replied that I was and then, like I've said, he asked me if I would be interested in the biggest story of my life. Well, that was just too generic, so I asked him what sort of story he was talking about.' Owen paused to readjust his seating position.

'And his reply?'

'It was a peculiar one,' Owen recounted it. 'Because he said that *initially*, what would grab the public's attention would be the murders – a series of them.'

'Initially?' Hunter asked.

'That was the word he used, yes.'

'And did he also use that exact combination of words – "murders – a series of them"?'

'He did, which I found intriguing, so of course I asked him for a specific number. A series was again, too generic. His reply was – "enough for the FBI to consider it a serial-murder case".'

Now Hunter understood why when Owen was cold-reading Agent Fisher, asking her how many bodies had been found, he started the count with three. Not one or two. A serial killer is defined by the FBI as a murderer who kills three or more people on three or more separate occasions, with a cool-off period between those murders.

'That surprised me even more,' Owen said.

'Why?'

'Because I had no idea the FBI was involved. And if the Feds are involved, then we really are talking big case here.'

'But according to what you just told me,' Hunter retorted, 'the caller never told you that the FBI was involved. All he said was "enough for the FBI to consider it a serial-murder case". That doesn't really imply involvement.'

'Granted,' Owen accepted. 'And my next question was exactly that. I asked him if the FBI *was* involved. His answer was a laugh.'

'A laugh?' Hunter found that strange.

'Yep.'

'What sort of laugh?'

Owen looked back at Hunter.

'Was it a nervous laugh, a short laugh, a long laugh, a sarcastic laugh, a crazy-sounding laugh . . . ?'

Owen made a face at Hunter. 'OK, now you're really asking too much. It was a laugh, you know? Just a laugh that obviously meant "hell yeah, the FBI is involved".'

Hunter knew that he was indeed asking too much. That was the psychologist in him talking.

'OK,' he said. 'Did you ask him why he used the word *initially*?' Hunter asked.

'I didn't have to,' Owen said. 'Because what he actually

said was that *initially*, what would grab the public's attention would be the murders – a series of them, but the real story went much, much deeper than that.' Owen paused and, while regarding Hunter, rubbed his wrists again. 'So that's something that we'll need to talk about when it's my turn to ask the questions. I'll need to know what the real story behind these murders is.'

'Of course,' Hunter agreed with a perfectly straight face.

'Great,' Owen said before continuing. 'So the caller asked me again if I wanted the story or not. My reply was "Of course I do, but first, for credibility, could you tell me who you are?" He told me that who he was wasn't important. What was important was that I listened carefully.'

The caller obviously knew how to entice an ambitious reporter, Hunter thought.

Owen reached for his coffee, forgetting that the cup was empty.

'Do you think I could get another one?' he asked. 'It helps.'

'That can be arranged,' Hunter replied as he slightly turned his head in the direction of the two-way mirror to his left. 'Please continue.'

'Well, he told me to listen, so I did. He began by saying, "Note down this address," which I did. It was Timothy Davis's address. Then he said something on the lines of "You have two and a half hours to get there."'

Hunter stood till, hands tucked into his pockets, his undivided attention on Owen's account of events and his physiological reactions. Hunter noticed no pupil dilation, no skin flush and no alteration in his breathing pattern. If Owen Henderson was lying, he was an expert at it.

'He told me that when I got to the address,' Owen

continued, 'I was to enter the house. He told me that the front door would be open. He told me that I needed to go downstairs into the house's basement and that was where I would find what I was looking for.'

There was a knock on the door to the interrogation room.

'Yes,' Hunter called out.

The door was pushed open by the officer who'd been standing outside. He handed Hunter a steaming cup of coffee.

Hunter placed it on the metal table.

'Thank you,' Owen said, reaching for it. 'I do like the fast service in here.'

Hunter disregarded the joke.

'So what came next?' Hunter asked.

Owen spent a few seconds watching the steam from his cup dance in the air.

'He told me that I should take an analogue camera with me, not a digital one.'

'The caller *instructed* you to do that?'

'Yes, that's what I just said, isn't it? And before you ask, no, I don't know why he wanted me to take an analogue camera with me. I just did as I was told.'

Hunter thought about it for a second. 'OK. What else did he say?'

'That was basically it,' Owen confirmed. 'The caller reminded me that I had two and a half hours to get to the address he had given me, then the call disconnected.'

'Did you ask him why two and a half hours? What would happen if it took you longer than that?'

'I tried,' Owen replied. 'But he told me not to interrupt him. He told me that if I wanted the story, I had to follow his instructions. That was it.'

Hunter walked from one side of the room to the other.

'So what made you believe him?' he asked. 'What made you think that that wasn't a prank call? Because, let's be honest here, who would really receive a call like that and follow it through, especially when you're asked to drive to a different city?'

Owen shrugged. 'I'm a freelance investigative reporter. We basically depend on tips to lead us to good stories. I had nothing else on my agenda for the rest of the day. My choices were to ignore the call and carry on doing nothing, or take a gamble. Do you have any idea of how many good and great stories are lost every day by reporters, just because they chose to disregard a tip?'

'I can imagine,' Hunter agreed. 'But I can also imagine how many bogus trips are made by reporters every day based on worthless tips. There must've been something there. Something that tipped the balance the other way.'

'Probably,' Owen accepted. 'But if I had to put it down to anything, it would have to be a gut feeling. After so many years on the job, you sort of develop a sense for it – a tingle at the back of your neck – a tightening inside your stomach – it's hard to say, but you feel it and a voice inside your head goes "do not disregard this one".' Owen sat back on his chair once again. 'C'mon, don't tell me that you don't know what I'm talking about. You might not be an FBI agent, but you're certainly a cop. A detective, no doubt. You guys depend on your gut feeling more than anything else. And so do we.'

Hunter had no argument against that comment.

'So how long did it take you to get there?'

'I left Phoenix pretty much straight away,' Owen replied. 'At 2:31, to be precise. I know because I checked the dashboard clock as soon as I turned on my engine, and I kept on checking the time almost every minute. I got to where I parked my car – the next street along from the address I was given – with twenty-five minutes to spare, at 5:38.'

'Why?' Hunter asked. 'Why did you park on the next street along? And why didn't you have anything with you? I mean – no cellphone, no wallet, no identification whatsoever? All you had was a camera. Why?'

Owen rested the cup on his lap.

'Because I had no idea what I was getting into,' he said. 'If I drove up to the house, that could've alerted someone, inside or outside the house. Having no identification, no phone, no anything would give me deniability in case I needed it. It was a decision I made on the drive down here. And it paid off.' He had another sip of his coffee. 'You all haven't visited the crime scene yet, have you? You got out of your FBI plane and came straight here, didn't you?'

There was almost a smirk in Owen's tone of voice.

'Why?' Hunter asked.

Owen held the suspense deliberately.

'Because Special Agent Fisher told me that a neighbor saw me breaking into Mr. Davis's house earlier today,' he finally revealed. 'Has anybody talked to this neighbor?'

All Hunter could do was quickly glance at the two-way mirror. He'd had a suspicion about the neighbor story. That had been the reason why he had asked Agent Williams to find out if anyone had interviewed the neighbor or not.

'I thought not,' the freelance reporter continued. 'Mr. Davis's house is pretty hidden from sight. It sits behind a world of vegetation. There's no way a neighbor from the next house could've seen anyone even approaching the front door or windows, let alone seen anyone breaking in.'

'We'll check on that,' Hunter said, playing the whole incident down before quickly moving on. 'So what time would you say that you got to Mr. Davis's house? At around 5:40?'

'Yes,' Owen agreed. 'I'd say that's about right. Give or take a minute.'

'And why didn't you say anything when the police got there?' Hunter asked. 'Why didn't you identify yourself as a reporter? Why did you play the silent game, followed by all that cold-reading theatrical crap?'

Hunter was pretty sure he already knew the answer, but for the record he needed to have Owen say it on tape.

'I'm an investigative reporter,' Owen replied. 'That's what I do. The caller didn't give me that much information over the phone. When the police arrived, I made an on-the-spot decision. I knew they would take me in anyway. I knew that I had nothing on me that could identify me. Saying something wouldn't have helped, so I decided to say nothing at all. I figured that the FBI would turn up sooner rather than later. I also knew that there wasn't a chance in hell they would voluntarily tell me anything about what I had just seen down in that basement. If I was to get anything, I would have to trick it out of them.'

The smile he gave Hunter was full of confidence.

'I know that I can pretty much cold-read anyone I want. Before becoming a reporter, I made a living by reading Tarot cards, palms, auras, rocks ... whatever clients wanted read. I figured that cold-reading an FBI agent wouldn't be any different than your regular John Doe.' He shrugged casually. 'I was right.'

Hunter first wondered how angry Agent Fisher would be right about then inside that observation room. Then he wondered what sort of sarcastic comment Garcia would be making. He waited a few seconds. No gunshots. Maybe Garcia kept his comment to himself.

'Right at the end of the call,' Owen said. 'That was when it got even weirder.'

'In which way?'

Owen thought back to the exact wording the man had used over the phone. It took him a few seconds to be absolutely sure.

'He said that we lived in a false world – a plastic world where real, natural beauty was the purest and rarest of art forms. The rarer it was, the more valuable it became. He said that true beauty could not be fabricated or copied, and for that reason, it was becoming extinct. He also said that true beauty should live forever and that he was making sure of that. He finished by saying that he hoped that I would be able to understand and appreciate true art.'

Fifty-Eight

The Pima County's Office of Medical Examiner, which was inside the east quadrant of the University of Arizona in Tucson, was an impressive building, both in size and architecture. Its design was punctuated by modern, sharp lines, and the building was fronted by terracotta tiles and large, squared, mirrored windows; a whole generation away from the historic-looking Coroner's Office in Los Angeles.

A Hawaiian-looking attendant greeted everyone from behind the reception desk in the entrance lobby, a dimly lit room that even at that time of night was air-conditioned to a few degrees below pleasant.

'Y'all must be with the FBI, right?' the attendant said, as he came off the phone.

'We are indeed,' Agent Brandon replied, displaying his credentials. 'Dr. Morgan is expecting us.'

'Yes,' the attendant acknowledged with a nod. 'He's on his way.'

Less than ten seconds later, the metal swing doors to the right and just past the reception counter were pushed open by Dr. Morgan.

'Agent Brandon,' he said, coming up to the group. His voice

sounded fatigued. He was wearing a blue lab coat, with a matching surgical cap.

'Doctor,' Agent Brandon returned the greeting with a handshake. 'Thank you so much for your time and cooperation. We understand that after-hours examinations are a very unorthodox practice and we really appreciate your help.'

'It's not a problem at all,' the doctor replied. 'Just doing my job.' He turned to face the others.

Dr. Morgan was a slight man, bent a little at his shoulders, with gray, thinning hair. He wore dark-rimmed glasses perched far up the bridge of his nose, and he moved slowly, as if his weight was just slightly more than his legs could handle.

After all the respective introductions and handshakes, the group, minus Special Agent Brandon, followed Dr. Morgan past the reception counter and through a set of metal swing doors that led them into a wide corridor with strip lights on the ceiling and linoleum floors so clean and shiny, it made everyone's shoes either click or squeak loudly with every step.

As they entered the corridor, they were all greeted by a cold, antiseptic odor that lingered in the air and scratched the inside of the nostrils like sharp, angry claws. Hunter and Garcia both hated that smell. No matter how many times they had set foot inside a morgue, neither seemed to ever get used to it, and by the look on both FBI agents' faces, they weren't very fond of it either.

Hunter scratched his nose and did his best to breathe mainly through his mouth. Garcia did the same.

They turned right at the end of the corridor and came to another set of double doors with two small frosted-glass windows at eye height.

'Here we are,' Dr. Morgan said, pushing the doors open and guiding everyone into a spacious, but bitterly cold examination room. Inside it, the antiseptic smell from the corridor outside lost most of its strength as it was replaced by a faint scent of industrial soap.

The theater itself wasn't much different from the ones Hunter and Garcia were accustomed to back in Los Angeles. Large double sinks against a corner of the room, metal counters with a multitude of tools, white floors, white-tiled walls and so on. The layout might've differed, but the contents were pretty much the same.

The center of the room was taken by a stainless-steel examination table. The body on it was completely covered by a white sheet. Above the table, powerful halogen lights in a circular formation bathed the entire room in great brightness.

Dr. Morgan approached the body, taking slow, hesitant steps, as if each step got him a little closer to sadness.

Hunter, Garcia and both FBI agents followed him, positioning themselves to the right of the examination table. Dr. Morgan walked over to the other side and pulled back the sheet, revealing Timothy Davis's naked body. His eyes had sunk deeper into their sockets. His lips had lost all their fullness and his skin looked rubbery, almost non-human, but despite all that the peaceful and serene look that Hunter had identified on the victim's face when he first saw the crime-scene photos back in the SUV was still there. Just like the previous three victims, Hunter was certain that Timothy Davis hadn't died in pain. He hadn't suffered.

On his torso, the famous Y incision that started at the top of each shoulder, ran down the front of his chest and concluded at the lower point of the sternum had been stitched up with thick, black surgical thread. The board on the east wall showed the final weight of Timothy Davis's internal organs.

As the sheet was pulled back, Hunter immediately noticed the incredible discoloration of the skin.

'I've been a pathologist for thirty-one years,' the doctor began. 'And in those years I've seen things that truly beggar belief, but what we have here . . .' he shook his head, 'should belong in a Hollywood movie, not in real life.' He repositioned himself by the head of the table. 'If any of you could give me a hand in turning the body over, I'd like to start with what's visible.'

Hunter and Garcia stepped forward to help the doctor. Once the body had been flipped over, Dr. Morgan took a second observing his guests before speaking again.

'From the lack of surprise on everyone's faces, I'm guessing you were all expecting to see these carvings on the victim's back.'

Silence ruled the room for just a couple of seconds.

'Unfortunately,' Agent Fisher replied, her eyes still on the corpse on the table, 'this isn't this killer's first victim, Doctor. The carvings are just one of his signatures. So yes, we were expecting to see them.'

Once again, and now knowing what to look for, Agent Fisher tried to silently decipher the markings right there and then, but this time the lines across the victim's back seemed longer. The carvings seemed more compact and closer to each other, with fewer immediately identifiable letters. She tried to blink the tiredness and the headache away, but it didn't work. She would need a lot more time to figure out this one.

Instinctively, just like a competitive schoolkid, she peeked at Hunter. His eyes were slowly moving from one cut to another, the look on his face sturdy, full of focus.

'What are they, if I may ask?' Dr. Morgan tried his luck. 'Some sort of message?'

'Something like that,' Agent Fisher agreed.

'Do you know what it means?'

'Not yet, Doc.' She shook her head. 'The killer changes the message from one victim to another. They are never the same.'

Another quick peek at Hunter. His eyes had left Timothy Davis's body and had refocused on nothing at all. His expression had moved from deep concentration to deeply thoughtful. Agent Fisher knew he had figured out the message again.

How the hell can he do that so fast?

All of a sudden, the pensive look disappeared and Hunter blinked a couple of times before looking at Garcia.

Garcia had been Hunter's partner for long enough to be able to decode most of his partner's facial expressions. Without uttering a single word, Hunter had just told him that this made no sense.

Both FBI agents also noticed the peculiar look on Hunter's face and, though they were unsure of what it meant, they could tell that something wasn't quite right. But maintaining the secrecy of the investigation was still paramount, so neither of them asked the question. They knew that they would find out soon enough.

'If you've seen similar cuts before,' Dr. Morgan continued, 'then you probably already know that the killer uses a very sharp instrument to create them. Something just as sharp and precise as the medical scalpels we use in this facility. Every one of those markings was made by a single slashing movement.'

Both FBI agents gave the doctor a subdued head nod.

'So I'm sure you also know the killer's MO,' the doctor said. 'You know how he takes the life of his victims.'

'Asphyxiation by suffocation,' Agent Fisher replied. 'Yes, Doctor, we do know his MO.'

Dr. Morgan met the agent's stare with confusion.

'Asphyxiation?'

Even the air inside the room stood still.

'He wasn't asphyxiated?' Hunter asked.

'No, he wasn't,' the doctor replied.

'Are you sure?' The question came from Agent Fisher.

Dr. Morgan looked almost offended. 'Did you hear when I said that I've been a pathologist for thirty-one years? Yes, I'm very sure, Special Agent Fisher.'

'I'm sorry, Doc,' she said, feeling embarrassed. 'I didn't mean it as disrespect. I'm just truly surprised, plus I'm very tired.'

'It's OK,' Dr. Morgan said. 'Have all the previous victims died by suffocation?'

'They have,' Agent Fisher replied. 'Every single one of them.'

'Well.' The doctor indicated the carvings to Timothy Davis's back one more time. 'Since you've all seen something similar to this before, I can understand how this odd, "Zodiac killer" type of code failed to shock you, but if you were expecting this victim to have been asphyxiated, then you're all in for a huge surprise.'

Fifty-Nine

'I guess it's time for a break,' the man the FBI called The Surgeon said out loud, as he exited the highway, taking the slip road that led to a small truck stop with a faulty neon sign up front. He'd been driving solidly for the past three hours and he still had at least another three to go. He felt hungry, but not desperately so; what he really needed was a bathroom break and a coffee refill.

The truck-stop diner was reasonably sized – twelve seating booths, nine of them empty. Against the counter, the man counted ten rotating red bar stools. Their bases were fixed to the floor. A young couple, having their last bites of a hamburger meal, occupied stools number eight and nine, counting from the diner's entrance inwards. The old-fashioned, black-and-white checkered floor was spotlessly clean, which pleased the man. Outside, a Kenworth, a Peterbilt and a Volvo truck were parked side by side. The load of the Kenworth seemed to be about twice the size of the other two trucks.

As the man entered the diner, all three truck drivers, who were individually occupying booths one, two and three, curiously looked up from their food to check on the newest arrival. None of them paid the tall man more than a couple of seconds' attention.

As the man approached the counter, the short-haired, middle-aged waitress standing behind it smiled at him. It was a courteous and professional smile, the same greeting smile she gave every customer who walked through the diner's front doors. The red apron around her waist had a couple of finger marks on it – mustard, judging from their color. A pair of dark-framed glasses hung from her neck on a thin cord. Her nametag read *Nancy*.

'Hi there,' Nancy said. 'Please take any seat you like. I'll be right with you.'

Her voice, despite being warm and welcoming, sounded tired. Her face looked worn and defeated, which gave away the fact that she'd been working at the same place for way too long and by then had given up on any dreams that she once might've had when young.

'Thank you,' the man replied with a nod, and made his way to the last seating booth at the other end of the diner. He sat with his back against the wall, facing the entry door.

The menu was pretty much a box-standard, middle-of-the-road diner menu – burgers, sandwiches, hot dogs, mac-and-cheese, ribs and so on. The diner specialty was a meatball sandwich with the chef's own secret recipe sauce.

'So what can I get you?' Nancy asked. Her glasses were now perched high up on her nose and she held a notepad and pen in her hands.

'Do you have any meatball sandwiches left?'

Nancy looked back at the man and the courteous and professional smile returned to her lips.

'Darling, meatball sandwiches are our trademark. We have

them twenty-four seven, and they are always fresh, plus they really do taste amazing.'

'Sold,' the man replied. 'Can I also have a coffee refill in here, please?' He handed her a large travel coffee container.

'Of course.' Nancy took the container. 'Anything else? Our pecan pie is also quite fabulous.'

'Fabulous?'

'Indeed.'

'With that sales pitch, how can I refuse? I'll have a slice. And some still water, please.'

'Coming right up.'

It took Nancy less than five minutes to bring the man his order. She hadn't lied. The meatball sandwich was nothing less than spectacular. The pecan pie, truly fabulous. The coffee wasn't bad either.

The man ate like he had zero worries in life. When he was done, he paid his bill in cash and left Nancy a twenty-dollar tip. This time the smile she gave him wasn't her regular, rehearsed one.

As the man walked past the cash register, a clipping on the local bulletin board by the entrance door caught his eye. He paused and studied it for a long moment.

'No way,' he finally whispered to himself, adrenaline already refilling his veins. He almost threw his head back and let go of a loud, animated laugh, but he wasn't about to call any attention to himself.

The man took a quick peek over his right shoulder to see if anyone was looking. No one was. Nancy had gone back into the kitchen, the young couple at the counter had left minutes ago and the only truck driver left, the one in booth three, was too busy devouring his order of ribs.

'Hello, beautiful,' the man said, his eyes back on the clip-ping. In one quick movement, he ripped it from the board. As he placed the piece of paper in his pocket, he felt a strange kind of warmth envelop his entire body.

He now knew exactly who his next victim would be.

Sixty

Dr. Morgan's comment made everyone inside Autopsy Theater One look back at him with concern in their eyes.

'And what does that mean exactly, Doc?' Agent Fisher asked.

'Let me show you.'

The doctor nodded at Hunter and Garcia, requesting their help to once again flip the body over.

'When I first saw the body, just a few hours ago,' Dr. Morgan began, 'something struck me as odd straight away – the severe discoloration of the skin.' He indicated as he spoke. 'I know you have all seen more than your share of dead bodies and probably witnessed just as many autopsy examinations, so I'm sure I don't need to explain to anyone what post-mortem lividity is.'

The short silence that followed confirmed Dr. Morgan's assumption.

'Well,' he continued, 'Mr. Davis here showed none. No lividity whatsoever.'

'How is that possible?' Agent Williams asked.

Hunter's heart skipped a beat.

'Because there was no blood,' he said.

Garcia and both FBI agents looked at him.

'No blood where?' Agent Williams asked.

'In his body,' Hunter replied.

Dr. Morgan nodded. 'That's correct. The victim's body was practically drained of all its blood. His veins were dry. His brain resembled a lump of stale bread. I managed to obtain a small amount of blood from his heart, liver and kidneys, but I had to practically squeeze it out of them.'

The doctor used both hands to mimic a squeezing motion.

It made Agent Fisher cringe.

'The victim had no blood in his veins when he got here?' Agent Williams asked. He was starting to wonder if he was dreaming or not.

'That's correct,' Dr. Morgan reconfirmed.

'Wait a second,' Agent Fisher said, taking a step back from the examination table. 'Have I just been thrown into the Twilight Zone here? This isn't a vampire story, right?' She addressed the doctor. 'You're not going to tell me that he's got fang marks on his neck now, are you?' Reflexively her gaze traveled to Timothy Davis's neck.

'No,' Dr. Morgan replied. 'There are no fang marks on his neck. All we have is this small puncture and bruise to his left thigh and an even smaller one on the inside of his left arm.' He called everyone's attention to it.

Directly over the median-cubital vein on Timothy Davis's left arm, a small bruise could be seen.

'Was he a junkie?' Agent Fisher asked.

'I found no indications of it,' the doctor replied with a shake of the head. 'This bruise,' he said, referring to the one on the victim's left arm, 'is consistent with blood donation.'

'Wow, hold up,' Agent Fisher said, both hands up in the air. 'Are you trying to tell me that the killer managed to extract *all* of the victim's blood through a minuscule pinprick on his arm?'

'No, that's not what I'm telling you,' Dr. Morgan came back. 'What I said is that this tiny injury and bruising directly over the victim's median-cubital vein here is consistent with the kind of bruising one gets after donating blood, but I don't think this was the killer's extraction point.'

'Hold on a second,' Agent Williams said. 'When you say "all of the victim's blood", how much blood are we talking about here?'

'Judging by the victim's size,' Hunter commented, 'somewhere between five and six liters.'

'I'd say that that's a pretty good assessment,' Dr. Morgan agreed before addressing Agent Williams. 'You see, the estimated volume of blood in a human body is approximately seven to nine percent of its weight. In life, our victim would've weighed around one hundred and sixty pounds, give or take.'

'I'm sorry,' Agent Fisher interrupted the discussion. 'But I don't think that the volume of blood extracted, or how much the victim weighed when alive, is of any real relevance to us. What I want to understand is – how is this possible? You said so yourself, Doc – the blood could not have been extracted through his veins.' She faced the body on the table one more time. 'There are no cuts to his body. His throat hasn't been slit open. His wrists haven't been touched. How did the killer drain him of *all* his blood?'

'Well, there are two problems with your statement, Special Agent Fisher,' Dr. Morgan countered, his tone of voice tenacious.

She half-glared at him.

'One,' the doctor began. 'The volume of blood extracted

is of extreme relevance to us because that was the cause of death, not asphyxiation. Once a body loses over forty percent of its blood volume,' he explained, 'which in medical terms is known as a class four hemorrhage, it's pretty much game over. The strain on the body's circulatory system becomes too great to survive. The heart will no longer be able to maintain blood pressure and circulation. Major organs will fail and the victim will slip into a comatose state, preceding death. That condition is known as hypovolemic shock.'

'No suffering,' Hunter said.

'Indeed,' Dr. Morgan agreed. 'The worst the victim would've felt would've been a discomfort in his chest as the loss of blood triggered his heart to work overtime to try to get oxygen to tissues. With that, his blood pressure would've dropped very quickly, taking him into the comatose state I mentioned.'

Dr. Morgan filled his lungs with air before re-addressing Agent Fisher.

'And the second problem with your statement is – I didn't say that the blood could not have been extracted through his veins. What I said was that I don't believe that this pinprick wound to the victim's left arm was the killer's extraction point, which leads us to the only other injury the body has sustained.' He indicated the puncture-like wound on Timothy Davis's left thigh.

'What?' Agent Fisher looked even more puzzled, but this time she wasn't alone. Garcia also looked a little lost.

'Your confusion is completely understandable,' Dr. Morgan said in a tone that carried no arrogance, no deprecation. 'I was quite lost myself, but I had to deal with the facts – the victim's body showed only two injuries – the pinprick to his arm and the puncture to his leg, nothing else. I just couldn't see a way where whoever did this, whoever drained the victim of his entire volume of blood, could've done it by inserting a sixteen-gauge needle into his arm. That left me with one option – the wound to his leg.'

'OK, but how?' Agent Williams this time. His attention had gone back to the injury on Timothy Davis's leg. 'How could the killer have sucked all the blood out of the victim's body through a small incision in his leg?'

'That's what got me as well,' the doctor admitted. 'In all my years as a pathologist, I've never seen anything quite like this. If the victim had been decapitated and left upside down, his body still wouldn't be this drained of blood.'

'So what's the answer?' Agent Fisher queried. 'How did the killer manage to do this through a hole in his leg?'

'Very cleverly, and that's the reason I've taken so long with this autopsy. I've been racking my brain to understand how this could be possible. I had to dig through his leg wound and inside his body for some sort of clue . . . something to point me in the right direction.'

'And did you find anything?'

'I did.' Dr. Morgan readjusted his glasses on his nose and gestured for everyone to follow him to the other side of the autopsy theater, where a human-body diagram hung from the wall. 'But I need you to understand that this isn't a certainty, by any means. What this is, is an educated guess taking into account the wound we have here and what I found during the post-mortem examination. So please stay with me here a moment, OK?'

Everyone's eyes settled on the diagram. It depicted the main veins and arteries in the human body.

'We'll have to wait for toxicology to identify the agent,' Dr. Morgan began. 'But for the killer to be able to work without the victim putting up a fight, he would've had to have sedated him. Toxicology will tell us what was used.'

Everyone nodded.

'Now for what I've found,' the doctor continued. 'The puncture in his leg was very carefully and expertly made to tap directly into the victim's left external iliac vein.' He indicated the vein on the diagram. 'Now here comes the very clever and equally difficult part, but if I've got this right the killer inserted something like a four-and-a-half catheter through the leg puncture and into the victim's external iliac vein. That is essentially a large connecting vein that connects the femoral veins to the common iliac veins. At the level of the fifth lumbar vertebra the left and right common iliac veins come together and become the abdominal vena cava. As the vein approaches the heart it becomes the inferior vena cava.'

On the diagram that hung from the wall, it all looked like one long vein, traveling from halfway down the leg all the way up to the heart.

'To put it simply,' Dr. Morgan clarified, 'this is basically a massive vein that travels to and from the heart. It's similar to a major city road that crosses several neighborhoods. Though the road remains the same, as it crosses from neighborhood to neighborhood, it acquires different names, that's all.' Dr. Morgan's hands moved away from the diagram. 'Are you all familiar with the system of inferior vena cava?'

Hunter nodded once; everyone else shook their heads.

Dr. Morgan looked back at him curiously.

'I read a lot, Doc.'

'OK,' the doctor replied, before addressing the rest of the

group. 'The inferior vena cava brings de-oxygenated blood from the lower body regions – legs, back, abdomen and pelvis – to the right atrium of the heart, and that's why the killer would've had to use a long catheter. He very slowly and carefully guided the catheter through the victim's vein – or veins, as it changes name like I explained – and into the victim's heart.'

As the doctor explained his theory, Garcia and Agent Fisher began to slowly cringe.

'At first,' Dr. Morgan carried on, 'I thought that the killer would've needed some sort of pump to pump the blood out of the victim's body.'

'Didn't he?' Agent Fisher asked.

'Well yes, and that's the real clever thing about all this.'

'He used the most natural pump of them all,' Hunter said. 'He used the victim's own heart.'

'What?'

Dr. Morgan nodded, looking impressed.

'Without a doubt a very clever, think-out-of-the-box idea,' he said. 'As I've explained, as the victim's volume of blood decreased, the heart would've begun pumping faster, sending more and more blood into the catheter.'

'But as soon as the blood volume dropped to under sixty per cent,' Garcia said, 'as you've also explained, game over. The heart would stop pumping. So how did he get the rest of the blood out of the body?'

'Great question, and the only way I can think of is by doing it manually.' He directed the group back to the autopsy table and used gestures to explain. 'First aid. As if he was trying to resuscitate the body. Both hands on the chest, over the heart, and then you pump. One, two, three, four . . . To get the blood from the victim's arms, I guess that the killer would've had to lift them up one by one and just squeeze the blood out of them and back into the heart. A few more pumps and voilà – one completely dried-of-blood victim.'

'That's absolutely insane,' Agent Fisher said, shaking her head.

'Perhaps,' the doctor agreed. 'But nevertheless effective and seriously clever.'

Sixty-One

'The markings to his back,' Agent Fisher asked Hunter as soon as they stepped outside the main building. 'You deciphered them, didn't you? You did it in there.'

Hunter paused at the top of the first flight of stairs and looked back at her with fatigued eyes. 'I think I did, yes.'

'You *think*?'

'It's been a long day,' Hunter clarified. 'I'm tired, my brain is tired, my eyes are tired.'

'Nevertheless, while in there, you did make out the Latin phrase that the killer carved into the victim's back, right?'

Hunter's silence was a resounding 'Yes'.

'Do you think you might've gotten it wrong? Made a mistake?'

This time his silence meant the opposite of his first. Agent Fisher heard them both loud and clear.

'OK, so what was it? What was the Latin phrase the killer used this time?'

Hunter looked around. Despite them being alone, he didn't think that the top of the stairs at the Pima County's Office of Medical Examiner in Tucson was the best place for them to have that conversation.

'Shall we maybe talk in the car?' he suggested.

'Yes, I think that would be best,' Agent Williams agreed.

As they all got back into the SUV, Agent Brandon looked like he was about to tell the group something, but he never got the chance.

'Could I have a quick look at that?' Hunter asked Agent Williams, referring to the large envelope Dr. Morgan had handed him inside Autopsy Theater One. From it, Hunter retrieved one of the Polaroid photographs that showed the carvings to Timothy Davis's back.

Agent Fisher scooted over toward Hunter to study the image, but gave up within seconds. If Hunter had already connected the lines and letters to create the new Latin phrase the killer had carved into the back of his fourth victim, what was the point in racking her brain to put that sick puzzle together? She certainly could do without the stress, especially considering the nuclear headache she'd been carrying around with her since she stepped out of that private jet.

'So what does this one say, Robert?' This time the question came from Garcia, who was sitting to Hunter's left.

Hunter scratched his chin before looking at Agent Fisher. As he pronounced the Latin words, he indicated on the Polaroid with his index finger, as if asking her to double-check he hadn't made a mistake.

'*Pulchritudo habitantem in interius.*'

Agent Fisher's eyes followed Hunter's finger like a duckling following its mother. The lines connected perfectly to form the letters. The letters connected perfectly to form each of the four words.

Once he showed it to her, it seemed so easy.

'That seems to be correct, yes,' she finally agreed.

'And in English that means what?' Garcia asked. 'Beauty ... where this time?'

'Resides on the inside?' Agent Fisher phrased her reply as a question while her gaze settled on Hunter. This time, she was the one asking for confirmation.

He nodded. '*Pulchritudo habitantem in interius* translates as "beauty resides – or beauty lives, or beauty is – on the inside". The exact wording may vary, but I guess the meaning is pretty much the same.'

'Beauty lives on the inside?' Agent Williams repeated the phrase, adding to it a bucket of doubt.

Hunter faced Agent Brandon, who was sitting in the driver's seat. 'How are we doing on that film we retrieved from Owen Henderson's camera? Anything?'

'Yeah,' Agent Brandon replied, handing Hunter a new envelope. 'It's all done. I went to pick it up while you guys were in there. I just haven't had the time to hand it over.'

Hunter tore open the envelope and pulled out a thick bunch of colored eight- by ten-inch photographs.

Everyone leaned toward him as he began flipping through the photos.

The first fourteen images were all full-body shots of Timothy Davis lying on the hospital-style bed in the basement of his house. The pictures were taken from a variety of angles and distances. Hunter didn't linger on any of them for too long.

The next eleven photos were close-up shots of the victim's face and the odd wound to his left leg. Again, Hunter flipped through those seemingly without too much concern, until he got to the last five photographs.

The impression that everyone got with the final five shots

was that Owen Henderson had started going through the motions of documenting the room where the body had been found. He had taken a photo of each of the four walls.

It looked like Timothy Davis had made his basement room into a shrine to his late wife, Ronda.

The first photo was of the wall to the left of the entrance door. Pushed up against it was an antique-looking, white dressing table with a matching tri-fold vanity mirror on it. Hanging from the corners of the mirror were a couple of gold necklaces. Both of them had crucifixes as pendants. Fixed to the leftmost corner of the mirror was a four- by five-inch colored photograph of Timothy and his wife on their wedding day. He was standing behind her with his arms around her waist. Their smiles seemed brighter than the sun up in the sky above them. At the opposite end of the mirror was another photograph of the couple, this time showing Timothy and Ronda as they cut their wedding cake. Their faces were the definition of happiness.

On the dressing table, a few items had been meticulously arranged, almost to the point of OCD. There was a hairbrush, a comb, a small jewelry box, a chrome eyelash curler, two nail files and two clear glass jars. The first one held a multitude of makeup pencils in several different colors and shades. The second one was overflowing with makeup brushes of all different shapes and sizes. At the center of the dressing table, pushed up against the base of the mirror, were three half-full perfume bottles.

Hunter flipped to the next photograph. It showed the basement room's far wall. Four female garments hung from hooks that had been fixed to it. A thin, see-through protective plastic cover kept all four items from getting dusty. The first garment, on the far left, was Ronda's wedding dress. The second and third items were two very elegant long evening gowns. The last item was a severely worn blue jeans jacket with two small rips on the right sleeve and a missing front pocket. Next to each of those items was a framed photograph of Ronda Davis wearing them.

Hunter moved on to the next photo. It showed the wall to the right of the entrance door. It was covered from floor to ceiling in more framed photographs of Timothy and Ronda at various locations – the beach, the mountains, dinner parties, their home ... everywhere. Some of them were from a long time ago, when the two of them were still in college. A few individual ones showed them as kids.

The next photo was of the fourth and last wall, the one with the entrance door. Pushed up against it, to the right of the door, was a wooden console table. On it, a single portrait photograph of Ronda, a blue vase with a bouquet of red roses and a small open jewelry box with just one item inside it – her wedding ring.

The last photograph in the whole set showed the ceiling. It was painted white, just like the walls. At the center of it, a flat chrome lamp with three spotlights supplied the small room with more than enough light. A few water infiltration spots could be seen against two of the corners, which had caused some mold to grow around them.

'Is this it?' Agent Fisher asked Agent Brandon.

'That's all we've got, yes. The film in the camera was a thirty-six-exposure roll. The last six frames were blank.'

Hunter flipped through those last five photographs one more time, his brain working overtime to try to piece things together.

'*Beauty lives on the inside*,' Garcia said. 'So how does that link to the crime scene as a canvas or work of art? Beauty lives inside of what? Inside that room? Is the killer now trying to be philosophical, saying that beauty lives inside us all, we just need to find it, so we can understand his work? Does he consider blood a beautiful thing? What . . . ?'

'Maybe the killer is talking about the room,' Agent Fisher said, nodding at the photos. 'He could be talking about what the room symbolizes.'

'What the room symbolizes?' Garcia asked.

'The undying love between the victim and his late wife.' Agent Fisher's tone was calm, totally lacking annoyance. 'Just look at these pictures. Once you're inside that room, you're surrounded by that love. There's no way you can escape it. Love and sadness reside side by side in there. It practically drips from those walls. Now think about it for a moment – not only murdering Mr. Davis inside that room, but also leaving his body there, surrounded by this "shrine" he created for his wife . . . the shrine he created for their love – that is probably what the killer considers a work of art. Once again, I think his Latin phrase is talking about the entire composition here, like a tribute to love – a love that after Mr. Davis's wife passed away, lived only on the inside: on the inside of that room – on the inside of him. Like the blood that ran through his veins. That's why he killed him by draining his blood. It's all, just like before, symbolism. And you might also be correct about what you suggested – "beauty lives inside us all".'

Garcia's eyebrows lifted.

'If the killer is using this murder to symbolize love,' Agent Fisher explained, 'then it's true that love lives inside us all, just like the blood that runs through our veins.'

'What about the victim selection?' Hunter asked.

Both agents looked back at him curiously.

'Why did the killer pick these four people as his victims?'

Agents Fisher and Williams were back at the same question they had been asking themselves in their new office.

'There has to have been a reason why the killer knocked on those four doors,' Hunter concluded.

'Sure there has,' Agent Fisher replied. 'But it doesn't mean that we'll be able to understand it or even explain it. Maybe in the killer's eyes these four victims were the ones who better suited his work. Remember, he's not after them as people; he's after them as objects – the best match for the big picture, for whatever sadistic art piece he's creating. That's why he doesn't hurt them. So yes, there probably was something quite specific about the victims that drove the killer to them, but that's something we might never understand. We might never be able to explain it because it could be something that is specific only to the killer and no one else. No matter how hard we try, we might never see things through his distorted eyes.'

Hunter knew that that was very true. Catching murderers didn't necessarily mean that they would understand the way they thought, their motives, their reasoning . . .

'How about the traveling?' Garcia asked. 'Even if the killer had a specific type of person in mind, let's say, one who best matched whatever crazy art piece he wanted to create, like you suggested, why pick them from four different cities . . . four different states?'

Agent Fisher went quiet.

'The killer's first murder was committed in Detroit,' Garcia added. 'A city with a population of almost 700,000 people. I'm sure he would've had no problems finding an eighty-four-year-old ex-janitor who also lived in Detroit for his second outing, or a young and attractive model for his third, or an African American male for his fourth. Why go from Michigan to Kansas, to California and now Arizona? What was so special about these four people that made him cross state lines just to get to them?'

'Maybe it's not about them being special,' Agent Fisher suggested. 'Maybe traveling is just part of what he does as a job. He could be a sports scout, or a pharmaceutical salesman, or something along those lines. Something that forces him to hop from city to city. He would then use the convenience of his job to choose his victims, picking them from different locations, knowing full well that that fact alone would make finding him a hell of a lot harder.'

Garcia thought about it for a moment, but his brain was too tired and everything was still too fresh for him to be able to think logically. In the space of less than twenty-four hours they had gone from a single victim back in LA, to four, spread over four different states. Absolutely nothing made sense at the moment and the craziest of all theories was the one that best matched the facts they had.

Hunter stayed quiet, but he couldn't help thinking that the murders seemed too elaborate for the killer to be picking his victims due to the convenience of a traveling job.

All of a sudden Agent Fisher's eyes widened, as a new thought exploded inside her head.

'Passenger manifests,' she said, addressing Agent Williams. 'If the killer really is traveling because of the job he does, then there's a chance he flies to wherever he's got to go, including the murder cities. If that's the case, his name will be on passenger manifests. We need to get in touch with every airport in

Detroit, Wichita, LA and Tucson, maybe even Phoenix. Let's get a team checking every airline's passenger manifests and cross-checking them all with each other. We've got to search at least three weeks each side of the murder date, inclusively. If we're lucky, we might get a name repeating itself flying in and out of all these four cities.'

'It's a hell of a long shot,' Agent Williams agreed. 'But it's definitely worth a try. I'll get a team on it first thing in the morning.'

Sixty-Two

Agent Brandon had gotten everyone a room at the Lodge on the Desert, a hacienda-style boutique hotel situated on five acres of land, right in mid-town Tucson. The place was as stunning as it was grand, featuring as its backdrop nothing less than the imposing Santa Catalina Mountains.

'Damn,' Garcia whispered as he and Hunter stepped out of the car and collected their bags. 'The FBI does have it a lot better than we do. Just look at this place. If the LAPD were banking this trip, we'd probably be sleeping in the car.'

'May I carry your bag for you, sir?' a young porter asked in a tone that sounded way too cheerful for that time of the morning.

Garcia smiled back at him. 'You certainly may.'

'And you, sir?' the porter addressed Hunter.

'I'm OK,' Hunter replied, slinging his bag over his right shoulder. 'It's not a heavy bag.'

Check-in was done quickly and smoothly, thanks to the three large capital letters that graced the top of the reservation page on the receptionist's computer screen. Maybe those letters were also the reason why the five best rooms available were allocated to them.

'It's 4:22 a.m.' Agent Williams said as he collected his key. 'I'd say that we all need to get at least four hours' sleep. So how about we all meet down at the breakfast room at eight thirty?'

Everyone agreed.

Hunter's accommodation was number 221, a spacious Old El Paso decorated room, just past a cactus garden in the hotel's west wing.

As he closed the door behind him and allowed his bag to slip from his shoulder to the floor, Hunter felt exhaustion take hold of every corner of his body like an untreatable illness. Right then he knew that nothing, not even his insomnia, would be able to keep him from falling asleep. Not this time. But despite how tired he felt, he decided to have a quick shower before bed. He was sure that he could still smell the stomach-churning scent from the morgue on his skin.

Hunter undressed by the plush and very comfortable-looking king-sized bed, before making his way into the bathroom.

'Wow,' he whispered under his breath as he paused by the door. He was unsure of what had impressed him more – the Mexican Talavera tiles that no doubt brought a lot of color into the bathroom, or its sheer size – about equal to his entire living room. The soft and relaxing scent of primrose and lily of the valley that loitered in the air was also a very nice touch.

Inside the shower enclosure, Hunter closed his eyes, leaned forward, rested his forehead against the colorful-tiled wall and allowed the strong, lukewarm water jet to massage the tense muscles on his neck, shoulders and upper back. If there was such a thing as heaven, this had to be its wet version.

The warm water relaxed him, but still his brain wouldn't fully disconnect. How could it, really, after the events of the past twenty-four hours? There was so much he needed to process that for the first time in his career, Hunter didn't really have a clue where to start. What should he analyze first? The murders themselves? The victims? The killer's MO? The killer's signatures? The messages? The crime scenes? The locations? The bizarre theory they had come up with? All of it at once?

Hunter could feel his head starting to spin inside his skull, so he decided to use the little strength he still had left to push all those thoughts to one side. He concentrated on scrubbing his whole body until he couldn't smell death on him anymore. By the time he turned off the water, his naturally tanned skin had acquired a light pink tint and his fingertips had wrinkled.

Back in the bedroom, without concerning himself with drying his hair, Hunter collapsed onto the bed. The sensation he got as his skin came into contact with the luxury white linen was that he had slumped onto a fluffy cloud. His eyelids didn't even flutter. They simply came down like heavy shutters at the end of a very long day. Less than a minute later he was asleep.

Sixty-Three

At exactly 8:25 a.m., Hunter stepped outside his room. As he did, Garcia rounded the corridor corner.

'Wow,' Garcia said. 'How is this for perfect timing, huh?'

Hunter closed the door behind him.

'I thought you'd be in the breakfast room already,' he said.

'In different circumstances, I would be,' Garcia agreed. 'But I really don't feel like facing those two by myself this early in the morning. I'm not a masochist, you know?'

Hunter chuckled. 'Yes, I guess I see your point. I don't think Special Agent Fisher likes you very much, Carlos.'

'Me?' Garcia's surprised face was almost sincere. 'Rubbish. Everyone likes me. I'm charming, good-looking, smart, and loads of fun to be around. What's there not to like?' He lifted his arms up to about chest height, spread them wide and used both hands to point at himself. 'Plus, I'm Brazilian. Everyone likes Brazilian people because we can samba.'

'Can *you* samba?'

'Can I hell. But that's beside the point. You're hungry, right?'

'Starving,' Hunter admitted. He didn't even have to ask. Despite how skinny Garcia was, he was always hungry.

'So,' Garcia asked as they made their way down the

corridor. 'How big and colorful are these rooms? Did you see the size of that bathroom?'

'Bigger than my apartment.'

Garcia laughed. 'That wouldn't be too hard, Robert. You live in a shoebox.'

'I like where I live.'

'Of course you do.'

Hunter and Garcia spotted Special Agents Fisher and Williams as soon as they entered the hotel's restaurant breakfast room. The two agents were sitting at a table by the floor-to-ceiling window on the east wall. They both wore their standard, FBI-issued sunglasses and dark suits. Agent Fisher's hair was loose and still wet from her morning shower.

Garcia held fast on a laugh. 'Are they both wearing sunglasses . . . inside? They are, aren't they?'

From the door, Hunter greeted them with a nod before making his way toward their table.

'Do we really need to sit with them?' Garcia whispered.

'I thought you said everyone liked you,' Hunter replied.

'And they do,' Garcia confirmed. 'But that doesn't mean that I have to like them back.'

'Maybe you can samba your way into their hearts,' Hunter said.

Garcia shook his head disapprovingly. 'Robert, you're brilliant at a lot of things, but making jokes on the spot isn't one of them. You'd best leave them jokes to me.'

'I thought that was a pretty good effort.'

Garcia wasn't the only one who wasn't in the mood for a reunion that early in the morning. As soon as Agent Fisher saw Hunter and Garcia at the entrance to the breakfast room, she leaned over toward her partner.

'I told you we should've picked a table at the back,' she murmured. 'Hidden from everyone. Now we're going to have to share ours.'

'I thought you liked Detective Hunter,' Agent Williams whispered back.

'And I do. I've got absolutely nothing against Robert. It's his partner who gets on my nerves.'

'Oh, it's Robert now, is it?'

She shrugged at him. 'Whatever.'

Despite keeping their voices to a whisper and turning their heads a little sideways as they spoke, Hunter had no problems reading their lips.

'Good morning,' Hunter said, coming up to their table.

'Morning,' both agents replied in unison.

'I thought you would've preferred a table at the back, hidden from everyone.' Hunter couldn't resist.

Both agents looked back at him, wondering.

'In view of all the new developments,' Agent Fisher announced even before Hunter and Garcia had taken the seats across the table from them, 'Director Kennedy has authorized a press conference. Special Agent Brandon is organizing it as we speak. A very condensed press release will be sent to all the major news channels this afternoon. At the press conference, we'll be answering a very select number of questions and that's all. I will not allow it to turn into a media circus. The whole thing won't take more than ten minutes, fifteen tops.'

'Hi, welcome to the Lodge on the Desert hotel,' a brunette waitress in her early twenties said, approaching their table as soon as Hunter and Garcia took their seats. The smile on her lips was fake, but still terribly welcoming. 'What can I get you this morning?'

'What's the biggest breakfast you have?' Garcia asked, returning the smile.

'That would be the Lodge on the Desert Arizona full breakfast,' the waitress replied. 'It includes—'

'It's OK, darling.' Garcia stopped her. 'I'll have it anyway. Whatever is in it, I'll eat it. Just bring it over.'

'How would you like your eggs done?' the waitress asked.

'Over easy, please,' Garcia replied.

'And your steak?'

Garcia did a double take. 'There's a steak?' He sounded truly surprised.

'Twelve ounces,' the waitress confirmed, studying Garcia's frame. 'It's a pretty large dish. Most people aren't able to finish it all. If you prefer I can ask the chef to hold the steak, or you could go for a less substantial dish.'

'Nope, steak is just fine. Bring it on.' Garcia smiled. 'As for finishing it all – challenge accepted. I'll have my steak medium rare, please.'

Hunter decided to skip the cooked breakfast and stick with the choices on the buffet. Agent Fisher and Agent Williams followed his example. All four of them ordered black coffees.

'The press release,' Hunter said to Agent Fisher, once the waitress had moved away from their table. 'What is it going to say?'

'Not much,' she replied with a headshake. 'But so we don't get a nasty surprise through a newspaper, I will have to mention everything that that goddamn freelance reporter knows. I won't leave him any trump cards. He and his cold-reading party trick can go screw themselves. Because of him, I'll have to mention the approximate timeframe of when the murders started, number of victims and so on, but I will not disclose any names. Not now. I also won't mention anything about the carvings, the killer's signatures, or his MO, and I will certainly not mention anything about the killer believing he's making art out of his victims.'

As if on cue, Special Agent Brandon walked through the breakfast-room doors and approached their table.

'Good morning, everyone,' he said, taking a seat next to Agent Williams. He looked and sounded a lot more rested than everybody else at that table put together. 'The press conference has been scheduled for today at nineteen hundred hours,' he announced. 'We'll be using the conference room here at this hotel. It's spacious enough.'

'That's fine,' Agent Fisher said.

Agent Brandon turned to face Hunter.

'And you were right about Mr. Davis's neighbor – Mr. Christopher Pendleton – the person who was supposed to have made the 911 call. He didn't. Nor was he supposed to be on vacation until the day after tomorrow. Mr. Pendleton runs his own law firm in downtown Tucson. He said that he only got home yesterday at around nine in the evening and was as surprised as anyone else to see all those police cars around his neighbor's house. When I knocked on his door this morning, about an hour ago, he told me that that was the first time anybody had asked him anything.'

'Does he live alone?' Garcia asked. 'Wife? Kids? Was anybody at home during the day yesterday?'

'He's divorced,' Agent Brandon replied. 'Two kids, both in college. The house is empty the whole day, most days.'

'Was there any sign of a break-in?' Garcia again.

'None whatsoever. The house is also alarmed. There was no breach.'

'Did Tucson PD confirm phone numbers after the 911 call?' Agent Fisher asked, annoyance already back in her voice.

'Apparently not,' Agent Brandon confirmed.

'So the killer made the 911 call,' Agent Williams concluded.

'That's the most likely scenario,' Agent Brandon agreed.

'Why?' Agent Fisher again. 'Why would the killer first call that shitty reporter, get him to the house and then call 911? Where's the sense in that?'

'He did it because he wants the press conference to happen,' Hunter said, his memory quickly connecting several facts.

'What?' Agent Fisher looked unsure, though she wasn't the only one. 'The killer wants the press conference to happen? I don't follow.'

'Well,' Hunter began. 'We all know that the killer was the one who called Owen Henderson back in Phoenix yesterday afternoon, right?' He didn't wait for a reply. 'We're now also pretty sure that the killer was the one who made the 911 call. He added the bullshit story about the neighbor coming back early from his holiday because it would give the call a lot more credibility, also giving us the impression that we had gotten lucky. Now think back to yesterday. Owen Henderson told us that he arrived at Mr. Davis's house at 5:40 in the afternoon, give or take a minute.' Hunter faced Agent Brandon. 'You told us that the 911 call came in at exactly 5:42 p.m., isn't that right?'

'Yes, that's correct,' the agent confirmed.

Hunter's gaze rounded the table and he shrugged.

'Now, does anyone here think that was a coincidence?'

Sixty-Four

The girl opened her eyes and slowly rolled over on the bed to have a look at her alarm clock, though she didn't really have to. Like always, she woke up just as the sun began infusing its first light into the dense night sky.

For a moment, the girl didn't move, her eyes fixed on the dim red glow of the digital timekeeper on her bedside table. Then, as the stupor of sleep finally began to dissipate, her lips stretched into a timid smile.

'It's Friday,' she whispered to herself.

With those words, the timid smile gained confidence before the girl rolled over again, this time to face the ceiling.

'It's Friday,' she told herself one more time, her voice a lot more animated than a second ago.

'Yes it is. Yes it is. It's Friday.'

Her words came out dancing to a silly melody that she had made up on the spot. As she sang her improvised verse, her hips shook from side to side and her head bobbed up and down to her own crazy rhythm.

The reason behind all that happiness was simple – today she would see him again, just like she had last Friday, and the Friday before last, and the Friday before that one.

They always met at the old park, the one behind the ugly, disused school. No one played there anymore. No one walked their dogs or rode their bicycles there anymore either. With the school closure just a few years back, the whole area was slowly forgotten, which suited them just fine.

'No one can know about our meetings, OK?' he had told the girl the first time they had met, four weeks ago. 'They won't let us meet if they find out.'

'Yes, I know,' she had replied. 'My mother really wouldn't like that.'

With every meeting they got a little more comfortable with each other, and that was another reason for the girl's barely containable happiness. Last Friday they'd held hands for the first time. It had made her feel like she had never felt before – warm inside, goose bumps on the outside, happy all over. She really hoped that he would hold her hand again today.

That thought alone brought a new smile to the girl's lips and a new, more animated rhythm to her improvised song. Her arms punched the air in front of her one at a time in a syncopated movement.

'OK, OK,' she told herself, bringing her enthusiasm down several notches. Before she could see him again, she had to go to school, and before that she had to get ready.

She turned and checked the bedside clock one last time. Definitely time to get up.

She swung her feet over the bed and sat at its edge. Right then, an idea came to her – before leaving for school, why not sneak into her mother's bedroom and hide one of her perfume bottles in her school bag? Her mother wouldn't mind, would she? She had so many of them. Plus, she wasn't stealing it; she was just borrowing it. She would return it when she got back.

Maybe she could even borrow a pair of earrings – those shiny ones her mother only wore on special occasions. Those were beautiful. Everybody loved them, and if she wore them, he would love them too, wouldn't he?

'Yes, of course he would.'

Maybe he would even love her.

Sixty-Five

The reality of what Hunter had just suggested hit everyone square in the face.

'There's only one way the killer could've placed that call at the exact time Owen Henderson stepped into Timothy Davis's house,' Hunter said.

'He was still there,' Agent Williams said.

Hunter sat back on his chair.

'I don't think that he was still inside the house,' he said. 'Too risky, but he was certainly close enough to have seen Owen Henderson arriving. Once he was sure that Owen had entered the house, he made the 911 call, probably also knowing that Tucson PD's response time would be under five minutes.'

'Wait a second,' Agent Fisher interrupted. 'If the killer really waited for the reporter to enter Mr. Davis's house before making the 911 call, then I think you might be wrong, Robert. You said that you think that the killer did all this because he wanted the press conference to happen, but I don't think so. Let's try to look at this logically. If the killer called 911 as soon as he saw the reporter entering the house, obviously it was because he wanted the reporter to be picked up by the police. If he wanted the reporter to be picked up by the police, it was because he wanted the reporter to talk to us. Clearly he knew that we would be interrogating anyone found at the crime scene. So, if he wanted the reporter to talk to us, it was because he wanted the reporter to try to get as much information out of us as he possibly could, which was exactly what happened.'

'Yes and no,' Hunter replied.

Agent Fisher stared at Hunter blankly.

'Yes,' Hunter explained. 'The killer wanted Owen Henderson to be picked up by the police and he wanted him to talk to us, but no, the intention wasn't for him to get information out of us. The cold-reading idea came from Owen Henderson himself, not the killer. There's no way the killer could've predicted how the interrogation would play out. Owen Henderson wanted to get information from us because he's a reporter and that's what they do. The killer's intention was to make *us* aware that now an ambitious reporter knows about the murders.'

'What that means,' Garcia jumped in, 'like I've mentioned before, is that now there's no way we can keep this whole thing under wraps anymore – if we don't say anything, Owen Henderson will. To put it simply, Agent Fisher, the killer has just forced us to call a press conference.'

Agent Fisher considered everything for a long moment.

'So you think that this killer is your typical, textbook, attention-seeking serial killer?' she asked. 'He did all this because he wants to be on the news?'

'Nothing typical about him,' Garcia countered. 'But why not? From the level of emotional detachment this killer has shown toward other human beings, even animals, there's no doubt that he is a high-grade psychopath and, as such, I'm sure he truly believes that he is indeed superior to everyone else around him ... in every sense.' Garcia paused, allowing his words to sink in for an instant. 'People like fame, Agent Fisher. They like to be remembered. Revered if possible. It's a fact. To some, it doesn't even matter if that fame is good or bad. Fame and notoriety can both be very powerful motivators, especially for people who believe that they are much more than what they really are.'

It was Garcia's turn to hold Agent Fisher down with a serious stare.

'You said so yourself, remember?' he continued. 'Certain killers want not only us, but the whole world to know how great they really are.'

'He's got a point, Erica,' Agent Williams commented.

'Is it really hard to believe that a killer who goes through all this trouble and preparation with every single one of his murders,' Garcia added, 'would want recognition for his work? Think about it – the professional removal of body parts, the Latin clues, the completely crazy way in which he drained one of his victims of *all* his blood, the canvas-like staging of the crime scenes, everything. He's showing off. What good is creating works of art if no one is able to appreciate them? This guy wants to be recognized for his ... "talent".'

While trying to organize their thoughts, all three FBI agents regarded the two detectives sitting opposite them.

'All right, that's a valid argument,' Agent Fisher finally accepted. 'But if this killer is after notoriety, why not go straight to the press with everything? We already agreed that he probably photographs his crime scenes for his own pleasure, for his "gallery of the dead" or whatever, so why not send a copy of everything to a newspaper or a TV station? That would guarantee him prime-time viewing, wouldn't it? Why go through such an elaborate plan, sending a reporter to the crime scene so he could get arrested . . . so we could talk to him . . . and so on? Doesn't all this sound too nuts to anyone?'

'Once again,' Hunter replied. 'Credibility.'

'Excuse me?'

'If he contacts the press himself,' Hunter explained, 'his story would lack credibility – he could be just another psycho looking for attention. Whatever photos he sends in could've been created using image-editing software. But even if they want to believe his story, any newspaper or TV station would have to confirm it either with the FBI or local police departments before printing or broadcasting anything. The story could very easily be played down by law-enforcement agencies and instead of prime time he would get a bottom corner on the fifteenth page.'

'But if the Federal Bureau of Investigation breaks the story in a national press conference,' Garcia said, jumping into Hunter's train of thought, 'he gets the credibility, the prime time and the ego boost he's after because this would be you, the FBI, admitting that you're struggling with the case.'

Garcia's words seemed to enrage Agent Fisher.

'Well,' she countered, 'the FBI certainly won't be admitting struggling with anything. Not in this press conference. I will not inflate this freak's ego in any way, shape or form. Actually, for this conference, we think that it would be best if the two of you stayed away from the cameras and let us do all the talking. After all, this is primarily an FBI investigation.'

Garcia fixed his ponytail while consulting Hunter with a simple look. Not that he needed to. Hunter hated being in front of cameras.

'Sure,' Hunter agreed. 'That's absolutely fine by us.'

Sixty-Six

After two more bathroom breaks and a total of almost seven hours behind the wheel, the man whom the FBI had initially called The Surgeon finally parked his car on his driveway. It had been a terribly long and awfully exhausting trip, but by all means worth every second, every drop of sweat, every bated breath. His latest piece of work had been exquisite. He wasn't shy to admit it. If he could actually put a price on it, he would have to say that Timothy Davis had been his most valuable item yet – inspirational.

The man couldn't help wondering how astounded the police, the FBI, even the coroner would be once the true extent of his ingenuity and intelligence was revealed through the autopsy examination. A catheter threaded directly through the inferior vena cava? Simply magnificent. Truly the work of a superior mind. No doubt that now they would have to at least recognize his genius, even if they didn't understand it.

The man loved the little 'wits' game he'd been playing. He was proud of how perfectly puzzling, how deceiving, how ambiguous the clues he'd left at every scene were, and they had to be. In a case like this, he had no doubt that the FBI would've turned to their NCAVC's Behavioral Analysis

Unit – the topmost elite – the best of the best when it came to puzzle solving. But were they, really? Had they actually figured anything out yet? Would they ever understand the grandeur of his vision, or see the importance of his work?

Despite how much the man enjoyed the game he'd created, he would be lying if he didn't admit that he was somewhat disappointed with the 'best of the best'. So far it had pretty much been a one-sided affair. By now, he had expected to see something on the news, or to hear something on the radio, or to at least read something in a newspaper or on the internet, but after over two months, he hadn't read a word or heard a sound about his work anywhere. Even after Los Angeles.

True, the man had never really cared much for cats. In his view they were animals without a purpose. All they ever did was eat and sleep. They were also disloyal, unashamedly befriending anyone who offered them food. But that wasn't reason enough to kill them – the man acknowledged that. No, back in LA the man had placed the cat inside the freezer simply for the shock effect. He believed that that would have rubbed up the police and the FBI the wrong way. It was simply the logic of this crazy world – take the life of a human being and people might get angry – take the life of a domestic animal and people will get utterly outraged.

But that wasn't all. Also solely for the shock effect, the man had practically painted the walls, the furniture, the entire room in blood – and still, even after Los Angeles, not a word about his work anywhere. But things were about to change. The man had made sure of it. Bringing the freelance reporter into the action had been another simple but cunning idea.

'There's no more denying it now,' he said out loud while staring into his own eyes in the rearview mirror.

But his trip to Arizona had proven even more fruitful than he had expected, because by sheer luck, in a truck stop in the middle of shit-kickers-country USA, he had found her.

Just a girl.

Just a young girl.

But perfect in every sense.

From the moment he'd laid eyes on her photo, pinned to that dirty bulletin board inside that greasy diner, he knew his collection would be getting a new piece. Now that he was back home, all he had to do was research her, devise a brand-new plan and then set it in motion, and he just couldn't wait to get started.

Sixty-Seven

Twenty-eight minutes. That had been how long it had taken Agent Brandon to drive from their hotel in downtown Tucson to Timothy Davis's house in Catalina Foothills. By most standards the house was certainly impressive, but still modest when compared to the other four on East Miraval Place.

Owen Henderson hadn't lied. Timothy Davis's property was surrounded by thick, overgrown vegetation. There was no way anyone could have seen into the house or grounds from a neighboring window, never mind witness someone breaking into the place.

On the driveway, two white forensics vans were blocking a silver Buick Encore. Leaning against one of the vans, a forensics agent, dressed up in a blue Tyvek coverall, was just finishing a cigarette. Her charcoal hair was bunched up into a messy bun at the top of her head. She too looked like she'd been up for most of the night. As Agent Brandon parked the black SUV on the road outside, the forensics agent stubbed out her cigarette, cleared a couple of loose hair strands from her face and walked back into the house.

Hunter, Garcia and all three FBI agents stepped out of the SUV, signed the crime-scene manifest and followed the footsteps of the forensics agent, rounding the driveway to the house's front porch, but as they got to it, Hunter paused, turned around and regarded the area before him.

'Something wrong?' Agent Fisher asked, noticing the intrigued look on Hunter's face.

Hunter's gaze moved left, in the direction they had come from. From where he was standing, he couldn't see the road, the entrance to the driveway, or any of the vehicles parked on it.

'Have forensics checked the live fence?' he asked Agent Brandon, indicating the thick, desert-like shrubs that surrounded the house.

'The fence?' Agent Brandon asked in reply. 'You mean like – in the bushes?'

'Yes, *in* them.'

'I know they've processed the outside of the house, including the driveway, but I don't think they've gone as far as checking *in* the live fence. Why?'

'I think it would be a good idea if they did,' Hunter replied before explaining. 'The killer placed the 911 call pretty much the second Owen Henderson entered this house.' He pointed to the driveway. 'The problem is, this front porch cannot be seen from the road, the driveway, or any of the neighboring houses.' He turned to face the live fence. 'But to make that "second-perfect" call, the killer would've needed eyes on this door.' He shrugged. 'Where would you have hidden?'

'I'll be damned,' Agent Fisher said, her eyes, just like everyone else's, slowly running the length of the live fence in front of them. The thick bushes would have provided anyone with a perfect hiding place, while allowing them a clear view of the house's front door.

'I'll get them to start on it straight away,' Agent Brandon said.

Once they entered the house, they lost no time exploring any of the rooms, moving straight down into the basement and the crime scene. They'd been correct in the impression they'd had from the photographs Owen Henderson had taken – the entire space had indeed been transformed into a shrine to Timothy Davis's late wife, Ronda. What no one could've guessed from the photos was that the nauseating smell of death that inevitably accompanied most crime scenes didn't linger in that room. Instead, a light lavender scent graced the air, as if every object in that basement had been infused with Ronda Davis's favorite perfume – a fact that somehow seemed to add an extra layer of sadness to an already heartbreaking scene.

'I hate to admit it,' Garcia said, coming up to Hunter, who had spent the last ten minutes studying the photograph-covered wall to the right of the entrance door. 'But Agent Fisher was right. This room slowly swallows you into this choking combination of love and sadness, as if both feelings really did reside side by side on these walls. It elates you and rips you apart at the same time.' Garcia looked around, as if he were searching for something. 'It's like some strange soul-draining quicksand. The longer you stay in here, the more divided you get.'

'And do you think that was done on purpose?' Hunter asked. 'I mean, do you think that the killer knew about this room beforehand? This . . . love and sadness sanctuary?'

Garcia pondered the thought for a minute. 'If we're correct about this whole "crime scene as a canvas" theory, if the meaning behind the killer's Latin phrase used here – "beauty lives on the inside" – really refers to the beauty that lived inside

Timothy Davis, maybe even inside this room, like Agent Fisher suggested, then he had to have known about it. No way this could've happened by chance, Robert.'

'That's the problem, Carlos,' Hunter said, his eyes still on the photographs that hung from the wall. 'How could he have known?'

Sixty-Eight

Agents Fisher and Williams had just joined Hunter and Garcia by the photograph-covered wall when Agent Brandon, who had stayed upstairs giving the forensics team a whole new set of instructions, walked into the room.

'You were right,' he said, his voice animated, his stare moving straight to Hunter. 'It was worth checking with blood-donation centers around town. Timothy Davis did donate blood recently. In fact, he did it yesterday at a Red Cross blood bank in central Tucson at around eleven in the morning. After his donation, he was seen talking to a tall man in the snacks room at the blood center. The information we got is that they were seen leaving together, and that was the last time Mr. Davis was seen alive.'

Agent Fisher first looked at Hunter as if asking, 'When did you instruct anyone to check with blood-donation centers?' before her gaze moved over to Agent Brandon with a new unspoken question: 'And why wasn't I informed about this before?' But the agent managed to swallow her pride and the question she finally asked wasn't a bickering one.

'Please tell me that this blood bank downtown has a CCTV system in place?'

'They do,' Agent Brandon replied, but didn't give anyone a chance to rejoice. 'But unfortunately, it isn't working.'

'What? Are you joking?' Agent Fisher looked like she was about to punch someone. 'How convenient.'

'No,' Agent Brandon clarified. 'The system hasn't worked for months. It didn't just all of a sudden stop working yesterday.'

'Months?' Agent Fisher queried, her voice moving up the irritation scale at least a couple of notches. 'And they never cared to fix it?'

'We're talking about the Red Cross here, Erica.' Hunter tried to calm her down. 'A volunteer-based movement where the budget is tight at the best of times. Fixing a CCTV system in a blood bank in Tucson probably isn't very high on their priority list.'

'Fine,' she said, throwing her hands up in the air. 'CCTV or no CCTV, we still need the names of everyone on duty at the blood bank yesterday morning, together with whoever else was inside that snacks room at that particular time. We need to talk to all of them, and we need to do that now.'

From his pocket, Agent Brandon produced a notepad.

'There were three volunteer nurses on duty at the center yesterday. A fourth volunteer took care of the snacks room. According to their records, there could've been as many as three other people in the snacks room at that time, but that hasn't been confirmed yet. The only other person we're sure was in the snacks room with Mr. Davis is the tall stranger, whom the blood center seems to have no record of.'

'No record?' Agent Fisher again.

Agent Brandon shook his head. 'Despite him being in the snacks room, which in theory you can only gain access to once you donate blood, no one can find him in yesterday's donor's list. This tall stranger doesn't seem to be in their system.'

'OK, so how the hell did he get into the snacks room?'

'Maybe the retina scan and the voice-signature security systems were also down,' Garcia joked, though his voice sounded serious. 'It's a Red Cross blood bank, Agent Fisher, not Fort Knox. The room was full of cookies and juice, not gold bars. He probably strolled in through the front door. Nobody would really scrutinize his presence there, would they?'

Before the agent could reply, Garcia turned and addressed Agent Brandon. 'What else have you got?'

'Well, all four volunteers who were on duty yesterday are back on duty today. All we need to do to talk to them is drop by the blood bank. And,' Agent Brandon informed everyone, but his nod once again went Hunter's way, 'forensics has already started going through the live fence outside. If you're right, with a bit of luck, we might get something.'

'Is the blood bank open?' Agent Williams asked.

Agent Brandon checked his watch. 'Yes, they opened a little while ago.'

'OK, so let's go,' Agent Fisher said, motioning toward the door.

Hunter would have liked to spend a lot more time inside that basement room, but preferably undisturbed and alone. Under the circumstances, there was nothing else he could do there.

Garcia didn't have to be asked twice. He, for one, was glad to get out.

Once the group was outside, Agent Fisher's cellphone rang inside her pocket. As she reached for it, Garcia, who was directly behind her, caught a glimpse of the caller's photo on the display screen. The image showed the smiling face of a teenage girl with Down syndrome.

'Oh!' Agent Fisher said, doing her best to hide the concern in her eyes as she addressed the group. 'You all go right ahead. I'll catch up with everyone in just a minute. OK?'

She brought the phone to her ear and though she kept her voice as quiet as she could, as she moved away from everyone, Garcia overheard her first few words to the caller.

'Hi, darling, is everything all right?'

Those words were flooding with worry.

As the remaining four rounded the house, moving back toward the driveway, Garcia looked at Agent Williams.

'Cruella DeVille has a daughter?' he asked, sincerely surprised.

The agent nodded. 'She does, yes. Heather. She's fourteen years old and as sweet as sweet can be. Funny, too. You'd fall in love with her if you met her.'

'Wow. I had no idea. She doesn't look like a mother, if you know what I mean.'

'Agent Fisher isn't a bad person, Detective Garcia. She's just—'

'Rude and a massive pain in the butt?' Garcia beat Agent Williams to the punch. 'And c'mon, call me Carlos. We're like old friends now. We've known each other for . . .' He looked at his watch. 'Almost twenty-four hours.'

Agent Williams smiled. 'Sure, Carlos, she can be rude at times, but I was about to use the word "dedicated". She's a very strong woman, who's been through one hell of a lot in the last few years.' He shook his head to indicate that that was all he was prepared to reveal. 'This job and her daughter are pretty much all she's got left, so every day, when she wakes up and grabs those credentials, she gives it one hundred and ten percent. Never less. Yes, to a lot of people she might come across as arrogant, intense, pushy, rude, and no doubt a pain in the butt sometimes, but the *one* thing you can always bet on is that she *will* get the job done. And she'll always have your back. No matter what situation you might find yourself in, if you ever need her, she'll always be there for you.'

They'd been sitting inside the SUV for less than ten seconds when Agent Fisher rejoined them. The only seat left was the one next to Garcia.

'Is everything all right?' he asked.

Agent Fisher had to do a double take. She had detected absolutely no sarcasm in the detective's voice. In fact, she could swear that there was concern in his words.

'Yes, everything is fine, thank you,' she replied, her tone a little skeptical.

Garcia smiled and once again Agent Fisher picked up no cynicism in his action. For some reason that prompted her to reveal a little bit more.

'I haven't been home for almost two weeks now. My daughter just wanted to hear my voice.'

'That's really nice,' Garcia said, his words sincere. 'So where is home, DC?'

Agent Fisher chuckled. 'Not for any amount of money. No, I'm also in California. Not that far from LA, actually.'

'Is that so?'

Agent Fisher nodded. 'Fresno. When I heard that I was flying to LA yesterday, I had high hopes of maybe making it back home, even if only for a night. Unfortunately, The Surgeon had other plans.' The agent's harsh look softened a touch. 'Have you got any kids?'

'No,' Garcia replied. 'My wife and I haven't decided if we really want kids or not.'

Hunter and Agent Williams were both sitting back on their seats, quite enjoying the scene playing out before them. Agent Brandon was also relishing the unusually cordial exchange between the two, but it didn't last very long. Just a couple of seconds later Agent Fisher was back to her normal self.

'Why aren't we moving yet?' she asked Agent Brandon as their eyes met in the rearview mirror. 'Go, go, go. We've got no time to lose here.'

Agent Brandon put the car into drive and hit the gas.

Sixty-Nine

Their trip to the Red Cross blood-donation center in down-town Tucson proved to be immensely disappointing. All three nurses on duty could clearly remember Timothy Davis – the very sweet African American gentleman who insisted on call-ing everyone ma'am – but none of them had any recollection of a tall stranger being at the blood center at around the same time Mr. Davis was there.

Inside the snacks room they found the same twenty-one-year-old volunteer who'd been tasked with monitoring that room the day before. He was the only one who could vaguely remember this mysterious tall man, but he was unable to give anyone any real details on the man's appearance. All the six-foot kid with acne-ridden cheeks could remember was that the man was quite tall, about three to four inches taller than him. He remembered that the man was wearing a baseball cap, but he couldn't be sure of its color. He also couldn't remember the man's attire. The kid never noticed the man's eyes; the man was wearing aviator sunglasses.

'Aviator sunglasses?' Agent Fisher asked.

'That's right,' the kid replied. 'A little bit like yours, though not as expensive-looking.'

'Did he talk to you at all?' Hunter asked. 'Say hello, good-bye, anything?'

'No, the man never spoke to me.'

'Do people usually?' Agent Fisher again. 'Speak to you, I mean.'

'Most of them say at least "hello" or "goodbye". Some ask if they can take a few cookies with them or what have you.'

'And you didn't find that strange?' the agent insisted. 'A man in a baseball cap and sunglasses . . . indoors, who didn't say a word to you?'

Garcia's eyebrows arched at the agent's comment about sunglasses indoors.

'I volunteer here whenever I can,' the kid explained. His voice was beginning to sound a little fearful. 'I was in an accident three years ago, and if it hadn't been for someone else's blood, I wouldn't be here now. So I donate blood every twelve weeks or so, and volunteer whenever possible. I know this might sound funny, but you do get to see a lot of people coming in here in dark shades, baseball caps and long coats. It's not really an odd practice. Some people are also very shy. If they talk to me, I always talk back. Try to make them feel as comfortable as I can. If they don't, I just leave them be.'

'And this tall man in a baseball cap and shades,' Agent Fisher said, showing the kid a portrait photograph of Timothy Davis. 'You remember seeing him talking to this man?'

The kid looked at it for a long instant. 'Yeah, for sure.' He nodded. 'They were talking by the cookie table over there.' He indicated the last of the three tables in the room.

'Do you remember seeing him coming into the room?' Hunter asked, pointing at the same door they had all come in from.

The kid took a moment.

'Actually no, I don't,' he finally replied. 'I don't remember seeing him coming in through that door at all, but he could've come in while I went for a bathroom break, or to pick up some more cookies and juice.'

Hunter turned and faced the other door, the one across the room from them.

'How about that door?' he asked. 'Is that door always open?'

'The exit door?' The kid nodded. 'Most of the time, yeah. It helps cool the room, you know? Many donors also like to take their drinks outside to escape how stuffy it can get in here sometimes. Some just step outside for a cigarette. Some people will spend a lot longer in here than they will donating blood.' He shrugged. 'As far as I know that door is only pulled to when it rains.'

'Where does it lead to?' Garcia asked.

'Just a back alley, really.'

Hunter faced Agent Fisher.

'There's your answer,' he said.

'To what?' she countered.

'To how our subject got in here. I had a quick chat with the girl at the reception desk,' Hunter explained. 'Contrary to everyone else at this center, she's not a volunteer. She's actually employed by the Red Cross. She deals with all the bookings and schedules and so on ... computer stuff. She's also the receptionist, which means that she's the one who greets everyone who walks through that front door, sits them down and makes sure that they have stuck to the blood-donation guidelines. She has to speak with everyone who enters this center.'

'And she doesn't remember our tall mysterious man.' Garcia could see where Hunter was going with his explanation.

'No, she doesn't,' Hunter said. 'She clearly remembers Mr. Davis. She said that it would be hard not to, but she does not remember any tall man coming in yesterday morning, whatsoever. My guess is that our subject simply sneaked in here through the back door. He knew nobody would really question him. He probably even had some sort of false bandaging around his arm just so he could blend in.'

'His arm was bandaged,' the kid confirmed. 'I do remember that.'

Hunter just made a face.

'Good call, Detective,' Agent Brandon said to Hunter, as the group finally left the Red Cross blood-donation center. 'Forensics seems to have found the spot where the killer hid in the live fence at Mr. Davis's house, just like you suggested. So far they've managed to retrieve a partial shoeprint, which is already on its way to our lab in Quantico. They are still checking for any fibers that might've lodged themselves in the bushes. With some luck, this might be our first real break.'

Seventy

To keep the number of reporters down to a minimum, one of the Bureau's favorite tricks when it came to press conferences was quite a simple one: issue the official press release, which would reveal the time and location of the press conference, as late as possible. The less time the press had to organize themselves the better. In the case of The Surgeon's investigation, the FBI's NCAVC decided to give the media only two hours' notice, which wasn't much, considering that the press conference was to take place in a boutique hotel in Tucson, Arizona.

The trick didn't work.

News of a serial killer roaming the streets of any US city was enough to get crime reporters jumping for joy. The news of a serial killer practically putting the entire country under siege was almost a once-in-a-lifetime event.

By 6:55 p.m., the conference room inside the Lodge on the Desert Hotel was packed to capacity. Broadcasting cameras and microphones seemed to be absolutely everywhere. Photographers and reporters were literally falling over each other for a better position even before anyone took the stage. Speculation ran around the room like kids out of control, with an army of voices interweaving to form a totally incomprehensible web of sound.

'Wow,' Garcia said, cringing at the noise as he and Hunter blended into the crowd by perching themselves between two cameramen right at the back of the room. 'This place is louder than a Sunday fish-market. Smells almost as bad, too.'

'Don't worry,' Hunter replied. 'This won't take long.'

At exactly 7:00 p.m., Agents Fisher and Williams entered the conference room. As Agent Fisher stepped up to the microphone podium on the small stage, Sunday fish-market turned into Sunday church.

'Good evening, everyone,' Agent Fisher began. She wore black straight-legged pants with a white satin blouse under a black blazer. Her hair was loose, falling down to her shoulders in ringlets. Her makeup was subtle and professional, but still elegant. Her posture was impeccable, oozing self-confidence. One didn't need to be a detective to know that she'd done this before.

'Hubba, hubba,' Hunter heard the cameraman to his right whisper to his friend. 'Is she an agent or a model? I wouldn't mind getting me a piece of that.'

'You know she carries handcuffs and a gun, right?' his friend replied.

'Hell yeah. Sign me up.'

'I'm Special Agent Erica Fisher with the FBI's Behavioral Analysis Unit,' the agent continued, before glancing at her partner. 'And this is Special Agent Larry Williams.'

Agent Williams greeted the room with a simple nod.

'I'd like to begin by saying that we're not here to make any sort of statement.' Agent Fisher's voice was placid but firm, full of authority. 'That was made in the press release you received this afternoon. What we're here to do is answer a few questions.'

She immediately lifted her hand, halting the loud murmur that threatened to engulf the room.

'But there are ground rules.'

She paused and let her eyes travel the room. Five seconds later they were back to absolute silence.

'This is a high-profile, ongoing investigation, which means that I will *not* discuss any avenues we are pursuing at the moment, so please don't even bother asking. We have very limited time to spare, so right now I'm prepared to answer questions for ten minutes only. That's all. Do *not* projectile vomit your questions at me. You want to ask me something, put your hand up like you were back in school. If I pick you, you are a lucky one. If I don't, don't start shouting your question over other people's voices. If this even hints at turning into a circus, this conference is over. I hope I've made myself clear.'

'OK, I take it back about wanting me some of that,' Hunter once again heard the cameraman say to his friend. 'She sounds like a nasty piece of work.'

Garcia didn't even try to hide his smile.

'All right,' Agent Fisher said from the stage. 'Your ten minutes start now.'

Hands flew up in the air. Most of them were holding microphones emblazoned with insignias – CNN, Fox, NBC, CBS, CNBC, Court TV, and even some international channels like the BBC, 9Live, France4, and several others.

Agent Fisher's gaze crawled around the room. She didn't recognize any of the faces.

'Please,' she pointed to an attractive dark-haired reporter who was sitting on the fourth row from the front.

'Thank you.' The reporter stood up and identified herself before asking her question. 'Lindsay Cooper, CBS News. In the FBI press release you say that this killer has claimed four lives so far. How certain are you of that number? And why can't the FBI disclose any of the victims' names at this moment?'

A Mexican 'yeah' wave circled the room.

Agent Fisher once again waited for the place to quiet down.

'Two questions in one,' she replied. 'You no doubt have experience in this.'

The room laughed.

'To answer your first question,' Agent Fisher carried on. 'We are one hundred percent sure of the number of victims so far. The reason we are not disclosing any of their names at the moment is because we have been asked by their families not to. We are respecting that wish.'

The reporter tried to tag her own question, but Agent Fisher quickly moved on to someone else.

'You,' she said, pointing at a tall and slim man, wearing a baseball cap and thick, round glasses. 'Red shirt, right at the back. What's your question?'

The man stood up. 'Alan Curry, representing the *LA Times*.' He pushed his glasses up the bridge of his nose. In his right hand he had a printout of the FBI's press release. 'Two months, four victims, four different states – other than that, your press release hasn't told us much else. My question is simple – how do you expect not to provoke countrywide panic with this kind of information? You haven't really told us anything about this killer. We don't know who to look out for, or what to look out for. Is this guy going after victims who are old, young, male, female, gay, straight, black, white, tall, short, blonde, brunette ... what? The four victims, has the killer picked them out of the streets, bars, clubs, colleges, parks, their own houses . . . where? Should we all be concerned about going out at night, or walking our dogs early in the morning? Did the victims share any characteristics that we should know about? Did the killer torture his victims? Is he likely to be timid and socially awkward? Are there any indications that he is an intelligent person, or the opposite?'

The man paused and looked around. All eyes were on him.

'C'mon, Special Agent Fisher,' he continued, his tone becoming a little somber. 'You need to give us a little bit more than this joke of a press release.' He raised the printout in his hand. 'You are the FBI's Behavioral Analysis Unit. When it comes to serial killers, you're supposed to be the utmost authority, not only in the country, but in the world. You study them, you collect them, you pick their brains apart, don't you? Two months . . . you must've had a team of criminal psychologists working non-stop to come up with some sort of profile on this guy, so where is it? What should we look out for? If this press release is all you can give us after over eight weeks of investigation, then it can only be for one reason – the utmost authority in the country doesn't have a clue where it stands, does it? There's no profile on this killer because you simply cannot come up with one.'

Agent Fisher immediately put up her hand, anticipating the explosion of voices that was about to come her way. But it never happened. Instead, every pair of eyes that a second ago had been fixed on the tall and slim man, darted toward the agent, but no one said a word. The only sound that could be heard inside the room was the incessant clicking of cameras.

'You're wrong,' Agent Fisher replied. Her voice still solid. Her self-confidence undaunted. 'Yes, we do have a very extensive profile on this killer, Mr. Curry, and the reason why we can't share it with any of you is because if we do, it will be all over the news and the papers by tomorrow, and guess what? Serial killers also watch the news. They also read the papers.' She paused so the whole room could absorb her words.

'If we reveal our findings on this killer now, it will give him a chance to alter his methods, to adapt, to evade the net that is already in place and quickly closing around him. We can't risk that, but I can tell you this, Mr. Curry.' Agent Fisher looked straight into the eyes of the reporter. 'This killer isn't intelligent, like you've suggested, he isn't smart, or talented, or creative, or gifted, or artistic, or anything else that he might think he is. No, he's just another pathetic loser. Another psychopath. Someone who probably blames society for his problems. Someone who, to make up for his many inadequacies, decided to go around playing God. But his days are counted, you can bet on that. We have figured him out and—'

'What the hell is she doing?' Garcia asked Hunter, his eyes growing wider with every word Agent Fisher uttered. 'It looks like she's trying to piss him off, and I'm not talking about the reporter here.'

'That's exactly what she's doing,' Hunter agreed.

Garcia listened for a few more seconds. 'That's not a smart move, is it?'

'No,' Hunter replied, transfixed by what Agent Fisher was doing on the stage. 'Angering this killer is not a smart move at all.'

Seventy-One

The man had been working at his desk for the past four hours. He had created ten different sketches – ten different plans. All he had to do now was decide which one he liked best, which one he could implement with most ease, but there was no real rush. After all, he had just added a brand-new item to his collection and he deserved a much-needed rest.

The man put down his pen, sat back on his chair and let his head drop back. He was tired and he could feel the muscles around his neck beginning to stiffen up, but more than that, he was hungry and he was thirsty.

In the kitchen, he switched on the small TV on the counter before pouring himself a large glass of unsweetened ice-tea. As he returned the glass jug to the fridge, an image on the small screen caught his attention. He used the remote control to turn the volume up.

Two crazy gunmen, armed with a high-powered, fully automatic assault weapon, had entered a rock concert in Barcelona, Spain, and opened fire on the crowd. The gunmen had managed to kill one hundred and fifteen people and injure another thirty-nine before they were both finally shot down by Spanish police. The attack lasted around forty-five minutes. The report included several shocking cellphone images shot from inside the venue by the fans themselves.

'This world is going completely nuts,' the man commented as he made himself a pastrami and cheese sandwich and divided it into four practically millimeter-perfect triangles.

While the news played out, showing more amateur images together with concert survivors' interviews, the man set a place at the six-seater table inside his kitchen. Drinks coaster, plate mat, napkin, cutlery and finally salt and pepper mills. That was always the order, and all of it always flawlessly aligned.

Like always, when eating a sandwich, the man started with the topmost triangle and worked his way clockwise. After he finished each triangle, which he would do with exactly two bites, the man would have two sips of his drink before returning it to the coaster. He would then dab the corners of his mouth with the napkin and return it to the right side of the plate mat before realigning everything once again. The process would repeat itself until his meal was finished.

As the man took his first bite of the last sandwich triangle, the news on his TV changed and the report about the atrocities in Spain was followed by a national bulletin.

'On a much more domestic note,' the TV anchorman announced, 'the FBI has held a press conference this evening concerning their investigation into the murders of four people. All of them victims of the same predator – a serial killer who has been roaming our streets for over two months now.'

The man stopped halfway through chewing.

'This is what Special Agent Erica Fisher had to say,' the news anchor continued.

The man put down his food and turned the volume up.

The report cut to the press conference held in Tucson,

which had already been edited by the station's news team. The segment started with Agent Fisher replying to the *LA Times* reporter's question, though his question was never actually shown.

After the agent's statement, the report cut to the news anchor once again.

'The FBI reassured the public that they are already closing in on the killer.'

For a moment the man didn't breathe. He didn't hear the end of the report either, all he could hear was the words that kept playing back, over and over in his head – *this killer isn't intelligent, he isn't smart, or talented, or creative, or gifted, or artistic, or anything else that he might think he is. No, he's just another pathetic loser. Someone who probably blames society for his problems. Someone who, to make up for his many inadequacies, decided to go around playing God.*

'Ha, ha, ha, ha, ha, ha.'

The man's laugh started slowly, like a locomotive leaving the platform. It was a quiet, reserved laugh, but as it gained momentum, it also picked up strength, echoing around the kitchen, with the man's shoulders bouncing up and down in an odd rhythm.

All of a sudden, the man went dead quiet. If anyone could see his eyes, they would've seen the focus, the determination in them.

'OK,' he said out loud, his head nodding a couple of times at the TV. 'You want to play? Let's play. How about a new game this time? We can call it "No More Mr. Merciful".'

Seventy-Two

'Hey,' Tracy Adams said, as she answered her phone after the second ring. 'Are you all right?'

'Yes, I'm fine,' Hunter replied. 'How are you?'

'I'm OK. Thank you.'

'I really wanted to apologize for having to cancel on you at such short notice . . . *again*.'

'But you've already apologized, remember?'

Like always, Tracy's voice was soft, her tone understanding, but Hunter did pick up a hint of disappointment in her pitch.

'Yes, but through a text message, which I would also like to apologize for.' Hunter's voice, on the other hand, sounded tired. 'It's been quite crazy over here and I just couldn't find the time to call, at least not for longer than a minute. I didn't want to call and then all of a sudden have to put the phone down on you because I had to rush off somewhere. Given the circumstances, a text message was my best option and even that had to be done in snatches.'

'It's all right, Robert. I know it's not your fault.'

Hunter got the feeling that what Tracy really wanted to say was: *It's all right, Robert. I'm used to it. It's not the first time you've cancelled on me, is it?*

Maybe it was the fact that they were in different cities, different states. Maybe it was the fact that distance was different from time in the way it affected people, but right then, Hunter missed her.

'I'll make it up to you when I get back to LA. I promise. I was thinking that maybe I could take you out for dinner somewhere. What do you think?'

Tracy went into a thoughtful silence, one Hunter could hardly blame her for. When he didn't cancel on her, he would usually cut their date short by having to rush out somewhere after a phone call.

'When do you get back, do you know?' she asked.

'I think we'll fly back tomorrow morning, or afternoon at the latest. There's nothing else we can do over here, really.'

Tracy went quiet again, but this time only for an instant. 'Wait a second, Robert, where are you again?'

Hunter had never told her where he had flown off to.

'Arizona.'

'In Tucson?'

Tracy's tone changed and Hunter couldn't tell if she was surprised, concerned, or both.

'That's correct,' he replied. 'How do you know?'

'I just caught the end of a news report on CNN – an FBI press conference in Tucson, Arizona, about a serial killer they've been chasing for some time now.'

'A little over two months,' Hunter said.

'Four victims?'

'Yes.'

'So *that's* the joint operation you were telling me about.'

'Yes.'

'This killer has been active for over two months?'

'Yes.'

Despite her curiosity, Tracy saw no point in pushing Hunter for answers she knew he would never give her. Instead, she brought the subject back to their date.

'How about Monday evening?' she asked.

The sudden change in topic did catch Hunter unprepared.

'I'm sorry?'

'Our dinner date,' Tracy explained with a half-laugh. 'I'm away for the weekend. I'm attending a conference in Sacramento until Sunday evening. I think I told you about it; I'm not sure. Anyway, I'll be back in LA by Monday morning. If it suits you, we can go for dinner on Monday evening.'

'Yes, that suits me just fine,' Hunter replied, a smile now also on his lips. 'Monday evening sounds great.'

Seventy-Three

Hunter, Garcia and both FBI agents did fly back to Los Angeles the next morning and the rest of the weekend went by in a blur of checking, cross-checking and re-checking.

By Monday morning, the IT experts in Quantico were still trying to breach Timothy Davis's laptop and desktop security, with absolutely no advance whatsoever. A separate team of analysts, also back in Quantico, had spent the last few days going over a monumental mountain of emails, texts and social-media messages sent to Linda Parker, but with over a quarter of a million followers all around the world, and having to backtrack everything to an indefinite point in time, the team couldn't even see the summit of their task, never mind get to it.

Though they were still searching, they'd also had no luck so far with the airlines' passenger manifests. To be on the safe side, Agent Fisher had put in a new request to include private jet companies.

The first real progress made by anyone came only on Monday morning. The FBI had finally managed to obtain a transcript of the telephone conversation between the killer and Owen Henderson, the freelance reporter the killer had called in Phoenix.

Owen had given Hunter a pretty accurate run-down of the entire phone call. Most of it, just like the reporter had described, had been nothing more than a set of instructions on how to get to Timothy Davis's house and what to do once he got there, but what had really intrigued Hunter had been the killer's final words to the reporter.

'We live in a false world – a plastic world where real, natural beauty is the purest and rarest of art forms. The most valuable of art forms. True beauty cannot be fabricated, copied, or duplicated and for that reason, it's becoming extinct, but true beauty should live forever. I am making sure of that. I hope that you will be able to understand and appreciate true art.'

Hunter had spent the entire morning dissecting those words, breaking down those sentences, searching for hidden meanings between the lines.

'Anything?' Garcia asked. He too had spent the last few hours scrutinizing the transcript.

'It doesn't make much sense,' Hunter said, slumping back on his chair.

'You think?' Garcia joked. 'We're talking about a killer who mutilates his victims, then uses their bodies to stage some sick scene that only he would consider art. Not to mention the cryptic Latin phrases that he likes to carve into their flesh. In other words – this guy is a freak, Robert, a lunatic lost in some crazy world inside his own head. I'm surprised he can actually string a sentence together. Wanting him to also make sense is maybe asking a little too much, don't you think?'

'No, I'm not talking about sense in what he said,' Hunter replied. 'I'm talking about sense in relation to what we have. He talks about natural beauty being the purest and rarest of art forms, but there's nothing natural about what he's doing.

He then tells us that it cannot be fabricated or copied. That it should live forever and that he's making sure of that, but if he believes that he's creating art, then in a sense he's fabricating it.'

Garcia mulled over Hunter's words. 'Maybe he means "fabricated" in the sense that it can't be mass produced. That his art is unique.'

'So why wouldn't he use the word "unique"?'

Garcia shrugged. 'Or who knows? Maybe he only said all that because he knew that we would interrogate the freelance reporter and all of this was devised just to confuse us even more, as if we weren't lost enough already.'

The second progress also came on Monday, late afternoon. The FBI forensics lab had finally managed to reconstruct and identify the partial shoeprint retrieved from the live fence by Timothy Davis's house. It had come from a Danner Quarry USA Boot, a company based in Portland, Oregon. Its size had been estimated to be anywhere between 11.5 and 12.5, which suggested something that they already knew – the person they were looking for would most probably be over six-foot-two tall. The problem they had was that the Quarry was Danner's most popular work boot, selling over 100,000 pairs yearly in the USA.

'One hundred thousand pairs?' Captain Blake commented, leaning against the edge of Garcia's desk. Since officially this investigation was a joint effort between the FBI and the LAPD, she liked to keep herself in the loop just as much as the NCAVC director. 'Well that's not really a viable avenue for anyone to pursue, is it? No matter how many agents Adrian Kennedy pulls into this investigation.'

'I know,' Garcia agreed. 'But I wouldn't be surprised if the FBI gave it a try.'

Despite the ample space and the advanced technology, Hunter and Garcia didn't really take to their new temporary office inside the Los Angeles FBI Headquarters on Wilshire Boulevard. Every morning, it took them about five minutes each just to clear security at the entrance, and since it was a widely known fact that federal agents and City police officers didn't really see eye to eye, the level of animosity that came at them from pretty much every angle, regardless of Adrian Kennedy's orders, was at the best of times infuriating.

Hunter and Garcia still met with Agents Fisher and Williams every day, but with no real necessity for them to be in the Federal Bureau building, they preferred to work from their own office back at the PAB.

'And that's pretty much the only progress that has been made?' Captain Blake asked.

'Well,' Garcia replied. 'That and the fact that the "crime scene as an art piece" theory has solidified considerably.'

'Yes, but it's still only a theory.' She immediately lifted her hand at Hunter. 'I know. I know. Everything in an investigation is only a theory until the perp gets caught and the theory gets proven.'

The captain had heard that saying from Hunter so many times, she had lost count.

'I just hope you can either prove or disprove this theory before the killer decides to go out again.'

Seventy-Four

As Tracy and Hunter got to the WeHo Bistro in West Hollywood, just a couple of hours ago, the sun had begun tucking itself away behind the horizon line, transforming the sky above Los Angeles into a beautiful gradient sheet, but while they were inside, thick, dark clouds had repopulated the sky, covering almost every visible inch of it. As they came out, a thunder roar startled Tracy.

Hunter noticed the quick quiver of her shoulders.

'Are you OK?' he asked.

'Yeah, I'm fine. I just wasn't expecting any rain tonight.'

Tracy wore a black and white, knee-length strapless dress with a charming black bow around her waist. Her hair, which she had straightened for tonight's date, was loose, falling over her shoulders like a shining red shawl.

Hunter looked up at the sky. The clouds were indeed menacing. He took off his jacket and placed it on Tracy's shoulders.

'Here,' he said. 'It doesn't really match your outfit, but it will keep you warm.'

Tracy smiled back at him. 'Will you walk me home?'

'Of course.'

As they walked, the wind picked up considerably, with the army of black clouds above them gaining strength.

Tracy was glad she had Hunter's jacket.

They reached her apartment block in less than fifteen minutes and as they climbed the short flight of stairs to the entrance lobby, Hunter paused, his body language a little cryptic.

'You're not going to come up?' Tracy asked, taking a step closer to him. Her green eyes sparkled behind her black-framed cat-eye glasses. Even in her high heels she had to tilt her head up to look into his eyes.

Hunter didn't reply.

She stepped closer still, so close that he could smell her hair.

'I think you should come up,' she whispered, standing up on her toes to put her lips close to Hunter's.

Their lips didn't touch, but he could feel her warm breath against his skin as she breathed. Her eyes blinked and the sparkle in them became desire.

Even from up close her skin was smooth and clear.

'I really think you should come up,' Tracy whispered again, this time slowly moving her head forward until their lips finally touched. As they did, she parted hers ever so slightly, but that was where she stopped, waiting, applying no extra pressure, controlling her urge. She wanted Hunter to take the initiative, to show her that he wanted her as much as she wanted him.

As Tracy breathed out again, Hunter knew he was lost.

He closed his eyes and kissed her.

Seventy-Five

As Hunter rolled onto his back, Tracy lay motionless, her breathing labored, her whole body glistening with sweat, her chest rising and falling in a crazy rhythm, as if she was hyperventilating.

'Oh my God,' she said, once she had finally caught her breath. 'I think I need a cigarette.'

Hunter turned his head to look at her.

'You don't smoke.'

'After this, I might have to take it up.'

They both laughed.

'I wouldn't mind a drink of water either,' Tracy said. 'Followed by a real drink.'

'That would actually be quite nice,' Hunter agreed.

'I'll get us one,' Tracy added. 'As soon as my legs stop shaking.'

More laughter.

Tracy did get them a drink, eventually, before they made love again ... then again ... then again.

As they lay side by side, literally too exhausted to move, Tracy smiled to herself.

'Do you know what the most incredible thing about tonight

has been?' She quickly paused and corrected herself. 'I mean, second most incredible thing.'

'What was that?' Hunter asked.

'Your phone hasn't rung. Not once.'

'Unless we get a new victim,' Hunter said, clasping his hands behind his neck, 'there's no reason for a phone call.'

Regardless of how intrigued she was, Tracy stayed quiet. All she did was look back at him with interest. She knew that if Hunter wanted to talk, he would talk.

'We're all stuck,' Hunter continued. 'The entire investigation is stuck. The FBI, us, forensics . . . we really have nowhere to go at the moment.'

Tracy rolled her body on her side, placed her elbow on the bed and rested her head on her knuckles. Her eyes were still firmly on Hunter.

His stayed on the ceiling.

'Which is a horrible feeling,' he said, and though it looked like he was about to tell her a lot more, he didn't.

Tracy maintained her silence. Hunter's profession wasn't one that would benefit from positive-thinking comments like, 'I'm sure you'll get him in the end,' or 'You can do this. Believe in yourself.'

The reason Hunter had opened up to her, even if it had been just a couple of sentences, was because he felt the need to let off some steam, not because he was looking for comfort or reassurance. Tracy knew that very well. She was also very sure that Hunter knew if he ever wanted to talk, she would be right there.

When Hunter had gone quiet for long enough, she knew that that conversation was over.

'I don't suppose you're free sometime tomorrow, are you?' she asked.

'Possibly. Why?'

Tracy scooted over and rested her head on Hunter's chest. 'I think I've mentioned this to you before, but for one week only, the owners of the two biggest comic-book stores in the US are opening the doors to their private collections. Between them, they've got some of the rarest comic books ever written. I know that comics probably aren't your thing, but I was wondering if you'd like to come with me? Tomorrow is the last day.'

'I didn't know that you were into comic books,' Hunter said.

'I'm not a collector or anything, but I really do appreciate the art, the creativity and the imagination that is put into them. Plus, this really is a rare opportunity.' She pulled back from Hunter, rolled over on her stomach and held herself up on her elbows. 'C'mon, it could be fun. We don't have to stay long.' The mischievous smile was back. 'We could come back here.'

'I used to read a lot of comic books when I was younger,' Hunter revealed. 'A lot younger.'

'Really?'

Hunter nodded. 'I even had a favorite comic.'

'And which one was that?'

'Not a very well-known one, I'm afraid – *Morbius*.'

'What?' Tracy's head kicked back. 'The Living Vampire?'

Hunter's surprise was genuine. 'OK, I'm officially impressed now.'

'If you're into a comic like *Morbius*,' Tracy said, excitement lifting her voice, 'then you have to come.'

Hunter knew Tracy was right. It probably would be fun.

'Sure. Why not?' he agreed. 'What time do you have in mind?'

'Well, I have a lecture tomorrow at ten in the morning.

After that I'm free, but I'd like to re-dye my hair if possible. My roots are starting to show.' She tilted her head down a touch to prove her point.

Hunter froze.

Sometimes . . . no, make that 'most times', not even Hunter was able to explain how his thought process worked. Things just suddenly came to him. His brain would establish the most obscure connections, triggered by words, or images, or sounds, or whatever he had come across. Right then, in bed with Tracy, Hunter had just had one of those moments.

'Holy shit.'

Tracy looked back at him in horror.

'Are my roots that bad?'

Hunter jumped out of bed and began getting dressed as quickly as he could.

'Holy shit,' he said again, before rushing out of Tracy's apartment.

Seventy-Six

Agent Fisher stood almost motionless before the south wall inside their office at the FBI Headquarters on Wilshire Boulevard. Her arms were folded in front of her chest, her eyes glued to the large monitor on the left. In her right hand, she had a Bluetooth clicker and with every button press the picture on the screen would fade out, quickly giving way to a new one. Judging solely by how much attention she was paying to every image, one would be forgiven for thinking that she was seeing those photos for the first time, but that simply wasn't the case.

Agent Fisher had been looping through the same crime-scene photographs that she had scrutinized one zillion times before, but that image-looping process had become a morning ritual for her. She did it every day, as she walked into their office. Maybe she was hoping that a fresh, morning brain, aided by fresh eyes, would perhaps pick up a detail somewhere that, until now, they had all somehow missed.

That hadn't happened yet.

From his desk, leaning back on his chair and always nursing a cup of steaming coffee, Agent Williams went through the ritual with his partner.

Agent Fisher had just clicked onto the last of Linda Parker's crime-scene photographs when Hunter walked through the office door. Under his right arm he was carrying a significantly fat document folder. No one needed to ask to know that he hadn't slept. Agent Williams put it politely.

'It looks like you've been working for most of the night.'

'Some of it,' Hunter admitted.

Just as he got to his desk, Garcia walked into the office. He, on the other hand, looked completely rested.

There was something in the tone Hunter had used when answering Agent Williams that made both FBI agents turn and face him.

'Have you found something new?' Agent Fisher asked.

'I think so.'

Agent Fisher used the clicker to turn off the monitor before walking over to Hunter's desk.

Agent Williams was right behind her.

'I think we made a mistake,' Hunter said as the group gathered around his desk.

'A mistake?' Agent Fisher asked. Her uncertainty was mirrored on Garcia's and Agent Williams' faces. 'A mistake about what?'

'About this killer's crime scenes. About them being a canvas. About him seeing himself primarily as an artist.'

The confusion on everyone's faces didn't go away. In fact, Hunter's words had the opposite effect.

'Let me show you,' he said, as he cleared his desk, placing everything except the computer monitor and the keyboard on the floor to his right. He then retrieved four pieces of paper from one of the printer trays and placed them on his desk. Next, he wrote down the four different Latin phrases the killer had carved onto his victims' backs. For clarity, he wrote their English meaning just under the Latin words. That done, he reached inside the fat file he had brought with him and retrieved a portrait photo of each victim, placing them next to the corresponding phrase.

'This investigation has been a cryptic maze from the get-go,' he began. 'This killer likes to play mind games and I think Adrian was right.'

'About what?' Agent Williams this time.

'About the killer testing us.' Hunter pointed to the four pieces of paper on his desk. 'There's no doubt that the carvings are clues meant for us. And we know that because at first view those clues are hidden. The victims are always left lying on their backs. The carvings are not a visual element in his canvases, if that really is what he's aiming for, or even an element in the shocking effect of his murders, because no one will see those carvings until the victims are moved, and that will only happen once the investigative team gets there. Still, after the carvings have been revealed, we have to put everything together – the symbol-like lines, the oddly split words, all of it – to finally form a sentence . . . in Latin, which automatically adds an extra layer to his cryptic game.'

'Ambiguity,' Agent Williams said.

'Precisely,' Hunter agreed, once again indicating the four sheets of paper on his desk. 'Every single one of these phrases could have more than one meaning, a meaning that doesn't necessarily have to refer to the crime scenes themselves, but whichever way we choose to look at these clues, it does seem like the killer has gone to great lengths to shroud everything in as much confusion as he could.'

'Well,' Garcia cut in, 'it looks like he's done a fantastic job so far, because right now he's got all of us chasing smoke.' He looked at both FBI agents. 'And he's had you guys chasing after your own tails for over two months now.'

Agent Fisher looked at him sideways.

'And that was what Adrian Kennedy meant when he suggested that the killer was testing us,' Hunter clarified. 'The killer made his clues cryptic and ambiguous for a reason – in his mind, delusional or not, only those "worthy" would be able to decipher them, but deciphering the clues was only half of the test. They also needed to be understood, and to the killer, only those with the right vision, higher intelligence, or whatever, would be able to truly understand them ... to truly understand *him*.'

'And what you're saying is that we misunderstood those clues?' Agent Fisher asked.

'Yes,' Hunter confirmed. 'I think we did. We thought that they were the killer's way of telling us that he saw himself as an artist, right?'

'Yes,' Agent Fisher agreed firmly.

'Well,' Hunter said, 'the clues are certainly telling us something about him, but they're not telling us that he's an artist.'

Everyone paused in anticipation.

'They are telling us that he's a collector.'

Seventy-Seven

It was as if Hunter had cast a flash paralyzing spell on everyone inside the office, because for the next five seconds no one spoke, no one moved, no one even blinked.

'What?' Agent Fisher broke the spell, quickly followed by Garcia, then Agent Williams.

'What?'

'What?'

Awkward looks all around.

'So what is he collecting?' Agent Fisher asked.

Hunter took a deep breath before speaking because he knew how crazy he was about to sound.

'Human rarities.'

Surprise and bewilderment came together to form a very peculiar look, which masked everyone's faces.

'Human rarities? What does that even mean?'

'OK,' Hunter said, calling everyone's attention to the first photograph on the left. Next to it was the Latin phrase the killer had carved into the victim's back.

'Kristine Rivers,' he began. 'Our very first victim. The killer scalped her and took out her eyes. Now have a look at this.' From his folder, Hunter retrieved the personal file the FBI had compiled on Kristine Rivers and placed it on the table. He then indicated two fields displayed right on the first page.

Hair color: Red.

Eye color: Blue.

'Now remember,' Hunter stressed, pointing to Kristine Rivers' portrait on the desk. 'This is her official profile, so we're not talking about her *dyed* bright red hair here.'

On the photo, Kristine Rivers' hair, which had been styled into large curls, was fire-engine red.

'Beneath all that bright red color,' Hunter carried on, 'Kristine Rivers *was* actually a natural redhead.'

Hunter went back to his file and selected a new photo of Kristine Rivers. This one showed her sitting with two other girls on a bench somewhere. Her hair was loose, falling several inches past her shoulders, a gorgeous shade of natural red.

'According to what we have,' Hunter added, 'this picture was taken just a few days before Kristine Rivers was murdered.'

Garcia and Agent Williams still looked puzzled, but from the expression on Agent Fisher's face, Hunter knew she had caught on.

'Redhead women make up less than two percent of the world's population,' Hunter explained.

'And the combination of natural red hair and blue eyes,' Agent Fisher took over, 'is the rarest eye/hair color combo on earth.' She looked back at Hunter. 'I too read a lot.'

'That's right,' Hunter confirmed. 'The *combination* of red hair and blue eyes makes less than 0.5 percent of the world's population. The *rarest combination* on earth.' He indicated the Latin phrase the killer had carved into Kristine Rivers' back.

Pulchritudo in coniunctio – beauty is in the combination.

The puzzled look on everyone's faces seemed to intensify.

Hunter kept the momentum going by indicating the second photograph from the left.

'Let's move to our second victim,' he said. 'Albert Greene.'

The photo Hunter had placed on his desk was the same one Agent Williams had showed Hunter and Garcia back in their office when they met for the first time. The picture showed the old man looking up from a newspaper.

'As we all know,' Hunter continued, 'the killer took Mr. Greene's eyes, nothing else.'

Hunter's words prompted everyone to move in a little closer and concentrate their attention on the old man's eyes.

'Is there something special about them?' Garcia asked.

'There is,' Hunter confirmed. 'Something that wouldn't show in his personal dossier.'

'And what is that?' Agent Williams this time.

'Isn't there anything on this picture that seems a little odd to any of you?' Hunter asked.

Three pairs of eyes jumped back to the photo on his desk.

Hunter waited.

'I don't see anything,' Agent Williams replied first.

Agent Fisher was still trying.

'The newspaper,' Hunter said, giving everyone a clue.

Both FBI agents' attention shot to the newspaper Albert Greene had in his hands. They both squinted, trying to make out some of the headlines.

For some reason, Agent Fisher tried to identify the date on the paper's front page.

Garcia's gaze, on the other hand, kept moving from Albert Greene to the newspaper then back to Albert Greene.

'No glasses,' he finally said.

Hunter nodded at his partner.

'What?' Agent Fisher looked unsure.

'He's not wearing any glasses,' Garcia said again.

'Albert Greene was eighty-four years old,' Hunter said. 'Most of us, even if we already wear glasses, will begin to experience a significant decline in our reading sight from around the age of forty-five. That decline will naturally progress as we get older and our eyes get weaker. But that wasn't the case with Albert Greene.'

'You got that from a picture?' Agent Fisher countered. 'He could've been wearing contact lenses here.'

'He wasn't,' Hunter affirmed. 'I spoke to his daughter on the phone earlier today. He had a few health issues, but for some reason, his vision never deteriorated, at least not at the rate that was expected. Albert Greene never wore glasses. He never needed them.'

'Never?' Agent Williams looked unconvinced.

'When he got to the age of sixty-five,' Hunter said, recounting what he'd been told by Greene's daughter over the phone, 'his daughter *made* him go to an optician with her because she just couldn't believe that he didn't need glasses by then. She thought he was just being his stubborn self, but no. According to her, the optician was surprised at how good Mr. Greene's vision was.'

'At the age of sixty-five?' Agent Fisher questioned. 'But Albert Greene was eighty-four when he was murdered. His vision could've easily changed in those nineteen years.'

'You would've expected it to,' Hunter agreed. 'But apparently that wasn't the case. Mr. Greene's daughter told me that since that first visit to the optician, she made him go back every year for a checkup.' Hunter shook his head. 'Nothing.

Year after year, the results were always the same. Mr. Greene's vision held steady like a fort. Two years ago, just after his eighty-second birthday, she took him to a clinic to see an ophthalmologist, not an optician, because she just couldn't believe the results anymore. She was starting to think that the opticians were getting things wrong. After a battery of tests, the ophthalmologist confirmed that Mr. Greene's vision had indeed deteriorated, but at a much, much slower rate than what would be considered normal. At eighty-four years old his vision was as good as might be expected of a person less than half his age.'

'How's that even possible?' Agent Williams asked.

'That's the problem,' Hunter replied. 'It's not supposed to be, but there have been a few isolated cases registered around the world where a person's organ has failed to age at the normal rate – eyes, liver, auditory system, heart – the cases are few and far between, but they do exist. It's a type of nerve and muscle hypertrophy. Mr. Greene was one of these rare cases; his eyes were unique.'

Hunter indicated the Latin phrase that corresponded to Albert Greene – *Pulchritudo in oculis aspicientis* – 'Beauty is in the eye of the beholder.'

Agent Fisher was starting to get fidgety.

'There's one more detail,' Hunter added. 'Can you remember the job Albert Greene did before he retired?'

'Janitor,' Garcia replied. 'He was a school janitor his whole life, isn't that right?'

'Not his whole life,' Agent Williams corrected him. 'For his last nine working years he was the main CCTV control-room operator for Maple Hills high school.'

'That's correct,' Hunter said. 'In other words, he was

an observer. He spent his days watching students through video cameras.'

'So?' Agent Fisher failed to see the relevance.

'Fuck!' Agent Williams didn't manage to keep his remark quite under his breath.

Agent Fisher's surprised eyes shot in his direction. Despite having worked with him for over seven years now, she couldn't remember ever hearing Agent Williams curse.

'By definition that's what a "beholder" is, Erica,' Agent Williams clarified. 'An observer.'

'Given how much thought this killer puts into everything he does,' Hunter said, 'I don't think that that was a coincidence. *Beauty is in the eye of the beholder.* The killer isn't talking about us being able to see the beauty in what he did. He's literally talking about the *eyes of the beholder.*'

'This is absolutely mad,' Garcia said.

'What about Linda Parker – the LA victim, and Timothy Davis from Tucson?' Agent Williams asked. 'How do they fit into this new . . . "collector" theory of yours?'

Hunter held everyone's stare for an extra second.

'Well,' he said. 'This is where it gets even more interesting.'

Seventy-Eight

Hunter placed a new photo on the table for everyone to see. It showed Linda Parker's skinned body lying on blood-soaked sheets inside her bedroom.

'As Dr. Hove suggested,' he began, indicating the amputations the killer had performed, 'despite the professional standard of the amputations, we assumed that the killer had taken Linda Parker's hands and feet to aid the job of skinning her body, but it appears that we have assumed wrong.'

'The killer wanted to keep her hands and feet?' Agent Williams asked. 'Why?'

'Late yesterday,' Hunter explained, 'our Operations team finished compiling a very extensive dossier on Linda Parker, including a thorough section on her modeling career. We already knew that the bulk of her work came from catalog shoots, right?'

Everyone nodded.

'OK, what we didn't know was that Linda Parker was one of the most requested hands, feet and cosmetic models in Los Angeles, shooting for catalogs and adverts that ran all over the world, not only in the USA.'

Hunter retrieved a pile of photographs from his folder and placed them on his desk.

'These are just a few of the photos Operations have sent over.'

He began flipping through the first batch of photographs – a series of close-up images showing only Linda Parker's hands and feet. The images advertised a variety of products, ranging from false nails to jewelry, to sandals, to nail varnish, to moisturizing creams and beyond.

'There's a reason why Linda Parker was one of the most requested models when it came to these sorts of adverts,' Hunter explained. 'Her hands and feet were considered perfectly balanced and symmetrical.'

'Perfectly balanced and symmetrical?' Agent Fisher intervened. 'What does that mean?'

'It's got to do with the shape, curvature and the size ratios: how long the fingers and toes are in comparison not only to each other, but also to the palms and feet.'

'You're kidding, right?'

'Not even a little bit. In the same way that clothes companies look for specific-sized models for specific items, shoe, jewelry, and cosmetic companies look for models with the most perfect hands, feet and skin they can find. That alone can boost sales by about five to ten percent.'

'I'll admit,' Agent Williams said, his attention still on the photos Hunter was showing them, 'her hands were very attractive. Very delicate.'

The next series of advert photographs Hunter showed them were facial and body close-ups of Linda Parker, all of them advertising a variety of cosmetic products.

'Her skin was also considered ideal for cosmetic advertisements – no blemishes, no marks, no freckles ... nothing. So much so that in the past two years, she graced the cover of no fewer than fifteen dermatological magazines, not only in this country, but also abroad.'

Hunter showed them all fifteen magazine covers.

Silence once again ruled the room.

Hunter indicated the phrase the killer had carved into Linda Parker's back.

Pulchritudo Circumdat Eius – 'Beauty surrounds her.'

Garcia's brain was the first to engage.

'As in the skin that surrounds her body,' he said in a thoughtful tone. 'Not the room that surrounded her dead body.'

'Precisely,' Hunter agreed. 'The killer wanted her skin. He wanted her hands and feet because they were "perfect".'

Hunter spread the photographs over his desk.

Eyes moved in all directions, jumping from picture to picture, trying to take in everything.

'So if we follow your line of thought,' Agent Williams said, 'there has to be something special about Timothy Davis's blood.'

Hunter placed Timothy Davis's autopsy report on the desk and flipped it to the second page, where he indicated the third entry from the top.

Blood type: AB-

From his folder, Hunter retrieved the FBI file on Timothy Davis that Agent Brandon had given them back at the airport in Tucson. The information he was looking for was right on the first page. He placed the file on the desk, next to the autopsy report.

'Timothy Davis's mother's name was Anjana.' He indicated on the file as he explained. 'And though she was born in the USA, she was of Asian-Indian descent.

His father's name was Terrence and he was a Deep-South African American, born and raised in Madison, Alabama.' He brought the autopsy report back to the top of the pile before clarifying. 'AB Negative is the rarest type of blood in the world. In the USA, it comprises less than two percent of the population. That number drops significantly when we divide the population into ethnic groups. In African Americans the frequency is less than 0.3 percent. In Asian Americans less than 0.1. If you combine the two ethnic groups together . . .'

Hunter once again indicated the information concerning Timothy Davis's mother – Asian-Indian descent – then the information concerning his father – African American.

'We're talking a negligible number of the population here. When it comes to blood type, due to his heritage, Timothy Davis was one in five million. He had the rarest of all blood types running through his veins.'

Hunter indicated the Latin phrase the killer had carved into Timothy Davis's back.

Pulchritudo habitantem in interius – 'beauty lives on the inside.'

'The killer's phrases aren't allusions to his crime scenes. They aren't a set of instructions on how to look at his work. They are direct references to what he takes – eyes, hair, skin, feet, hands, blood . . .'

Hunter returned to his folder.

'We have one more detail,' he said. 'The phone conversation between our killer and Owen Henderson, the freelance reporter he called in Phoenix. You have all received the official transcript yesterday, right?'

'Yes.'

'The killer's last few words to Owen Henderson over the phone,' Hunter carried on. 'After he gave Owen the instructions on how to get to Timothy Davis's house. At first, I couldn't make any real sense of what he'd said, but now ...'

Hunter placed a copy of the transcript on his desk. To emphasize his argument he had underlined a few key words.

We live in a false world – a plastic world where <u>real, natural beauty</u> is the <u>purest and rarest</u> of art forms. The most valuable of art forms. <u>True beauty cannot be fabricated or copied</u>, and for that reason, it's becoming extinct, but <u>true beauty should live forever.</u> <u>I am making sure of that.</u> I hope that you will be able to understand and appreciate true art.

'He's talking about *pure, true, natural beauty*,' Hunter said, once everyone had finished reading the transcript. 'A *rare* kind of beauty that *cannot be fabricated or copied.*'

'His victims' body parts,' Agent Williams concluded.

Hunter nodded once. 'And he finishes by saying, "True beauty should live forever. I am making sure of that." So how do you think he's making sure of it?'

Garcia and both FBI agents exchanged worried looks.

Hunter addressed Agent Fisher.

'I think you're right, Erica, the killer *is* probably creating some sort of "gallery of the dead", but not from pictures he takes at the crime scenes. He's creating his gallery from their body parts. To him, they're much more than simple trophies. They are items of true, rare beauty that cannot be copied or duplicated, and the only way he can make sure that those items will live forever is by preserving them.'

Hunter brought everyone's attention back to the photographs on his desk.

'He's not creating art. He's collecting it.'

Seventy-Nine

The door closed behind him with a muffled thud, but the man didn't move. Not for a while. He simply stood there, admiring the room he had created with his own hands.

It had taken him almost two years to transform the space down in his basement into exactly what he wanted, but the time and effort he had put into it had clearly paid off. The room – his gallery – was nothing less than magnificent.

The man closed his eyes and breathed in the stale air inside the oddly shaped room. As the air traveled into his nostrils, bringing with it a very familiar chemical scent, his skin turned into gooseflesh.

The man adored that smell.

He kept his eyes closed for a full minute, savoring every second, allowing the anticipation to build up inside him. He could feel his lungs expanding and collapsing with every breath, his heart beginning to increase its rhythm, his muscles tensing ever so slightly.

Satisfied and somewhat intoxicated by the ecstasy of it all, the man reopened his eyes, switched on the lights and refocused on the wall across the room from him. It was lined with long wooden shelves which had been divided into separate, different-sized compartments, each holding a clear glass jar illuminated by a special light, designed to best bring out the details of the jars' contents.

As the man approached his gallery he paused, smiling, admiring his own work . . . his unique collection.

The man lifted his right hand and allowed the tips of his fingers to brush against one of the jars. As his skin came into contact with the smooth, clear glass, a new wave of exhilaration shot through his body, filling him with energy.

He pulled back his hand and stared into the empty jar.

His plan was almost complete. His most audacious plan yet. Soon, that jar would be filled, but first he had to teach the FBI a lesson – one that they would never, ever forget.

Eighty

'But how about the crime scenes staged as a canvas?' Agent Fisher asked. 'Was that just a coincidence?'

'Maybe they never really were staged as a canvas,' Hunter said, and quickly decided to better explain his logic. 'We see what we want to see. That's the way the human brain works. At first, when you believed that Kristine Rivers' murder had been vengeance against Adrian Kennedy, you managed to link the killer's Latin phrase – *beauty is in the relationship* – to that theory, remember? You assumed that the killer was talking about a family relationship. The same happened with the second victim and the second crime scene. You linked that Latin phrase – *beauty is in the eye of the beholder* – to the theory you had at the time, believing that the killer was maybe referring to something Albert Greene had seen, which was improbable, but still plausible. It was the killer's third outing, Linda Parker, that put an end to the "payback" theory. You just couldn't link all three victims to a revenge act. Understandably, after spending two months going down wrong avenues and dead-end streets the FBI was frustrated. Then along came a new possible theory, which fitted the third crime scene well, but not the others. Still, frustration, pressure, desperation and the need for answers has a way of forcing the human brain to take different points of view, and that's what we did. We were desperate. We needed something we could work with because we had nothing. The art-piece theory was a possibility, so just like with the payback one, we shaped our point of view, we found an angle and we made it fit.'

'And aren't we doing the same with this new "collector" theory?' Agent Fisher asked. 'I'll admit that it does fit into place a little better than anything we had before, but it isn't any less crazy. And figuring out what this killer is actually doing – whether it's creating works of art with his crime scenes, or collecting rare human body parts, which he extracts from his victims so he can preserve them – doesn't really get us any closer to catching him.'

'I'm not so sure about that,' Garcia said, beating Hunter to the punch.

'What do you mean?'

'If Robert is right about this,' Garcia explained, 'if what this killer is really doing is collecting rare body parts to create his own gallery, or to make a casserole, or whatever, then Robert's theory would also explain the one thing that we were having trouble linking to the "art" theory.'

'And what would that be?' Agent Fisher asked.

'The victim-selection process.' This time it was Agent Williams who beat Garcia to the punch, his tone thoughtful, his eyes back on the photos on Hunter's desk.

'The victim-selection process,' Hunter agreed, rearranging some of the photographs. 'How are these victims being chosen? Why are they being chosen? That was the one piece of the puzzle that we just couldn't slot into place. The best we could come up with was a random selection process, but if this killer really is collecting rare body parts, then there's nothing random about his victim selection. On the contrary, it's *very* specific. That's why he travels. He'll go to wherever they are because these people are unique, and what they have to offer him – *real, natural beauty – cannot be fabricated or copied.*'

Agent Fisher's jaw tensed. If Hunter was correct, then the victim-selection process was not random. The killer wasn't driving around, picking his victims off the streets by flipping a coin. He knew who his victims would be beforehand and that gave them something they could work with.

'So how is he finding them?' she asked, her voice gaining a new, excited tone. 'How would anyone find people with rare conditions or something unique or special about them like rare blood type, rare eye color, or whatever? Medical records?'

'Very possibly,' Agent Williams agreed, excitement also finding its way into his voice. 'The information the killer would've needed to guide him to most of his victims could've easily been found through medical records, with the exception of Linda Parker.'

'The killer wouldn't need her health records to find out about how perfect her skin, her hands and feet were,' Hunter cut in. 'That information was available on her website and on every single one of her social-media pages. And since she's registered as a public figure, all of her profiles are visible to absolutely everyone.'

'Still,' Agent Williams said, 'our best bet right now is indeed health records, isn't it?'

'Sure,' Garcia replied. 'But I think maybe we're forgetting something here. There's no Universal Health Records Archive; no national unified database for medical records, which means that running a search across the whole of the United States for something like specific blood types, or specific eye/hair color combinations, or anything else using only health records is impossible, so how is the killer able to do it? Unless he has managed to tap into the database of every major hospital in the USA, which is a pretty impossible task, how is he—'

'Health insurance,' Hunter interjected.

Everyone looked at him.

'You're right,' he said to Garcia. 'Health records can't be shared, but health-insurance companies do have central data-banks and the information in them *can* be shared between all the branches and subsidiaries of the same insurance group, no matter which city they're in. If the killer has managed to hack into the database of any of the top health-insurance companies in this country, he would have access to millions of health records from people all over the land. Finding his victims would be just a question of time.'

'So our first step would be to check which health-insurance company each of our victims were with,' Garcia said.

'I'm on it,' Agent Williams said, reaching for his cellphone.

'How easy do you think it would be to hack into a health-insurance company database?' Garcia asked.

'Not easy at all,' Hunter replied. 'But I know just the person to ask if it can be done and how it can be done.'

Eighty-One

Michelle Kelly, the head of the Los Angeles FBI Cyber Crime Division, had just finished a meeting with two of her top programmers when Hunter, Garcia, and Agents Fisher and Williams walked into the large and uncomfortable cold room.

As she clocked the two detectives, Michelle paused, looking somewhat confused.

Hunter and Garcia also immediately spotted her across the room from them. How could they not? Michelle Kelly looked nothing like a typical FBI agent. She also looked nothing like most people would expect an uber computer and networks geek to look like.

Thirty-year-old Michelle Kelly was five-foot-eight, with long dyed black hair and a spiked fringe that fell over her forehead in a teenager's skate-punk way. Her deep-green eyes were heavily framed by black eyeliner and purple eyeshadow. She had a thin, silver-loop nose-ring going through her left nostril and a second loop-ring that pierced the right edge of her bottom lip. She wore black jeans and a black T-shirt with a lime-green skull. Above it, were the words *Killswitch Engage*.

'Detectives Hunter and Garcia,' Michelle said, as she

approached the group. Though confusion still masked her face, her tone was warm and welcoming. 'To what do I owe the pleasure?'

They shook hands.

'Do you know each other?' Agent Fisher asked.

'Yes,' Hunter replied. 'Michelle and the FBI Cyber Crime Division helped us solve a serial-murder case a couple of years ago.'

'Hi,' Michelle said, extending her hand at the two FBI agents. Both of her arms were covered in tattoos from wrist to shoulder. 'I'm Michelle Kelly ... or ... official title – Special Agent Michelle Kelly. I'm the head of this division.'

If Agent Fisher tried to hide her surprise, she failed miserably.

'You are the *head* of the Los Angeles Cyber Crime Division?' she queried.

Michelle frowned at her. 'That's right. Why? Is there a problem?' Her eyes moved sideways to Hunter as if asking, *Who the hell is this bitch?*

'No,' Agent Fisher replied. 'No problem at all.' She backpedaled like a pro. 'I was just expecting to see someone who looked more like a mad professor than a rock star.'

'Thank you,' Michelle replied. 'I'll take that as a compliment.'

She took a step back and regarded the group for no more than a split second.

'It's obvious that this isn't a personal visit.' Though Michelle addressed everyone, her stare settled on Hunter. 'So what can I do for you guys this time?'

'Is there a more private place we can talk?' Agent Fisher asked, looking around the large open-plan room, which seemed to be in a league of its own when it came to high-tech

equipment. Lights were blinking on and off just about everywhere she looked. The walls were covered by mega-monitors
showing maps, moving images and lines of code; she had no
idea what they meant or what they were used for. A multitude
of desks, with agents typing frantically at their computers,
were scattered around the space.

'Sure,' Michelle replied. 'Follow me.'

She guided them to her office, located at the far end of
the floor.

'Better?' she asked, as she closed the door to her office
which, though spacious, was crammed with books.

'Much,' Agent Fisher replied. 'Thank you. This is quite a
sensitive case.'

'Aren't they all?'

Michelle waited for everyone to take a seat before taking
hers behind her desk. 'So what is this about?'

Agent Fisher took the lead and gave Michelle the run-down
on what they needed.

She listened without interrupting.

'We already have a team checking if the victims were all
with the same health-insurance company,' Agent Fisher said in
conclusion. 'What we need to know is how difficult it would
be to hack into one of these databases and search them for
anything specific.'

'From the outside,' Michelle began, 'terribly difficult.' She
held the suspense for a few seconds. 'But it can be done. And
if your killer really is finding his victims that way then I'm
willing to bet that the only database he hacked into belongs to
the GlobalAmerica Health Group.'

'The largest health-insurance group in the USA,'
Hunter said.

'That's them all right,' Michelle agreed. 'A few months ago we investigated a breach into one of their servers. They have over one million physicians, six thousand hospitals, and seventy million subscribers, but the very interesting fact, at least where you guys are concerned, is that they have an integrated information and technology platform called Optum, which is pretty much used in four out of every five hospitals in the US, regardless of whether the hospital is part of the GlobalAmerica Health Group or not.'

'Wait a second,' Agent Fisher stopped her. 'Are you telling us that if anyone hacks into this Optum platform, they would be able to access records from everywhere, irrespective of which insurance group the patient might be with?'

'Pretty much,' Michelle replied.

'Sonofabitch!'

'There's also a chance that the killer works for a branch of the health-insurance company,' Michelle added. 'Or any of the hospitals that use the Optum platform. In that case, accessing any patient health files would be a hell of a lot easier. The downside to that – to the person who is accessing the files that is – is that if those records were accessed internally then it will be much easier to track the digital trail.'

'Is there any way we can find out if certain files were accessed recently?' Agent Fisher asked. 'And in that case, by whom?'

'We can try,' Michelle replied. 'If the files were accessed internally, then our chances of finding out who did it increases exponentially, but if Optum – or any health-insurance database – was hacked from the outside, things get harder.'

'How much harder?' Agent Fisher asked.

'Depending on how good the hacker is,' Michelle came back, 'how well he was able to cover his tracks, it may range from "a hell of a lot harder" to "impossible". I won't really know until I try it.'

'Can you try it?' Hunter this time.

They held each other's stare for a moment, which seemed to bother Agent Fisher.

'Sure,' Michelle finally replied, her gaze now moving to the two FBI agents. 'But I will need an official request for that. After all, this is the FBI.'

'Get started,' Agent Fisher said, getting to her feet. 'You'll have the official request within the hour.'

Eighty-Two

Hunter and Garcia had gone back to their office at the Police Administration Building and by lunchtime, the information on which health-insurance company each of the four victims had a plan with had come back to them. For the first time they seemed to have caught a real break.

Kristine Rivers had a student health plan with Direct Healthcare. Albert Greene had a senior-citizen policy with Cambridge Health Plans. Linda Parker was with Prime US Healthcare Services, and Timothy Davis with AtlantiCare Health. All four of those companies were subsidiaries of the GlobalAmerica Health Group. Their records shared not only the same central database, but they could all also be accessed via the Optum integrated information and technology platform.

'So you think that the killer is finding his victims through their medical records?' Captain Blake asked.

'Right now,' Garcia replied, 'it seems like our best bet, Captain.'

'And how is he getting to the database?'

'Two ways of doing it: internally – if the killer works for any of the companies under the GlobalAmerica Health Group, or for a medical establishment, like a hospital or a clinic with access to this Optum platform, and externally – by hacking into the system from the outside. What we're doing,' Garcia explained, 'is checking to see when was the last time that any of the victims' medical records were accessed. With that, there's a chance that we'll be able to follow some sort of digital trail and figure out who accessed them. It can take a while though, if we ever get anything.'

Captain Blake took a step back from Garcia's desk and regarded both of her detectives for several seconds.

'When was the last time you had a day off?' she asked.

'What?' Garcia came back.

'A day off. When was the last time you had one?'

Garcia looked at Hunter for help.

'I'm not really sure,' Hunter said. 'A while ago. Why?'

'Have you two looked at yourselves in the mirror? You guys could audition for *The Walking Dead* right now and get the part, do you understand what I'm saying? You have been on this case for about a week now, isn't that right?' The captain didn't give them a chance to reply. 'And just before that you were on that triple-homicide case, weren't you? The one in Bixby Knolls?'

'That's correct,' Garcia confirmed. 'The father who raped and murdered his three daughters.'

'Well, so that's it,' Captain Blake said, her voice as commanding as it had ever been. 'You guys are taking the next two days off. I don't really give a damn about what Adrian Kennedy or the FBI has to say. This is a joint operation, which means that you are still under my command. You were supposed to take a break after the Bixby Knolls murders anyway, so finish whatever it is that you are doing here today, then go home and get some sleep, and take the next two days off. From what you told me, unless this killer gives you a brand-new victim, there's nothing else you can do, other than wait for Cyber Crime.' She paused by the door to their office. 'It's not a request.'

Eighty-Three

Hunter finally left his office at around 7:30 p.m. Despite being a workaholic, he had to admit to himself that he welcomed Captain Blake's orders with open arms. He had needed to check his diary to find out the last time he and Garcia had had a day off: twenty-three days ago. Forty-eight hours off the clock, even if he didn't sleep that much, would certainly recharge his batteries and re-sharpen his brain. Maybe he could even spend some of that time with Tracy.

That thought made him smile.

Suddenly, and seemingly out of nowhere, as Hunter took the exit onto Soto Street in the direction of Huntington Park, a black Ford Fusion appeared on his left and cut in front of him. Hunter had to swerve hard right not to clip the Fusion's bumper.

'You have got to be joking.'

Hunter's surprise came not due to the Ford's maneuver, but to the fact that that same black Ford Fusion had pulled exactly the same move, at that exact same junction, the night before, just as Hunter drove home. Hunter had taken notice of the license plate.

'That's it,' Hunter said to himself. 'I'm pulling him over.'

But as Hunter stepped on the gas in pursuit of the Ford Fusion, his thought process did another somersault, jumping from A to Z in two seconds flat.

That was when he realized something he'd been missing.

Eighty-Four

The phone on Hunter's desk inside their temporary office on the eighth floor of the FBI building on Wilshire Boulevard rang at exactly 7:56 p.m. There was no one there except Agent Fisher, who had been working on a report for the past few hours. She dug her heels onto the floor and kicked her legs, pushing her chair away from her desk and sending it in the direction of Hunter's.

'Special Agent Erica Fisher,' she said, as she answered the phone.

A second of hesitant silence.

'Did I dial the wrong extension?' the female voice on the other side asked.

Agent Fisher immediately recognized who the caller was – Michelle Kelly – the head of the LA FBI Cyber Crime Division.

'Hi, Miss Kelly,' Agent Fisher replied. 'No, you haven't. This is Detective Hunter's desk, but I'm the only one in the office right now. In fact, Detectives Hunter and Garcia prefer to work from their shoebox office back at the PAB. Is there anything I can help you with? Do you have any news for us?'

'I do,' Michelle replied.

Those two simple words took Agent Fisher's heart rate from resting to one-hundred-yard dash.

'What have you got?'

'It took us a while longer than we expected,' Michelle began. 'But we've made some progress.'

'I'm listening.'

'Albert Greene's medical records were accessed via the Optum integrated information and technology platform exactly twelve days before his murder.'

'Internally or externally?'

'Externally,' Michelle replied. 'Someone hacked into the system.'

'Can you trace it?'

'We are working on it, but I can tell you this – whoever this guy is, he's no amateur. He knows his way around cyberspace.'

Every hair on Agent Fisher's body stood on end.

'But that's not all,' Michelle announced. 'Timothy Davis's medical records were also accessed externally. Would you like to have a guess at how many days before his murder?'

'Twelve?' Agent Fisher's eyes widened as she said the number.

'Exactly, and here's the kick – the same with Kristine Rivers' records – accessed externally via Optum twelve days prior to her murder. Linda Parker's records weren't touched.'

'The killer wouldn't need her medical records to gather the information on her,' Agent Fisher said.

'Anyway,' Michelle carried on. 'Twelve days prior to every murder – you know what that tells us about this killer, don't you?'

'That he's methodical,' Agent Fisher replied.

'Very,' Michelle agreed. 'Probably almost to the point of

OCD, which would mean that he also doesn't like to stray from routines, and that can increase our chances of tracking him down.'

'So where are we right now with that?'

'Crawling stages.'

'But you've picked up a trail, right? I mean, finding out about the records being accessed externally and all.'

'More like we've picked up a scent rather than a trail,' Michelle clarified. 'But yes, we do now have a starting point, and we're going after him with everything we've got.'

Eighty-Five

The man had spent almost an entire week putting the final touches to his plan and making sure that everything would work exactly in the way he had schematized it. It was a complicated and bold plan. A lot more daring and complex than anything he had done so far. Every detail had to be perfect. There simply was no room for mistakes, but then again, the man never really made mistakes. He was way too smart for that.

Today, after purchasing a cheap pre-paid cellphone and an old-fashioned Polaroid camera, all the man needed to do was a couple of last-minute tweaks to the system; nothing major, just an adjustment here and there, and he'd be able to run his final test tonight. If everything went to plan, and there was no real reason why it wouldn't, he would be hitting the road in the early hours of the morning and by tomorrow, he would have her.

Then the real fun would start.

As always, the man had already made the trip to where the girl lived. That was how he worked. Once he had identified a target, step two was always to go see them for himself. No matter where in the country they were. It gave him a much clearer idea of who the target really was and how to best approach him/her. He would, at least twice before he took them, stake them out for a period of never less than twenty-four hours each time, looking for patterns, routines, anything and everything that could make the job of taking them easier.

Only once had he deviated from this – while researching Linda Parker, whose daily schedule proved to be too elusive, too unpredictable. And so the man had decided to actually approach her beforehand.

Posing as an international photographer, he had booked a three-hour photo session with the model in a studio not that far from where she lived. It had been a risky move, the man knew that, but he also knew how to cover his tracks, and there was no way anyone would be able to track him through that photo-session booking.

But the man hadn't needed to resort to any tricks with this new girl. She had the most predictable routine of them all, which, in a way, was expected, given who she was.

The man checked his watch, powered down his computer and sat back on his chair. As he envisaged what was about to unfold in the next few hours, he felt as if his body was being pricked by a thousand needles, injecting him with some new drug that electrified his veins.

The man smiled as he caught a glimpse of his reflection on the dark computer monitor.

It was time to go work on his disguise.

It was almost time to go get the girl.

No more Mr. Merciful.

Eighty-Six

'Don't eat so fast, Chiquita,' the live-in babysitter said, as she poured the girl another glass of apple juice. She always called the girl 'Chiquita', which meant 'little girl' in Spanish. 'Why are you eating so fast?'

The babysitter, who was fifty-four years old, with short black hair and kind, dark-brown eyes, still spoke with a slight Puerto Rican accent, despite having lived in America for forty years.

The girl had one more spoonful of her chili con carne before responding.

'Because it's delicious . . . and I'm hungry.'

The babysitter frowned. 'It's not any different from all the other times I prepared you chili con carne.'

'Well, it tastes delicious to me,' the girl replied, having another spoonful. 'It's delicious every time.'

'Delicious, huh?' the babysitter said. 'Thank you, Chiquita. Still, delicious or not, don't eat so fast. It's going to give you a stomach ache. You're supposed to chew your food before swallowing it. And drink your juice.'

'I am,' the girl replied, having the last of her dinner before reaching for her glass of juice, which she drank down in three large gulps. 'There . . . see?'

'What's gotten into you today, Chiquita? Do you want to feel sick?'

'No. And nothing has gotten into me. Everything is perfectly fine.' The girl got up from the dinner table and placed her bowl and her glass in the dishwasher.

The babysitter could easily tell that there was something different about the girl, but whatever it was, it seemed to be something good. Since that morning, the girl had this happier air about her.

'I think I will go finish my homework and then go to bed,' the girl said.

'Don't you want your dessert?' the babysitter asked. 'We still got cheesecake.'

'Umm. Maybe not tonight.'

'OK,' the babysitter said, making a face. 'What's wrong, Chiquita? There's got to be something wrong. You never skip dessert.'

'There's nothing wrong,' the girl replied, shaking her head. I just need to watch what I eat. I don't want to be a big fat balloon.'

'What?' the babysitter said, almost in shock. The girl was a million miles away from being overweight. 'Did someone at school make a comment on your weight?'

'No.'

'You can tell me, Chiquita. Did someone tell you that you needed to watch your weight?'

'No. Why? Do you think I need to watch my weight?'

'Of course not, Chiquita. There's absolutely nothing wrong with your weight, but I want to know where this silly idea to skip dessert came from.'

'Well,' the girl replied with a shrug. 'I saw this program on

TV about eating sweets every day and how people got fat from it. I don't want to be like that.'

'Oh, you saw it on TV, did you?'

'Yes.'

'Chiquita, you don't have to worry about that. They were talking about people who eat junk food all the time – candy bars, chips, cookies, pizza, or whatever. You don't do that, do you?'

'No.'

'No, you don't. You eat healthy and you have a dessert with your meal every day, which is good for you.'

The girl just looked back at her babysitter.

'Here,' the babysitter said, as she opened the fridge door. 'You're having your dessert. There's nothing wrong with having a dessert after a meal.'

The girl didn't want to argue. 'OK, but just a small slice then.'

'A small slice it is. And don't eat it too fast.'

The girl took no notice of the babysitter's last few words, devouring the whole thing in three bites.

'OK, now I'm going to go finish my homework and go to bed.'

The babysitter wanted to ask the girl if she wasn't going to watch some TV with her, like they did most nights, but after the comment the girl had made about the program she had watched, the babysitter thought that less TV wouldn't be such a bad idea.

'OK, Chiquita. Let me know if you need any help with your homework.'

'No, thank you. I'll be fine.'

The girl practically skipped out of the kitchen and went upstairs.

There certainly was a reason why the girl felt so happy – it was Wednesday evening, which meant that she would see him again the day after tomorrow. The past Friday, at the park behind the disused school, he had held her hand again, but this time, as they said goodbye, he kissed her on the cheek. The girl had never been so happy. He had also commented on her perfume, the one she had borrowed from her mother's room. He said that it was very nice. The girl hadn't managed to find her mother's sparkly earrings, but it didn't matter because he kissed her anyway. Now, the girl just couldn't wait for Friday to come.

'Just tonight and one more sleep,' she told herself.

She finished her homework, turned off her bedroom light and tucked herself into bed, but she was too excited and her brain couldn't stop imagining scenarios of what would happen as she and the boy met on Friday – holding hands, hopefully another kiss – who knew? When the girl finally fell asleep, she still had a smile on her face.

Her eyes blinked open again when she heard the door to her bedroom being pulled open.

Oh no, she thought. *Did I miss my alarm? I never miss my alarm.*

But that thought disappeared almost instantly, as her eyes moved to the alarm clock on her bedside table – 00:17 a.m.

'Lucia?' the girl called out her babysitter's name in a sleepy voice.

There was no reply, but the girl heard footsteps entering her room.

'Lucia?' she called again, as she reached for her bedside lamp.

As the light came on, the girl's eyes went wide with shock

and her muscles stiff with fear. Towering over her bed was a tall and strong-looking man, whom she had never seen before. The look in his eyes was cold, the expression on his face uncaring, but what petrified the girl was the fact that the man's gloved hands and some of his clothes were covered in blood.

'Hello ... Chiquita.'

Eighty-Seven

It was the last of Hunter and Garcia's two days off and for the first time in years, Hunter did stay away from his desk, spending most of his time in Tracy's company. He had spent last night at her apartment and though she had asked him if he wanted to stay the night again, Hunter had politely declined, saying that he wanted to run a few searches against a couple of FBI databases.

He had lied, which Hunter hated doing, but he wanted to take it slow with Tracy. He liked her . . . a lot, actually, but he had way too many demons running around inside his head to be able to simply step into a relationship in the same way a regular person would. Back in his apartment, Hunter read for a few hours before finally going to bed.

To put it in simple terms, there are essentially two types of insomnia. The first and most common one of the two keeps the subject from falling asleep. Regardless of how tired they might feel, or how dark and silent they might be able to make their surroundings, as soon as they finally lie down and close their eyes, their brains will shift into a new gear they didn't even know existed. The body will feel exhausted, but the brain will be wide awake. No position will ever be comfortable enough and sleep eventually becomes as elusive as the pot of gold at the end of the rainbow.

The second type is even more debilitating because it will allow the subject to fall asleep easily at first. It will permit them to go into a deep sleep, which we all experience during the first third of our sleeping time, before torturously waking them up as if an angry fire alarm had gone off inside their heads. Once they are awake, most people who suffer from this type of insomnia will not be able to fall asleep again for the rest of the night.

Unfortunately for Hunter, he suffered from both types.

He'd been asleep for just under two hours when his brain decided to hit the fire-alarm switch.

'Oh, give me a goddamn break,' he mumbled as he opened his eyes and woozily stared at the ceiling. He could picture his brain laughing at him.

So you thought you would get some real sleep this time, did you? Oh, Robert, you are so easy to fool.

Hunter turned to one side and closed his eyes again, willing sleep to come back, but that just caused his brain to laugh harder.

What are you doing? Are you challenging me? We both know who'll win this battle, don't we? Sleep time is over for you, my dear friend.

Defeated, Hunter sat at the edge of his bed and switched on the bedside lamp.

Cursing his brain, Hunter staggered into the bathroom and washed his face. As he reached for the bathrobe hanging from the hook by the shower enclosure, he heard his cellphone ring on his bedside table. He rushed to it.

'Detective Hunter,' he said into the mouthpiece. 'UVC Unit.'

'Robert, it's Erica. We've got a lead.' There was an excited quiver to Agent Fisher's voice.

'What?'

'Cyber Crime has managed to track the external connections that were made into the Optum platform.'

'All of them?'

'That's right. It took them almost three days to track the entire path because the connection was bounced through five different locations. A pretty clever move, according to Cyber Crime, but not clever enough. The connections all originated from the exact same location, and guess what? The location is in California. Less than a hundred miles outside Los Angeles.'

'What? Where?'

'Riverside County,' Agent Fisher replied. 'The property is an old horse ranch just south of Skull Canyon, about an hour's drive away.'

'Who's the owner?'

'The ranch used to belong to a Mr. Thomas Brewer, who died nine years ago. His wife had passed away five years before him and their only son was killed in action in Iraq in 2005. There's no record of a new owner. It seems like the place has been abandoned since Mr. Brewer's death. We're on our way there right now. You coming?'

Hunter felt a whoosh of warmth start at his temples and slowly spread through his whole body.

'What's the address?'

'I'm sending a map with all the coordinates to your phone right now.'

Eighty-Eight

Once Hunter joined Corona Freeway heading south, it took him exactly fifty-two minutes to reach exit eighty-five, leading to Indian Truck Trail. From there it was another four minutes until he reached Temescal Canyon Road. Two minutes later Hunter got to the dirt road Agent Fisher had indicated on the map she had sent him. The road was narrow and bumpy, surrounded by hills, bushes and rough terrain. The sky, dense with menacing clouds, cast a particularly dark night where not a single star could be seen.

Hunter drove for another eight minutes until he saw Garcia standing in the middle of the road, signaling him with a flashlight. He instructed Hunter to switch off his headlights and pull up by some heavy bushes on the right, where Garcia's Honda Civic, a Chevrolet Malibu and an Audi A6 were already parked.

'When did you get here?' Hunter asked, as he stepped out of his Buick and zipped up his jacket.

'About three minutes before you,' Garcia replied. 'I got the call around two in the morning.'

'Yes, so did I. So what have we got?'

'Just around those trees.' Garcia indicated a cluster of low trees a few yards in front of them. 'In a night this dark, head-lights can be seen from miles away. This is as close as we can get in a car without announcing we're coming.'

They rounded the trees and climbed up a short but steep hill covered by shrubs. Agents Fisher and Williams were crouched down behind a couple of leafy bushes.

'That's the ranch,' Agent Fisher said, indicating through the bushes while handing Hunter a pair of binoculars. He repos-itioned himself and had a look.

The property was about two hundred and forty yards in front of them. There were only two buildings – a two-story wooden house with squared windows on the right and a long and wide stable on the left. Both structures looked old, uncared for and in serious need of some heavy repairs. The place also looked deserted.

'Cyber Crime traced the Optum platform breaches to this location?' Hunter asked, handing the binoculars back to Agent Fisher.

'That's right. All three of them, but it doesn't look like anyone actually lives here. Did you notice the state of the place? Most of it is falling apart. If Cyber Crime got this right, then my guess is that the killer probably searched around for a place like this – abandoned, unclaimed and far from prying eyes. You drove up the dirt track, right?' She looked around just to emphasize her point. 'There's nothing around here but hills and rough terrain. No neighbors. No roads. No animals. Nothing. In theory, this place is a safe house. The killer could do whatever he liked in there without ever worrying that he might get caught or disturbed.'

With the number of abandoned and shut-down properties increasing every year all over the land, Hunter didn't find it at all surprising that this killer had perhaps settled on a disused location to run his operation from. Over the years, he and Garcia had chased a number of perpetrators who had done just that – used abandoned buildings as their 'headquarters', or to dump bodies, or to rape and torture their victims before murdering them ... the applications varied, but the examples were plenty.

'Do we know if there's anyone in there right now?' Hunter asked. 'It looks empty.'

'There's someone in there, all right,' Agent Williams countered. 'I got here about twenty minutes before you guys. See the top window on the right?' He indicated the house. 'About fifteen minutes ago, a light came on briefly before being switched off again. We haven't seen anyone leave.'

'Can I have those binoculars again?' Hunter asked.

He spent another minute studying the property and its grounds. No dogs, and he couldn't see a vehicle anywhere, but then again, a car could easily be parked at the back of the house, or inside the stable.

Hunter turned around and looked down the hill they had climbed. 'So are we waiting for the strike team?'

'They're on their way,' Agent Fisher replied. 'But we're not waiting.' She quickly decided to explain before the next obvious question came her way. 'This killer acts alone, we all know this. If he's in there, and it looks like he is, then the odds are totally in our favor. Four armed and highly trained law-enforcement officers against one probably unarmed civilian.'

'Probably,' Garcia said, as he zipped up his jacket and readjusted its collar. The wind had started to pick up, bringing with it a strong smell of damp soil. Rain was clearly imminent.

'He has no reason to be,' Agent Fisher retorted. 'He's not

waiting on a strike. Like I've said, this is probably his safe house. The only place where he feels secure enough to let down his guard. Add to that the fact that he's completely oblivious to the fact that we've made this location. He might be in there walking around naked while covering himself in ice-cream. I've checked with Cyber Crime – they've covered their tracks. They guaranteed me that there's no electronic, cyber way the killer could've been alerted that his connections to Optum have been traced.'

'And you really think that instead of waiting for the strike team, the four of us storming the property right now is a good idea?' Garcia asked.

'Yes, I do.' Agent Fisher's voice was firm. 'Whoever accessed the medical records of Kristine Rivers, Albert Greene and Timothy Davis did it from that house, twelve days prior to their murders. We know that there's someone in there right now. Maybe that's what he's doing again, searching for a new victim, scanning the Optum platform. If he finds what he's looking for, he might not come back here for days, weeks, months even. Remember, we don't have a name or a face. All we have is this location, which on paper belongs to no one. What that means is that if he's in there and we miss him now, we have no other way of tracking him down until he comes back here again, by which time it will probably be too late for whoever he might be selecting right now.' She paused and looked back down the hill. 'If you'd rather wait for the FBI strike team to get here, be my guest, but I'm going in.'

Neither Hunter nor Garcia could argue with Agent Fisher's reasoning.

'Fine,' Garcia accepted. 'We're in. So how are we—'

'Light,' Agent Williams announced, this time indicating

the stables. A faint light was seeping through some old wood boards on the far left.

They all went silent and still.

Agent Fisher used the binoculars to have a look.

'Can you see anything?' Garcia asked.

'No, nothing.'

The light stayed on for less than a minute before being switched off again.

Hunter borrowed the binoculars one more time, spending another full minute regarding the ranch.

'I haven't seen any movement,' he said. 'So he's either still in the stables, or I've missed him as he walked back into the house.'

'So how do you guys want to do this?' Garcia asked.

'I think our best option is if we split up into two teams of two,' Agent Williams replied. 'One enters the stables, the other the house.'

'Do we have any sort of communication device?' Garcia asked. 'So the two teams can stay in touch?'

'I've got two headsets in my trunk,' Agent Williams announced.

'That will help,' Hunter said.

Agent Williams quickly ran back to his car and picked up the headsets, handing one to Hunter and one to Agent Fisher.

'Larry and I can take the stables,' Agent Fisher said, checking her Glock Model 22 and making sure she had an extra fifteen-round clip with her. 'You two the house. What do you say? We'll use the headsets to keep in touch.'

'No problem,' Garcia replied. 'But if I'm going into possible close combat with deaf ears, I'm taking the Twins with me. Hold on.'

'What?' Agent Fisher made a face, but Garcia had already rushed back down the hill. A minute later he was back, carrying with him a sawn-off double-barreled shotgun.

'Meet the Twins,' he said, indicating his weapon. 'The bad boys of close combat.'

'You give your weapons names?' Agent Fisher asked.

'Boys with toys,' Garcia replied. 'What can I say?'

She shook her head. 'If possible we would like to take him alive.'

'Haven't killed anyone in my career yet.'

They checked their weapons and tested their headsets. All was in order.

'We'd better get going before the rain gets here,' Hunter said. 'If our shoes get wet, once we enter that house, each step will sound like a duck being strangled.'

'Let's do this,' Agent Williams said.

They took off in the direction of the house.

Eighty-Nine

Hunter, Garcia and both FBI agents walked as fast and as stealthily as they could, and considering that they had opted to keep their flashlights switched off so as not to give away their approach, they bridged the two hundred and forty yards between their last position and the ranch in almost no time. Their dark clothes also helped them blend into the night, in case anyone was looking.

As they got to where the old gates to the ranch would have been – about forty yards from the house – they all heard a distant sound like a car engine running in low gear.

'What's that noise?' Agent Fisher asked.

'Generator,' Garcia replied. 'Probably somewhere at the back of the house.'

Hunter also noticed some fresh tire tracks on the dirty road leading into the ranch. They rounded the stables and disappeared toward the back of it.

'OK, this is where we split,' Agent Fisher said, looking up into the sky. The wind had strengthened a few notches in the last two minutes. The smell of damp soil now seemed to be part of the night. Rain was just minutes away. She paused and looked at both detectives. 'Stay safe.'

'Wait,' Garcia said, as he reached into his pocket and handed her a hairband. 'Here, for your hair. You don't want it flipping onto your face while you're chasing the bad guy, do you?'

She shook her head. 'This is my good-luck charm. Only once I chased a perp with my hair tied back. That was the only time one ever escaped me.'

'OK.' Garcia returned his hairband to his pocket.

Agents Fisher and Williams made their way toward the large stable building, while Hunter and Garcia carefully approached the dilapidated house on the right. Hunter used his flashlight to examine the front door. There was no lock. Its frame was old and split in places, and most of the dark-green paint that had once covered the door and the rest of the house had long ago cracked and chipped away, thanks to the elements.

'We've got to find another way in,' Hunter said.

'Why?'

'Check out those hinges,' Hunter replied, flashing his light at them. 'They're covered in rust. We open this door and even under cover of the generator's noise, those hinges will sound like an alarm.'

'Great!' Garcia looked right, then left. 'So which way do you want to go?'

Hunter pointed right.

Once again, being as careful as they possibly could not to make any noise, they rounded the house to the right. As they made it to the side of the property they halted. A faint light showed at one of the second-floor windows.

'The killer being upstairs isn't necessarily a bad thing,' Garcia said.

Hunter agreed with a nod.

'Team A, this is team B,' Hunter whispered into his headset. 'What's your location? Over.'

A second later Hunter's earpiece cracked into life.

'We have just entered the stables, over,' Agent Fisher whispered back.

'We've got a light on the second floor of the house,' Hunter said. 'You guys might be in an empty building over there, over.'

'Not sure about that. We've also got a light here. Inside one of the enclosures. Can you see any movement? Over.'

'Not from where we're standing. We're still outside the building. How about you guys, can you see any movement? Over.'

'Same as you. Not from where we're standing.'

There was a short silence.

'I think it's best to proceed as planned and maintain radio contact. Over.'

'Ten four. Over and out.'

Hunter passed on the news to Garcia.

'Oh, that's awesome.'

The first ground-floor window on the right side of the house was completely gone. No glass, no frame, nothing. All that was left was a huge hole in the woodwork.

'I guess we've found our way in,' Garcia said.

Hunter quickly checked the floor inside the house directly under the window – no glass.

'I'll go first,' Garcia said.

'Careful with the floorboards,' Hunter said. 'They might crack, squeak, or both, so step lightly.'

'Sure, Dad.' Garcia smiled. 'Here, hold the Twins.' He handed his shotgun to Hunter.

'I can't believe you actually named your gun.'

'You liked that, didn't you? My pistol is called Big Baraboom.'

Hunter just shook his head.

Garcia got through the window hole without any problems. As his feet applied pressure against the floorboards they squeaked, but very lightly.

Hunter passed the Twins back to his partner.

'The floorboards feel quite solid for such an old and uncared-for house,' Garcia said.

Hunter handed him his H&K Mark 23 pistol and quickly cleared the window.

The room they landed in was square, with an old three-seater sofa pushed up against one of the walls. The sofa had long ago lost all its cushions and a few of its springs could be seen through the large rips in its fabric. Against the opposite wall was a tall and very wide bookcase. Out of its twelve shelves, only three remained. The floor was practically covered in old paperbacks. A tipped-over coffee table was in the center of the room, which carried a strong smell of damp, old paper and rotting wood.

Hunter hand-signaled Garcia – *Cover formation. I'll take lead.*

Garcia nodded.

Hunter switched on his flashlight, held it in his left hand with an inverted grip and brought it under his right arm – wrist against wrist – creating a cross where the left wrist supported the right one, his weapon hand. He held both at chest height with his right arm extended.

Garcia held his flashlight under the barrels of the Twins. Being a shotgun, his weapon came up to shoulder height.

Hunter moved forward, taking extra-light steps.

Garcia was right – the floorboards felt a lot more solid than

Hunter had expected. They did squeak, but not loud enough to alert anyone.

Hunter stepped over *Moby Dick*, *The Three Musketeers*, *The Sun Also Rises* and several other classics before finally reaching the door, which was flat against the floor outside the room. With his back against one of the walls, Hunter peaked around the doorframe – first right, then left. The next room also seemed absolutely still.

Hunter signaled for them to move on.

As they took their first step over the flat door, their bones practically jumped out of their bodies.

BANG, BANG.

From outside the house, coming from the direction of the stables, they heard two gunshots.

Hunter and Garcia locked eyes, fear and confusion swimming around in them. Neither had to say a word to each other.

They turned and dashed like a couple of Olympic runners toward the house's front door.

Something had gone horribly wrong.

Ninety

'OK, this is where we split,' Agent Fisher said, looking up into the sky.

The agents left Hunter and Garcia behind and quickly made their way toward the stables building. Once they got there, they flattened their backs against the wall to the right of the two large, sliding, barn-style doors. The doors hadn't been slid all the way shut, leaving a gap between them of about a foot and a half.

'Now that's lucky,' Agent Williams said, nodding at the doors. 'We can make it through that gap without having to touch the doors.' He quickly flashed a light on the door rails. They were in a terrible condition.

'I'll go in first,' Agent Fisher said, but Agent Williams stopped her by placing a hand on her left shoulder.

'No, Erica, I'll go first. You cover me.'

'Always the protective gentleman,' Agent Fisher said, winking at her partner.

Neither of them had any trouble clearing the gap between the doors.

The inside of the building looked pretty much like what most people would expect a stable to look like – a long and wide corridor, flanked on both sides by individual horse enclosures. The concrete that paved the corridor was old, warped and cracked. The enclosures had clearly been modified and were a little different from most regular stables. There were no windows, openings, flaps or metal bars where one could look into the enclosure to check on the animals. Instead, they all had solid, sliding wooden doors, which were all shut. There must've been about twelve to fourteen enclosures on each side of the corridor, but what really made them pause as they cleared the stable doors was the fact that on the left, toward the end of the long corridor, they could see a dim light coming through the cracks on the wood panels from one of the enclosures.

'So what do we do?' Agent Williams asked, his voice a barely audible whisper. 'Do we start at this end and check every enclosure, or do we move straight down the corridor and start with the lit one?'

Before Agent Fisher could reply, her headset cracked into life and she heard Hunter's voice loud and clear.

'Team A, this is team B. What's your location? Over.'

. . .

Once Agent Fisher ended her transmission with Hunter her eyes found her partner's. 'I don't like this, Larry. Not even a little bit.'

'What's going on?'

'There's a light on in the house as well,' she replied. 'Second floor. Just like us they can see no movement. Not yet.'

Agent Williams looked down the corridor at the faint light coming from one of the enclosures.

'You're right,' he finally said. 'I also think that the best thing to do is to proceed as planned. So how do you want to do this?' he asked again. 'Do we start at this end and check every enclosure, or do we move straight down the corridor and start with the lit one?'

'I don't know,' Agent Fisher whispered back. 'The light could be a trick.'

At that exact moment a muffled clang came from the first enclosure to their left, as if something had been dropped onto the floor.

Both of their hearts missed a beat.

'Did you hear that?' Agent Fisher asked.

Agent Williams nodded and quickly signaled her to get ready.

With ballerina steps they approached the enclosure. Agent Williams signaled his partner to ready herself at one side of the door, while he positioned himself at the other. The plan was for Agent Fisher to quickly slide the door open. Agent Williams would then storm the enclosure first, quickly followed by Agent Fisher. The two of them had performed similar maneuvers during different investigations countless times before. They both knew exactly what to do.

They readied their weapons and flashlights and signaled each other that they would go on the count of three. Agent Fisher used head nods to count them in.

One. Two. Three.

In one powerful yank, Agent Fisher pulled the door open. It traveled down its old and rusty rails uneasily, but still fast enough to surprise anyone who'd been hiding inside the horse enclosure.

As the door slid open, Agent Williams, who had his back against the wall outside, quickly rotated his body clockwise and into the horse enclosure, his right arm extended in front of him, his eyes alert, his weapon searching for a target.

A split second later, Agent Fisher appeared to his left, her weapon just as hungry as his.

Their eyes moved in every direction, finding nothing. The enclosure was empty, but their attention was immediately drawn to a second door located diagonally across from where they stood. It was an internal door that linked to the next enclosure along, and it was wide open.

'The enclosures link internally,' Agent Fisher whispered.

Agent Williams nodded and signaled for them to take cover formation. He would take the lead.

Moving three paces in front of his partner, Agent Williams began making his way toward the open door, his attention on edge, his weapon ready to fire. As he got to a few feet from it, he turned to signal Agent Fisher again, but paused in total confusion.

Agent Fisher's weapon was raised and aiming straight at his heart.

'I'm sorry, Larry,' she said in a quivering voice. Her eyes drowning in tears.

'What?' Agent Williams was the image of perplexity. His weapon arm had relaxed, as his brain tried hard to make sense of senseless. 'What are you talking about, Erica?'

'I'm so, so sorry,' she said again. Tears began rolling down her face.

'Sorry? Sorry for what?'

'For this.'

Agent Fisher squeezed the trigger twice in quick succession. The bullets exploded against Agent Williams' chest with maximum impact, rupturing muscle, shattering bone and perforating his heart in two places.

Ninety-One

Hunter and Garcia exited the house in the direction of the stables at full speed. As if on cue, as soon as they hit the ground
outside, the rain that had been threatening finally arrived . . .
and it seemed angry. Its raindrops were the size of grapes.

'Officer down,' Hunter heard Agent Fisher's voice come
through his headset. 'Officer down.'

'What?' Hunter called over giant strides. 'What happened?'

In no time at all the two detectives had reached the stables,
squeezing through the gap between the two sliding doors with
a simple body twist. Their weapons were up and ready, their
breathing labored, their clothes drenched in rainwater.

They looked left, then right – nothing.

'Over here.'

They both heard Agent Fisher's voice coming from the
horse enclosure to their left. Hunter and Garcia lost no time,
immediately rushing to it. As they entered the square pen, they
saw Agent Fisher kneeling by a pool of blood, cradling Agent
Williams' lifeless body in her arms. A few feet behind her was
a second door, which stood wide open.

'Jesus, what happened?' Hunter called out, kneeling next
to the agent.

Garcia stood by the first door, guarding the entrance like a hawk.

The rain, pelting down against the old roof full of holes, filled the stable with a deafening drumming-like noise. Water drips began appearing everywhere.

'Too many enclosures,' Agent Fisher explained in an anxious voice, her eyes full of tears. 'We decided to split up. I took the right side and Larry took the left one. I had just entered the first enclosure on the other side when I heard the shots.'

'Have you called it in?' Hunter asked. 'Have you called for an ambulance?'

'Yes, but what good will that do, Robert? He's gone, can't you see? He's gone.'

Hunter looked up at the opened door. 'Did you see anyone? Did you see the shooter?'

'No, I didn't see anyone, but it looks like the enclosures all connect internally. He could be anywhere right now.'

Hunter looked back at Garcia.

'No one has exited the stables,' Garcia said. 'At least not through the door we came in. If anyone had I would've seen it.'

CRANK.

They all heard a loud noise coming from outside the enclosure. Hunter and Agent Fisher jumped to their feet.

CRANK.

It happened again.

Weapons in hand, all three of them stepped outside the enclosure as cautiously as they could. There was no one there.

'Shit,' Agent Fisher said. 'The doors.'

'What?'

'When we got here,' she clarified, 'every single door was shut.' She indicated the door to enclosure number five on the right side and then the one to number six on the left. They were now both open.

'Where the hell is the strike team?' Garcia asked. 'Shouldn't they be here by now?'

Agent Fisher didn't reply.

'So what now?' Garcia again.

'Well, I'm not waiting,' Agent Fisher said, stepping to one side to avoid a leak from the roof. 'I'm going after this bastard. You guys do what you think you should do.' She began moving toward the second enclosure on the right.

'Wait,' Hunter called, as he turned and faced Garcia. 'Stay with her. I'll take the left side.'

'I don't need a babysitter,' Agent Fisher replied, before using the back of her right hand to wipe tears from her eyes.

'No one is babysitting anyone, Erica,' Hunter came back. 'We need to split up and there're three of us. No offense, but you're a bit shaken up and your eyes are full of tears. Your reflexes are not the same as they were a moment ago. So I'll take the left side, you two take the right. Go.'

'No,' Agent Fisher retorted. 'If you take the right side and we take the left one, the corridor between both sides stays clear. The killer might get past us without us noticing him. Better would be if you take the left enclosures, Carlos takes the right ones and I'll hold the corridor. If he runs from one side to the other, I'll spot him. It gives us a better chance.'

'She's got a point, Robert,' Garcia agreed.

'OK,' Hunter said. 'Anyone see anything, shout. Let's move.'

Repeating the same maneuver Agent Fisher had performed with Agent Williams when opening the door to the first enclosure on the left just moments ago, she helped Garcia with the door to the first enclosure on the right.

Hunter went back to the one on the left, skipped over Agent Williams' body on the floor and entered the second enclosure through the internal door.

It was empty.

So was the one Garcia had entered. It looked identical to the one they had just come from, with an internal door that linked the first enclosure to the second one. The door was open.

Garcia moved fast but quietly, his eyes covering every direction as he took each step. He placed his back against the wall to the left of the opened door, readied himself and rotated his body counterclockwise into the next room.

Empty.

Directly in front of him was the internal door that linked that enclosure to the next one. Garcia moved to it.

The rain outside, and some of it inside, had strengthened considerably. The drumming noise against the old roof now sounded like a Death Metal concert.

Once again, Garcia placed his back against the wall to the right of the door, but before he was able to perform his rotating maneuver, he saw Agent Fisher walk in through the same connecting door he had just walked through. She had tears in her eyes.

Instinctively he lowered his weapon.

'Are you all right?' he asked. 'Has the killer come through the corridor?'

Agent Fisher raised her weapon, pointing it directly at Garcia's chest.

'I'm sorry, Carlos.'

'What?' Garcia's shock was so intense, he practically froze.

'This wasn't supposed to go like this.'

'You've got to be joking.'

Garcia tried to move, but his weapon was down while Agent Fisher's was locked on to her target. There was no contest.

As Garcia tried to bring his weapon back up so he could fire, Agent Fisher squeezed her trigger three times.

Some say that your whole life flashes before your eyes just before you die. In Garcia's case, a single memory ... a single image flashed before his eyes a millisecond before the three bullets exploded against his chest and blood splattered against the wall behind him.

The image he saw was of his wife, Anna, smiling at him.

Ninety-Two

Hunter had just entered the third horse enclosure on the left when he heard the three loud shots coming from across the corridor from him.

He had never been one to believe in premonition, or sixth sense, or cop's intuition, or whatever anyone would like to call it, but right then, as the sound of those three shots traveled through the air and into his ears, he felt as if a ghost had walked straight through his body and taken with it a part of his soul.

Disbelief had frozen him in place and it took Hunter's brain an extra half a second to reengage. As it finally did, he shot out of the enclosure like a guided missile.

'Carlos,' he called out as he reached the stable corridor, his voice loud enough to power through the thundering rain. 'Erica.'

No reply from anyone.

'Carlos.'

Nothing.

Hunter made an on-the-spot decision and, assuming that he and Garcia were moving at the same pace, quickly approached the door to the third enclosure on the right and snatched it open.

Empty. There was no one in there, but as Hunter took a couple of steps into the room and waved his flashlight around, he saw blood splattered against the frame of the internal door that linked enclosures two and three.

'No. No. No.' Hunter rushed to it and his heart sank into the darkest of holes. On the floor, resting in a pool of his own blood, he saw his partner.

At that exact moment, Agent Fisher entered the enclosure through the door across from the one Hunter was at.

'No,' she cried out, her voice shaking, her eyes red from tears.

'What happened?' Hunter asked, dropping to his knees to cradle Garcia.

'I don't know,' she replied. 'I was guarding the corridor as planned. Then I heard the shots and rushed in through the first enclosure.'

'He's got a pulse,' Hunter said, after placing two fingers on Garcia's carotid artery, his voice fearful and hopeful at the same time. 'He's got a pulse. Where the hell is the ambulance?'

CLANG. CLANG.

From just outside the enclosure they were in, came the loud sound of two doors slamming.

Hunter's eyes flashed fire.

'Stay with Carlos,' he ordered Agent Fisher as he jumped to his feet and readied his weapon. 'Keep applying pressure to the wound and call for an ambulance now. I'm going after this sonofabitch.'

'I'm coming with you,' Agent Fisher came back.

'No. You're staying here with Carlos. Keep him talking. Don't let him doze off. And call for that goddamn ambulance.'

Hunter rushed out of the enclosure, determination and anger driving him like an autopilot.

Out in the corridor, Hunter checked left and right: nothing but rain coming down from roof leaks just about everywhere.

Which way, Robert? he asked himself mentally. *Right or left, which way? Pick ... now.*

He chose right, away from the front door they had squeezed through and toward the enclosure that was still lit. He walked slowly. Each couple of steps came with a full three-hundred-and-sixty-degree check – left, right, behind him, move on. He had taken his seventh step when heard a weird noise coming from his headset. It lasted for just a second. He paused and looked both ways. Nothing. He took a step back.

Vruuummm.

There it was again. It sounded like static interference.

'What the hell?' He moved his head forward then backward a couple of times.

Vruuummm, vruuummm ... vruuummm, vruuummm.

Hunter narrowed his eyes and once again looked right then left. He saw nothing. He couldn't dwell on it any longer. He had to move on, but as he took another step forward, he heard Agent Fisher call him.

'Robert.'

Hunter looked in the direction her voice had come from.

She was standing by the door to the fourth enclosure on the right, the one he had just passed. Her gun was pointing straight at him.

'Please drop the gun, Robert,' she said, her voice shaky.

'What?' Hunter tried to blink the confusion away.

'The gun, Robert, drop it.'

Hunter's brain froze. Absolutely nothing made sense. 'What?'

'NOW, Robert.'

Hunter lifted his left hand to signal her that he would do as he was told. Slowly, he placed the gun on the ground.

'Kick it,' she commanded.

Hunter kicked it to her.

'You shot them, didn't you?'

'I didn't know I would have to shoot them,' she said, tears once again coming to her eyes.

'There's no strike team coming, is there? No ambulance either.'

Agent Fisher shook her head. 'I didn't know I would have to shoot them. I didn't want to, but he's got my daughter.' Her eyes wandered right. 'No. He deserves an explanation. They all did.'

'What?'

Hunter followed Agent Fisher's eyes, but there was nothing there. Suddenly he realized what he'd been missing. Agent Fisher wasn't addressing him. She was addressing whomever she was talking to through the earpiece in her right ear. That was why she had her hair down all the time – to hide the earpiece.

Hunter's eyes moved around the place one more time. The static noise he'd heard just a moment ago. He now knew it had been electronic interference against his own headset. Broadcasting cameras, probably.

Somebody had been watching them this whole time.

Hunter felt a tight knot grip his throat from the inside. How could he have been so oblivious?

'He's got my daughter, Robert,' Agent Fisher said again, tears now rolling down her face, her voice uneven. 'She's fourteen years old and she's got Down syndrome. If I don't do what he tells me to . . . he's going to kill her.'

Hunter kept his eyes on her weapon arm. It was almost as shaky as her voice.

'She's all I have and I'm all she has. Can't let him do it, Robert. I can't let him take her from me.'

Hunter's gaze moved to her face. Her eyes were begging him for his forgiveness.

'I'm sorry, Robert,' Agent Fisher said. There was sincerity in her tone. 'I'm so, so sorry, but I have to protect my daughter.' She steadied her weapon hand.

Hunter had no idea how many times Agent Fisher squeezed the trigger this time, but he only heard the first shot, and for some reason, that single blast sounded a lot louder than any gunshot he had ever heard.

Ninety-Three

Several hours earlier

On Wilshire Boulevard, somewhere on the short stretch between Beverly Hills and Westwood Village, was a canyon of high-risers one row deep. The buildings seemed a little out of place in Los Angeles, as though someone had stolen a piece of Manhattan's Upper East Side and placed it inside LA's suburban grid. The apartment the FBI had allocated to Special Agent Erica Fisher was situated on the sixth floor of one of those buildings.

Agent Fisher had left the FBI Headquarters late and driven to a little Vietnamese café she had discovered just a block away from her building, but instead of having her food at the café, just like she had done the three previous times she'd been there, tonight she got her dinner to go. She still hadn't spoken to her daughter today and she wanted to give Heather a call before her bedtime.

Agent Fisher had just placed her food on the kitchen counter when the video intercom by her front door rang, which made her frown. She wasn't expecting any visitors, though Agent Williams sometimes dropped by unannounced.

'Hello,' she said into the microphone.

The person she saw on the video screen was a young and clean-shaven man, wearing a brown baseball cap.

'Parcel for Erica Fisher.'

Agent Fisher wasn't expecting any deliveries, but the FBI had a habit of sending her files without forewarning her.

'Can you leave it with the concierge?'

'I need a personal signature, ma'am.'

The agent studied the man through the small screen. 'Which courier company are you with?'

'Deliver LA, ma'am.' The man raised his credentials so the camera could pick it up. 'We deliver at any time. Day or night.'

'Stay there, I'll come to you.'

It took Agent Fisher less than a minute to get down-stairs again.

'Erica Fisher?' the man said as the agent met him in the building's lobby.

'That's me.'

The young man handed her a square cardboard box – twenty inches by twenty inches and about seven and a half deep.

She looked at it with intrigue. It was clear that that box hadn't come from the FBI.

'Could I please get a signature, ma'am,' the man said, hand-ing her an electronic sign pad.

'Who is this from?' she asked, searching the back of the box for a sender. There was none.

The man shrugged. 'I simply pick them up from the depot and deliver them, ma'am.'

'And the company you work for is called Deliver LA?'

'That's correct.' He handed the agent a calling card.

Agent Fisher signed the pad and handed it back to the man.

'Have a nice evening,' he said, before exiting the building and getting back on his bike.

Back in her apartment, curiosity got the better of Agent Fisher and she quickly used a kitchen knife to break the seal on the box. She pulled the lid open and paused, confused. Inside it was a cellphone sitting on top of a black leather coat.

'What the hell?'

All of a sudden, the cellphone inside the box rang, frightening Agent Fisher and making her jump.

'Motherfucker.'

She stared at it for a few seconds.

'What is this? Am I in the Matrix now?'

The phone was still ringing.

She regarded it for a few more seconds before finally picking it up.

'Hello?'

'Hello, Special Agent Erica Fisher.' The voice that came through the earpiece was male; he sounded middle-aged – perhaps somewhere between thirty and forty-five years old. The man also spoke in a boring monotone and with a slight accent. One that Agent Fisher couldn't quite place.

'Who is this?'

'Well, this is the person you called "just another pathetic loser". A psychopath. The person who you said blames society for his downfalls. The person who, to make up for his many inadequacies, decided to go around playing God.'

'What?'

'Yes, Special Agent Erica Fisher. Remember the press conference back in Tucson? I'm the one who isn't intelligent, or smart, or talented, or creative, or gifted, or artistic, or anything else. Those were your words, were they not?'

It finally dawned on Agent Fisher who she was speaking to and she felt sweat beads starting to form on her forehead.

'If you remove the coat from the box,' the man continued, 'you'll find an envelope under it. Inside the envelope there are some photographs, which I'm sure you'll find very interesting. Why don't you have a look at them?'

'What are you talking about?'

'Have a look at the photographs, Special Agent Fisher.' The man's tone was firm.

She removed the coat from the box and reached for the envelope, quickly tearing it open. There were five Polaroid photographs inside it. As she looked at them, her heart stopped.

All five photographs showed Heather, her daughter, tied up to an uncomfortable-looking bed. The girl didn't look hurt, but her eyes were cherry red and the skin around them was raw from so much crying. Agent Fisher had never seen her daughter look that sad.

'Wha . . . ? The agent tried to breathe. 'What is this?'

'This is exactly what it looks like, Special Agent Fisher. I have your daughter. The reason I used a Polaroid camera is so that you know the photos aren't a trick. No editing whatsoever. This is real and this is happening.'

'You sonofabitch,' Agent Fisher yelled down the phone. 'I swear to God that if you hurt one hair on her head I will kill you, do you hear me? I WILL KILL YOU.'

'I hear you, all right.' The man's voice stayed as calm as a librarian's. 'Now do you hear me?'

'She's fourteen years old, you sick freak, with a mental age of ten, or haven't you realized she's got Down syndrome?'

'Oh, I certainly have, and if you think I give a damn about that, then you shouldn't have the job you do. I'm a psychopath, remember? You diagnosed me yourself. Psychopaths display no emotions toward other human beings, or have you forgotten that, Special Agent Fisher?'

Agent Fisher couldn't think straight. All she could think about was her daughter.

'She's fourteen years old,' she said again, this time fighting back tears.

'If you want your daughter to live,' the man said, 'you'd better do exactly as I tell you. If you don't, I promise you I will skin her alive. I'll take her eyes, too.'

'Oh my God . . . no.'

'I trust you've seen what I can do, so you know this isn't an empty promise. Rule number one: do not disconnect from this call. If you do, your daughter dies.' A very short pause. 'What's rule number one?'

Agent Fisher did her best to hold back her tears, but her voice was still shaky.

'Let me talk to her. Let me talk to my daughter.'

The man was already expecting that request. It was only natural.

'What's rule number one?' the man asked again.

'Do not disconnect from the call,' Agent Fisher replied. 'Let me talk to Heather. Let me talk to my daughter.'

'Sure, but before I do that, I want you to put on the coat that's inside the box.'

'What?'

'The black leather coat, put it on,' the man ordered her again.

'Why?'

'Put it on, or I will hurt your daughter right now, and remember – do not disconnect from the call.'

As Agent Fisher picked up the coat, she noticed it was heavier than she expected.

'What is this coat?'

'Put it on.'

She did as she was told. 'OK, it's done; now let me speak to my daughter.'

'Left internal breast pocket,' the man said. 'There's a small switch there. Switch it on.'

'What? You've got to be kidding me, right?'

'It's not a bomb, Special Agent Fisher. I'm not a terrorist,' the man explained. 'Four of the buttons on that coat are cameras that transmit using the connection on the phone you're holding. Those cameras need to be on, so use the switch in the pocket and switch it on . . . NOW.'

Agent Fisher knew she had no other choice but to trust what the man was telling her. She reached for the switch, found it, closed her eyes and flicked it on.

No explosions.

Agent Fisher breathed out.

'There we go,' the man said. 'Now wave your hand in front of the coat, please.'

Once again, Agent Fisher did as she was told.

'Now let me speak to my daughter.'

'Sure,' the man replied, 'But keep that left hand in front of the jacket, so I know you're not using it to dial your phone. If I even suspect that you're trying to contact anyone about this, your daughter dies, is that clear?'

'Yes.'

'Mommy?' Agent Fisher heard Heather's sweet voice come through the earpiece.

'Heather, darling.'

'Mommy, I don't like this man. He's not nice. Can you come pick me up?' She sounded like she'd been crying . . . a lot.

'Yes, darling.' Agent Fisher swallowed her tears. 'I'll go pick you up in a moment, OK? You just sit there and wait for Mommy.'

'Are you coming now?'

'Yes, honey, I'm on my—'

'Sorry to interrupt,' the man cut in. 'But this was getting too soppy for me.'

'What do you want?' the agent asked, anger dripping from every word.

'Right now I want you to listen. Inside your right pocket there's an earpiece – Bluetooth. It will fit into your ear perfectly. Switch it on and put it in your ear. It will free your hands.'

'Done.'

'Now let me see both of your hands. Place them in front of the coat.'

Agent Fisher followed the instructions she was given.

'Fantastic. Now place the phone inside your internal right breast pocket.'

She did.

'That phone has a talk-time battery life of twenty hours. More than enough.'

'Enough for what?'

'You better stop interrupting me, Special Agent Fisher. It's very annoying. And KEEP YOUR HANDS IN FRONT OF THE COAT.'

Agent Fisher obliged.

'If this phone call gets disconnected, your daughter dies. No questions asked. If I suspect that you're trying to contact or signal anyone at any moment, your daughter dies. No questions asked. If you do not execute the orders I give you through the earpiece immediately, your daughter dies. No questions asked. If you take off the earpiece or the coat, your daughter dies. No questions asked. If anyone notices that you are on the phone to me at any time, your daughter dies. No questions asked. One of the button cameras on your coat points directly at your mouth, so do not try anything stupid or your daughter dies. No questions asked. Is all that clear?'

'Yes.'

'So, are you ready for an adventure?'

'Go fuck yourself.'

'Oh, I forgot. One more rule. You curse at me again, your daughter dies. No questions asked.'

Agent Fisher began trembling from a combination of anger and fear, not for her life, but for her daughter's.

'OK,' the man said. 'Grab your car keys. We're going on a road trip.'

Ninety-Four

The first thing that the man instructed Agent Fisher to do was to change her shoes into something a lot more comfortable. 'Shoes you can run in', were actually the words he used. After that, he told her to pack her regular weapon, jump in her car and drive south, joining the US-101 from North Los Angeles Street.

'OK,' Agent Fisher said as she finally got onto the freeway. 'So where am I going here?'

'Oh, we're taking a ride to a great little horse ranch I found.'

'Why?'

'Because it's a great place for a stand-off.'

'A stand-off?'

'Well, I'll explain as we get nearer.'

Agent Fisher knew that she had to keep the man talking for as long as she could. As long as he was talking he couldn't be hurting Heather, and that was all that mattered right then.

'Why are you doing this?'

'Because you called me a "pathetic loser", you called me dumb – well, not in so many words, but you did. You said that I was an inadequate person. What do you think, Special Agent

Fisher? Do you think that you can just go around spreading lies about people and not suffer any consequences? Sorry, but that's not the way the world goes.'

'You're doing this,' Agent Fisher asked in disbelief, 'you've kidnapped my daughter because you want an apology?'

'Oh, no, no. It's way too late for an apology now. But you'll see what I want in due time. It's not my fault if you are not worthy of my work. It's not my fault if your intellect is too constricted to understand the magnitude, the importance of what I'm doing.'

'You mean collecting body parts?'

The man went quiet for a moment.

'What?' Agent Fisher pushed. 'You think we haven't figured that out?' She was careful not to sound too aggressive. She had no idea what sort of temper the caller had, but she could guess. If he got so offended as to kidnap her daughter just because she called him a 'loser' in a press conference, who knew what he would be capable of if she insulted him in a direct conversation? 'Your Latin clues were very clever. It took us a while. We considered several different theories, but we got there in the end.'

'I'm glad that you have finally figured out the clues, Special Agent Fisher, but the real question is: do you understand it? Do you see the importance of what I'm doing?'

'No, I don't,' Agent Fisher admitted. 'You're killing people to rob them of their body parts. What's the grand vision there? What is the master plan behind any of that?'

'You really don't see it, do you, Special Agent Fisher? We live in a screwed-up world, a false world where almost nothing is real anymore. Everywhere you look, most of what you see is fake, even the bodies you see – fake cheekbones, fake lips, fake noses, fake hair, fake eyelashes, fake breasts, fake muscles, fake bums, fake smiles, fake teeth, fake nails, fake skin color, eye color, hair color ... everything. Our whole lives are nothing more than one huge lie. Online we have one thousand friends, but in real life we barely have three. We pretend to be what we're not, to impress people we don't like. In cyberspace we lead a fantastic life – we post pictures and statuses that suggest one thing, when in reality we are just the opposite. We lie, we cheat, we steal, we deceive, we pretend ... we do anything to maintain the fake appearance that we are happy with ourselves ... happy with our lives, without realizing that what is actually making us miserable is the lying, the fakeness, the pretending. The more we lie, the sadder we get, but we can't stop it. We've all been sucked into this false world that no one can get out of, so we just have to keep on going. Keep on pretending. Keep on lying. We are all con artists. All of us.'

The man paused for breath.

'Me? I am simply visionary enough to be able to see what is real, what matters most, what is really valuable in this world, but unfortunately we can't collect "truth", so I decided to go after the next most valuable commodity on earth. True beauty. The kind that cannot be fabricated, copied, or duplicated, no matter who you are or how much money you have.'

Keep him talking, Agent Fisher kept on telling herself.

'You don't really know what you've done, do you?' she asked.

'I know exactly what I've done.'

'Do you know about your first victim, Kristine Rivers? Do you know who she was? Who she really was?'

The man went quiet.

'She was the niece of the FBI's NCAVC director. Do you know what that means? It means that the Bureau will *never* stop looking for you. *Never.*'

Agent Fisher paused, allowing the man to savor those words.

'I wasn't lying when I said that the net is closing around you,' she continued. 'There are tens of agents working this case, each covering a different aspect of the investigation. You won't be able to hide forever. We'll get to you sooner rather than later, but I can help you.' Agent Fisher's voice took a tender tone. 'Please just let my daughter go. I know you don't really want to hurt her. You don't really want to hurt an innocent fourteen-year-old girl whose understanding of this world, this false world you hate so much, isn't like ours. Please, just let Heather go and I will testify on your behalf. I promise you. I'll tell the court how merciful you were.'

'Enough,' the man said, his voice angry. 'Do you really think you can win me over with your soft talk?' The man laughed. 'I WAS merciful, or didn't your pathologists figure that out? There was never any torture. Never any pain. No suffering. Once they were gone, I placed them in the most respectful position there is – resting placidly on their backs. They should be thankful to me. Do you know why? Because I immortalized them. And now you want to talk about helping me out? You make me laugh. Who's pathetic now, huh? As for being able to hurt an innocent person? Why don't you ask Lucia, your daughter's babysitter?'

Agent Fisher felt her stomach churn. 'What have you done?'

'Let's just say that there was a lot of blood.'

'What have you done?' Tears came into Agent Fisher's eyes.

'One day what I'm doing will be understood, Special Agent Fisher. My collection will be understood. It will be seen as the most valuable collection on this planet. You'll see. Just give it time.'

Agent Fisher heard keyboard clicks coming through her Bluetooth earpiece.

'OK, you're coming up to an exit on the right. I want you to take it.'

Agent Fisher followed the caller's instructions until he told her to park by some heavy bushes on the side of the dirt road she'd been driving on for the past few minutes. They were in the middle of absolutely nowhere.

'Now what?' she asked.

'Now I want you to get on the phone and call the rest of the investigative team. The team that were with you in Tucson. All three of them. Tell them that you have got a lead on a suspect, or anything you like, but be convincing, because you'll only have one chance. Get them to come to you. You guys are about to storm the suspect's hideout place.'

Left with no options, Agent Fisher had to do as she was told.

'I'm impressed,' the man said after she made all three calls. 'You have actually figured out about the Optum platform.'

Agent Fisher squeezed her eyes tight in anger. To convince Hunter, Garcia and Agent Williams to come meet her, she had told them that Cyber Crime had managed to track the breach to the Optum platform. Now the killer knew the FBI knew about how he was gathering information about his victims. Even if she managed to get out of this, their only lead on how to actually track this killer down was now lost.

'Anyway,' the man continued. 'Now we wait. Don't worry. I'll guide you through every single step. I'll even tell you what

to say, if the situation warrants it. And don't try to do anything silly, because I have eyes everywhere. The entire ranch is
covered in cameras and from where I am, I can control lights,
doors, noises, anything I want. All you need to do is follow the
script exactly how I tell you and little Heather here won't have
to worry about the big bad man.'

Ninety-Five

The man did guide Agent Fisher through absolutely every single step of the way, sometimes even telling her exactly what to say. He was also the one who had created the noise that had first startled Agent Williams. Through his cameras, he had watched as both agents approached and entered the first horse enclosure on the left. As Agent Williams moved to the internal door that linked enclosures one to two, the man ordered Agent Fisher to shoot her partner.

'What?' she had whispered back in a quiet voice that escaped her partner's ears.

'You heard it right, Special Agent Fisher. I want you to shoot him. Don't hesitate. If you do, I swear I'll start cutting your little girl. Shoot him. Shoot him NOW.'

'I'm sorry, Larry. I'm so, so sorry.'

'Sorry for what?' Agent Williams had asked.

'SHOOT HIM, or this little ugly bitch will start bleeding.'

'For this.' She squeezed the trigger twice.

'OK, now get ready, because here come the other two.'

The man had watched as Hunter and Garcia exited the house and dashed toward the old stable building. He controlled the opening and closing of enclosure doors to give the impression that there was someone else in there with them. He also told Agent Fisher what to say when Hunter had suggested that she and Garcia team up to check the enclosures on the right.

'OK,' the man had said. 'Let's take out the guy on the right first. He has just entered the second enclosure. Go after him and shoot him dead. Shoot him three times, not two. Go . . . now.'

Once Agent Fisher had followed her orders, the man told her to run back to the first enclosure and wait.

On one of his monitors, the man watched as Hunter rushed out of the enclosures on the left, following the sound of the gunshots. When Hunter had entered the third enclosure, the man told Agent Fisher to also rush back into it and put on a good show, pretending she had just got there.

The man was pleasantly surprised with how good an actress Agent Fisher could be.

'Don't worry about finishing this one off,' the man had said once Hunter had ordered Agent Fisher to stay with Garcia and call an ambulance. 'He will bleed out anyway. Just let him suffer. Let's go finish this. Let's go take down this last one and I promise you, you will see your daughter again.'

The man observed as Hunter returned to the corridor between the two enclosures and slowly began moving forward.

'OK,' he said to Agent Fisher. 'Move to the fourth enclosure. You'll come out just behind him. Let's go end this.'

The man listened as Agent Fisher told Hunter to drop his weapon and kick it toward her. When she told him that her daughter had been taken from her, the man's eyes widened.

'What are you doing, Special Agent Fisher? You better get back to the plan or your daughter dies.'

'No,' Agent Fisher had replied. 'He deserves an explanation. They all did.'

The man thought about it for a split second. So what if she told him why she was doing what she was doing? He would die anyway.

'OK, go ahead. Get it off your chest.'

As the man watched Hunter through the camera buttons on Agent Fisher's coat, he got a bad feeling. There was something about the man he was watching that bothered him. To him, Hunter looked dangerous. A lot more dangerous than the other two. He decided it was time to end that game once and for all.

'All right. That's enough. I want you to shoot him. I want you to shoot him NOW, or I will rape this little bitch before I cut her, do you hear me? Shoot him. Shoot him NOW.'

BANG.

Ninety-Six

Hunter had no idea how many times Agent Fisher squeezed the trigger, but he only heard the first shot, and for some reason, that single blast sounded a lot louder than any gunshot he had ever heard, but still Hunter never closed his eyes. He would not give her or whomever it was that was watching them through the cameras the pleasure of seeing him flinch. Instead, Hunter looked straight into Agent Fisher's eyes.

He saw the tears and the anguish in them. He saw the undying love of a mother who needed to protect her child. He saw the turmoil she was going through, the emptiness reflected from her soul. He also watched as her weapon hand was practically blown to pieces by the shotgun blast that came from her left.

A twelve-gauge shotgun cartridge releases tens of lead pellets. Upon exiting the gun barrel, the pellets spread out like a 'ball of death' traveling toward its target. That ball of death hit mainly Agent Fisher's hand, nearly obliterating it, but some of the pellets did hit her arm, chest and stomach, causing blood, muscle and bone to splatter in all directions. Her gun was catapulted across the floor and her body dropped to the ground like an empty sack of potatoes.

Hunter's eyes shot to his right and he saw Garcia standing there with smoke coming out of his shotgun. Hunter blinked twice to make sure he wasn't seeing things.

'Fucking bitch,' Garcia said, now looking at Hunter. 'She shot me three times.'

He noticed the mesmerized look on Hunter's face.

'What, you think that when I went back to my car to pick up the Twins here that was the only thing I picked up?' He shook his head, unzipped his jacket and used his knuckles to knock against the Kevlar vest underneath it. 'Oh hell no. I also grabbed my second-best friend here – Mr. Not Today. There's a reason I keep it in the boot of my car.'

'But you're bleeding,' Hunter said.

'One of her bullets grazed the inside of my left arm.' Garcia lifted his arm to show the wound. 'Hurts like a motherfucker.'

Hunter rushed to Agent Fisher's body on the ground. She had fallen inside enclosure number four on the right, just by the door.

Garcia was right behind him. 'Shall I shoot her again?' he asked as he got to Hunter.

Hunter lifted a finger to his lips while shaking his head at Garcia. He then pointed at his ear and made a circular motion with his finger to indicate that there were others listening.

Garcia halted.

A few more gestures told Garcia that there were cameras around.

As Garcia took a step back and began scanning the walls inside the enclosure, this time for cameras, Hunter quickly checked Agent Fisher. She was still alive, but losing a lot of blood through the horrible wound on her right arm. Hunter took off his belt and used it as a tourniquet to reduce the bleeding before searching her pockets. He found the cellphone the man had sent her, but it was shot, completely destroyed by one of the shotgun pellets.

'Motherfucker,' Garcia said as he identified a tiny camera above the inside of the door to the enclosure. He moved to the tip of his toes and grabbed it off the wall. It was round and small, the size of a coat button. 'No microphones,' he said to Hunter. 'This is a visual aid only.'

'Whoever this guy is,' Hunter said, 'he's got no ears here anymore. The phone is shot to pieces.'

'How is she?' Garcia asked.

'Alive, but she's losing blood fast. We need an ambulance here, now.'

'I'm on it.'

'And wrap something around your arm wound,' Hunter said. 'Before you bleed out, too.'

'I'm on it.'

While Garcia called for back-up, Hunter called Adrian Kennedy. As they waited, Hunter stayed with Agent Fisher while Garcia went around the stables collecting every camera he could find. There were thirty-two in total – one inside each enclosure and four on the center corridor.

It took the FBI back-up team and the ambulances less than forty minutes to get there. Adrian Kennedy was inside a jet and on his way. Agent Fisher was still alive, but the paramedics didn't sound very hopeful about the chances of her actually surviving.

'So the killer's got her daughter?' Garcia asked, after Hunter had told him the little he had gathered just before Agent Fisher got shot. His arm had already been bandaged up.

'That's what she said.'

'So chances are, she's dead.'

'I'm not so sure,' Hunter replied.

'How come?'

'Your shotgun blast obliterated the cellphone in her pocket, which means that the killer lost ears on this place immediately. He had eyes, but no ears anymore. What he saw through the cameras was Erica getting shot by you and falling to the ground like a corpse. He probably thinks she's dead.'

'She still might be,' Garcia said.

'But not yet,' Hunter retorted. 'Anyway, if the killer thinks Agent Fisher is dead, what's the point in killing her daughter? Remember, this is a killer who has always been merciful with his victims. He never tortures them. He's not after that kind of pleasure.' Hunter shook his head. 'No. I don't think he's going to hurt her. I think he'll just let her go.'

Right then, Hunter felt his cellphone vibrate inside his jacket pocket.

'Detective Hunter, UVC Unit,' he answered straight away. He listened for several seconds, his expression changing from tired and worried to completely surprised. 'You're kidding. Send those photos to my cellphone now. I'll wait and I'll call you back.'

'What's going on?' Garcia asked.

'Hold on,' Hunter replied, his attention fixed on his cellphone, waiting for it to beep announcing a new text message. It did ten seconds later.

A minute after that, Hunter was on the phone to Adrian Kennedy again.

Ninety-Seven

Through one of his monitors, the man watched as Garcia suddenly appeared to Agent Fisher's left and, quick as a flash, pulled the trigger on his sawn-off double-barreled shotgun.

'NO!' the man screamed, his voice resonating against empty walls, but it was already too late. The shot hit Agent Fisher with utmost precision, sending a crimson mist up in the air and the agent to the ground. Immediately, all the monitors that were broadcasting the images picked up by the camera buttons on Agent Fisher's leather coat went blank. His audio feed also died instantly.

'Shit!'

The man knew that the cellphone in her pocket had been hit.

He checked his other monitor for the images coming from the cameras inside the stables. Agent Fisher had fallen inside horse enclosure number four on the right, just by the door, but the camera for that enclosure was directly above that same door, which meant that she had fallen in a blind spot. With no eyes on her, the man couldn't tell if she was still alive or not. All he could see, from one of the cameras on the corridor, was the edge of her feet, and they weren't moving.

Then, all of a sudden he saw Garcia look up at the camera above the door and reach for it.

He'd been made. That was unfortunate, but instead of being angry, the man smiled at himself. It didn't matter if they found the cameras, the phone, the leather coat, or anything else. He was already counting on that happening. Maybe not this soon, but he knew that they would eventually find them. Still, it didn't matter because none of it was traceable. The cameras hadn't been bought in a shop. He had put them together himself from parts bought from a variety of different outlets. The jacket he had purchased in a goodwill shop. There was nothing in that ranch that would give the FBI any clues to who he was or how to find him. He now knew that the FBI knew about his Optum platform breach, but he was a computer whiz, and he knew that there was no way they could trace any of those breaches back to him.

It was a pity that his little game had ended this way and so soon, but it had certainly been fun.

The man switched off all the monitors and sat back on his chair. He felt tired, exhausted even. He hadn't slept in fifty-one hours, and now that his revenge against Special Agent Fisher was complete, the fatigue hit him like a plane crash. He decided that he would rest for a little before returning to the girl. He had no use for her anymore. The girl had no mother. Even if Special Agent Erica Fisher survived, she would spend the rest of her life in prison. He might as well end the little girl's misery.

Maybe he would be merciful one more time.

Ninety-Eight

It's astonishing how light and darkness can completely alter one's perception of time. Take, for example, every casino in the United States. The intensity of the lighting in their gambling floors is controlled and constant – twenty-four hours a day, seven days a week – just the right balance of brightness and colors so as not to overexpose and tire the human eye. Consequently, gamblers often lose track of time. What to them might feel like an afternoon spent at the tables, turns out to be a day and a half.

Heather Fisher was being subjected to the exact same experience, but in total darkness and without the luxuries of a Las Vegas gambling floor. Her notion of time had left her long ago.

After the man had allowed her to speak to her mother on the phone, he had put her in that dark room and Heather had waited and waited and waited. Her mother had said that she was coming to pick her up, but she still hadn't turned up. After waiting for what seemed like an eternity, Heather had cried herself to sleep.

The girl missed her mother dearly, but what had really made her sad was the fact that she had been unable to go to the park after school to meet the boy. She really liked him. He was just like her, different, but they understood each other and they always laughed together. She liked that very much. She liked when he sat next to her, when he held her hand, when he smiled at her, and she had felt the warmest of feelings inside when he kissed her cheek last Friday.

The man had taken away her cellphone, so she had no way of telling the boy that she couldn't be there. She was terrified that the boy wouldn't want to go to the park to see her anymore. That he wouldn't want to sit next to her again, or smile at her, or hold her hand.

Why was that man so mean? She had never done anything to him.

When Heather woke up again, the room was as dark as it had always been. She felt hungry, thirsty and cold, and the mattress she was lying on felt like it was made out of cement. Every muscle in her body hurt, especially the ones on her neck. As she sat up, blood throbbed in her ears, making her feel dizzy. Her clothes felt soaking wet and they didn't smell so good. She really didn't like that.

Tears welled up in the girl's eyes again. She couldn't understand what was happening to her. Why was she in that room? Who was that man? Why did she have to sit in the dark? And why didn't her mother come pick her up like she said she would? Her mother never lied to her.

Then a new thought came to the girl. Maybe the man was the boy's father. Maybe he had found out that his son, Thomas, was meeting her at the park after school and he didn't want that, he didn't want his son sitting next to her, or smiling at her, or holding her hand. The man didn't want that because she was different. But Thomas was also different and she really, really liked him. If she could, she would sit next to him every day.

Heather closed her eyes and the tears became sobs. She cried for a long while before she heard footsteps approaching from outside the small room. She quickly wiped the tears from her eyes and jumped to her feet.

'Mommy?' she called, feeling her way in the darkness toward the door. 'Mommy, I'm here.'

Heather heard a key being inserted into the door lock. It turned once, twice, three times.

'Mommy?'

The door was finally pulled open and light spilled into the room from the corridor outside. Heather blinked, turning her face away from the door. The sudden bright light hurt her eyes.

'Mommy?' she called one more time.

'No,' the man replied, his voice firm and strong. He used the remote control in his left hand to switch on the lights inside the room.

Heather blinked a few more times before her vision finally could handle the brightness.

The man stepped into the room and allowed the door to close silently behind him.

Heather shivered.

'Mommy isn't coming for you.' The man returned the remote control to his trouser pocket, from where he retrieved a pair of latex gloves. 'Nobody is ever coming for you ... Except me.'

Ninety-Nine

The FBI Special Weapons and Tactics team convoy was made up of three black SUVs. There were five specially trained assault agents in each vehicle. The team leader was Special Agent Trevor Richardson, an ex-military black-ops officer with over seventeen years' experience in covert operations. His team was the best the FBI had to offer and they were all pumped up and ready to strike.

The address they had took them to a very quiet street on the outskirts of Chula Vista, the second largest city in the San Diego metropolitan area, Southern California. There were only three houses on the street, all of them back from the road and far enough from each other for one to be able to throw a loud party without ever bothering the neighbors. The specific house they were after was by far the largest one on the street, tucked away right at the top of the hill. The team had already acquired the architectural blueprints for the property. It showed a massive two-story building with six bedrooms upstairs, all of them en suites and three of them very oddly shaped. Downstairs there was a large kitchen, a dining room, a living room, a study and an extra room that could be absolutely anything – a games room, a projection room, a lab, a gallery ... whatever the owner had decided to make of it, really. The basement was enormous and though they knew of its existence, its layout was a complete mystery to the team.

From the outside, the house was also the most imposing on the street, with a large, very well-cared-for front garden and a driveway that ended in a wide cobblestone courtyard, with a three-car garage to its right. The car parked in front of one of the three garage doors was an Infinity QX80 – the exact vehicle they were looking for.

The car and the house were registered to Arthur Weber, a thirty-four-year-old computer whiz and entrepreneur who, at the age of twenty-five, had become a millionaire several times over, thanks to the success of his mobile applications company – Walking Gadgets. He had sold the company two and a half years ago for an absolute fortune and since then, at least according to what the team was able to gather in such a short time, had become somewhat of a recluse, withdrawing from social life almost completely. Mr. Weber had never been married, had no children and no siblings. His mother had raised him alone, as his father had walked away from them even before he was born.

The sun was about forty minutes away from rising when the three FBI SUVs pulled up outside the gates of Mr. Weber's house.

'OK, everybody, listen up,' Agent Richardson said, as all fifteen agents gathered around in a circle. 'As I've explained before, we're splitting into three teams – Alpha, Beta and Gamma. Gamma team will enter the house and immediately proceed upstairs. Beta team will take the ground floor and Alpha team will venture into the unknown that is the basement. I will be leading Alpha team. Collins will head Beta team and Gomez Gamma team.' Richardson checked his watch. 'The sun will be up in just over thirty minutes and I want this all wrapped up by then.'

'Roger that, sir,' fourteen voices said in unison.

'Now here's the deal,' Agent Richardson continued. 'Whoever this guy is, he has no clue we're coming for him this morning, so surprise is on our side here and we want to keep it that way. No loud noises. Once inside, hand signals only between team members. Team leaders will maintain minimum radio contact. The point to remember is that if this is our guy, he's responsible for at least five deaths, one of them a fellow agent. He's smart and very resourceful, but the good thing is, he shouldn't be carrying a weapon. The bad thing is, like I've said before, he's got a little girl hostage, who he might be keeping in the house. We have no real intel on that and for that reason, I want all of you to be on your toes. The girl's name is Heather. She's fourteen years old. She has Down syndrome and she's the daughter of an FBI special agent.' He lifted up a tablet, on its screen a portrait photograph of Heather. 'This is her and she's our priority today; is that understood?'

'Yes, sir.'

'The idea is to take Arthur Weber alive, so deadly force is to be used only if absolutely necessary, but if that necessity shows its ugly face, I want you to drop him without hesitation.'

'Roger that.'

Agent Richardson looked around his elite squad of men – fourteen 'don't fuck with me' badasses whom he would trust with his life.

'All right,' he said in conclusion. 'Once in there watch your six and cover every corner. Lock and load, Godspeed and let's go get this sonofabitch.'

One Hundred

All three teams moved fast and stealthily, easily clearing the gates and the front lawn in absolutely no time at all. The FBI had already been in contact with the alarm company that serviced Arthur Weber's house and the whole system had been switched off without the owner's knowledge, so no one had to worry about bypassing circuits or disconnecting wires.

As they approached the house, Alpha team rounded it to the back door, while Beta and Gamma teams stayed with the front one.

'Beta and Gamma teams in position, over,' came the announcement from the Beta team leader over their headsets.

'All right,' Agent Richardson replied, nodding at the team agent who had slid a fiber-optic tube under the back door. The tube was connected to a five-inch monitor screen.

'Clear,' the agent said, nodding back at Agent Richardson before moving to the door locks.

'Alpha team is also in position, over,' Agent Richardson replied.

'Done,' the agent said, as he finished picking the locks.

'Back door is breached,' Agent Richardson said into his microphone. 'We're going in, over.'

'Front door is breached,' came the reply from Beta team leader. 'We're going in, over and out.'

Wearing the latest technology night-vision goggles, all three teams entered the house from both doors, cruising through rooms they knew only from a floor plan like ghosts through a cemetery.

Gamma team rushed through the front door and reached the stairwell that led to the house's second floor in three seconds flat. A second later the entire team was upstairs.

Beta team followed Gamma team in, beginning their sweep of the ground floor through the entry foyer, before moving on to the living room.

Alpha team entered the house through the kitchen. The door that led them to the basement was identified on the blueprint and sat next to a large double-door fridge on the south wall.

'It's unlocked,' the first Alpha team agent who got to the door hand-signaled his team leader.

He's probably downstairs, Agent Richardson thought, and signaled the rest of the team to proceed in two-by-two cover formation. He would take point.

The door led to a wide concrete stairwell. There was a light bulb above their heads, just past the door, but it was switched off. Agent Richardson hand-signaled his team that they were moving down to the next door at the bottom. In between the first and second doors there were twelve steps.

The door at the bottom was also unlocked. There was no light from the other side. Another signal told the agent behind Richardson to push the door open while the rest of the team stormed into the next room. Fingers counted down from three . . . two . . . one.

The team thundered through the door and into a wide room where the wall across from them was lined with wooden shelves. Those had been divided into separate, different-sized compartments, each holding a clear glass jar. A laboratory-like smell lingered in the air.

What the actual fuck? Agent Richardson thought, as the entire team focused their attention on the contents of the jars.

The team cleared the room and moved to the second door – also unlocked. It dropped them in a corridor where the walls were cinderblock, the floor concrete and the ceiling white, with long strip lights. These were on.

To prevent the team from going blind, their night-vision goggles immediately adapted to the new light. Still, the team quickly removed them.

The corridor was straight for about ten yards before bending left.

The team moved silently and cautiously.

'This is Gamma team leader,' Agent Richardson heard the voice come through his headset. 'Upstairs is clear. Neither of the subjects is up here, but we did find a control room of sorts. There's a makeshift control desk and no less than ten monitors. We did try switching them on in case they could give us an idea of where the girl is located, but all we got were snowing screens. If they were receiving images from broadcasting cameras anywhere, it's all been disconnected. There's also a board covered in schematics of what looks to be plans for remotely activated engines and light switches. According to the schematics, the engines are to be placed on sliding doors somewhere, so they can be opened or closed remotely, so be extra vigilant, over.'

'Roger that, Gamma team,' Richardson replied. 'We suspect

the subject, at least one of them, might be down here in the basement. Secure that control room and those schematics and await further instructions, over.'

'Roger that. Do you need any help down there? Over.'

'That's a negative, Gamma leader. Over and out.'

As Alpha team rounded the corridor corner, they saw two doors, both of them on the wall to their left. There was light seeping from under the first door. The same wasn't true for the second one.

Richardson hand-signaled his team that they would storm through the first door. Once again the team got ready.

One of Alpha team's agents placed his back against the wall to the right of the door and very carefully tried the handle. A couple of seconds later, while keeping the handle all the way down, he nodded at Agent Richardson, indicating that the door was unlocked.

Up came the finger count.

Three . . .

Two . . .

One . . .

The agent with his back to the wall swung the door open in one very smooth movement. A millisecond later, the other four members of Alpha team blasted through into the room beyond.

One Hundred and One

'Mommy isn't coming for you,' the man had said as he returned the remote control to his trouser pocket and began gloving his hands. 'Nobody is ever coming for you . . . Except me.'

Maybe it was the sincerity in the man's tone of voice, or maybe it was because the girl sensed danger in every word he spoke, but as he got to her and placed a hand on her left shoulder, the girl lost control. The fear that had begun as butterflies in her stomach rapidly spread throughout the rest of her body, manifesting itself in irrepressible shudders, forcing the tears that had welled up in her eyes to finally roll down her cheeks.

Without being able to move, frozen in place from pure fear, the girl wet herself.

The man looked back at her in disgust. As he circled around the girl, positioning himself directly behind her, the door to the small room they were in was pushed open and, in a blink of an eye, five FBI agents stormed in.

Despite how shocked the man was, he was able still to quickly slide his hand from the girl's shoulder to her neck and bring her close against his body.

'Don't move!' five different voices shouted at the same time.

The aims of five different assault rifles targeting the same two-square inch spot over the man's chest.

'Let the girl go,' Agent Richardson commanded. His voice was calm but overflowing with determination.

The man said nothing in reply, his big and powerful hand completely covering the girl's neck, his fingertips rounding it to her nape. He wouldn't need a second hand to snap the life out of her.

'Let the girl go,' Agent Richardson commanded again. 'It's over. You know you can't win.'

'I wouldn't be so sure of that,' the man said, his eyes moving down to his hand before returning to the five agents before him.

Heather tried to breathe through her nose, but the air seemed to travel into her nostrils in chunks, making her entire head shake with the effort, her tears now wetting the man's hand.

'It's OK, Heather,' Agent Richardson said. Though he was speaking to the girl, his eyes never left the man standing behind her, holding her by the neck. 'Your mommy sent us. We work with her. We're going to take you home, sweetheart.'

The girl tried to speak, but the man's grip against her neck was too tight and all her vocal cords were able to produce was a meager squealing sound.

'It will take me just a split second to break her neck,' the man said, his eyes playing a tug-of-war with Agent Richardson's. 'You know that, right?'

'You really want to talk calculations?' Agent Richardson replied. 'OK, I think I can do that. If you were lightning fast, it would take you maybe a second to do what you said you would do, but you would need both hands to be able to do it that fast. With only one hand it would take you one, possibly two seconds more, and remember, you would still have to be lightning fast to be able to accomplish that. The problem you have is that we're all carrying modified M16 assault rifles with high-velocity ammunition. That means that a round will leave the barrels of our weapons at an average speed of 2,750 feet per second, or 1,875 miles per hour. The distance between our weapons and you is about eight feet, give or take a couple of inches. If we throw that into the equation, we'll get that any one of our rounds would reach your chest in about 0.00002 of a second. I can't really compare that to anything to give you a better example because nothing in this world can travel that fast. So, like I've said, whichever way you look at this, you've lost. You and the girl are coming with us, whether you want it or not. The girl will be unharmed, there's absolutely no doubt of that, but you've got a choice – unharmed, or in a body bag – and I'll give you three seconds to make that choice. Three . . .'

In the eye tug-of-war the man could see he was losing.

'Two . . .'

Fingers tightened against triggers.

'One . . .'

The man let go of the girl's neck.

One Hundred and Two

Three days later

'Agent Fisher is out of danger,' Adrian Kennedy announced to Hunter, Garcia and Captain Blake. He had flown in from Washington again that morning. 'She lost her hand. It was amputated at the elbow.' His eyes moved to Garcia, who didn't shy away from the tough stare.

'How about her daughter?' Hunter asked. He was sitting back on his chair, fingers laced in front of his chin, elbows resting on the chair's arms.

'Have you met her?' Kennedy asked.

'No, unfortunately not.'

'You should. She's the sweetest girl you'll ever meet, plus you were the one who saved her life.'

'I would like to one day,' Hunter replied. 'Anyway, how is she doing?

'She's all right. Obviously a little shook up and a bit upset because her mother has lost her hand, but she'll be fine.'

'Since we're on that subject,' Captain Blake cut in, 'what's the full story on that, Robert? How did you go from pretty much being ambushed to finding out the killer's address?'

Hunter shrugged. 'I was trying to put some facts together and an idea came to me,' he explained. 'We knew that this killer traveled. He had already taken four victims in four different states. With that in mind, we were trying to sieve through airlines' passenger manifests, looking for a name that repeated itself arriving or leaving those four cities in the vicinity of the murder dates.'

'Yes,' the captain said. 'You told me about that long shot, but you got nothing from it.'

'You're right,' Hunter agreed. 'We didn't get a single name from those manifests, but that was because the idea we had was right, but the method was wrong.'

'How so?'

'When the searching through passenger manifests was suggested,' Hunter replied, 'we didn't know that Arthur Weber was a collector. We were still working with the art-piece theory then, but once we figured out what he was actually doing, some of the parameters on that search had to be altered. Arthur Weber was collecting body parts, which meant that after murdering his victims and harvesting the selected piece, he would have to transport them back to wherever he kept that collection – his gallery, so to speak.' Hunter shook his head. 'There was just no way he would be doing that through any means of transport that would involve more than one passenger – himself. He just couldn't risk getting those body parts past airport security, or into a bus or a train. What if something went wrong with the luggage? Or there was an accident? Or whatever? Too many unknown factors, and someone like Arthur Weber would never risk that.'

'So he would've driven everywhere,' Captain Blake concluded.

'That's right,' Hunter agreed. 'The second factor that got me thinking was that to obtain the pieces for his collection, Arthur Weber would've driven absolutely anywhere in the country, no matter how far, which suggested that he would have a good and strong roadworthy vehicle. Probably quite comfortable, too – something like a mid-sized to large SUV.'

The captain didn't find it hard to follow Hunter's logic.

'In possession of those new parameters,' Hunter continued, 'I called Adrian, who called the US Department of Transportation. They were the only ones who would already be equipped to run the sort of search I had in mind.'

'Traffic cameras,' Captain Blake said. She had now clearly tapped into Hunter's thread of thought.

Hunter nodded. 'The ones that covered all the entries and exits to those four cities. I asked him to start with the murder dates and then move forward a day at a time, not backward. The way I figured, the killer could have arrived in any of those cities on the day of the murders or any time prior to them – days, weeks, even longer – that would depend on how much preparation he would've needed for each murder, which I'm sure varied from victim to victim. But once he had his piece, chances were that he had nothing else holding him to the city in question and he would've probably wanted to get the hell out of there as soon as possible.'

'So the search was only looking for license plates registered to SUV vehicles,' the captain sai, 'leaving those cities on specific days, which probably reduced the amount of data considerably.'

'It certainly did,' Hunter replied. 'But it still took us two days to get a match. Arthur Weber's SUV, an Infinity QX80, was picked up on the I-94 leaving Detroit a day after Kristine

Rivers' murder. It was picked up again on US Route 400, on its way out of Wichita, the day after Albert Greene's murder. Then again on the I-5 leaving Los Angeles in the direction of San Diego the day after Linda Parker's body was found, and one last time on the I-19 leaving Tucson the day after Timothy Davis was killed. Too much coincidence, but we still took a huge risk, because we had no time to make any proper checks. I received that information on the day of the ambush, about an hour or so after the paramedics got to us, and that was when I called Adrian with an address and a name.'

'I didn't care if we had had the proper checks or not,' Kennedy took over. 'A little girl's life was now at stake and I wasn't about to risk it due to a technicality, so I immediately dispatched FBI's top SWAT team. Given the limited intel they had on the location and on the subject, they did an amazing job.'

'And this Arthur Weber really did have a human-body-parts gallery in his house?' Captain Blake asked.

'He did,' Adrian confirmed. 'Down in his basement. You haven't seen the pictures yet? I've sent them to Robert and to Detective Garcia.'

'No,' the captain replied. 'And to be honest I'm not sure I really want to. I did read the file we now have on Arthur Weber. His mother home-schooled him, right? She forced him to learn Latin and Greek and she was obsessed with perfection – physical, that is.'

'That's exactly right,' Garcia said. 'Though her home-schooling was more like a prison than a school. Arthur Weber wasn't allowed outside. He grew up completely isolated and until the age of twenty-two, his only human interaction had been with his mother, who was a totally domineering and

overzealous woman, completely obsessed with physical perfection, an obsession that drove her insane. By the age of
forty-five, she'd already had thirty-eight cosmetic surgeries.'

'Thirty-eight?' Captain Blake cringed.

Garcia nodded before continuing. 'But unfortunately her
insanity didn't stop with her. She also wanted her only son,
Arthur, to be physically perfect, or at least what she considered
to be physically perfect. Remember when I said that until the
age of twenty-two, Arthur Weber's only human interaction
had been with his mother?'

'Yes.'

'His first non-mother interaction was with a cosmetic surgeon.'

'She forced him to have surgery?' Captain Blake asked
in bewilderment.

'Fifteen of them,' Garcia confirmed, before showing the
captain a portrait photograph of Arthur Weber. 'This is him at
the age of eighteen.' He showed her a second photo. 'And this
is him at the age of thirty.'

Captain Blake's jaw dropped open. 'Are you for real? This
is the same person?'

There wasn't a single facial feature on Arthur Weber's first
picture that was recognizable on the second one. His eyes,
nose, jawline, cheekbones, brow, mouth, lips, chin, teeth and
ears all looked different.

'He looked much better before all the procedures,' Captain
Blake commented.

'Also,' Garcia carried on, 'probably just to please his mother,
Arthur Weber started studying medicine at home – reading
books, watching videos, searching the internet . . . whatever.'

'Now would be a good time to mention Arthur Weber's IQ,'

Hunter cut in. 'Rated at one hundred and fifty-two, which would put him comfortably inside the genius bracket.'

Captain Blake frowned at him.

'What I'm trying to say here is that from books alone he could learn just as well and as easily as if he'd attended classes in an Ivy League university. And that was where all of his medical knowledge came from – books.'

'How about his computer company?' the captain asked. 'Where did that come from? Wasn't that how he made his fortune?'

'It was,' Hunter replied. 'And it all came from his genius. From what we've gathered, Arthur Weber was a natural when it came to computers. He started messing around with them at a very early age and it all just made sense to him – the codes, the electronics . . . all of it. He started creating his own applications at the age of ten. From there it all escalated naturally. He set up his company at twenty-three and by twenty-five, he was already a millionaire.'

'So what happened with him?' the captain asked. 'His mother's obsession with physical perfection just rubbed off on him?'

'In a reverse sort of way,' Hunter said, nodding.

'What does that mean, Robert?'

'It will take countless therapy sessions for anyone to be able to properly get to the bottom of it,' Hunter explained. 'And that's only if Mr. Weber decides to talk, but his mother's obsession no doubt left him with much deeper scars than simply physical ones. Scars that no plastic surgeon can ever fix. But the catch was, unlike his mother, and probably *because* of his mother, Weber didn't seek to be perfect himself. His mother had tried that on her and on him and it hadn't worked.

He knew that. He could see that. Chances are that he even hated her for it, but he still admired perfection. He had to. It was drilled into his brain probably since he was a baby.'

'So he searched the country for people with perfect body parts?' Captain Blake asked skeptically.

'The rare and unusual ones,' Hunter replied. 'But not in a freaky way, in a more natural, rare way.'

'So he didn't actually hate those people for being perfect,' Captain Blake concluded. 'He envied them.'

'We think so, yes,' Hunter agreed. 'That's probably why he never hurt any of them, but again, the real truth about Arthur Weber's darkest demons will only come out if he ever decides to speak up.'

'His mother passed away three and a half years ago.' Garcia took over again. 'From complications from one of her plastic surgeries. That probably messed his mind up even more. A year after she passed, he sold his company and the speculation is that he began planning his collection then. With his computer knowledge, tapping into the Optum integrated information and technology platform to obtain his victims' medical records wasn't much of a problem. The rest, as they say, is history.'

'Did he have any more victims lined up?' Captain Blake asked. 'Does anyone know?'

'Apparently, yes.' Kennedy was the one to reply this time. 'A seventeen-year-old girl from Sentinel, a very small town in Arizona. She had complete heterochromia, with one dark-brown eye and the other light blue. An extremely rare condition.'

'She has no idea that her life has just been saved, does she?' Garcia asked.

Kennedy simply shook his head.

'And where is Arthur Weber now?' Captain Blake asked.

'In the infirmary of one of our Federal Detention Centers,' Kennedy replied.

'Infirmary?' Hunter asked.

'Yesterday morning he came down with a very bad case of food poisoning,' Kennedy clarified. 'Arthur Weber had a very OCD personality. At home he never deviated too far from his preferred meals. It appears that his stomach hasn't really approved of our federal facility's cuisine. Not yet, anyway.'

The comment brought a smile to everyone's faces.

One Hundred and Three

That morning, due to a broken-down truck by exit road number four, it took Tyler Weaver exactly twenty-eight minutes and thirty-one seconds to drive the nine miles between his house and his work place. That was about twelve minutes more than usual. Parking the car took him another forty-eight seconds. The walk between the staff parking lot and the staff door were responsible for another thirty-three seconds. Security check, clocking in, dumping his bag in his locker and a quick trip to the bathroom added another eight minutes and forty-nine seconds to his time. Grabbing a quick coffee at the staff room and the final walk down the corridor that led to the control room took another one minute and twenty-seven seconds – which meant that in total it took Federal Detention Center infirmary control-room guard Tyler Weaver exactly forty minutes and eight seconds to go from his door all the way to the worst day of his life.

Guard Weaver felt his heart go from resting to tachycardia as he got near the west wing control room – the infirmary's maximum-security wing. The square control room with large bullet-proof glass windows was never, ever left unattended, having always a minimum of two officers inside it at any time of day or night, but from halfway down the corridor Guard Weaver could see no one, which was worrying fact number one. Worrying fact number two was that the control room's assault-proof door was wide open and unattended; but the most disturbing fact of all was the large blood smear that Guard Weaver could see against the inside of the control room's bullet-proof glass.

'No, no, no ...' His voice got louder as he went from walking to the fastest sprint he'd ever done. With each step, the large ball of keys that hung from his belt bounced loudly against his right thigh.

Guard Weaver reached the control-room door in two seconds and nightmare became reality.

On the floor inside the control room, Guards Vargas and Bates lay in one massive pool of blood, both of their throats slit.

'Jesus Christ!'

Guard Weaver had to step over Vargas's body to reach the blood-splattered cell monitors. Only one maximum-security prisoner was supposed to be in the ward that day. Guard Weaver checked the monitor broadcasting the images from infirmary cell one.

Empty.

Lying in another pool of blood inside the cell was another body, who had been stripped naked. Guard Weaver immediately recognized the body he could see on the monitor as belonging to Guard Torres.

He felt his airways constrict. Breathing became a struggle.

'Shit, shit, shit.'

Though he knew it was way too late, the first thing Guard Weaver did was raise the alarm, then with trembling fingers he called the FBI Academy in Quantico.

One Hundred and Four

'Special Agent Larry Williams' funeral will be in two days' time,' Kennedy said, as he got ready to leave Hunter and Garcia's office. 'It will be held in Washington DC. I just thought you'd like to know, in case you guys can make it.'

'He was a great agent,' Garcia said.

'He was one of my best,' Kennedy came back.

'So what will happen to Special Agent Fisher?' Captain Blake asked.

'Not a special agent anymore,' Kennedy replied. 'And once she leaves hospital she will go to prison; there are no questions about that. There will be no trial, as she already said that she wouldn't contest any charges brought against her.' There was undeniable sadness in Kennedy's eyes. 'She was also a great agent, but first and foremost she was a mother. Nothing can compete with that. She simply followed her heart. She did what she had to do to save her daughter.' Kennedy paused by the door to Hunter and Garcia's office. 'She told me to tell you that she will be forever in your debt, Robert.'

'In my debt? For what?'

'For saving her daughter's life. She told me to tell you that you managed to do what she had failed to.'

Right then, Kennedy's cellphone rang. He retrieved it from his pocket and brought it to his ear.

'Director Adrian Kennedy,' he said into the phone.

The next several seconds were spent listening. Within the first five seconds, Kennedy's facial expression morphed to confusion. Five seconds later, to disbelief. Five seconds after that, to shock and anger.

'What do you mean, *he's gone*?'

Those words prompted Hunter, Garcia and Captain Blake to look back at Kennedy expectantly.

'He killed three guards?'

'What's going on?' Garcia asked.

Kennedy lifted a hand, signaling him to wait.

'So he waltzed past security, just like that?' Kennedy's hoarse voice was getting louder with every word. 'What kind of amateurish, shit security do we run down there? It was supposed to be a *maximum-security* facility. Do they even know the meaning of the word *maximum* or *security*? I want a nationwide APB to go out now, and I mean NOW. I'm on my way back.'

Kennedy disconnected from the call. The look in his eyes as he looked back at Hunter was overflowing with sorrow.

'What's going on, Adrian?' Hunter asked, his voice unaltered.

'He's gone,' Kennedy replied. His voice, on the other hand, was unsteady, the look in his eyes now vacant. 'He's escaped.'

'Who escaped?' Garcia jumped to his feet. 'Arthur Weber escaped?'

'No,' Kennedy replied. 'Not Arthur Weber.'

Fear shot up Hunter's spine like a derailed train because he already knew the name Kennedy was about to throw at him.

'Lucien,' Kennedy said.

Hunter closed his eyes.

'Lucien?' Garcia asked, his gaze playing ping-pong between Hunter and Director Kennedy. 'Who's Lucien?'

'Lucien Folter has escaped,' Kennedy confirmed. His entire demeanor had changed. It now seemed leaden with anguish.

Garcia had never seen his partner look the way he did right at that moment. If he didn't know better, he could've sworn that Hunter looked almost scared.

'Robert, who the hell is Lucien Folter?'

Acknowledgements

My most sincere gratitude goes to my agent, Darley Anderson, and everyone at the Darley Anderson Literary Agency for their never-ending strive to promote my work anywhere and everywhere possible.

And to Jo Dickinson, my incredible editor; as well as everyone at Simon & Schuster for their tremendous support and tremendous hard work.

Kara Louise, for her tolerance, her understanding, her belief, and frankly for putting up with me.

About the author

Born in Brazil of Italian origin, Chris Carter studied psychology and criminal behaviour at the University of Michigan. As a member of the Michigan State District Attorney's Criminal Psychology team, he interviewed and studied many criminals, including serial and multiple homicide offenders with life-imprisonment convictions.

Having departed for Los Angeles in the early 1990s, Chris spent ten years as a guitarist for numerous rock bands before leaving the music business to write full-time. He now lives in London and is a Top Ten *Sunday Times* bestselling author.

Visit www.chriscarterbooks.com or find him on Facebook.

FIND OUT MORE ABOUT
CHRIS CARTER

Chris Carter writes highly addictive thrillers
featuring Detective Robert Hunter

To find out more about Chris and his writing,
visit his website at

www.chriscarterbooks.com

or follow Chris on

facebook: https://en-gb.facebook.com/Chris-Carter

All of Chris Carter's novels are available
in print and eBook, and are available to
download in eAudio